As the Eagle Flies

by
J. D. Oliver

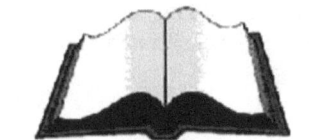

CCB Publishing
British Columbia, Canada

As the Eagle Flies

Copyright ©2009 by J. D. Oliver
ISBN-13   978-1-926585-14-7
First Edition

Library and Archives Canada Cataloguing in Publication

Oliver, J. D., 1939-
As the eagle flies / written by J. D. Oliver – 1st ed.
ISBN 978-1-926585-14-7
I. Title.
PS3615.L4816 A8 2009   813'.6   C2009-900175-6

Disclaimer: This is a work of fiction. The characters, incidents and dialogues are products of the author's imagination and are not to be construed as real. Any resemblance to actual events or persons living or dead is entirely coincidental.

Extreme care has been taken to ensure that all information presented in this book is accurate and up to date at the time of publishing. Neither the author nor the publisher can be held responsible for any errors or omissions. Additionally, neither is any liability assumed for damages resulting from the use of the information contained herein.

Publisher: CCB Publishing
               British Columbia, Canada
               www.ccbpublishing.com

Chapter One

I leveled our Twin Engine Cessna off at eight thousand feet, just like the flight plan I had filed said I would. Looking down, I could see Cheyenne shrinking smaller and smaller. Jake and Dad were already asleep in their seats; they had partied pretty hard last night.

Me? I had consumed my usual two drinks. Dad had hit it a little harder than usual. Jake now, he had sneaked a few when he thought I wasn't looking. Jake was only 17, and had the usual teenager attitude, you know, they know everything and us oldsters don't know anything. Yeah he considered me old at 26. Dad wasn't even old in my sights, he was only 52.

The plane was handling pretty good, even though we were right at the weight limit. Our saddles and tack were pretty heavy. The three of us weren't all that heavy, we were all muscle and bone. In our line of work, it kept us right down slim. We were on the Rodeo circuit, had been for the last year.

Jake rode Bulls and Bareback, he was pretty good, yeah and it was going to his head. I could see trouble in the future if we didn't get off of the circuit. Dad and I, we team roped. And I rode saddle bronc. I made my ride last night, but the pickup men were slow and I got drilled in the dirt pretty good.

Jake missed his mark out of the chute on his bareback ride, but won second place money on his bull. Dad and I took second in the team roping. We picked up ten thousand between the three of us. Not a bad night.

We didn't pack any horses along. When we team roped we

always were able to use someone else's horses, for part of the purse of course. The other contestants didn't mind, as long as they got their share. Dad and I were pretty good, we almost always placed in the money.

Being we had this plane we made a lot of Rodeos. Jake was in fifteenth place and if he kept it up we'd be going to the finals. I was really starting to get worried about Jake, his ego was getting bigger with each win. I can remember Mom telling me that pride always goes before a fall. I sure missed her.

Mom was a full blood Cheyenne, Northern Cheyenne that was. Dad had married her when she was just sixteen. Dad was a German, on both sides all the way back. Mom had died two years ago, a drunk driver had hit her head on, she never had a chance. Dad had taken it pretty hard, of course us kids did too.

I guess that's why we were on the circuit. I was in Iraq when it happened. I came home on emergency leave, my time was almost up anyway. Our place was in the Big Horn Basin. It had been in Dad's family for over a hundred years. The Oil and Gas people had been trying to get a hold of the ranch for years.

Dad was pretty well broke up over Mom's death. Not enough to sell the place to Oil people, but enough to put it in a partial nature conservancy. That way it could never be developed or subdivided. We have caretakers living on it. We bought this plane with the money we got from the conservancy. I guess it was like having your cake and eating it too.

The next Rodeo was in Santa Fe. I don't know why I said I would fly at 8,000 feet, it was way to low to get over the Rocky Mountains, so I went up to 15,000, to make sure. Our plane was pressurized and I had made sure we had plenty of oxygen in the tanks. I was a Navy pilot, they sure were pissed when I resigned my commission.

But hell, it was my decision. You see, it was starting to bother me, I didn't mind shooting at planes and things that were shooting at me. But when I didn't know who were in those buildings that I dropped my bombs on, that was what I couldn't do anymore.

Besides, Dad and Jake needed me. One thing about this Rodeo business, it kept your mind off of the past, that is, except at times like this, when you were 15,000 feet in the air and the plane was on Auto Pilot.

I dug out the map. I always liked to know what was below me, just in case. I studied it, looking at any place that a plane this size could land. A person never knew.

Anytime you flew over the mountains, the turbulence was always worse. It was getting rougher so I took it off auto.

I looked down, we were just passing over Monarch Pass. The air was crisp and cold. The temperature said it was forty below outside. Of course it wasn't that cold down there, being it was the middle of summer. But there sure was a lot of snow on those mountains. I sure hoped they were wrong on this global warming thing, but I knew they weren't. I guess we weren't helping it any, flying a plane like this.

It was a good thing that this plane had big gas tanks, so we could get from Cheyenne to Santa Fe without stopping for fuel. The turbulence was getting better, so I checked my settings and put it back on auto.

Dad stirred and opened one eye. "Where are we?" he asked.

"Well right now, we're close to the New Mexico state line. Are you okay? You had about one too many last night?" I said.

"Yeah, I'm okay. Next time I do that, stop me, alright?" Dad said as he looked around for his hat. Like any old cowboy he just wasn't comfortable without it being on his head.

"Don't worry, I will. The only reason I didn't stop you last night is, that you really hadn't tied one on since Mom died. So I figured you had one coming."

"Well you're right about that. Grieving takes awhile. Your mother will always have a place in my heart, but I guess there is no use in getting maudlin about it, we can't change things, we just have to learn to live with them." Dad said, as he found his hat and screwed it down.

"There's a bottle of water beside your seat and some aspirin, it should help some," I said.

Jake was still sawing logs. I can remember when I was a teenager, I could also sleep for hours. Dad poured some aspirin in his hand and gulped them down with water for chaser. "When do you figure on getting to Santa Fe?" Dad asked.

"Oh, should be there in under two hours, we're making good time." I said, as I felt a little vibration. I checked all my gauges. Everything looked normal, all except the oil pressure on the right engine was just a hair lower than it was the last time I looked. I took it back off auto pilot.

Dad hadn't felt the little quiver. If I hadn't spent the last few years in a plane, I probably wouldn't have either. I looked at the map again. There it was again, a little stronger this time, I never looked up from my map. I looked down; we had just passed over Route 64.

The mountains were on my left, but up ahead I could see a nice valley with the Rio Chama River running along the west side of it. The little town of Abiquiu lay on the southern end of the valley right on the river. I would try for it, they might have a landing strip. Dad had noticed that we were starting a downward glide.

"Are we getting close to Santa Fe?" he asked.

Now I never did like to lie, so I didn't, "Nope, we're not." The plane quivered again. I looked at Dad and said, "Did you feel that?"

"Yep, sure did. What was it?"

"There's a problem in the right engine, I'm going to set her down at the first field I find. We can fly on one engine, but I don't like to. You see the oil pressure gauge, it's slowly coming down and I don't want to ruin that engine, but I might have to feather it, I hope not," I said, just a little wisp of smoke could be seen coming from its cowl...

"Shit, I guess we don't have a choice. Get up here in the co-pilot's seat and look down there, see if you can find a good spot to land," I said, as I killed the right engine. The plane lurched sideways before I could correct it, but then I got control and straightened it out.

Jake woke up. "What the hell are you doing, can't you fly this thing?" he said.

"Just fasten your seat belt and take that pillow and put your head between your legs, we're going to have to make an emergency landing." That shut him up, right quick. He wasn't as tough as he thought he was.

Dad said, "I see a place, it's a might short, it looks like it used to be a strip. See over there by them buildings?"

I banked the plane a little to get a good look. He was right, it was short, but hell a Carrier deck is shorter than that, but then again a Carrier deck has landing cables and a fighter jet has landing hooks. But what the hell....

I did one fly by, just to get a good look. I could see a man standing down there looking at us. He started to herd some cows off the grass strip. He was thinking anyway.

Chapter Two

I came around and lined myself up, the wheels were down and locked. There was a fence that I would have to clear at the start of the runway. I came in low and as soon as I was just by the fence; I set her down with full flaps and brakes locked. The wheels were throwing sod every which way.

The man had chased the last of the stock out of our way. I got her stopped just before I ran into the fence at the end of the runway, or I guess I could say pasture. I sure put some grooves the full length of it. I suppose I would have to pay for that.

I turned around and tapped Jake on the shoulder, "We've landed, you're safe now." He looked up, his face pale as a ghost. He looked around and didn't say a word. For a man who could ride a two thousand pound bull, he sure let a little emergency landing spook him.

As we were getting out, the man who shooed the stock away was walking toward us. He was an older Mexican fellow, with a big smile. "That was a good landing Senor, the Gods must of have been with you. Welcome to the Ranchos de Chama. My name is Miguel." He said, holding his hand out to shake.

I took his hand and pumped it, "Thank you for clearing the runway, I'm Clay, this is my brother Jake and this is my father, Karl Bronson. You sure saved our lives."

"You're welcome Senor. Do you want me to get the tractor and put your plane in the hanger?" He said pointing to a large hanger setting on the East side of the runway. I hadn't even noticed it.

"Yeah, I guess, sure. That right motor has some problems, do you know of a good aircraft mechanic?" I said.

"I used to work on the Patron's airplane, perhaps you would like me to look at it?" he said with a smile.

I looked at him, closer. He had a twinkle in his eye. Now I knew better than to judge people by first sight; this was a case in point. He was more than met the eye. "Yes, of course I would," I said.

He went to get the tractor, it was equipped with an aircraft hitch. He pulled it over and backed it in the hanger. He said, "Perhaps you would like to get your overnight bags, I will take you to the main house and introduce you to the Senora. She will be glad to have you stay with them."

"Are you sure, we could just bunk here in the hanger?" Dad said.

"That would hurt her feelings, you must come to the main house," he said.

"Okay, sure, we'll come, we're sorry for suggesting otherwise." Dad said. We retrieved our bags. Jake still hadn't said a word. There was an old 47 Chevy pickup parked beside the hanger, Dad and Miguel got in the cab, Jake and I, jumped in the back. Jake mumbled, "I guess we're going to miss that Rodeo in Santa Fe."

"I do believe you're right. But I guess we need the rest anyway." I said. The main house was a mile up a tree lined lane. This sure was a fancy place. I could see Dad and Miguel laughing and talking in the cab. They seemed to hit it off pretty good.

The main house was a classic Mexican Villa, in the Santa Fe style. We pulled up and as we were getting out, the main door opened; a women stood there smiling. Miguel said, "This is my wife, Ester. She's the Home Manager for the Senora. I run the Ranchos." Turning to his wife, he said, "Ester is the Senora ready to receive visitors?"

"Of course, she heard their plane land; she is expecting them. Come in please, Juan will take your bags to your rooms." A young boy appeared and took our bags and hurried off down a cool hallway. The walls in the house must have been three foot thick.

She showed us into a parlor where a woman was bending over a fancy antique crib. She stood up and turned to face us. She was in her middle forties or so, she said, "Welcome to our home. My name is Felicia Cortez," she held her hand out, Dad took it and bowed low over it. I couldn't believe it; I had never seen him do something like that. He kissed the back of her hand, she did a little curtsy. What was more, he had taken his hat off at the first sight of her. Jake and I grabbed our hats off and mumbled a greeting of some kind.

Dad said, "My name is Karl Bronson, these are my son's Clay and Jake. She turned to us and smiled. She was beautiful, not that Jake and I were interested, but Dad sure was.

She said, "My Hacienda is yours as long as you need it, I heard your plane coming from a long ways off and knew you would land here. We've already had our noon repast; can I have the cook bring a snack before supper?"

"Uh, no we're alright, perhaps just something to drink?" Dad said. She clapped her hands, a young girl scurried in. "Juanita, some ice tea please?" The girl turned and scooted off. Miguel and Ester had disappeared. Felicia showed us to some overstuffed cowhide leather chairs. She settled into her chair like a queen setting down. Which I guess she was; queen of this place anyway.

The girl came back with a pitcher of ice tea and glasses along with some scones or something. She poured our glasses full. When she passed the bread, both Jake and I took a handful. Dad didn't.

There came a whimper from the crib. Felicia said, "Oh, my Grand Daughter is waking up. She wants fed." Felicia looked directly at me. She said, "Clay, if you would be so kind, please take the baby to my Daughter-in-law, she will nurse her. It's down the hallway the second door on the left, just knock lightly and go right in."

I was stunned, too stunned to protest. I went over and picked up a four or five months old baby girl, she had dark brown hair, she gurgled at me and smiled. It was strange; I picked her up, just like I had been doing it from her birth. Dad and Jake were staring at me, that's okay, I was staring at myself.

I knocked, turning the knob, I went in. There was a young women sleeping in a big old style bed. She had blond hair. I went over and stood beside her, I cleared my throat. "Uh, Miss, your Mother sent me in with the baby, she's awake."

She opened her eyes; they were blue, she looked at me, her eyes focusing. Suddenly she was wide awake. She sat up, "What time is it?"

"Uh, I believe its somewhere around three in the afternoon." I said, as she sat up in bed. She had on a light night gown, open at the throat. "Shit, she let me sleep too long again. Alita was colicky all night; I guess I was just tired out. Here, give her to me." She said as she opened her night gown. It fell off of her shoulders, exposing both breasts! She didn't even blink. Alita locked on to her left breast, sucking mightily. "My name is Faith, what's yours?

"It's Clay, look I'm sorry, I shouldn't be in here, but your Mother sent me in. I guess I was just too surprised to protest. Besides, when I picked the Baby up, it, it just seemed like she was mine, weird huh?"

"My Mother-in-law, not my Mother. Her son, my husband

was killed along with her husband in a plane crash about a year ago." She was looking at me with a small smile on her face; as her eyes twinkled at my discomfort.

She glanced down at the baby and then her other breast. "Nice huh?" she said, indicating her right breast. "They sure are bigger with all of this milk."

"Uh, yes, I should be embarrassed and you know what? I am. But anyway; may I set down beside you?"

"Yes, sure. I'm not this way with everybody. But it seems like, I don't know, I have been expecting you. I know I've seen you in my dreams."

I sat down, she reached over and took my hand. It fit naturally into mine. I leaned over as she raised her lips to mine. The baby burped. We both laughed. "I guess I had better get up, here take her, she needs changed, there is a changing table over there. I'm going to take a shower." Faith got up, I took the baby. She dropped her gown and walked toward the bathroom. My eyes followed her all the way till she pulled the shower curtain.

I didn't have any trouble changing Alita; although I had never changed a baby before in my life. The shower turned off, Faith stepped out, grabbing a towel she smiled at me. I stood there with Alita in my arms, still staring. She got dressed in a peasant skirt and blouse, she didn't bother putting on underwear.

"Come on, let's join the others. Felicia's daughter should be home anytime. She took some stock to town; a few old cows. Her name is Alona, she's sixteen. A regular pistol." Faith grabbed my hand, I followed along.

As we came in, Jake and Dad turned to look, they both stood up. I said, "Dad this is Faith and Alita, the baby's name is Alita." Then I introduced them to her. I was still holding the baby. Jake was looking back and forth between Faith and me.

Dad had politely greeted Faith, then turned his attention back to Felicia.

Faith said, "Is Alona back yet?"

"No, not yet, I'm sorry I hadn't told them about Alona; she is my daughter, she took some stock to market, we're expecting her anytime. Jake, perhaps you could meet her at the barn and tell her we have company?"

It was Jake's turn to be stunned. He nodded numbly, and left. Faith come up and took my elbow, "Would you like to see the barn? We can go along."

"Sure, I think maybe Alita would like the fresh air." Now how would I know if the baby would like fresh air?

Faith said, as we closed the massive front door, "I think Felicia and your Father would like some time alone. Did you see how her eyes sparkled? I think she likes your Dad."

"Wow! I don't understand what's happening. But I like it." I said. We heard Miguel's old pickup coming down the lane. He stopped beside us. "I had some time, so I checked the right engine on your plane; I can find nothing wrong with it, Senor."

"Huh? Not even some oil on the engine from a leak? There was smoke coming out from under the cowl."

"No Senor, I even started it up; the oil pressure was normal. I could find nothing wrong. But yes, when you were landing I seen the smoke you speak of, but now it is fine."

Faith looked up at me, "You silly boy, of course there was nothing wrong with your plane. You were meant to come here. We were expecting you."

"You mean that just happened so we would land here?" I said. She nodded, while taking my hand and putting my arm around her waist.

As we stood by the corral, we could hear a truck coming down the lane from the highway. It was a brand new diesel 5 ton stake truck. It came roaring in and slid to a stop. A young dark haired girl in jeans and western shirt jumped out. She quickly glanced at Faith and me, then turned her gaze to Jake. They stood there staring at each other.

"Alona, this is Jake, the one you're staring at. And this is his brother Clay, he's mine. The father to them both is in the house with your mother. It's like the Eagle told us; you remember, in our dreams?"

Alona drew some circles in the dust with her boot toe. She was looking at Jake through lowered eyes. A small smile was growing bigger, showing her pearly white teeth. She said, in a voice just above a whisper, "Jake, would you like to see my Barrel Horse?"

"Yeah, sure I would, do you Rodeo?"

"Yes, of course. I know you do too. Did you win last night?" Jake had his composure back. I seen his chest puff out some, he said, "Sure did, I guess you could call it that anyway, I took second place money on a pretty bad bull. Anytime I stick for eight seconds; I call that winning."

"I call that winning too." She said, as she motioned for Jake to follow her. She wouldn't have had to do that, because he sure would of followed on his own. Course he was a couple of steps back so he could appreciate the view.

Faith gave me a wink, as we watched them walk off toward the barn. "I think they like each other, don't you?" Faith said, then added, "Would you like to see our swimming hole? It's just a short way. Alita likes to crawl in the grass, there's a lot of shade there."

"Sure, I reckon." I said, as I adjusted Alita's position in my right arm, as I still had my left arm around Faith. The swimming hole was a natural slow backwater off of the river. The grass grew right down to its edge.

Faith sat down cross legged with her peasant skirt flared out around her. She said, "Just put her down beside me." I did so. Alita immediately started to crawl toward a Dandelion plant. She picked it and started to put it in her mouth, I grabbed it and said, "Hey not in your mouth; let's put it in your hair." I put it above her ear, she gurgled at me. Then I picked her up and went to set beside Faith. Faith took her and put her in her lap. Alita leaned back between her breasts and started to doze off.

It was pleasant sitting there in the shade and listening to the water and the birds and the bees. Faith cocked her head at me and said, "Well, what do you want to know about me?"

"I reckon just about everything. You seem to know more about me, than I do you." I said, as I took her hand in mine, and looked at the well manicured nails. Then I said, "I've never seen a ranch girl with nails like yours?"

"There's nothing to say that a ranch girl can't keep herself up, just because she lives on a ranch, is there?"

"No, of course not. But I get the impression that you haven't always lived on a ranch, have you?"

"No, I haven't, you're right. I grew up in the Napa Valley in California. I had a Basketball scholarship to Arizona State. That's where I met Theodore, he was an Agriculture Major there. We got married right after graduation."

"Basketball? You don't look like a basketball player." I said.

"What does a basketball player look like?" Faith said, pinching my hand a little bit.

"Well you know, sort of butch, I guess?" She pinched me a little harder.

"Do you think I look Butch?" She said.

"No, not the least little bit, you're beautiful. But on second thought, from what I seen in your room, you have muscles in all the right places." She smiled.

"Yes, and I bet you do too. Would you like to go

swimming? Alita is asleep."

"Well, yeah, I guess. But we don't have any suits; we'd have to go back to the house to get them." I said.

"We don't need suits, nobody can see us." Faith said as she laid Alita in the grass. Then she stood up and said, "Come on, stand up, I'll help you with your clothes." I did as instructed. Ever since we got here I was doing what I was told. I guess I was still in shock. She unbuttoned my shirt and pushed it back off of my shoulders. Her fingers made a trail down toward my belt buckle, before I knew it, I was stepping out of my jeans. She started to pull my shorts down, I stopped her.

"Not till you're, you know, take yours off." I said. She smiled and dropped her skirt, like I said she didn't put any underwear on. Then she slowly took her blouse off. I stood there transfixed. Then she reached out and pushed my shorts down a ways, then used her right foot to push them down all of the way. She had a big smile on her face.

I said, "Hold on a second. Do you know what you're doing? I'm sort of old fashioned. I'm not saying that I've never had sex before, but somehow, between you and me, I want something more. What about you?"

"Of course silly, we're going to get married. I told you I've had dreams about you. And I don't mean in just a general way. I know every bit of your body. For instance, I haven't seen your backside, have I? No…what would you say if I told you that you have a heart shaped birthmark on your right hip? Now think about me, you may not think you have ever seen my body before, but think hard, close your eyes and tell me where I have a mole, you couldn't of seen it before in the bedroom, because it's hidden."

I closed my eyes. Her body came into my mind. On her inner thigh, up close to her groin was a mole, it couldn't be seen, where it was at. She was right I had seen her in my dreams, in a very intimate way. I thought they were just sex dreams; I didn't know they were about anybody in particular. I opened my eyes, she was standing close up to me. "See, I told you." Then she took my hand and we got in the water.....

We lay beside each other, drying in the soft breeze. Alita was still sleeping. Faith's breasts were swelling with milk, one of them was dripping a little bit, I wiped it away. Faith sighed, "I suppose I had better wake Alita up, I feel like an old milk cow that needs milked." Alita latched on with enthusiasm. I sort of envied her.

"I guess we had better be getting back, I should help set the table. Ester does all of the cooking, they think I don't know how." I held Alita while Faith got dressed, then Faith took her and I started to get dressed. Faith watched my every move.

We walked back hand-in-hand. Alita was gurgling and cooing and pointing to all of the animals. "Faith," I said, "you know this is not going to happen again till we get married?"

We stopped walking, Faith looked up at me and said, "Yes," in a soft voice, "I know, it's just that I couldn't help myself. Even before Theodore died, I had dreams about you once in awhile. I didn't know what they meant, then. I thought they were just sex dreams, like you know everybody has."

"I know, I have been having the same dreams and I thought that was just what they were, dreams. But now we know that they were more than that, color me old fashioned, but I believe that sex and marriage go hand-in-hand." I said, as I leaned over and kissed her.

We continued walking, with Alita on my right hip and Faith pressed tightly up against me on my left side. I can remember my mother carrying Jake on her hip; just like I had Alita. It may not be manly to carry a baby that way, but it sure was easier.

When we got back to the house, Jake and Alona were just

coming from the barn. They weren't holding hands, but they might just of well had been. They were walking side by side, joking and laughing. Alona's eyes sparkled, they couldn't take their eyes off of each other.

When they seen us approaching, they stopped in their tracks, and stared. I couldn't blame them, you really couldn't tell where Faith left off and I began; as close together as we were. Plus I guess with the baby thrown in the mix, we were quite a sight to them.

Alona said, "Faith, Uh, what's going on, you just met him?"

"Not really, we've known each other for quite awhile; you remember, our dreams. Anyway, we're getting married." Faith said.

"What about Teddy, he's only been dead for not even a year; don't you think that it's a little fast?"

Jake spoke up, "Uh, Alona, I know my brother; he usually doesn't do things on the spur of the moment. If they are going to get married, knowing him, I'm sure it's forever."

"Well, I guess so, it's just that it took me by surprise." She turned to look at Jake, their eyes met, she forgot all about us.

As the four and half of us went into the hall setting room, we seen Dad and Felicia setting there, sipping Margarita's. Felicia turned to us and said, "Would you like a drink, I can ring for one?"

I said, "Just some Ice Tea for me and the Mrs. The kids there might like some soda pop."

Felicia, looked at Faith, "Ah, I thought so. Karl and I have just been discussing your up coming marriage. Would you like to make it a double wedding?"

I thought my announcement would take them by surprise, but they had turned the tables on us. All four of us stood there dumbstruck. Alona said, when she found her voice, "you mean you two are getting married also?"

"Yes, we weren't in as big of a hurry as Clay and Faith, but since they are getting married, we might as well do the same. No use to have two big weddings; when one will do." Dad said. Then he took Felicia's hand and kissed it. Her eyes were just as happy as my new wife's were.

Felicia looked at Alona and Jake, "I'm sorry, but you two will just have to wait, you're way to young to get married."

"Huh, Uh," Jake stammered, "we hadn't even thought about getting married, have we Alona?"

"Well…no, not yet. But I do like you Jake. But marriage at this time, no, I guess not." She took Jake's hand, "We can wait, can't we Jake?"

"Yes, of course, we both are too young, you sixteen and me only seventeen."

Dad said, "Damn right you will wait. Even though your hormones are in high gear right now. Oh I know Clay and Faith aren't a very good example. But hey, they're a lot older than the two of you. They have waited their turn. The same goes for Felicia and me, we're almost three times your age, so I guess we have the right."

Felicia said, "That's right Karl, I can remember my Grandfather saying, 'just because I have a little snow on the roof, that's no sign the furnace has gone out'."

Alona said, "Really Mom, that's gauche, I've never heard you talk that way, for heavens sake act your age." Felicia, stuck her tongue out at her daughter, Faith giggled and took Alita from me and handed her to Felicia, "Here Felicia, hold your Granddaughter; Clay and I have to set the table for dinner." Then she took my hand and hustled me out of the room.

As soon as we got out of the room, she plastered herself against me and kissed me. She pulled away and looked into my eyes. I guess I broke the spell when I said, "Uh, Honey, you just left two wet spots on my shirt, don't you have a nursing bra to absorb some of that?"

"Oh you, of course I do." Then she kicked me lightly in the shins. Of course it didn't hurt, she was still barefoot. I pulled her back against me and kissed her, for a long time...I didn't care if my whole shirt got wet.

"We broke and she said, "I don't know why I'm making so much milk, I have enough milk for three babies. I guess I should donate some; is there some place that can be done?"

"I don't know, maybe you could ask your doctor, he might know?" I said.

"Yeah, I guess I will call her tomorrow. I'll have to use the breast pump again tonight, I think I have a lot of bottles in the refrigerator. No use to waste it, I guess."

How did I go from a care free bachelor to a husband and father, in a matter of hours? It wasn't as if I didn't like it, because I did. But it sure was mighty fast.

"The dishes are in the cupboard, over there. You set the table, I'm going to call my Doctor, she said I could call her anytime." Then she went to the phone in the hall. Set the table? I had never sat a table before in my entire life. "Hey, how many places do I set?" I called after her.

"Eight," she called back, "Miguel and Ester eats with us." I went to the cupboard, all of the time trying to remember how my Mother used to set the table. I had just finished when Faith came back. "She said we could come in tonight, she would meet us in her office. She said there was a shot she could give me; to cut the flow down a little bit. Will you drive me in?"

"Of course, blow in my ear and I'll follow you anywhere." I said.

"Oh, I'll do more than that, after we're married." Then I got another kiss...

After supper, Faith fed Alita, then left her in the care of Alona and Grandma. We went out to the five car garage. In one of the spots was a restored 50 Ford Pickup. It was cherry apple green in color. Faith said, "This was Teddy's pride and joy, it looks stock, doesn't it? But it's not, there's a fairly new Mustang V-6 under the hood; he said it was supercharged. I haven't driven it, in fact I've never even rode in it. He had just finished it the week before he was killed in that plane crash. Do you want to take it?"

"Yes, of course. I would love to, I've always been a little bit of car nut myself." I said, as I slid behind the wheel. Of course that was after I helped Faith in the passenger side. It did have seat belts and after market airbags.

The transmission was a dragsters dream, it was one of the sidebar shifts, it wasn't just a three speed though, it was a five speed. It took me a few seconds to get the hang of it. The motor just sat there and growled. Oh yeah, there was one other thing that wasn't stock; a built in child restraint seat. I guess he was thinking ahead.

I felt a little funny, it was like stepping into another man's shoes. I guess I shouldn't worry, Faith sure wasn't. We couldn't set side by side; cause of the child seat in the middle. I guess that was okay, we were buckled in anyway.

I idled out of the garage and down the lane. When I hit the county road, which was paved. I goosed it, it fish tailed from side to side before I could get off of it. "Whew, this is one hot rod," I said, Faith said,

"Isn't it though. Oh, you were talking about the truck, yes it is too." She said with a smile. I looked at her, "Patience, my love, patience." I said with a leer.

We pulled up in front of the clinic. I went around and opened the door for Faith. I reached in to help her out, she grabbed me and pulled me down and kissed me. Of course I put up a fight, NOT!

She was leaking again, that cut our kiss short. "Damn, that sure puts a damper on my ardor," she said.

"Yeah, mine too. But I guess that's good, at least till we get married. I sure hope that shot the Doc is going to give you works." I said.

The Doctor was waiting for us. She was a young Navajo girl. Turned out this was her first practice. She looked at me, "Sioux?" She said.

"Uh, no, Northern Cheyenne. Close, but no cigar." I said.

"I hope you don't smoke!" She said.

"Uh, that was a joke, of course I don't smoke."

"Good. Because second hand smoke is bad for babies, well really for anyone." She said.

I was starting to think she didn't have a sense of humor, that was till I caught the twinkle in her eye. "Oh, you were just pulling my leg." I said.

"Well Duh, I was starting to think you didn't have a sense of humor. Come on in, we'll give you a quick once over Faith, then we'll see about that shot."

I followed her in. The Doc glanced at me, then said to Faith, "Where did you pick him up?"

"He fell out of the sky, he's mine and I'm keeping him." Faith said.

"Well, I sure don't want him, he's all yours." Doc said. "Although he is sort of cute."

"Hey, I'm right here. Are you both blind?"

"Stifle it Edith, if you want to stay in here while I check your wife over." Doc said.

"Hey, you called her my wife, how did you know we're getting married?" I said.

"Well, what else would you be doing with Faith, she's not a

floozy, you know?"

"Yes, Doc, I do know that. And I'm not either. Do you know anyone who can marry us?" I said.

"Yeah, me. I'm the Clerk and Recorder and the Justice of the Peace for the Chama area. As such I'm licensed by the state."

I looked at Faith, "Is that right, can she do that?"

"Yes, not only that, but being a doctor she can give us our blood tests." Faith said.

"What's your name Doc? I asked.

It's Pretty Otter, Gail Pretty Otter. So how did you come to fall out of the sky?"

"Well, we didn't really fall out, the starboard engine on my Cessna was giving a little trouble; we had to make an emergency landing." I said.

"You said 'we', who else was with you?" Gail asked.

"My Dad and Brother. My Dad's name is Karl and my brother's name is Jake. Our last name is Bronson. Oh, by the way, as far as the wedding goes; Dad and Felicia are getting married also."

"What? Felicia Cortez is getting married? I can't believe it, really?" Gail said.

"What's wrong with her getting married?" I asked.

"Nothing really, it's just that with the Spanish Land Grant; you do know that her place has been in her family for three hundred years? I see that you didn't, but anyway when she got married the first time she didn't even take her husbands name, she kept her maiden name of Cortez. And speaking of the land grant; Faith, would you tell Felicia that there has been some lawyers poking around? They wanted to see her title, I told them to piss off."

"Well you can rest assured that Dad isn't interested in her property, that is outside of the intimate kind. My Mother died two years ago. We still own our ranch in the Big Horn Basin. We don't need more land." I said.

"I'm sorry if I gave you the wrong impression, I didn't think your Dad was. It's just that I can see trouble on the horizon; is your Dad sure he wants to get involved?"

"Sure, why not? We're fighters, always have been. We especially like to take the underdog's side." I said.

"Alright, let's forget about that. Since you guys are getting married, I guess I had better give you both a quick once over. When is the last time you had a physical Clay?"

"When I was mustered out of the Navy. I guess it's been about two years."

"Okay, but I think I'd better check a few things; we'll draw some blood and a urine sample and I suppose we had better check your prostate."

"Why my prostate, what for?"

"Well I think Faith would like to know that you're in good operating condition, plus also I had better check you for testicular cancer." Gail said, then added, "do you want separate examining rooms, or are you both comfortable right here?"

"Oh, I want to stay in the same room," Faith said, with a diabolical giggle.

"Alright, Clay there's a specimen cup in the bathroom, over there. You give me some urine, I'll give Faith her shot and take a blood sample from her. Just leave the bottle on the sink when you come out."

I went in and did what she asked. Then I came out and sat beside Faith on the exam table. Gail pulled a couple of vials of blood out of me. Then said, "Okay, stand up and drop your drawers."

"Are you sure we have to do this?" I said, as Faith reached over and unbuckled my belt. "Yes, I'm sure," Gail said. As she snapped some latex gloves on, she too had a diabolical grin on her face.

"Turn your head and cough," She said, I did so. "Well there's no hernia's anyway, stand still so I can feel for lumps."

Faith said, "Can I do that, I should know what to look for, shouldn't I?"

"Sure," Gail said, "just feel all around, you can tell if there's something amiss."

"I don't feel anything." Faith said.

"Good, turn around Clay and bend over, here's a tissue, sometimes you might leak a little bit." I think she really took delight in my discomfort. I know my face must have been bright red.

"No, that's fine too. You can just throw that tissue in the garbage. You can get dressed now."

"Do you do that to everyman that gets married?" I asked.

"No, of course not. Faith just wanted to see if you were a good sport or not; you are. But really, a man should get checked every year for prostate cancer, it didn't hurt you any did it?" Gail said.

"No, it was just embarrassing is all. But come to think of it, I would a lot rather have a woman doctor do that than a man. I always felt uncomfortable when a man doctor did that. With you it wasn't so bad."

"That's just because my fingers are smaller." She said, then added, "would you two like to get a cup of coffee?"

I looked at Faith, she nodded. "Sure," I said, "do you know of a place?"

"Why wouldn't I? I'm a local around here, you know. There's not too many choice's in a little town like Abiquiu; my cousin has a small Café. He needs the business anyway, you two being a couple of money bags, you can leave a big tip."

"Oh, we can, can we? But yes, I usually do anyway, especially if the waitress is cute." Faith kicked me. "But not anymore, even if their ugly, I'll leave a big tip." Faith kissed me.

"Alright, I'll take my car, you two can meet me there, Faith knows where it's at."

It was a little bigger than Gail had led me to believe. Gail was already inside, she was setting at a corner booth. She waved us over. There were perhaps ten people already there, Natives with a long history in New Mexico, mostly Navajo and Mexican, a couple of whites. Or what could be called whites, now all of the races were so intermixed, it was hard to tell, look at me.

We were sipping our coffee, when Gail said, "You know, Faith's condition made me think of something my mother told me. You've heard of the 'Long Walk', haven't you?"

"Yeah, I have, I don't know about Faith, how about it Faith have you?"

"Perhaps, something about the Indian wars, wasn't it?" Faith said.

"But what does that have to do with Faith being a milk factory?" I asked.

"That was what I was coming to, it's a little bit yucky, but not really. You see it was a matter of survival. The year was 1864. The Army had completed the burning of all of our crops and orchards; we had no way to sustain ourselves. In short we lost. Kit Carson was the officer in charge, he told us he would make sure we were treated fairly. They were going to relocate us from our homes, it started at Canyon de Chelly in Arizona. They made us walk, men, women and children from our homes to Bosque Redondo in Eastern New Mexico.

Anyway, they didn't provide them with enough food; over three thousand perished on that walk. My Great Grandfather was just a small baby. My Great, Great Grandmother had the same condition as Faith, she made lots of milk. So what they did was to give her the food, in turn she fed both the baby and my Great, Great Grandfather on her milk. I told you it was little bit yucky, but when you think about, it wasn't that bad, they all survived anyhow."

"I don't see anything yucky about that," Faith said, "but I guess, some people probably would, but not me."

"As long as were telling survival stories," I said. "My Great Grandmother survived the Sand Creek Massacre. That was on Dec. 28, 1864. On Sand Creek, Chief Black Kettle was camped there with Cheyenne and Arapaho families. Chivington and 700 so-called Colorado Militia. That was when he said, 'Kill them all, big and small, nits make lice.' Out of 123 dead, a hundred of them were women and children."

We three sat there for awhile, not saying anything. I finally spoke up, "Of course those two depredations were only two things that happened. There were many more. In the whole world things like that are going on everyday: Still! It has never stopped. But Hell, there's not much we can do about it. I guess the only thing we can do; is for us not to be a party to any of it."

Gail took a deep breath and said, "So, when do the four of you want to get married? I can have the paper work ready tomorrow."

"That's fine with us," Faith said, "but I had better call you in the morning, after we talk to Felicia and Karl." On that note, we all said our goodbyes. Faith and I got back in the Pickup. It snapped to life, with a throaty growl. "So how fast does this thing go? I asked Faith.

"I don't' know this is the first time I've every rode in it. But Teddy did say that he could bury the needle, whatever that means." She said.

I looked down at the speedometer, it read up to 140. I don't think I would like to go that fast, but it was nice to know it could. When we got back to the Hacienda, Alita was awake and hungry. The four of them were playing cards, Texas Hold Em. Alona was winning. I looked at Jake, for once he wasn't a sore loser.

Dad and Felicia were playing by remote control I think, because they couldn't take their eyes off of each other. Which made me glad, Dad deserved some happiness again.

Faith had taken Alita into the bedroom to feed her. The poker game broke up. Alona went off to bed, Jake went to his own room. I guess I was supposed to sleep with Faith, my bag was in there anyway. And I think Dad's was in Felicia's room.

The three of us were having a short nightcap. I told Felicia about what Gail had said; that some lawyers were poking around the records.

She said, "Yes, I know. They have been trying to overturn my Spanish Land Grant. They haven't made any progress though. But still I'm worried, you know how some of these crooked lawyers are; if they can't find a loophole they will try to make one."

"You know, there is one thing about loop holes; they sure resemble a hang man's noose," Dad said. "That old saying, 'give a man enough rope and he's libel to hang himself'; it sure could prove true in this case."

"Oh yeah, one more thing, Gail says that she can marry us, she wants to know if tomorrow is fast enough?" I said.

Dad put his arm around Felicia, she smiled up at him, she said, "No, it's not fast enough, but I guess it will have to do. That is if your Dad doesn't mind living in sin for one night?"

"I sure don't mind, as long as we tie the knot first thing tomorrow, does that go for you too, son?"

"I reckon I don't have much choice, if I don't go in there; she will just come out and drag me in, but that suits me to a tee."

Chapter Three

As I closed the door quietly behind me, Faith said, "I'm not asleep, but Alita is, would you put her in her crib? Lay her on her back, not her tummy."

I laid her on her back and covered her up to her chest with a light flannel blanket. She stirred a little bit, but didn't wake up. I heard the bed squeak as Faith got up and went to the bathroom, I glanced around, all I seen was her naked backside as she padded away.

I sat down on the bed and pulled my boots off. One of my socks had a hole in the toe. I was setting there contemplating that, when Faith came back.

"What's the matter, how come you're not undressed?" She said, standing there with her hands on her hips, with her head cocked to one side looking at me. I looked back, she sure was pretty. I think she was the first natural blond that I had ever seen.

"Uh, no reason, I guess I was just waiting for you to tell me, I didn't want to assume anything." I said, as I started to unbuckle my belt.

"Land sakes, you sure are something, what do you mean you don't want to assume anything? We're getting married tomorrow, here let me do that, you're all thumbs."

Alita slept all night, it must have been just after daylight when I heard her whimper, I got up and got her, I changed her diaper before I woke Faith and put Alita in her arms. Then I went and got in the shower. As soon as I was dried off, Faith handed me the baby. And she stepped in the shower. I laid Alita in the middle of our bed, she just giggled and smiled at me; I think she liked me.

I got my bag out and was looking through it for clean underwear; I couldn't find any. I was still rummaging when Faith came out, drying herself, she said, "What are you looking for?"

"It seems I don't have any clean underwear." I said, standing there in my all-together.

"No problem, on the right side of the dresser, top drawer, it's full of men's underwear. You don't mind do you?"

"Huh? You mean they were his?"

"Yeah, but I threw away all of the used ones; these are brand new, they have never been washed. I don't know why I kept them, sort of a hope chest I guess. Anyway, were my hopes realized?"

"Well, I would say so, that is if I fit the bill?" I said, walking toward her, she met me half way, jumping up, she put her legs around me and one thing led to another; as I backed her toward the wall. Alita wasn't paying any attention to us, she was busy playing with her toes.

We had a late breakfast with Dad and Felicia. It was just the four of us; everyone else was already about their chores, including Jake and Alona. Gail showed up before the noon hour, she had all of the needed paperwork.

We had the wedding at two PM, in the yard under the big cottonwood tree. There were about forty people there, some from town, Gail had told them about the wedding. And of course all of the people from the Ranchos de Chama.

The rest of the day turned out to be a big fiesta. Everyone had brought some kind of food dish; plus of course the Ranch had supplied enough to feed an army. Some of the ranch hands played on their guitars and whatever. It was the best wedding that I had ever been to; of course I guess because it was mine.

The next day Dad and Felicia left for a short honeymoon. They said they were going to Mazatlan. Miguel drove them to the airport in Santa Fe. Faith and I decided to stay right at the Ranch, what could be more romantic than here?

The Rodeo in Santa Fe was a week long affair. There was four days left, Jake had called and he could still compete. Alona was entered in the barrel racing anyway. So we went to the Rodeo. I didn't have a roping partner, but I did sign up for saddle bronc.

We took the quad cab with a horse trailer behind for Alona's horse. It sure was nice that Faith was nursing; we didn't have to take bottles along, but of course the diaper bag was a necessity. We got rooms at the Holiday Inn. Yeah, Jake and Alona had separate rooms.

That horse of Alona's was a good one, she took second place money the first day. Jake was in top form, he placed third in the bull riding, second in bareback. I got bucked off, I don't think my mind was on my riding. Besides it sure was nice having Faith to assuage my wounds.

The second day though, I did better, I took second place money. I had to show my wife that I wasn't a complete duffer. Of course she knew that I wasn't. She liked my riding capability.

I don't know why we got rooms for Jake and Alona; cause they slept in the stables with her horse. Turns out someone was messing with the horses. I guess it was the sign of the times when a horse wasn't safe anymore. But they did come back to their rooms to take showers; so I guess the cost wasn't a complete waste.

The second night there, we were laying in bed talking, right after we put Alita down for the night. Faith said, "You know, you haven't told me much about yourself?"

"I haven't? What do you want to know? You know my Dad and Brother, you know my mother died from a drunk driver. You know we have a ranch in the Big Horn Basin. I told you I was in the Navy, so what else is there?"

"You personally, what makes you tick? Oh, I know what turns you on. And that you're a caring and gentle person. You said that you were in Iraq, tell me about that?"

"Are you sure you want to hear about that? I guess you are or you wouldn't of asked. Okay, here goes. Like I said, I was a Navy Combat Pilot, our Carrier was in the Persian Gulf. I flew both daylight and night missions, pretty routine stuff, they gave you a target, you went in and dumped your load and headed back. That was all except this one time, I was on a night mission, but before I could unload I was hit with a SAM missile; you know a Surface to Air Missile. It took off one wing, I ejected. Have you ever parachuted to earth at night? No, I suppose you haven't. Anyway it sure is different at night, sort of pretty though.

I came down on the outskirts of this little town. The first thing I did was bury my chute. I made sure my locater beacon was on. You know so they could find me. Are you bored yet?" I said, as I did a few navel maneuvers around her navel...

"Stop that, I'm not bored, I want to hear all of it."

"Alright, well this town was controlled by Al Qaeda, I went toward some buildings, just on the edge of town, like I said it was night and I was always pretty good at playing hide and seek at night; I enjoyed flitting from shadow to shadow. I heard and seen a bunch of guys talking in Arabic in the courtyard of this one house. Now I could understand Arabic, but can't speak it too good.

Now these guys weren't locals, they were Al Qaeda, for sure. I got up real close, when I buried my chute, I also buried my flight suit and helmet, all I kept was my .45. With my complexion and hair color, you couldn't tell me from one of them. Anyway, they were getting this young guy ready for a suicide mission, they were strapping the C4 to him.

There must have been about thirty of them, with more in the house. In fact I was sure this house was supposed to be my intended target. They were talking that young fellow up pretty good; telling him how he was to get all of these virgins when he got to his Valhalla or some such.

Anyway they got him all cinched up and were telling him how to set it off; turns out they had a remote control; it was nothing but a cheap cell phone that they were showing him how to use it, I was also paying attention. But to make a long story short, this young fellow put the remote in his pocket. Then they all trooped in the house, for a last drink or something. But lo and behold that remote fell through a hole in his pocket, no one noticed it but me. So after they went in the house, I picked it up and ran.

It was an hour or two before dawn. I suppose that bomber was to go to marketplace or something, anyway I got myself at least a block away, then I pushed the proper button on that phone.

All hell broke loose, there must have been more munitions in that house than you could shake a stick at. Like I said, I was at least a block away, I was knocked flat, I must of passed out for a few minutes. When I came to, the whole block was on fire. I had roofing nails sticking out of me like a pin cushion. I got up and headed away from that town.

Funny thing, as I was waiting for rescue, I got to thinking, you know about all of those innocent lives those suicide bombers were taking. Then I thought about how I dropped bombs, not knowing who was really down there. Could I be guilty of taking some innocent lives myself?

That's when I decided to call it quits. Of course, it turned out that all of those nails in me sort of put me on the ineligibility list anyway. I couldn't fly combat anymore."

"Is that where all of those little scars came from?" Faith said, as she traced all of the scars with her finger, till she found the proper spot. She wasn't the only one who could play that game, I found her proper spot too!

As we were enjoying the afterglow, I asked Faith, "So, what about you? Tell me some things from your background."

"Well, as I already told you, I'm from the Napa Valley. My folks own a winery. I played high school basketball, in fact I got a scholarship for Arizona State. I played ball for them too. I'm pretty good, I would of went Pro, except I met Teddy. There's not really too much more; I was about six months pregnant when their plane went down. The only thing that kept me sane was knowing that I had this little person growing in me. And of course those dreams that I kept having about you."

"You know, I played basketball in High School too. We'll have to play sometime.

Of course, I bet you're better than me." I said.

"I don't know about that, you're pretty good in getting the ball in the basket, yourself." Faith said.

"Yeah, you could be right, I was always pretty good at the slam dunk." I said, Faith countered with, "Good, you want to do some 'one on one'?" One thing for sure she was an expert on the 'full court press'.

When we got back to the Hacienda, Dad and Felicia still weren't home. That was okay; they both deserved their happiness. Miguel and Ester had everything under control. Of course they had been running the ranch, more or less, since the

Patron had died. One thing for sure; they sure didn't need my input. The everyday running of the ranch was none of my business.

But I was a little interested in how everything worked. I asked Alona about it. She said that Felicia kept the books, but that she let Miguel and Ester handle the everyday things.

She said, "But Mom keeps a close eye on everything, she does it without being 'bossy' though. I guess she has what they call 'tact'. I try to learn from her, but sometimes I'm so impulsive."

"Don't feel bad about that, it's only normal, you're only sixteen." I said. We were setting on the front veranda swing, the two of us. She turned and looked at me, "Can I be honest with you?" She said, as she twisted a ring on her right hand.

"Sure, why not? What's on your mind?"

"Do you think Jake likes me? I mean, I'm having all sorts of feelings for him. But I don't know how to react. Like you said, I'm only sixteen, but you know, *I want*. Is that wrong?"

"Uh, you *want*? Want what?" I said. Knowing full well what she was talking about; stalling for time till my brain could get around it.

"You know what I'm talking about. I can't talk to Mom about it, or Faith either, but you seem like a big brother to me, what should I do?"

"I'll tell you what my mother told me when I was sixteen. 'slow down', I know you're hormones are racing each other to see who wins. You have to ask yourself; what do you want out of life? That is do you want a life, or do you want a baby tucked under each arm? Now I'm not saying that is what will happen to you, but it could. You see, I was ready to settle down when I met Faith, she was what I was looking for. But I'm ten years older than you are…. Now Jake, he's a man, right now at seventeen, his brains ain't in his head, there a little lower in his jeans. In time he's going to be a fine young man, that's when he will make you a good husband."

"Yes, in my mind, I know you're right. Thanks for being honest with me. Jake did tell me he wants to go to college, I do too. And if we mess around and have a kid, that will mess things up for sure. I guess that's where self control comes in."

"Yes, it helps if you have a goal and work toward it, but life is a series of goals, it takes a bunch of small ones, to get to the big one. Just remember one step at a time, Alona, one step at a time." I said, as Faith came out of the house with Alita, she motioned for Alona to get up and move, then she handed the baby to me and sat down.

As Alona went in the house, Faith asked me, "What were you talking to her about?"

"Life. Just life. Like all teenagers, their hormones are in high gear, she just wanted to know how to slow them down."

"Oh, and you know how to slow them down huh? What about your hormones, are you going to slow them down?"

"Oh, I know about hormones, I've had a lot of practice in corralling them. My hormones? Nope, I'm not going to slow them down one little bit. I'm married, I don't have to anymore."

"You had better not slow them down, they belong to me now." Faith said, as she snuggled up close. Alita blew bubbles and giggled.

This was one of those moments when everything was perfect. A person doesn't have very many of them in life. The Devil sees to that. My mother said that the Bible said to oppose the Devil and he would flee from you. I had been trying to do that all of my life, but it seems like he would come back around and bite me in the butt. This time I was going to ambush him.

How was I going to do that? They say that nature abhors a

vacuum, but Mom told me that the Devil loves a vacuum. If you had a empty brain, he was sure to fill it. I guess the trick is, to keep it full. But full of what?

That I didn't know, exactly that is. But what I did know; was that family could take up a big share of that space. And now I had one, a ready made one. Perhaps it would be enough.....

Dad and Felicia got back the next day. They both had good suntans. They had taken a Taxi from Santa Fe. Turns out they had stopped in Abiquiu to see Gail. When they had left for their honeymoon they had told Gail where they would be staying, not us. Anyway, she had called them; turns out some high priced lawyers had shown up with some papers that claimed that their clients had a claim on the Rancho.

"Gail told us that she was sure they were counterfeit. But that it was just a smoke screen for something else, she didn't know what." Dad said.

"Yes," Felicia said, "my lawyers said not to worry about it. But I can't help thinking that these people wouldn't go to all of that trouble; if they didn't have something up their sleeve."

I said, "Who are these people, did Gail know?"

"Well, yes and no. It was a company, 'Fantasies Incorporated.' From Los Angeles. It was signed by a man named Dipper Tick." Felicia said.

"Dipper Tick, you have to be kidding." I said.

"No, that was the name on the papers. Gail said that she took the papers, but didn't file them, she just put them in her desk drawer." Dad said.

"Well is the guy still in town?" I asked.

"She thinks he is, at the Bed and Bug; it's a bed and breakfast place on the edge of town." Felicia said.

"Bed and Bug? You mean they have bed bugs?" I asked.

"No, it's owned by another one of Gail's cousins, he just named it that for a joke." Felicia added.

"How many cousins does Gail have anyway?" I asked.

"I don't know for sure, I think a lot of them she just calls her cousins. But most of the Navajo are closely related anyhow." Felicia said.

I sat there thinking. For some reason I had a flash back to my younger years, on the Northern Cheyenne Reservation in Montana. My Grandfather was a Medicine Man. He taught me a lot, mostly on how to be observant. That's what a Medicine Man did anyway; observe everything around him. Especially nature. They never practiced magic; anymore than Nature itself did. Granted nature is somewhat of a miracle in itself. Again, that's all he did was observe and practice what he saw.

And that's what he taught me; take advantage of everything around you. Like I already told you about being shot down in Iraq, and how I was able to stay in the shadows. I looked at Felicia and said,

"Would it be alright with you if I did a little investigating of this Dipper Tick?"

"I suppose, but they could be dangerous, you might get hurt." Felicia said, looking at my father.

Dad said, "Don't worry about Clay, he can take care of himself; he's hell on wheels."

Faith spoke up, "Hey lets slow down a bit, if Clay is going to go poking around, I'm going with him, we're a team. There is more than enough breast milk in the Fridge, Grandma can watch her for a few hours."

Felicia said, "Are you sure Honey, you haven't been too active lately?"

"Yes, I'm sure. You forget I was a basketball all star, plus I was also very good in gymnastics. I can handle myself." Faith said, as she got up and started pacing the room.

The phone rang, it was Gail, turns out we didn't have to go see this Dipper Tick this night; cause he had checked out and went to Santa Fe. Faith stopped her pacing and said,

"That doesn't change anything, we can go to Santa Fe, can't we?"

"Yeah sure, sweetheart, but not tonight and when we do, we'll be gone more than overnight, what about Alita?" I said.

"Well, we'll... we'll, just take her with us, that's what." Faith said, with a stubborn set to her jaw.

"Yes, we can. All I want to do is just poke around a little anyway. What better cover than having my family with me. We'll make it like a holiday, it'll be fun." I wasn't as upbeat as I sounded, the best laid plans of mice and men always have a way of getting messed up. I guess you could call that Murphy's Law. But in knowing that you can be forearmed.

Dad cleared his throat, "Just what kind of poking around are you planning on?"

"All I want to find out; is who's all back of this business, 'Fantasies Incorporated'. Is it just this Dipper Tick or are more people involved?"

"Well, can't a lot of that be found out on the... What do they call it? I know, the Internet." Dad said.

"Yeah, I guess, but I'm sure Gail can do that for us." I said.

"Gail? Why her, I know all about computer's; you forget I went to College and I like to think I'm a modern girl, or woman now, I guess, since I have a baby and on my second husband."

"And your last husband by the way, but not your last baby, I plan on giving you several more." I said. "But if you want to you can get on that box of transistors tonight or do you want to wait till morning?"

"I can wait till morning. I had other things planned this night, you know, I, uh, told you about it?" She nervously glanced at Felicia.

Felicia smiled, "Don't be embarrassed, Karl and I, have the same thing planned. For every night the rest of lives; that's the goal anyway. Of course that might change when we get old; like in our nineties." Then she took Dad's hand and they disappeared into their private little world; their bedroom.

Faith looked at me and smiled and crooking her finger she beckoned me to follow her. She didn't have to ask me twice.

Alita was already asleep in her crib, we both stood there looking down at her. "Faith," I said, "just how old is she, I figured she was about four or five months old?"

"She's six months, in fact I think we're going to have to start feeding her some solid food, you know, baby food in a jar."

"Yeah, good idea. I sure don't know anything about babies, but I guess we'll learn together." I said.

"Well, it's a good thing that I did a lot of baby setting; I'm not a complete dunce about it, you know."

"I didn't mean to say that you were. I'm sorry if it came out that way. You'll have to forgive me, it's just that having a baby is so new to me, plus also a pretty wife like you. So I might make a few blunders along the way." I said, as I picked Faith up and took her to bed.

"You haven't made any blunders so far," Faith said with a moan.

While Faith was getting things together the next morning, I went out and checked the pickup over. The ranch had their own gasoline tanks, so I filled it up. The pickup box was covered with a metal cover, with a lock at the back. When you unlocked it, it raised by itself on pneumatic arms, pretty neat, all kinds of room to store stuff out of the weather, plus you would have to have a cutting torch to break into it.

38

Faith came out of the house with two suitcases, all of the clothes the three of us would need for awhile. I stored them in back, Faith said, "Honey, the stroller is in the hall closest, would you get it please."

The stroller was where she said it would be. Plus on the back closet wall, there were gun racks; there must have been ten rifles, plus five pistols. I picked up a compact 9mm, it had a ten shot clip. It fit right in my inner jacket pocket, not even a bulge. I looked around for extra clips, I found three of them. Why I took that pistol, I really couldn't say, just a hunch, besides it didn't weigh all that much.

When I got back to the truck Faith was waiting for me, "Uh," I said, "aren't we forgetting something?"

Faith looked around, "I don't think so sweetheart." She said with a straight face. Then she smiled, "don't worry Grandma is changing her; they'll be right here. Did you actually think I would forget Alita?"

"No, I guess not. But you know I'm not the sharpest knife in the drawer." I said, giving her a hangdog look.

She snuggled close and kissed me on the cheek, "don't you worry Baby, you're sharp enough for me." Now that perked me up, right smart. Now there's one thing I had found out about women when I was just a little squirt; 'don't act any smarter than you need to be'. Of course that doesn't work with all women; just those that love you.

Felicia came out with Alita on one arm and the diaper bag in the other, Dad was right behind her. I really don't think that they were going to let each other out of sight.

Dad said, "Now you kids be careful; we don't know if this Dipper Tick is dangerous or not. Do you need any money?"

Faith said, "No, we don't need money; I've got plenty." I added, "Don't worry, all we're going to do is just try and find out who this guy is; personally. Plus, I think we'll make this a little vacation for the three of us, just have fun."

Faith took Alita and buckled her in the built in car seat. We said our goodbyes to the folks. I don't know where Alona and Jake were; probably off doing chores or something. I hoped it wasn't something.

I sure like this truck it handled like a dream. I was finding more out about it all of the time. Turns out it also had an electronic stabilizer system built in; to keep it from rolling over. Teddy must have been quite the engineer or just spent a lot of money getting someone else to do it.

I looked over at Faith, "Say Honey," I said, "you said that you had plenty of money. Just what did you mean?"

"Just that, you might say that I'm rich. You see Teddy had a life insurance policy, the face value was two million, but it had a double indemnity rider; for accidental death it doubled. Four million, tax free. I haven't touched any of it. It's just drawing interest. But I do have an ATM card."

"Well I guess that's good. I have about a hundred thousand in my bank account, plus about three thousand in cash in my billfold." I said.

"Yeah, I know what's in your billfold, I looked. I just wanted to make sure you weren't carrying any condoms in there. I was happy to see that there weren't any. You can feel free to look through my purse anytime you want to." Faith said.

"Now that's a funny thing. My mother told me when I was just verily walking; you don't ever get in a woman's purse. That's one thing I will never do, unless it's an emergency."

"I don't have any secrets to hide from you." Faith said.

"That's not the point, a woman's purse is more personal then seeing her naked. A man has no purpose in a woman's purse." I said.

"Do you have that hang up about your wallet?" Faith asked.

"No, of course not, a man doesn't carry any secrets in his

wallet, they're all in his head. And a smart wife can dig them out of there with no trouble at all. You might say, what you see is what you get." I said.

"Is that right? Can I get what I see anytime that I want it?" Faith said, with a sly smile.

"Yep, anytime. But tit for tat, that goes for me also." I said, right back.

"Of course, sweetheart, I wouldn't have it any other way." Faith said, licking her lips.

We got on Route 84, which ran through Abiquiu and then on to Santa Fe. We didn't stop in Abiquiu, just slowed down so we wouldn't get a ticket. The next town of any size was Espanola, we did stop there, Faith had to use the facilities. Would you believe they still had a full service gas station?

The attendant was a young white man. I hadn't paid much attention as to how Faith was dressed, but he did. Faith was wearing a light summer dress, of course in the pickup, it had worked itself up to show pretty much all of her legs. When she swung around to get out, it showed all of her legs, clear up to her panties. Then when she reached in to get Alita, that must have been quite a sight also.

I had to tell him twice, to top off the tank. Couldn't blame him for looking; Faith was a 10 for sure. But in my eyes she was clear off the scale. He was taking his time, washing the windshield and checking the air pressure in the tires, just waiting for her to come back. I couldn't help but smile, in his shoes I would of probably did the same. When Faith and Alita came back, he stood there with his mouth open. I reached over and pushed his jaw shut, "Careful there Pardner, you'll catch flies in there," I said, as I paid him. I slipped him an extra five, he didn't even notice....

Faith said, "Would you get me a Soda?"

"What kind?" I said. "A Diet Cola is fine." She said. I

went to the machine and put a dollar bill in, out came one. Of course there was no change. The machine beside that one, dispensed bottled water, I got two of them, one for Alita and one for me. That attendant was still standing there staring at Faith.

As we got back on the road, I said. "Do you always get a reaction like that?"

"What reaction? What are you talking about?"

"You know, that attendant."

"Oh, him. Sometimes, but usually not so overt. Are you jealous?"

"No, not really. When you have the most beautiful woman in the world, I guess you have to get used to it." I said, patting her knee.

"Thank you Sweetheart, that was nice of you to say that. But you know you're no slouch yourself. I have noticed how women look at you also. And yes, I am jealous, so there!

"You have no reason to be. I would never cheat on you. My Mother would rise from her grave and give me hell, if I did." I said.

Alita was asleep in her car seat. Faith was nodding off herself. I turned the radio down low, so as not to disturb them. I was reflecting back over the past couple of weeks.

So much had changed in my life and you could say in Faith and Alita's also. I wasn't disappointed on how my life had changed. I don't think Faith was either.

Alita was at that age where her personality was starting to kick in; she was a happy child. She sure smiled a lot at me anyway. Or maybe I just tickled her funny bone, somewhat like a clown would.

I seen some flashing lights up ahead. Looked like the Highway Patrol had somebody stopped. I slowed down and started to move to the left, to give them the required room. I was just about past them, when I seen a flash and the Patrolman staggered back from the window. I knew what had happened; he had just got shot.

I whipped the truck around far enough to block the car from moving. Faith woke up, "What's going on?" She said.

"Stay down, don't get out!" I said, as I got out and reached in my jacket pocket for that 9mm, that I had put in there from the hall closest.

There were three men in that car. The one who shot the Patrolman was just getting out when I had blocked them in. I had automatically looked at the Cop, he was hit in his right shoulder, he was stunned, but if he didn't bleed out he would be Okay.

The shooter turned his pistol my way, I shot him through his left eye. The other two were already out of the car, a bullet whizzed by my ear. He was a piss poor shot. Another bullet flattened itself against the back window of the truck.

I took a little more time with this one, I hit him in his right forearm; his pistol flew away, he went down screaming. The other guy threw his gun down and screamed, "Don't shoot, I give up!"

Faith jumped out of the truck with her cell phone stuck to her ear, "I called 911, their on the way." I walked over to the guy who gave up; I clipped him behind the ear with the butt of my pistol; he went down like a rag doll. Since I had to check on the Cop, I didn't want this Yo-Yo changing his mind and shooting me in the back. The other guy was down on his knees moaning and crying.

The officer that was down, was just coming out of it. I sat him up and took his shirt off, the bullet had passed clean through. I used some of his tee shirt and plugged the hole, it didn't look like there was any major damage to any main arteries.

Faith had come over too, she said, "Just take deep breaths, help is on the way, they said they were only about ten minutes away, I gave them the mileage post that we are close by." She said to the Cop, he nodded, Faith laid him back down and put his jacket under his feet to raise them up, so he wouldn't go in shock. Then she looked at me, "Perhaps you had better put a tourniquet around that idiot's arm, otherwise I'm afraid he will bleed to death." I glanced over at him. "Go on Honey, if you didn't want him alive, then you should of shot to kill." She said, as cool as could be.

They were as good as their word, another Cruiser and an ambulance pulled in not five minutes later. They hustled the injured Patrolman into the ambulance and it took off. It wasn't five minutes later that another one showed up, along with a Cruiser with the shift Captain in it. The first thing he did was play back the video from the Trooper's car.

It was all on there. He came over to me. "I want to thank you for stopping to help, I'm sure they would of finished him off, if you hadn't of intervened. May I see you're I.D.?"

"Sure." I said, I pulled out my billfold and showed him my Wyoming Driver's License and my Military I.D. card. "Navy huh?" I nodded. "Well, again thank you Lieutenant. I see you're driving a New Mexico truck, is that your wife?"

"Yes, we've only been married for a little over two weeks. She's from the Ranchos de Chama, she was married to Teddy Cortez, he was killed a little over a year ago in a plane accident."

"Yes, I remember that, I was the first one on the scene. Him and his Father were both killed. Well Son, you've married into one of the oldest family's in New Mexico, you realize that don't you?"

"I don't know, I guess." I said, when I heard a moan. "Oh

Yeah, don't forget that guy down in the ditch there, I had to put him out, he's not shot. But I didn't want to get it in the back while I was seeing to your trooper, so I just clipped him behind his ear."

"Yeah, I seen him down there. They'll get to him. Have you ever seen these guys before?" He asked me.

"No, I haven't, I don't think Faith has either or else she would of said something. We were heading for Santa Fe, is it Okay if we leave? Our baby is asleep in the truck."

"Sure, I guess. As long as you stay there for a couple of days; just in case I need to get more details. But that video pretty well tells the tale."

All of the while all of this had been happening the traffic hadn't stopped; they just slowed down to rubber neck. Faith was waiting beside the truck, as I walked up I noticed where that bullet had hit the rear window of the truck. I reached out to touch the spot. The residue wiped away at my touch.

"I'll be dammed, that's bullet proof glass; did you know that?" I asked Faith.

"No, I didn't, but Teddy was always a nut for details. Look Alita is still sleeping; all of the shooting didn't even wake her up. Where did you get that pistol?" Faith asked.

"In the hall closet; when I went to get the stroller. I don't know why I picked it up; premonition maybe?" I said.

"No, more like dumb luck, wouldn't you say?" She said, as she pulled me close and kissed me, "you saved that guys life, I bet his wife would like to thank you."

"Yeah, I suspect, but I didn't do anything special it was like instinct just took over; I wasn't even thinking. I said, as we both got in the truck and went on our way.

Faith looked over at me, "Did you notice that he didn't ask you for your gun?"

"Who didn't?"

"The Captain, you're supposed to have a permit for a concealed weapon in this state."

"Knowing Cops, I bet he will get around to it. Why do you think he wants us to stick around in Santa Fe, for?" I said. Then Alita woke up, hungry of course. By the time she had her fill, we were on the outskirts of Santa Fe.

We drove around a little while; till we found the most expensive looking Motel. I didn't want to stay in a Hotel. I liked having my vehicle close at all times. The place had all of the amenities of a Hotel anyway, plus I could park right in front of our door.

This place had a four star restaurant too; anyway that's what the ad on the dresser said. After supper, on the way back to our room, I noticed the swimming pool; it was also close by our room. "Did we bring any swimming suits?" I asked Faith.

"Sure, I have my Bikini, I tried it on before we left, I can get back in it since I lost all of the baby weight. I even have a small one piece for Alita, I got it when I had a baby shower. And yes, I have one for you too."

"I guess that answers the rest of my question; do you want to go swimming?"

"Yes, of course we do. And don't worry Alita won't pee in the pool. She never does pee in her bath water; she did once in awhile till she was about three months old; but one time I told her not to do that and she hasn't since."

"Well I wasn't worried about that, it didn't even come to mind. But it's good to know." There was only one other couple in the pool; maybe because it was mid-week. I don't think they appreciated us coming in. The women had her top half off; she hurriedly pulled it up as her cheeks were turning red. Faith smiled at her and nodded, I think that made her feel better, her husband or friend swam away to the other end of the pool.

When Faith got in the pool with Alita, the woman swam over. That's one thing about a baby; she's an ice breaker. "Oh what a pretty baby, she looks just like your husband," she cooed.

"Why thank you," Faith said. "I thought so too. Your friend seems a little shy," Faith added.

"That's my husband, we're newly-weds. You know how it is when your on your honeymoon and there is no else in the pool. He didn't want you to see that he was aroused; he is sort of shy." Then she called to her husband, "Frank, can you come back over now?"

He swam toward us, his face was starting to lose its red blush. The woman said, "My name is Fern Blake, this is my husband Frank Blake."

I said, "My name is Clay Bronson, this is my wife Faith and our daughter, Alita. We're on a little vacation. We're from Abiquiu. We ranch there." I said, shaking his proffered hand. "Are you from close by?" I asked.

Fern answered, "Yes, we're both from right here in Santa Fe. Frank is the clerk and recorder. I work in the office also, or I guess I should say I did; I had to quit when we got married. He didn't want anyone to think he was playing favorites; you know how office politics can be."

Fern bent over a little and started talking baby talk to Alita. I didn't want to mention it, but when she pulled her top up, the back hook must of come unlatched; her bra top was floating free, exposing her breasts. I caught Faith's eye, she seen what I was trying to tell her.

"Uh, Fern. Would you like me to fasten your top? It seems to be a little loose."

Fern looked down, "Sure, can I hold Alita while you do that?" She didn't bat an eye. Faith let her take Alita then Faith fastened her bra. Fern said, "You know I used to teach swimming at the Y, we used to teach baby's this young to swim, would you like me to show you?"

"I suppose so, is it dangerous?" Faith said, with a little trepidation in her voice.

"No, of course not, mostly it involves showing you how to teach her." They, the three of them moved to the shallow end of the pool. I looked at Frank and said...

"Well Frank, how long have you been the clerk and recorder?"

"Let's see, I am 35 now and I got the job when I was 25, so ten years I guess. You say you Ranch around Abiquiu, what's the name of your Ranch?"

"Ranchos de Chama." I answered.

"I've heard of that ranch, it's a Spanish Land Grant isn't it?" Frank said.

"Yes, it belongs to my mother-in-law; Felicia Cortez. How come it rang a bell?" I asked.

"Strangest thing, yesterday was my last day of work; that is before we took two weeks off. Anyway there was this guy came in and he wanted to look at the plats of all of the Spanish land grants in New Mexico, especially those of the Ranchos de Chama."

"Would his name happen to be Dipper Tick?" I asked.

"Why yes, that was his name, how did you know?"

"He's been poking around Abiquiu also. Did he want to know anything in particular about them?"

"Yes, he was interested in the mineral rights, I told him that most all of the land grants kept there own mineral rights. I suppose a few of them have been sold off." Frank said.

"Let me ask you this; is there anyway any of these Spanish land grants can be contested?"

"I suppose anything is possible, but to my knowledge none of them have been overturned. But there are a lot of crooked lawyers out there. Like I said, anything is possible these days. Just look at how this administration is twisting the constitution."

"Yes, I know, all of these illegal phone taps for one thing." I said. "Did you let him see those plats?"

"No, I did not. He even offered me a bribe, I just laughed in his face. I like to think that I'm a good judge of character. He struck me as a pompous egotistical ass of low moral fiber." Frank said with a sniff. I had to smile to myself, here he was just about to put it to his new wife in a public pool. Well, can't say as I blamed him much though, they were alone, at first.

"Thank you Frank, for that heads up on him. Do you know where he's staying in town?" I asked, not really expecting an answer.

"Why yes, at the Plaza; it's the biggest Hotel in town." Frank said.

I looked over at the women, Alita was swimming under water between the two of them. I did hear at one time; that if you got children young enough they took naturally to the water. I glanced back at Frank, he was staring at his wife, licking his lips. I called to Faith, "Perhaps we had better get out; I think Alita has had enough for one day."

Faith glanced at me quizzically. I looked sideways at Frank, she understood. "It's bedtime for Alita," Faith told Fern. "Perhaps we will see you at breakfast, that is if you get up that early," she added.

Alita really didn't want to get out; she just made one small protest, then acquiesced, she was a bright child. As we were walking back to the room, I said, "So you think Alita looks like me?"

"No, I did not say that; Fern said that she looks a lot like her father, I just agreed, that yes she does. I just didn't tell her that you were not Alita's father. It was none of her business. I think she is the type of person that likes to gossip, I just didn't give her any." Faith said, as her off hand slipped down the back of my swim trunks.

Chapter Four

The next morning we were laying in bed sipping our morning coffee; when there came a knock on the door. I slipped on my robe and palming my pistol behind my back, I answered the knock.

It was the Highway Patrol Captain from yesterday. He said, "May I come in?" I noticed that he had the morning newspaper in his hand, "Sure come on in, do you want a cup of coffee?"

"Yes, I would like one." While I was answering the door Faith had got up and put her robe on, she went and got him a cup. "Do you take cream or sugar?" She asked.

"Just black would be fine thank you so much, I'm afraid I haven't had breakfast yet; this will hit the spot." We sat down at the table. He took a sip and then opened the paper to the front page; "you both take good pictures, evidently one of those cars that passed yesterday was a reporter for the daily Bugle. I don't know how he got your names; probably from one of my Officers." He held the paper up, in big blazing headlines, it read: 'Local Rancher and Wife save the life of Highway Patrol Officer.'

In smaller letters underneath it said. "Local rancher and his wife, Clay and Faith Bronson; save the life of Officer Kenneth Holden. After seeing Officer Holden get shot, they stopped their vehicle and shot and killed the wanted murderer Ted Wayland and his cohort; 'Boat Lewis', who was also a wanted criminal from the Los Angeles area. The third man in the vehicle they knocked unconscious, no name is available for him at press time." It went on, but that's all I read.

I looked at the Captain, "That guy I shot in the arm, he died?" I asked.

"Yeah, I guess so. Turns out he was a bleeder; they couldn't get it stopped, I guess he was in the wrong line of work. By the way, my name is: Courtney Lopez. Yeah, I know, most people think Courtney is a girl's name, you can just call me Cort. It's simpler that way."

I reached out and shook his hand. He added. "Oh yeah, by the way, I will need that pistol. I brought you another one, brand new, just like yours, same make same model. Also I brought you a permit for it. Didn't want you packing that thing illegally. We need yours for evidence. Yeah also, the both of you will have to go the inquest. Just routine stuff. But it won't be till next week, will you stick around or come back for it?" He asked.

"I don't know for sure; we have some things to check on here. The newspaper gave the names of those guys, but do you know what they were doing in this neck of the woods?" I asked.

I don't know for sure; but the guy you knocked out was a lawyer from L.A. any way that was what his I.D. said. Worked for some big law firm; I didn't pay much attention to their name. Of course he clamed up right away, asked for his lawyer. That pistol he had beside him, he did threaten you with that didn't he?"

"Well, he had it in his hand and it was pointed at me at one time, but when he seen the other two go down, he shucked it right away." I said. "So I guess you could say that he would of taken a shot; if he thought he could of got away with it."

"That's good enough for us, we'll charge him with assault with a deadly weapon."

"What was his name anyway?" Faith asked.

"Delbert Westinghouse. He did sort of fit that name didn't he?" Cort said.

"Well, I would say more of a Dilbert, not Delbert." Faith said.

"Yeah, there is some what of a distinction between the two, isn't there?" I said.

Faith said, "Yes sweetheart, there is, I would much rather be a Del; instead of a Dil." Faith got up; Alita had woke up and was hungry. Faith picked her up and sat on the bed and turned her back and proceeded to feed her.

"Well, I suppose I had better be going. I'll let you know when that inquest is. And if you decide to go home let me know, Okay?" Cort said....his face turning red.

"Honey," Faith said, turning around with Alita on one breast and the other bare, "do you think we have time for me to get my hair done. I noticed there is a Beauty Shop here?"

"Sure do you want me to call for an appointment, and then we can go to breakfast?" I said. As I dropped my robe and reached for my pants.

"Would you really do that for me? Teddy never did anything that he didn't consider manly." Faith said as she switched feeding outlets.

"Sure, what's the big deal about calling for a hair appointment for you? I'm not the one getting my hair done." I said, as I buckled my belt and went to the phone. Turns out she could get in about 10:00 this very morning. We finished getting dressed, the three of us. One thing about Alita; she was a happy child. She never cried or fussed unless of course she was hungry or had a dirty diaper. I guess I would be little cross also if I was hungry or had crapped my pants.

When we got to the dinning room, Frank and Fern Blake

were already seated and was reading the morning paper and sipping their morning coffee. They both looked up as we entered. The look on their faces was one of two very perplexed people.

The hostess seated us at the next table to them. Franks expression was one of almost fear, bordering on envy. Now Fern was another story altogether; her eyes were flitting back and forth between the two of us. You could tell she full of millions of questions. Well maybe not millions, but a lot anyway. Faith smiled at her and that was all it took; here she came and pulling up an extra chair she sat down. The only thing that saved us was the fact that her food came a couple of seconds later.

We ordered, also we ordered some cream of wheat for Alita, this was to be her first time; out side of prepared baby food. She really liked it. Of course we didn't feed her all that much; just enough to know that she liked it.

The Blake's were done with their food and drinking more coffee by the time we finished eating. Faith looked at her watch, she had ten minute's before her hair appointment. As Fern came up, Faith said, "I'm sorry we don't have too much time to talk, I have a hair appointment at ten."

"You do? So do I, perhaps we can talk there, if that would be alright?" Fern said.

"Sure, that would be fine, here Clay, will you take Alita for me?"

"You bet, she's no problem at all." I said. As I wet a napkin and washed her face. The baby's face; not Faith's. Alita just made a little face, as all kids do when you wash their faces. Then she grabbed the wet napkin and gave it a toss, it landed in Frank's coffee cup.

"Oh, I'm sorry Frank, here let me call the waitress, she will get you a clean cup." I said.

"No, don't, I've had enough anyway, we were just killing time; till you folks got done so we could talk to you."

"Okay, come set over here. What's on your mind?" I said.

"Well, we read the morning paper; we couldn't help but see your pictures and read the story. Those men, the two you killed and the other one were with that Dipper Tick in the office the other day. I just thought you would like to know." Frank said, as he was twisting a napkin into knots. Alita was watching him, she looked at me and motioned for me to give her a napkin to play with. I did.

Frank was still talking, but I wasn't paying much attention; I was watching Alita. She tore off part of the napkin; dipping it in what was left of her cream of wheat she rolled it up into a ball and then she tossed it toward Frank's coffee cup that held her other napkin; it landed in the coffee cup on the other table. Then she tore off another piece and did the same thing. Damn, she was not only bright, but she hit what she was aiming at. I never told her to stop it; I just handed her more napkins.

The waitress had been watching us, she was a blue eyed red head. I bet she was as Irish as they came. She came over, "Is there anything more that you want?" She said as she laid more napkins on the tray of Alita's high chair.

"No, I don't think so, just the bill I guess." I said, as I winked at her. No I wasn't hitting on her, she knew what I meant. She reached out and ruffled Alita's hair.

Frank's voice came back into my consciousness. "So therefore, I just wanted to let you know if there is anything I can do for you, be sure and let me know."

"I will Frank, but if they come back around; this is my satellite cell phone number," I wrote it down on a piece of napkin and handed it to him. He looked at it. I continued, "Just call anytime, either Faith or myself will answer it."

Alita and I went back to our room, I changed her diaper and

asked her, "Do you want to go swimming?" She gurgled and clapped her hands. I took that as a yes. I put her little swimming suit on her. And changed into mine. There was a young family with three small children already in the pool. They were trying to teach the kids to swim. It's a fact that most kids that grow up in the high desert do not know how to swim. They have a hard time finding water deep enough to swim in. This family looked like they were of that fold.

I sat Alita down in the shallow end; she sank to the bottom and then started to swim along the bottom and then she came up for air and then back down. The mother of the family was staring at us.

"How in the world did you teach her to do that?" She asked me.

"I didn't, my wife and Fern Blake gave her a lesson yesterday. I guess she's just a natural," I said. Her children were watching. Her youngest was probably just under two, she watched for a little bit, then she just dropped under water and started to do the same thing as Alita was doing. The younger children start to swim, the better they do.

We spent the next hour there; helping the other two children, they also picked it up fast. The parent's names were Harry and Sally, I didn't pick up on their last name. But I did find out they worked for a ranch not to far from our own. They were on a small vacation.

Alita and I had just came back to our room, when Faith got back. I was stunned; in walked a dark haired brunette. Alita stared at her. So did I. "What, what did you do?" I said.

"I had it dyed, do you like it?" She said. Now my Mother didn't raise any idiots.

"Yeah, I think I do," I said. "But, you're sort of mismatched aren't you?" I said.

"I already thought about that," she said, holding up a small box, "this dye is made especially for pubic hair, will you help me with it tonight?"

"Sure, I guess so. But why did you want to dye your hair?" I asked.

"Cause. You know, maybe you don't; but I was a blond with Theodore. I want to forget about him, not that I haven't, but, this is my new life, the only thing I want to remind me of him is Alita. Are you sure you like it?"

"Yes, I definitely do. It makes you look not only sexy; but deadly so. I could almost call you Elmira. Wow! Too bad Alita isn't asleep."

"Oh, that can wait, we have all of our lives to look forward to." She said, as she kissed me and plastered herself against me. She untangled herself, then sighed and said, "I guess I had better tell you the truth; I was never a natural blond. I'm sorry if I deceived you. Are you mad at me?"

"No, of course not. I fell in love with you; not the color of your hair." I said, kissing the nape of her neck. She moaned a little bit, then said,

"Honey, you had better stop that; Alita is staring at us." I pulled back, not because of what she said, but because our phone was ringing.

It was Cort, "Sorry to disturb you," He said, "but the inquest was put on fast forward, it's this afternoon, can the two of you make it?"

"Sure, no problem, but we'll have to bring Alita with us; we don't have a baby sitter. Will that be Okay? I said.

"I don't know why not, that'll be a good touch anyway. That Dipper Tick made bail for Delbert Washington; even though it was set at five hundred thousand. I half way hope he jumps bail; we could use the money."

"Will they be at the inquest?" I asked.

"I don't know why they would; it's just a coroner's inquest.

I'm sure after they see the video from the patrol car there won't be any doubt as to the rightness of the kills." Cort said. He added. "I'm sure you will be cleared; then you won't have to stick around any longer, that is if you don't want to."

"Yeah, we'll see, thanks a lot Cort, what time is the inquest?"

"Two PM, is that alright?"

"Sure, we can make it, at the court house, right?"

"Yep, see you there." Then he hung up. I turned to my wife; did you hear all of that?"

"Yes, what do you want me to wear? Something sexy or something prim and proper?"

"I think I would go with prim and proper; of course you could wear gunny sacks and you would still look sexy. But do your best to tone it down."

"In that case, I had better go buy something. Can you watch Alita for a half hour more? They have a boutique here, so it won't take long."

She was a good as her word; she came back in a dark gray suit with the skirt down to her knees, along with a pair of medium high heels. I was at a loss for words.

The more clothes she put on the sexier she looked. I didn't say anything, it wasn't her fault, she was just born that way.

I just put on clean jeans and shirt along with my boots and hat. I did make sure I put the new pistol in my overall jacket pocket. I had already put the gun permit in my billfold. We fed Alita before we left.

They had a metal detector at the court house, I showed them my permit. Turns out it just wasn't a regular permit; it was police officers permit and as such it allowed me to carry the gun into court houses; just like a police officer would.

When the guard handed the permit back to me, I looked at it, closely this time. It said that I was a special agent for the state of New Mexico. I wondered what kind of a special agent?

After I stowed my billfold in my jeans pocket, Alita held her arms out to me. I took her, I think she liked her new Dad. I know I really liked her. Faith straightened her suit jacket and arraigned her skirt. Everyone was staring at her. Blond or brunette, red or purple, her hair color made no difference. She was a bombshell no matter which way you looked at her.

Cort was right; the inquest was over in a matter of minutes. It was more or less a formality. The coroner ruled it justifiable. As we were walking out, I asked Cort, "Hey, I just read this permit; what kind of an agent am I supposed to be?"

"A special agent appointed by the Governor, he is concerned about these land speculators. The Governor is a friend of mine. I told him about Dipper Tick, turns out he's not the only one who has been poking around. He wants you to look into it; see if my maybe organized crime might be trying to move into our state. I'll bring your I.D. and badge over later."

"Uh, I really don't know about this, just what would I have to do? And who would I report to?"

"This really isn't that kind of job; like you have to clock in and stuff. The Governor just wanted you to have the proper authority. They did a background check and your record is squeaky clean. And oh, by the way, it doesn't pay anything."

"Well in that case, how could I turn it down. Do I at least get an expense account, car, or anything?" I said with a smile.

"No, no car. But if you have any legal expenses or anything like that, just submit a request for reimbursement." Cort said, with a lopsided grin.

"You mean if someone sues me, the state will pay for it?" I said.

"Well you are an employee of the state, that would be only fair. Wouldn't it?"

"Fair? Yeah, I guess. I think it all depends on what side of the word 'fair' that you're standing on. But yeah, if I find anything out, I'll keep the state informed. That would be only 'fair' wouldn't it?" Cort sort of looked a little crestfallen, at what I had just said. He didn't know quite what I meant. That was okay, I didn't either.

As I was buckling Alita into her car seat Faith was watching me, she said, "Honey, are you Okay, you look a little glum?"

"I'm alright. I was just thinking that's all. A lot has happened to us since we left the ranch. I don't think that I'm too happy about it. How could I be; I just shot and killed two men. Granted they deserved it, but just the same it grates on a person."

"I would say that I know how you feel, but that would be false, how could I? I've never had to kill anyone. Oh, there were times I would of liked to, I suppose, but in retrospect I'm glad I never have. But you just remember, you saved that Officer's life, and I would say his life was worth ten of people like you shot."

"Yes, I know Honey. I guess what's happening to me is just a delayed reaction. It's happened to me before; after some operations that I've been on. I sure get tired of this world at times. But, you know what? You and Alita make it all worthwhile; life that is. So what do you want to do the rest of the day?"

"I know, let's play like tourists. We can go down to the old part of town and sightsee and shop. Would you like to do that?" Faith said...

"Sure Sweetheart, I guess that would be fun. I don't think that I ever have." I said, as I started the truck and worked my way into the line of traffic.

Tourist season was in full swing, we did find a parking

space in a lot that was specially made for tourists. As we were parking, a car with Montana plates parked beside us. It was an older couple, he looked to be in his late 60's, her in her early 60's or late 50's. They were dressed in typical western style. Much like us really.

As we were putting Alita in her stroller, the woman couldn't help but make a fuss over her. "Oh, how cute, how old is she?" She asked as she talked baby talk to Alita. Why women do that I have no idea. "Almost seven months." Faith answered.

"She looks just like her Father," the women said, looking at me.

"Yes, we've been told that before," I said, then added, "Where about in Montana are you from?"

The older gentleman said, "Judith Basin, I have a ranch there, we're just down here for a little vacation. Are you from here?" He asked me.

"Well, yes and no. My mother-in-law has a ranch in the Chama Valley, my folks have a place in the Big Horn Basin. But Faith and I, we have each other and of course our daughter Alita."

"Well, then you have the world, don't you?" He said.

"Yes, we do. My name is Clay Bronson, this is my wife Faith, and of course you have already met Alita." I reached out to shake his hand.

He said, "I'm Charles Hester, this is my wife Edith."

We chit-chatted, for awhile, like strangers will, then parted for our different ways. They were pretty much doing just as we were, playing the tourist. Like I mentioned before they were dressed much like people from Montana usually are; boots, jeans, western get-up. He was carrying his billfold in his right hip pocket, the same as me. Now why I noticed that, was beyond me. Perhaps it was because every time I was out in public I was always conscious about my wallet. I sort of kept one hand on it, not literally, but in mind. Oh yeah, she had her purse on a long strap over one shoulder. Easy pickings, right?

They were a couple of shops ahead of us, when I noticed some pick pockets setting them up for hit. "Look Faith, their being set up." I said, she looked up from a window that held turquoise jewelry.

"Yeah, two men and a woman, right?"

"Yep, well really a man and a woman, plus it looks like a kid. I think the man is the distraction and the woman is the Dip; and I think she hands off to the kid. Or vice-versa I guess it could be. Let's get close, I'm getting a little bored anyway, I need some action."

"Bored? How can you be bored, you have a brain, don't you?" Faith said, as we maneuvered the stroller through the crowd.

"Yeah, I have a brain, but all it wants to do is think about you naked." I said, leering at her.

As we were doing this, Alita was listening to us and picking up on our vibes, you might say. I may be mistaken but I think she knew what we were talking about. The pickpocket's, not the other, she hears that all of the time.

We got there just as the man sort of stumbled in front of the older couple, the older gentleman reached out to steady him and the woman made the dip. Just as she had his wallet clear, my hand clamped like a vise on her wrist. Her eyes flashed up at me, but she didn't struggle.

The interference man made a dive at me, Faith pushed the front of the stroller into his path, he tripped over it and fell flat on the sidewalk. Faith stepped on his neck and held him firmly to the concrete. Every time he tried to struggle, she pressed a little harder, cutting off his wind. The hand off kid stood there, not knowing what to do.

If looks could kill, I would be dead… The woman's eyes were spitting fire at me. "You ought to mind your own business, if you knew what was good for you." She said.

"Strange thing about that, I never do know what is good for me. And evidently you don't either. If the three of you are pro's, you're not very good." I said, as I took the billfold out of her hand and handed it back to Charles.

Just then a cop showed up, after a short explanation he took both of them into custody. The kid was still standing just around the corner, peeking at us. We didn't say anything to the cop about the kid. The kid didn't think anybody knew he was with them. I jerked my head at Faith, nodding toward the kid. I took the stroller and continued to talk to the Hesters. Faith moseyed over closer to the kid. I could see that she was talking to him.

After agreeing to let the Hesters buy us supper, I walked over to where Faith and the kid were still talking. As I got closer, I could see that I was mistaken, he wasn't a he, he was a she, but she was still a kid, looked to be twelve or thirteen.

She had short red hair and freckles. Faith turned to me, "Clay I would like you to meet, Rosie O'Claire, an orphan. That is till the two pickpockets became her foster parents. They were training her in the ways of the nefarious. And since we have removed her meal ticket, I guess we're stuck with her for awhile anyway."

"So Rosie", I asked, were they from Santa Fe, or what?"

"No", she said, in a pleasant contralto voice, "they have a place in Las Vegas, Nevada. They said they had a short job to do down here, they just got a call the day before yesterday, we got down here last night. They had a picture of the old couple they tried to rob. Their car is over here, I have a key to it."

"Well, how about that, do you have clothes in the car?" Faith said.

"Yes, I have an over night bag; with one change of clothes and my tooth brush and stuff."

"Okay," I said, "lets go get your stuff, plus I would like to see what they left in the car; like papers and whatever." We walked over to a late model 'caddy'. In the cubby hole was an envelope, with said picture, plus a short note from; *guess who, nobody but Dipper Tick.* It read, 'get Charles Hester's wallet, he carries his social security card and a certified copy of his birth certificate with him. I need it to get in his safe deposit box'.

I took the envelope with me. I don't know how he was going to get in that safe deposit box without a key, but who knows, maybe he had his ways. I knew the two pickpockets would make bail right quick. Dipper Tick was probably in there right now trying to get them out.

I asked Rosie, "Do you want to stay with them, or go with us, it's up to you. Do they have legal custody of you or what?"

"I want to go with you, Blackie, that was the guys name, tried to get in bed with me the other night, but she caught him. I know it would only be a matter of time till he raped me. And I don't think this foster thing was legal anyway. They knew somebody at the orphanage, I was sort of handed out the back door late one night."

"Do they know you had that key to their car?" Faith asked.

"No, I had an extra key made, they did not know. I was going to steal their car and get away the first chance I got." Rosie said.

"Alright then, you put your overnight bag back in the car; is there anything in there that you simply can't live without?"

"Yes, my birth certificate, my parents were killed in an auto accident, I carry my birth certificate and social security card in there."

"Get them out, but leave the bag; we'll buy you anything

you need. I'll jimmy the door lock, so it will look like someone broke in. But how do we know someone won't break in before they get out of jail anyway?"

As we were walking back to the truck, Faith asked Rosie, "Just how old are you?"

"I'm twelve, I'll be thirteen in December."

"Only twelve, you seem much older than that, I guess you've led a hard life. How long ago did your parents die?" Faith asked.

"Five years ago, they were both orphans themselves, so we didn't have any relatives; that I knew of anyway."

"Well, I guess that's why you seem much older. Experience wise, you're like in your twenty's. What about schooling, what grade are you in?"

"I don't know, I haven't gone very much. But I do a lot of reading. And I have been taking some courses on the computer, I'm pretty smart, I guess." Rosie said.

We arrived at the truck and right away I seen we had a problem. The cab of a 1950 Ford Pickup, especially with a built in car seat, was not big enough for the four of us.

I stood there scratching my head, Faith spoke up, "you know I never really liked this truck anyway. But I know who does, the man who did most of the work on it has a shop just a few streets over. When Teddy died he tried to buy it from me, but at that time I wasn't thinking straight. Maybe he has something bigger? Should we go see?"

"Yeah, I guess so." I said, "But maybe Rosie can sit on your lap, if it's just a short way?" We put Alita in her seat, and we all piled in, Faith and Rosie were a little cramped, but they'd live.

His shop was behind a southwest style house with a lot of trees around it. As we pulled into his driveway and shut it off, he came out of the shop; he must of heard us. We all got out, he recognized Faith right away. "Hey Faith, you ready to sell me that truck, looks like you need more room?" He said. He was young man, a little older than me, say in his thirties.

"Yes, Hector I am," Faith said, then added, "but not just sell, I would like to trade for something bigger but with all of the trimmings."

"I have just the vehicle for you, a new Durango I just reworked, the same goodies that your truck has. I'll trade you for just 5,000 difference."

"5,000 huh? Yeah, but you see, mine's a classic, the Durango is just a new truck, a dime a dozen. I'll tell you what, I know how bad you want this truck. I'll trade for 3,000 difference, how's that?" Faith said.

"Alright, if you wasn't Teddy's widow, I wouldn't do it. But cash, no credit cards." Hector said.

Faith looked at me, "Sweetheart, will you pay him? I don't have that much cash on me."

"Yeah, no problem." I said, as I pulled out my billfold and counted out 3,000. I know why she traded him down, she knew I only had 3,000 in cash with me. Faith handed Hector the money, then said,

"Hector, this is my husband, Clay Bronson. This is Rosie O'Claire a new friend of ours. I assume you have the title for this vehicle?"

"Sure, and already notarized. What about yours?"

"It's in the cubby hole, I'll sign it." And she got it out and did the same. Then we changed our stuff over. He was right about one thing; the Durango had a child car seat.

"Oh yeah, that switch on the dash turns on the turbo-charger, be careful with it; make sure you have plenty of room ahead before you hit it. Otherwise on cruising speed it only runs on four cylinders, it kicks up to all eight when you give it a little gas. It even has a full tank of gas; I suppose yours is on empty." Hector said with a grin.

"You're wrong about that, its full, I don't let my gas tanks get below the half way mark, that way you'll never run out of gas," I said.

As we left, Faith looked back, a little wistful, I thought. I said, "We didn't have to trade your truck, we could of just paid cash for this vehicle."

"No, that's fine. It belonged to Teddy. A person's car is very personal, it's something like a dog, it should only belong to one person. With Teddy I was a blond, now I'm back to my normal hair color. With you I want everything to be new." Faith said.

"Honey, that's fine, but there is no way that you can cut all of your ties to the past. For instance, Felicia. She's Alita's Grandmother, that's a fact that you cannot change."

"I know that, it's just the more personal stuff, like my hair and vehicle. I don't want anything to stand between us." Faith said.

Rosie spoke up from the back seat. "You were married before?" She asked.

"Yes Rosie, I was." Faith said, "my first husband and Alita's Grandfather were killed in plane crash over a year ago. Clay and I have only been married for a short while. And also Clay's father, married my ex-mother-in-law."

I looked in the rear view mirror at Rosie, then said to Faith, "Do you think the boutique at the Hotel will have clothes to fit Rosie?"

"Yes, I know they have. The fancy kind anyway. For jeans and boots, we'll probably have to shop elsewhere. How about it Rosie, are you up for new wardrobe?"

"Oh yes, but I don't want to be any trouble, just the basics would be fine." Rosie said as she handed Alita her Teddy Bear. Alita giggled at her, Rosie's smile grew wide on her face.

I asked her,

"Do you like kids?"

"Oh yes, I used to baby sit them at the orphanage. How old is Alita?"

"Just a little over six months, we are just starting to feed her baby food, do you think she looks like Clay?"

"Yes, remarkably so, but he's not her father, is he?" Rosie said.

"No, he's not. But when anybody asks, just tell them that he is, because that's the truth, now." Faith said.

"I wish she was my sister." Rosie said, as she smoothed Alita's hair.

"Well, you have our permission to say that she is, if you want to." Faith said.

We arrived back at the Hotel/Motel, whatever you wanted to call it. On our way in I stopped at the desk. "We are going to have to have a bigger room, our daughter just arrived from home. Do you have a suite with two bedrooms?" I asked.

"Yes, it costs a lot more, double to what you're paying now, is that alright?"

"Sure, just put it on the same card that you already have, do you have someone to help us move our stuff?"

"Yes," she said, then she rang her bell and boy appeared and accompanied us to our old room. We opened the door to find a mess. Someone had rifled it. We backed out.

And called Cort.

The boy showed us to our new room. I didn't want to disturb anything in the old room till they had a chance to go over it for prints. I don't know what they could have been looking for; we hadn't left anything of importance in it. But I had hunch who was responsible for it.

When Cort arrived with the CSI team, he came by our new room. "Their hard at work, but I brought your new I.D. and

Badge. Boy, trouble seems to follow you around, doesn't it? I see you've added to your family?"

"Yes, this is Rosie O'Claire. We had a little run in with some pickpockets, she was kidnapped by them, but now she's not." I said.

"Yeah, I know. When I left the courthouse, a lawyer was already there, trying to get them sprung. They might even be out by now, so watch yourself. I know a federal judge who might help to straighten out who she belongs to, by the looks of it, I suppose you two want custody of her?"

I looked at Faith, she nodded, "Yes, you're right." I said, "I also believe those two pickpockets are in cahoots with Dipper Tick."

"Well, I would say that you were right, since it was him that showed up to try and bail them out." Cort said, then added as he left, "I'll keep in touch, you had better be sure and pack your heater with you."

I grinned and patted my pocket. I had to smile at Cort's use of the word 'heater'. He must of read too many Mike Hammer novels. I looked at the I.D. that Cort had given me, Special Agent, CSI division. For the State of New Mexico. Well I guess they had to put something on there. I still couldn't understand the why and wherefore of them wanting me to work for them. It just didn't make sense, I was a nobody.

I said as much to Faith, "Don't worry about it Dear," she said, "they must have their reasons. But we do seem to be right in the middle of things all of the time, don't we?"

"Yes, and I'm not sure that I like it. Now take this Charles Hester thing. I think we're getting into things a bit deeper. Anyway, when we have dinner with them tonight, we can find out a little more I guess."

"Sure, but right now Rosie and I are going to get her some new clothes" Faith said, then added, "you can watch Alita, can't you?"

Mr. Mom, that's me. But I really didn't mind. I changed her diaper then fed her some baby food, then rocked her to sleep. Before they got back, the hotel boy had delivered our belongings from the old room, the CSI team had left.

This new room had three bedrooms along with three bathrooms. The hotel boy came back with a helper and the crib from our old room. I had him put it in the bedroom that Rosie would be using, she could watch over her at night. That is if Faith would let her.

They came back loaded down with packages. Rosie's eyes were beaming. "I have never had so many new clothes, thank you both, so much." She said.

"You're welcome sweetheart," Faith said. Then to me, "where do you have Alita sleeping?"

"She's in the first bedroom, there, on our bed. The boy brought her crib, I had him put it in the next bedroom, I thought Rosie and Alita could sleep in there, is that Okay?"

"Yes, that is if Rosie wants to sleep in the same room as Alita?" Faith said.

"Oh yes, that would be perfect, I'd love to." Rosie said. Then she asked, "Is it okay if I take a shower and change into some of my new clothes?"

"Of course, we're supposed to meet the Hester's for supper. Here in the dinning room of our Hotel, their staying here also." Faith said.

"Oh," Rosie said, "do you think they know I was supposed to be the 'hand off'?"

"No, they don't know that, you've done nothing wrong Rosie so don't worry about it." I said.

Faith and I, went to clean up and change clothes also, but of course every time Faith got naked, one thing led to another, per usual.

Chapter Five

The Hester's were already seated when we got there. They weren't expecting Rosie, but it was no problem, the table was plenty big enough.

Edith Hester said, "I didn't know you had another child, she looks a lot like you Faith, that is all except for the red hair."

"Yes, doesn't she though, but I just dyed my hair, you should of seen it before." Faith said, smiling sweetly.

Frank and Fern Blake were seated at a table a short ways over. I waived at them, Frank got up and came over. "I heard you had an interesting afternoon. Did you know they were already bailed out?" Frank said.

"No, but it doesn't surprise me, these are the people that they tried to rob, Edith and Charles Hester." They shook hands, I continued, "This is Frank and Fern Blake, he's the clerk and recorder here in Santa Fe."

After some more small talk, Frank went back to his table. I was always somewhat of an introvert; not too good at small talk. Now Faith was just the opposite; an extrovert, at times you couldn't shut her up, that was fine though, I loved to hear her talk.

After we had ordered, I said, "Charles, do you know what they were after in your billfold?"

"Why, money, I suppose." He said.

"No, they were after your SS Card and the copy of your birth certificate that you always carry with you."

"How in the world did you know what I carry in my wallet?"

"I'm a special investigator for the State of New Mexico, the police knew, I guess the pickpockets most of told them. They also said that they wanted to get in your safe deposit box. What do you have in there that they might be interested in?"

"Nothing much, keepsake jewelry, a few mementos from our past, that's all." Charles said.

"Those mementos, could you elaborate on them?" I said.

"Sure, some of my medal's from the war, and a copy of a deed, on a Spanish Land Grant that my Great Grandfather gave to me. He sold the Ranch, but the deed isn't completely worthless, he kept the mineral rights."

"Ah, the mineral rights, worth more now than the land that covers them. That was what they were after. Where is this old ranch located?" Faith asked.

"It was over close to the Brazos Mountains, close to the Chama River Valley. But I believe part of it is in the 'Edward Sargent State Wildlife Area.' You can't drill for oil in there. Unless of course someone changes the rules." Charles said.

"Well the way their ignoring the constitution now, I'm sure some crooked politician can overcome that." Faith said.

Our food came and food being the more important; our conversation lapsed. Rosie had ordered steak and lobster, she had said that she never had lobster before, so I had told her to order what she wanted. Of course her eyes were bigger than her stomach. Which I knew would be the case, that's why I had only ordered a small steak, I ended up eating what she couldn't. I didn't like to waste food.

As we were drinking our after dinner coffee, I said to Charles, "I would suggest you not carry those documents with you, I don't know how they found out that you did carry them in your billfold, but I wouldn't do it anymore."

Rosie was feeding Alita a small dish of vanilla pudding for dessert, of course she got more of it on her, than in her. I sure could get used to this family stuff. Charles sat his coffee cup down and said,

"I suppose you're right, this world sure has changed. There was a time when we didn't even have to lock our houses much less worry about someone stealing our pocketbooks."

"Yes," I said, "the only thing that remains constant is change itself, much like the weather I suppose. But I wouldn't mind change so much, if it wasn't always for the worse."

"Sweetheart," Faith said, "don't be negative, some changes have been for the better; you know like health care, haven't they?"

"Yeah, I guess, if health care was available to everyone on an equal footing, but of course it's not." I said.

Faith quickly changed the subject, "So Edith, how long do you and Charles plan on staying down here?"

"We planned on going back next week; but now that this has happened. We might leave quicker." Edith said, looking at Charles.

"Yes, we've been here for a week already and there are some things that I have to take care of at home. Even though my Grandson runs the place now, I'm still in charge. I think we'll leave the day after tomorrow."

With that the party sort of broke up. As we were leaving the dinning room, I said to Charles. "Charles, I want to emphasize the seriousness of things now. With Crude Oil selling at over a hundred dollars a barrel, there isn't anything some of these oil people wouldn't do to get your mineral rights, even murder."

He stopped, I could see that he was mulling it over, "You really think so? They would stoop that low?"

"Yes, they started a war to get oil, they wouldn't hesitate to kill us small potatoes." I said. "Just watch your back, okay?"

He nodded, they went to their room and we went to ours. We put Alita down and she went right to sleep. Rosie's eyes were drooping also, her head had no more than hit the pillow and she was out.

Faith and I weren't too far behind them. Faith was asleep long before I was. I kept running things over in my mind. You know worry is nothing more than a circle of inefficient thoughts whirling around a point of fear. I always knew that, but trying to get your mind to stop doing that is another thing.

I must of went to sleep, because the next thing I knew I awoke from a bad dream. I couldn't remember all of it, something about getting shot. I lay there for awhile. I didn't want to wake Faith up, she needed her sleep. I looked at the bedside clock; one thirty. The bar would still be open, I decided to go get me a night cap.

Faith and I always slept naked, I was hugging her, I slowly disentangled myself, she stirred and muttered, but didn't wake up. I picked up my clothes and dressed in the common room.

I was right; the bar was still open. There were about nine of ten people still there. I went to the bar and ordered a blackberry brandy. I always notice things, when I came in I seen two people that I knew; those pickpockets Blackie and his wife, I never did get their last names. They had seen me when I walked in. They were in deep conversation, glancing my way every once in awhile.

Damn, I had forgot my gun. Here I told Charles to watch his back and I leave my gun in the room. I turned my back to the room and watched them in the bar mirror. There was a heavy glass ash tray on the bar, I was sort of playing with it, idly, more sub-consciously than not.

The bartender called for last drinks before closing. Most of the people got up and left, those two didn't. The bartender poured me another shot of brandy. I held the shot glass in my left hand. I seen that Blackie and his wife were walking toward me. She was reaching in her purse for something, I let them come.

She came up on my left, Blackie on my right, her hand was still in her purse. I felt the barrel of a pistol as she held it against my ribs. Now you see that is a mistake a lot of criminals make; they always have to grandstand. She should of just shot me right away. Instead she started to speak, "You son of a bitch," she said.

That was all the further she got, with my left elbow I pushed the gun to the side as I turned to smash her in the face with that heavy glass ash tray that I held in my right hand. I caught her right on the bridge of the nose. Her gun went off, just grazing my ribs, the shot wasn't a complete waste, it got Blackie right in the heart.

She lay there on the floor, out like a light, making a ghastly breathing noise through her smashed nose, the pistol still gripped in her hand. Blackie wasn't doing anything; he was stone cold dead.

The bartender looked like he was in shock, I said to him. "Would you please call 911, I think she needs a paramedic. And I would also like one, that shot seemed to of perforated my hide a little bit."

They got there post haste. Of course the cops came at the same time, I showed them my new I.D., they acted some impressed. The medics wanted to take me to the hospital, I said, "No, just sew me up right here." Before they were done, Cort showed up.

"I'm sorry Clay, I should of warned you, that they made bail." Cort said. Then, "Are you alright?"

"Yeah, I think so. That bitch tried her best to put me under. Her mistake was that she just wanted to palaver awhile before she did it. Remember that Cort; if you want to kill somebody don't stop to talk about it."

The medic finished with the stitches, "does that hurt?" He said.

"No, not since you shot it with Novocain. Is there anything special I should be doing with it?"

"Just don't get it wet. And you had better let a doctor see it on the morrow. I'll put a bandage on it. I wouldn't be doing any setups, if I were you." He said. I turned to Cort,

"How about it, do you need me any longer?"

"No, I don't think so, the bartender gave me the particulars. And there was also a surveillance camera. When you going home? There sure seems to be a high body count when you're around." He laughed, then added, "I was just kidding, I'll be by after lunch tomorrow. I have a little more info on that Dipper Tick. See you then, go on, go the bed."

I used my magnetic key on the door, looked like every one was still asleep, the clock said that it was three. Faith was still asleep, I undressed and got in, cuddling up close. She was on the right side of the bed, my wound was on my left side, so I could lie on my right side. It wasn't long till I fell asleep, with no dreams.

I was woke by Faith screaming, "What the hell, where did all of the blood come from?" She was setting up in bed looking at me. She had thrown the covers back, "There's blood all over you and the bed."

Her screaming brought Rosie on the run, she was carrying Alita. All three of them were staring at me. "Take it easy, I'm okay. I couldn't sleep last night, so I went down to the bar for a nightcap." I looked at Rosie, "Rosie, your old foster father is dead, and your foster mother has a broken nose."

Faith said, "Turn over, let me see your side." I did so, "What happened, it's still bleeding."

I told them the whole story. Faith said, "Come on, get in the bathroom, let me take that bandage off and see if I can't put a cork in that leak." I got up and walked to the bathroom, with blood running down my side. Faith yanked the bandage off, "That's a piss poor job of sewing, Rosie get my sewing kit out of my suitcase, will you. Get in the tub, don't bleed all over the floor. Take your shorts off, they're soaked with blood." I stood there in my altogether. Rosie came back and handed Faith the sewing kit. Faith said, "Rosie, use your free hand and hand me a wet washcloth, then put Alita in her high chair and come back and give me a hand."

Of course Alita wasn't about to be left in the next room, Rosie had to bring the high chair into the bathroom. Faith looked at Rosie, "You okay?" Rosie nodded, "Good, then put your finger here, put pressure on it. I'm going to cut those stitches, it's bleeding from somewhere deeper, I have to get down to it. Here let me hold that, you get me that book of match's from my suitcase." She looked up at me, "You're not going to faint on me are you?"

"Hell no, do what you have to, I'm okay." I said, with more bravado than I felt.

Rosie came back with the match's and then put her finger on the spot, Faith finished cutting the stitch's. "There it is, that little bleeder, Rosie light me a match and heat the end of this needle, I have to cauterize that blood vessel."

There was a little sizzle, then Faith said, "Rosie thread the needle with that cat gut thread. No, not that one, the other one." It didn't take her long to stitch it back up. Then Faith said, "I'm going to turn on the shower and wash the blood off of you, it won't hurt your 'owee'. I hadn't noticed before, but Faith was still naked, just like when she went to bed. I had left my shorts on when I came back and went to bed. Rosie didn't bat an eye at either one of us, she knew what was important and what was not.

After we had got dressed, Faith called the front desk and had them send a maid up. She was little bit upset, the blood had soaked down into the mattress. I told her we would pay any damage's. And that we were going down to eat. The maid said she would call maintenance for a new mattress."

As we were walking down to the restaurant, Rosie said, "Where did you learn to do that?" She was looking at Faith.

"Oh that, in college one year I had a part time job with a vet, I used to watch him do it, it looked pretty simple. And sure enough it was."

"But you had cat gut, in your sewing kit, who carries cat gut?"

"Oh, I've had to do that sort of thing before, I believe in being prepared."

While we were waiting for our food, Cort found us. I asked him to join us. The waitress came over and he ordered. Then he turned to us, "I'm afraid the woman died, seems a little bit of bone penetrated her brain. And again, they want an inquest, tomorrow to be exact."

"Are they going to want one every time I kill someone?"

"Again, I'm sure it's just a formality. Nothing to worry about." Cort said.

Rosie looked at me and said, "You've killed other people?"

Cort said, "Yes," and then told her about me saving that Highway Patrolman. Rosie smiled at me and said, "You're somewhat of a hero, huh?"

"No Rosie, I'm not, I was just in the right place at the right time. Now Faith here, she's the hero, and you also. Look at how you both saved my life this morning." I said,

Cort said, "What's this?" Rosie told him all about it.

"Clay, you had better go have that checked out," Cort said. Faith said, "Hey, you doubt my work?"

"No, of course not, but you're not a Doctor."

"No, I'm not, I work for free. Clay's alright, but just to be sure, I'll take him by the Hospital this morning, myself." And she did, along with Rosie and Alita.

We went in, they said that they were expecting me, Cort had called them. They ushered us into one of those little tent rooms. It only took about 30 seconds for the Doctor to show up. He looked at the wound, "Hey that's a pretty good job of stitching, did the paramedics do that?"

"No, my wife and daughter did, there was a bleeder the paramedics missed, she had to cut it open and cauterize it." I said.

"Huh, you did this? With no anesthesia or anything?" He said, incredulously.

"Sure, my husband is tough, he didn't even cry." Faith said, giving me a wink.

"Well, that's good, I would have. But we had better shoot him full of antibiotics, to ward off any infection." He rang for the nurse, then said to me, "I hear you're responsible for those two new bodies in the morgue?"

"No, I'm not. She killed him as she committed suicide. I just got in between them."

"Uhhuh," he said, then he seen my face, he flushed and went to meet the nurse. Faith looked at me and said, "Really honey, he didn't mean any harm."

"I know, it's just that maybe I'm feeling guilty." I said.

We sort of lazed the day away, anyway, I did. The girls all went shopping. I laid on the bed watching TV. Yeah, it hurt. I didn't want my family to know it did, but I think they figured it out, when I wouldn't go with them.

They, all three came back late that afternoon with more clothes and accessory's, for all of us. Faith had bought Rosie a video game that you could plug into the TV, you could play

Golf, Bowl and stuff like that, pretty realistic, you actually got exercise from it. What wouldn't they think of next?

I didn't feel like going out, so we just ordered room service for supper. Cort called and told us the time for the hearing; ten the next morning. I was feeling some better, just a little stiff. Faith changed the bandage, she said there was no sign of infection.

All four of us went to the hearing. Guess who else was there, yep, you're right, that Dipper Tick. He tried to speak, but the Judge shut him down right quick. He had that Delbert Washington with him. The Judge had them escorted out. Anyway, I was glad he was there, I got a good look at him, I bet I could recognize him in a dark alley.

Cort was right, it was just a formality. Especially after they seen the bar video, it sure made things simple, cut and dried. The Judge did say that I seemed to be a little bit of a violence magnet. Whatever that meant. Come to think of it, things did seem to be always happening to me.

As we came out of the court house, Dipper and Delbert were waiting for us, they came up to me and Dipper started calling me a murderer. Seemed he couldn't do it without yelling, of course there were members of the press there, which I am sure he called. I was a good boy, I didn't do anything. Faith was a bad girl though.

She got right back in his face, then she did something that was pretty neat, she sort of fell backwards making it look like Dipper hit her. I was watching and I could hardly tell that she was faking. She staggered back and then kicked him in the groin and when he bent over, she kneed him in the face. He was out like a light.

I yelled at the press, "Did you see that, that man hit my wife, did you get a shot of that?" The camera man for the local TV station said, "Yes, I got it all." There were a couple of police officers that seen it also, they turned Dipper over and cuffed him. Delbert was hopping up and down and screaming at the cops, they cuffed him also.

I gathered my family and we got the hell out of there. As we got in the car, I said,

"Honey, where did you learn to do that?"

"I told you I took gymnastics. That was nothing, I could of made it look much worse." Faith said, with a big grin on her face. Rosie looked at her and said,

"Will you teach me how to do that fake thing? Also how to do what you did to him, I liked that."

"Sure Honey, that was just self-defense, all women should know how to do that."

Alita was laughing and clapping her hands, her eyes were sparkling. That kid was very aware of what went on, sometimes she was down right scary, how smart she was.

Rosie handed her one of those vanilla cookies, the kind that sort of melt in your mouth. Rosie said, "I read some to Alita last night, she really likes it."

"I know Rosie, I try to read to her every chance I get. I'm really glad you are with us, you're just what she needs, a big sister." Faith said.

I said, "Well, what do you women think, do you think we should leave Dodge?"

"Huh? What do you mean leave Dodge?" Rosie asked.

"Get out of town, you know leave Dodge." I said.

"Oh, you mean like Dodge City, in the old west. Where would we go?" Rosie asked.

"Home, to the ranch," Faith said. "In the Chama River valley. Grandpa and Grandma are there, plus two cousins, you will like them." Faith said to Rosie.

"Do we have a big family?" Rosie asked.

"Well, not too big. Just the right size you might say. But

there are a lot people who work for the ranch, they have kids just your age. You'll have loads to do, all kinds of fun things." Faith said.

"You mean, I'll have kids to play with?" Rosie said.

"Sure, didn't you have kids to play with at the orphanage?"

"Not really, no one felt much like playing, they wouldn't let us do anything that made any noise. Then after Blackie and Mina took me, they wouldn't let me out of their sight. All they did was show me how to pick pockets and stuff."

"Oh, so you know how to pick pockets? Well that might come in handy some day, if done for the right reason," I said, "were you very good at it?"

"I guess so. Sometimes they let me do the dip and Mina was the handoff. I hated it; stealing that is. Do you believe that stealing is wrong?" Rosie asked me.

"You bet I do, very wrong. Look what it got Blackie and Mina, a ride on the big express to hell." I said.

"Do you believe there is a hell? I heard a preacher one time say that we were all going to hell; if we didn't join his church and give ten percent of everything we owned." Rosie said.

"One thing I do know, Rosie, is that if you get the proper meaning of Hell, Hades or Sheol, they simply mean the common grave of mankind. And aren't we going there anyway, some day?"

"Hey, that kind of talk is depressing, let's think of something happy, okay?" Faith said.

"Alright," Rosie said, "I didn't like that preacher anyway, he kept trying to touch all of the young boys." I looked at Faith and shook my head, we dropped it. We had arrived back at the Hotel anyway.

Chapter Six

Have you ever heard of the talking hills? It seems to me there was a poem or story about them. Also I read a story about traveling hills. Why do I mention them? Well my dreams this night were sort of like that.

I was camped in a valley with running water that was surrounded by hills. But when I camped there, one of hills seemed to be whispering to me. Of course I ignored it.

Thinking it was just the wind in the trees. But as I banked the campfire for the night, the ground shook, I thought, Oh Great, an earthquake.

I heard boulders rolling down the side of the hill closest to me, trees falling, a rush of air. The moonlight was bright. I could see the hill moving, heaving it's great mass. It was rising into the starry night sky!

I always believed that the hills were alive, but not this alive. The hill stood up, it was in the shape of a giant man; two hundred feet tall. He looked down at me, a rumble of thunder came from his mouth: "Clay Bronson," the thunder said.

In my dream, I answered, "Yes, I'm here." Just like it was natural to talk to the hills. The hill said, "Are you lost Clay?"

"No, I don't think so," I answered. "I don't know where I'm at, but I don't believe I'm lost."

"Ha, Ha," his laughter rang out, "spoken like a true son of the earth," he said, then, "yes, you will never be lost as long as you listen."

"Listen? Listen to what?" I said.

"To the sky above, to the earth below, to the wind in the trees, to the flight of the Eagle. To the mouse as it burrow's in the leaves of autumn. To the blood coursing through your veins. To creation itself. Listen Clay and it will save your life, not only yours but your family as well. Listen well Clay and creation will tell you the path to take."

His rolling thunder was still in my ears as I awoke to a summer time thunder storm going on outside of our window. Faith was wrapped around me, or me around her, whichever. Faith had her face buried up against my chest, I could hear her whimper a little in her sleep, as the thunder rolled across the night sky.

Rosie came in with Alita in her arms. "Can we get in bed with you, Alita's scared," Rosie said. In a flash of lighting, I could see Rosie's face, it was chalk white.

Faith had woken when Rosie spoke, "Of course, here get in beside me," she said, as we both scooted over to make room.

A clap of thunder shook the room. Alita whimpered and buried her face in her mother's bosom. Rosie scrunched up tight against them both.

"Wow! That's sure a humdinger out there, isn't it?" Rosie said, in a high falsetto.

"Nothing to worry about," I said. "I was just talking to him, he's just trying to make a point."

Faith turned her head and said to me, "What in the world are you talking about?"

"I just had a dream is all, it must have been due to the thunder, my dream that is. Nothing important, you know how dreams are?"

"Well I know how mine are, but yours must be something else, talking to the thunder!" Faith said.

"Well I really wasn't talking to the thunder, I was talking to a hill, his voice was like thunder." I said.

"Talking to a hill, are you sure it wasn't' a mountain, that thunder sounds a lot louder than just a hill talking." Rosie said.

"Oh, you believe me then?" I said.

"Of course I do, Dad." She said, "I know you could never lie."

I thought to myself, she called me Dad! That sounded sort of nice. "You're right Rosie, I wasn't lying; in my dream I was talking to a hill that stood up. He was about two hundred feet tall, he called me by name, it was quite life like," I said.

"I talked to a hill once," Rosie said, "only it wasn't in a dream, it was an actual hill, it was whispering to me, only thing was I couldn't make out what it was saying, I asked it to repeat what it said, but it wouldn't."

"That's strange, the hill spoke to me in a whisper first, I thought it was the wind, so I ignored it, but then it shook itself and stood up and called me by name." I said.

"You two are getting weird," Faith said, "go to sleep both of you. Alita is already back to sleep."

"Okay, I see you don't believe us, next time I talk to him you can join me." I said.

"Oh yeah, right, I can join you in your dream? I have never known two people to share a dream at the same time, have you?" Faith said.

Rosie said, Oh,Oh,Oh, I want to join you both, don't forget me please, next time take me too?"

"You got it, Rosie," I said, "let's go to sleep, before Mom spanks us both."

Faith whispered in my ear, "You wish."

Yeah, I did wish, but when you have two children in bed with you, wishing didn't amount to a hill of beans. But I did cuddle up tight against my wife, that was nice.

The next morning as we were eating breakfast in the Café,

Cort came in and sat down with us. "Boy that was quite a storm last night, the lighting hit a church steeple over on Oak Street. Burnt the whole church down. And Oh yeah, that Dipper Tick and his friend made bail early this morning. So that's twice they have made bail. But I think they just jumped that bail; I seen them fogging it out of town just now. I didn't follow them, I could care less. Did put out an APB on them though."

"Did you see which way they went?" I asked.

"Yeah, north, I don't think they were heading for L.A., but I could be wrong." Cort said.

"I think you're right. They weren't going back to California; wouldn't surprise me if they weren't heading for Montana." I said.

"Montana? Why in the world would they go there?" Cort asked.

"Because that's where Charles and Edith Hester are from, I think old Dipper is still after those mineral rights to his Spanish Land Grant."

"Have the Hesters left for home yet?" Cort asked.

"Nope, not since I see them setting over there in the corner." I said.

"Perhaps one of us should warn them" Cort said.

"Well, I reckon one of us should. But since I've already told them to watch their backs, perhaps you should take on that task?" I said. "And if I were you I would emphasize that Dipper and Delbert aren't above committing murder to get what they want." Cort got up and went over to do his duty.

The Hesters packed and left that day. Now me, I'm a worrier, if there's nothing to worry about, well I'll just poke around till I find something. I got to worrying about the Hesters. Damn, I couldn't get it out of my mind. Now I knew old Dipper wouldn't be able to get on a plane, not with that APB out on him, but he could just drive. Of course it would take him a couple of days to get there; probably have to detour around some towns and such. So I figured I had about two to three days to get there myself.

We also left for home that same afternoon. We called and let them know we was coming. Felicia was real glad when she heard about Rosie, said she'd have an extra room made up for her. But I told her that Rosie would bunk in with Alita. Faith was driving while I was on the cell phone, I added, "Would you have Miguel service and check over my plane, I have a flight to make." Felicia said she would and she didn't even ask where I was going. But my wife did, as she looked at me sharply and swerved the Durango a little.

"Where in the hell do you think you're going? And wherever it is, you're not going without us!"

I thought fast and changed one little thing about my plans, "Of course I wouldn't go anywhere without you, or the children. But as to where, the Hesters. I think they might need a little help, they're a nice old couple. I would hate to see them murdered."

"You didn't say where, I forgot where they were from?" Faith said.

"In the middle of Montana; the Judith Basin. I think the nearest airport is in Lewistown." I said.

"You know of course, that it is none of your business?" Faith said.

"Yeah, I know, but what about you, what would you do?" I said.

She thought about it, I could almost see her gears turning over, "I would do,.. the same as you,... of course." And she paused at each one of the commas.

"Good, I have Charles' cell phone number, I'm going to

call him and tell him to meet us. I'm not sure that Lewistown has rental cars or not. I think they do, but I was a little kid the last time I was there." I called them, they must have been in a dead zone, I got his answer recording. Told him to call me when they got home.

It was just coming on to supper time when we pulled into the ranch yard. Dad and Felicia were rocking on the front veranda. Jake and Alona were still out doing the evening chores. But Miguel and Ester came out of the house, along with some of their children.

Rosie's eyes were sparkling. It didn't take long before Rosie was running around with the other children. Alita tried to get down to join them.

My cell phone rang, it was Charles Hester. I told him the whole story and then: "I was planning on flying up there and give you a hand on this."

His answer: "We would be glad to see you, but I think we can handle this. But what you could do is send me a picture of those two yahoos. The Sheriff is a friend of mine. Also, the hands on my ranch are always packing, if you know what I mean. If they show up out here we take care of our own problems. Again, if you know what I mean."

I did. After I got off the phone with him, I called Cort. Cort e-mailed the Fergus County Sheriff pictures of Dipper and Delbert.

I hoped Charles knew what he was doing. I also hoped we knew what we were doing; but really does anyone know the right thing to do all of the time? I didn't think so.

Most of the time we make decisions and hope for the best.

After supper that night, the whole family was setting around drinking their coffee and discussing the happenings of the last week or so.

Jake came up with an idea, that none of us had thought of:

"Why don't we just drill for oil ourselves?" He said.

That took everyone by surprise a little bit. Alona added. "Yes, you know I learned in school that drilling for oil doesn't have to harm the environment. If it is done in the proper way and care is taken. And what is disturbed is restored."

"Yes," Jake said. "Most of the damage that is done, is done because of greed and speed."

I think I had been underestimating my little brother, as well as Alona. Faith spoke up, "We could start our own oil company, drilling company anyway?" She sort put it out there like a question. Felicia picked it up.

"Where could we find people who know how to drill for oil, without damage?"

"What about at the College's? Dad said, "You know everyone, well not everyone, but a lot of the university's are thinking 'green' these days."

"Yeah the Geologists, but what about the 'roughnecks', the guys who actually do the work? Where do we find those who have experience and also who think 'green'." I said.

"We talk to them." Faith said. "I mean we go where they are drilling for oil and scout them out. I'm sure there are some who don't like sloppy drilling practices."

I said, "I think I know where there is a lot of drilling going on, and a lot more to be done. That's on the Oil Shale deposits in eastern Montana and western North Dakota.

"Yes," Dad said, "I heard on the news just the other day that they have developed new technologies to recover that oil. And in order to get to that oil, they have to do it economically, that means they can't be sloppy and wasteful."

"Okay then, we are all agreed; we're going to beat the big oil company's at their own game?" I said. The vote went around the room, everyone raised their hands, even Rosie and Alita.

Alona raised her hand again, "but one thing; just us alone won't be able to get this going like it should. We need to get the other Spanish Land Grants on board, anyway those who haven't sold their saddles."

"Uh, one other thing," Felicia said, "how do we know there is oil under our land?"

"That is a good question," I said, "I don't think these oil company's would be so hot to get these mineral rights, if they didn't already believe there is oil here." I looked at Felicia, "Have you ever noticed anybody strange on your land?"

"I don't think so, wait, there was some college people that wanted to check all of our ponds and streams for some endangered species. I told them they could go ahead and look and I did see them all over the place. That was about six months ago."

"Well there you go, that was oil people, I bet. Did they ever do any seismic readings? Did you hear any explosions, or anything? I said.

"No, not really." Felicia said.

Jake spoke up, "Maybe they have some other way of doing that now, dynamite is a little archaic isn't it?"

"I don't know, I'm not a seismologist or a geologist. They probably do." I said.

Dad said, "So, you haven't told us the details on all of your adventures since you two went to Santa Fe?" Why he changed the subject, I don't know.

"Well, you've been watching the news I take it? Anyway, you seen what happened on the highway up there. We got there just at the right time, for Officer Holden anyway. And then of course, it seems they liked the way I handled that, they made me a Special Agent for the state. Here, see the badge and I.D." I passed it around, and then went on, "And, we stopped a pickpocket team. As a result of that the pickpockets had it in for me and they tried to kill me, but ended up killing themselves." I raised my shirt to show the bandage, "but they did manage to ventilate my hide, but my beautiful wife saved my life. That's about it," I said.

"He just hit the highlights," Faith said, "I'll fill you all in on the details in the morning, the children are tired and I have to change that dressing on Clay's side, I don't want it to get infected." With that the meeting broke up, Faith picked up Alita and Rosie came over and put her arm around me, we excused ourselves.

The next morning when I woke up I was alone in bed. I looked at the bedside clock, it was past ten. I must have been tired. My feet had just hit the floor when Faith came in. "How are you feeling this morning, does your side hurt?" She said.

"Not as much as my bladder, stand back, if you don't want to see Niagara Falls." I said, as I padded to the bathroom, she was right behind me, I lifted the seat and cut loose. "It's a good thing that I don't have a shy kidney," I said, glancing at my wife standing there smiling.

"Well, be that as it may, but you had better be careful with your aim, or you'll be mopping the floor." She said, as she put her hand on mine and corrected the aim. I was more than a little bit embarrassed. But grateful too, because I sure didn't want to mop the floor. When I finished she said,

"Stand there, I want to change your bandage again," then she jerked the old one off. "Owe!" I said, she poked around on it, "There's a little red area here, stand in the tub, I'm going to pour Hydrogen Peroxide on it." And she did..... when I stopped yelling she said, "Oh, quit being a big baby, come on, get dressed, I saved some breakfast for you."

She went back in the bedroom and laid my clothes out. I came up beside her, she turned and bumped into me, I grabbed her, my breakfast really got cold.

We let the idea of starting our own oil company jell for a few days. A lot of time an idea might sound pretty good one day and not the next. For one thing it sounded like it would be a hell of a lot of work, did we want to get tied up like that?

Dad and I were working with a couple of colts, getting them used to having something on their backs, when Dad said, "Clay, I'm not too sure about this oil thing. Felicia and I were talking last night. We wouldn't mind finding out if there is oil here. But we don't want to get tied up with our own oil company. If we could get some wildcat operator to work with us on shares, we'd probably do that."

"I think you're right Dad, Faith and I were of the same mind. Even though we don't have a stake in this ranch, we sort of feel like we're part of it."

"Well, you do have a stake in this place, Felicia redid her will, we're all part of it. I wanted her to wait awhile before she done it, to make sure that's the way she felt, but she said she was sure. She said as iffy as life was these days, she didn't want to put it off.

I tried to talk her out of it, but she insisted."

"Yeah, some people might think we were taking advantage of her, and that sure ain't the case. But it sure looks that way don't it?" I said.

"Yes, it does. And that bothers me. Shit, a little over a month ago, we didn't even know this place existed. Felicia and I have been doing a lot of talking. Turns out, she said that she had been praying for a miracle, and then in we flew, three men for three lonely women. Don't that beat all!" Dad said.

"Yeah, just like that engine acting up, and then we couldn't find anything wrong with it. Could be some higher power had a hand in it. One never knows." I said.

"So," I added, "Does she want us to look for an independent driller?"

"I think so, I told her I would talk to you, to find out what you thought. I'll tell her what you said, and let you know in the morning. I suppose I had better talk to Alona and Jake, they're part of this deal too."

Dad left me to deal with the Colts, one was sure a handful. I snubbed him uptight to the hitching post in the middle of the round corral. Then I talked real slow and easy to him, he started to quiet down. I rubbed him all over; to get him used to being touched. Now horses are a lot like people, you approach them the right way and you can do most anything with them. I told him I wouldn't get physical with him if he wouldn't get physical with me. We came to an amicable agreement: I'd go slow in getting that saddle on him and he wouldn't kick my lights out. Besides, I didn't want that wound in my side to start bleeding again, Faith would have my hide.

I turned around, Faith, Rosie and little Alita were setting on the corral rails watching me. Alita was sitting up there a big as you please, between Rosie and Faith, of course Faith had one arm around her. Rosie said,

"Can I help, I like horses, I think they like me too."

"Sure, hop on down here, and I'll introduce the two of you." Rosie got down, I loosed the rope a little to give the colt a little breathing room, he seemed quiet enough. As Rosie came up the colt turned his head and sniffed her, then he nickered softly. Rosie held the back of her hand to his nose. I seen the expression in his eyes soften. I gave him more slack.

Rosie was rubbing behind his ears, the next thing I knew she grabbed a hunk of mane and swung up on his back; he just danced a little. Rosie leaned forward over his neck and whispered something to him. I'll be damned if it didn't look like he smiled.

I took my rope off of him, Rosie gave him a little knee pressure and they were walking around the corral. I reckon

Rosie had herself a horse.

Rosie said, "Can we go for a ride?"

"We, who's we?" I said.

"Wind Walker and me?"

"Oh, you've already named him?" I said.

"Well, he is an Appaloosa and he said he can run as fast as the wind." Rosie said.

I looked over at Faith, she nodded. "Okay, but don't go too far, lunch is about ready," she said.

I opened the corral gate, they trotted out. Rosie still had a hold of his mane, otherwise she was just guiding him with knee pressure. Where she learned to do that, I wouldn't know. I didn't think she had ever been around horses before.

Felicia had come up to the corral as all of this was going on, she said, "She is a Caballo Espiritu Jinete. My Father told me that my Great Grandmother was one, also."

"A what?" I said.

"A horse spirit rider. Or just a spirit rider. They call them a spirit rider, because their spirit and the horse's spirit are one. They are very rare, you a very fortunate to have her as a daughter."

Rosie came trotting back, "Can Alita come with me?" She asked.

Faith looked at Felicia, Felicia nodded. "Yes, I guess so, just be careful." Faith said.

"I will be, she can sit in front of me, I will hold onto her. Windy is the one that thought of taking her along, he likes kids." Rosie said.

I looked at Faith, she looked back at me. She said, "One never knows what one gets when the bones are tossed, do they?" I just nodded. Bones? I've heard of tossing dice, but wait, Oh yeah, in the Bible they tossed 'bones'. I didn't know my wife was a Bible reader.

It was two hours later when they came back, Faith heard them coming, she went out on the veranda, "You missed lunch, aren't you hungry?" Faith said.

"Oh, we found an apple tree, and a wild plum bush, Alita liked the plums, they were soft, I had to chew the apple a little bit for her." Rosie said.

Alita had plum juice down the front of her, but she had a big smile. Rosie handed her down to Faith, then Rosie took Wind Walker back to the barn and grained him. At least she didn't have any tack to mess with, nothing to take off of the horse, cause he didn't have any on.

As Rosie came back, I asked her, "How did you know what was safe to eat?"

"Oh, that was easy, Windy ate some first, he even pawed up some root stuff, some kind of tuber, I think, he ate some first, so I tried it, it was good. I didn't give any to Alita though."

Alita wasn't that full, she reached into Faith's blouse, she wanted some milk. Faith was only too happy to oblige, she was getting a little full. It wouldn't be too long till she would start to wean her. Faith popped one out, and Alita latched on. There was a shawl on one of the veranda chairs, I draped it around Faiths shoulder's.

Faith smiled up at me, and mouthed the words, 'you big prude.' Yeah, I suppose I was. Faith and Rosie winked at each other.

When Alita had had her fill, she sat up and wiped her mouth with the back of her hand and reached her arms out to me. I took her, she pointed to her bottom. Sure, save the dirty jobs for me, that's just like a woman. I took her in the house and changed her. Faith followed us in, "You need a bath young lady, would you like to go swimming?"

All four us went to that swimming hole where Faith and I

fist made love, I made sure though that the women brought their swimming suits. And I brought something else, I never went anywhere, anymore without my gun, one never knows, does one?

I said they brought their swimming suits, and they had them on when they got in the water, but the next thing I knew they were tossing them on the bank. I got out and went and laid in the sun on the bank and went to sleep. Let the nymphs play, I didn't have to watch.

I was glad they didn't let me sleep too long, Faith woke me up, said I had better move to the shade or I would get a bad burn. She stood over me with water dripping down her thighs. "Where are the kids?" I asked. One big drop fell from her right breast and hit me between the eyes. "They went back to the house," Faith said, as she pulled my trunks down.

When we got back to the house, both kids were taking a nap. After that work out, I think we needed one also. But Dad and Felicia wanted to talk.

"Well, we talked to Jake and Alona, I guess we're all in consensus, to try and get an independent driller to drill for oil on our place." Dad said.

"Okay then, what do you want us to do?" I asked.

"Well we thought that you and Faith could hunt one up for us." Felicia said.

"Alright, Faith what would you say to a little trip to Montana?" I said, looking at my lovely wife.

"What about the children? Are they going with us?" Faith asked.

"That's up to you, I don't think it will be too dangerous. But then again we didn't think our trip to Santa Fe would be either." I said.

"Well, you could leave them here," Felicia said. "Just leave some breast milk in the Fridge. Since Rosie is with us now, she and Alita are together most of the time."

"Miguel has already checked and serviced the plane, so you could leave tomorrow." Dad said.

"I guess so. But let me give all of you some advice," I said, looking back and forth between them. "I think everyone on the ranch, the adults that is, should go armed."

Felicia said, "Goodness why?"

"Trust me on this, it's just a feeling I have. Times are changing, people have no natural affection. Also, this land grant thing, greed overcomes common sense. Just be prepared. As far as Rosie goes, you can consider her an adult and trust her the same."

Just then Rosie came in the room, carrying Alita, "What are we talking about?" she asked.

"I'm glad you're here, Rosie." Faith said, then she filled her in on our plans. Rosie said, "Don't underestimate the kids on this ranch, they can handle themselves. Did you know that Juan can kill a rabbit on the run at fifty yards with his sling?"

"No, I did not know that. But I tell you what, Rosie. You're in charge of organizing them. You're right most adults underestimate what kids can do. Let's hope the bad people do anyway. Along that line of thought, do you remember the movie 'Cowboys' with John Wayne? They were all kids, but they beat older men, because the men underestimated the boys."

"No, I never seen that movie, but I do understand what you're saying, that's why I was so good at pick pocketing, people never expected a kid to pick their pocket."

Dad and Felicia looked at each other, "What's this?" Dad said.

"Uh, I didn't fully explain about Rosie, she was taken against her will by those pickpocket couple we told you about. They had trained her to pick pockets. And oh yeah Dad, while we're gone, I was wondering if you would contact the ranch's lawyer and start making arrangements for us to legally adopt Rosie?"

"Sure, no problem. Is that what you want Rosie?" Dad asked her.

"Yes, oh yes, of course I do! This is what I've wanted all of my life." Rosie said, as she came over and gave Faith and I a big hug.

"Are you going to check in on the home place in Wyoming, as long as you'll be flying over it?" Dad asked.

"Yes, I thought I would. I know we don't have to worry about it, I'm sure Red and Daisy are running the place Okay." I said. Faith spoke up;

"Who are Red and Daisy?"

"Cousins of my Mother. We run about 500 Cow and Calf pairs. Red is the Foreman for us. Daisy his wife cooks for the hands and keeps the books. They are very competent." I said.

"How come you never mentioned them before?" Faith said.

"I don't know. Really the ranch belongs to Dad, I just didn't think it was important." I said.

"Felicia," Faith said, turning to her, "did you know about that?"

"Yes, of course, Karl told me all about it. Don't be mad at Clay. He's right, the Big Horn Basin Ranch is in Karl's and my name, now. As is this ranch. But we have already had a new will drawn up, all of you kids are in it."

"Oh, I wasn't worried about that, I was just upset that he didn't tell me all about it, you know how noisy I am." Faith said.

"And it's well that you should be sweetheart," I said, "don't worry, from now on you'll know everything. I guess it's just that so much has been happening, so fast. That our home place didn't seem important."

With that, the confab broke up. It was about an hour till supper time. So, we used the time to pack for our trip. I checked my guns over. It seems we had gathered guns like a ditch does tumbleweeds. But they were all standard size. Faith wanted something a little smaller. "I know," Faith said,

"In the hall closet, where we keep all the guns, Teddy had bought me a little .32 Auto. But he said he reloaded the shells. He took out the lead and shaved some of it off of the butt end. That way there was more room for extra powder, he said he changed it into a magnum."

"Well why don't you go get it, make sure you bring the ammo with it. I'll finish packing. That was one thing the Navy taught me, is how to fold and pack clothes."

We only took one suitcase a piece. We wouldn't be gone that long. Faith came back with the pistol, along with four extra clips for it and a box of shells. We laid out our clothes for the morrow. Jeans, boots, western shirts and overall jackets. With the needed hats by Stetson. I made sure the jackets were loose enough to accommodate the guns and extra clips.

Chapter Seven

That night in bed I got to thinking about Teddy, you know, Faith's Ex. On how he seemed to be somewhat of an over achiever. Faith rolled over and said, "What's wrong? How come you're not sleeping?

"What made you pick me? I mean, your late husband seemed to be perfect. And I know I'm certainly not."

"What brought all of this on?"

"He seemed to be able to do anything, so why did you want me?" I said. Faith sighed, and snuggled closer. Then she said,

"I know it may seem that Teddy was the perfect husband, but he wasn't. I'm not going to list all of his faults. But I know one of the reasons I wanted you and still do. But in order for me to explain that, let me tell you one of his faults. When we had been married for about a year. One of my friends suddenly became a divorced single mother. Teddy and I were talking, and he said that she was going to have a hard time finding a husband now." Faith gave another sigh and tried to crawl inside of me, then she continued.

"I asked him why? He told me, 'well she has a kid, I know I wouldn't want to raise another man's kid.' I couldn't believe he said that. I was very disappointed in him.

And do you remember what you said when you brought Alita to me, while I was sleeping? Anyway, you said that it was as if she was yours! Well, that cinched it for me, your goose was cooked. So go to sleep, or do you want to have sex?"

"Can't we do both? I mean sex first, then sleep?"

"You got it bucko, top or bottom? Faith said.

"Yeah," I said…….

The next morning our plans changed some. We had planned on going, the two of us. But seeing Rosie's downcast countenance, changed our minds. Alita also had a pouting lip on her, almost to the ground. How Alita knew that we were planning on leaving them home beats me. But as soon as we said they could go, she smiled. Big time.

It didn't take Rosie long to pack bags for the two of them.

The whole family followed us to the air pasture. You really couldn't call it an airstrip. As I stowed our suitcase in the plane. I noticed Rosie's was a little heavy. "What do you have in here, bricks?" I asked her.

"No, you said we should all go armed. I just got a weapon from the closet, along with ammo."

"Uh, do you know how to shoot?" I asked her with bated breath.

"Sure, I read up on it, nothing to it. I got on the internet last night, it showed me how." Rosie said.

"What kind of a gun do you have in here?" I asked.

"It's called an Uzi, for its size it holds more shells and shoots them faster. That's okay, isn't it?"

I looked at Faith, my eyes were asking her to step in here. She said, "Sure it is Honey. But we have a rule around here, we never draw a gun without intending to use it.

So don't go waving it around a like a kid, which you are not, we trust you."

Rosie was glowing, at the praise that she was not a kid. So far she had proved herself. After we got in the air, I asked Faith. "Just how many guns were in that closet?"

"A lot, besides the ones on the back closet wall, if you open that wall there is a room back there, it is full of guns and ammunition."

"Why in the world so many, were they expecting a war?" I said.

"I don't know. But have you ever noticed the gun slots in all of the outside walls. I guess the local Indians, about three hundred years ago, would come by and just take potshots at the house. Those walls are three feet thick. Teddy told me they believed in being prepared."

Being that we left from our own private airfield, I didn't file a flight plan. So when I reached 20,000 ft. I got on the radio with Denver and filed one. The plane was flying a like a new one. Which I guess you could say it was.

Alita wanted fed, so Faith and Rosie changed seats. Rosie was bombarding me with questions about the plane. Finally I said, "Just take the wheel, keep her steady." I showed her what did what, she learned fast. Then I had her do a few maneuvers, she was a natural.

"How come you're so good at this?" I asked Rosie.

"Oh, I looked up this plane model on the internet. They showed how to fly it. It was a little easier than I thought it would be. Must have been how you showed me, you're a good teacher." Rosie said.

"What's your I. Q. anyway?" I asked her.

"I don't know, I've never been tested. I've always been pretty good at tests. Do you like to take tests?"

"Heaven's no, I hate them. I've always liked practical application, you know hands on?" I said.

Faith said, from the back seat, "Does he ever."

Rosie said, "Huh, what?"

"You never mind her, Rosie, she's just funning you."

Rosie thought a little while, then said, "I know what she was talking about, I'm not a baby, you know."

"We know you're not, Rosie. But sometimes *we* act like it." Faith said.

I changed the subject, "Do you know how to set the course?"

"No, not really."

"Okay, this plane has the newest navigation system, just put in the coordinates and it will set the course, it uses satellites to guide itself by."

"Then it has Auto Pilot?" Rosie asked.

"Sure, like I told you, we just put in the latitude and longitude of where we want to go and the GPS guidance system will take us there, pretty simple, huh?"

"Well what if it malfunctions, how do we know where to go?" Rosie said.

"Well then we just use dead reckoning, I just look out the window to see where I'm at and then I say, I reckon we'll head that way, or I'm dead." I said with a laugh.

Faith said from the back, "Oh, you think you're so funny, but yes we do go by the landmarks that we can see, in conjunction with the map. But at night, if we don't have instruments, we can go by the stars, which help a little bit, but if it's cloudy we've pretty well bought the farm."

I turned and looked at Faith, "Hey, you didn't tell me you knew how to fly?"

"Of course I do. Teddy taught me." She seen my eyes cloud over, then she said,

"I'm sorry, I won't mention him anymore, I know he's starting to get under your skin."

I nodded at her, "well, it does seem like every time I turn around, up he comes again. I'm going to have to do some fancy foot work to live up to his memory."

"No you're not, you've already surpassed him in so many ways, remember, it's you I love." Faith said.

Alita had finished her repast, she sat up and wiped her mouth with the back of her hand, then held out her arms to me and said, "Papa". Faith said, "See there, those are her first words, you're the only father she knows."

I started to trade places with Faith, "Uh, perhaps you had better put those away," I said,

"What for, Rosie has seen them before? But just to please you I will." Then we traded places. Of course I was just in time to change Alita, seems like it always turned out that way. It wasn't long before Alita and I were fast asleep. Faith and Rosie could fly the plane for awhile.

I awoke when I felt the plane change course. "Hey, what's going on?" I said.

"Oh, I was just giving Rosie some exercise's to do, go back to sleep, we'll put it back on auto pretty quick."

"Where are we at?" I asked.

"We're over the mountains west of Denver, I think that is Berthoud Pass down there." I looked down, "Yep, you're right. How's the fuel?" I asked.

"We have plenty, it's just under three quarters of capacity. Nothing to worry about. I think this plane is a lot more fuel efficient than our old one." Faith said.

"That's one of the reasons I bought this model, it's supposed to use about thirty percent less fuel. So far I've been well pleased with it." I said.

All of this time Rosie had been making shallow dives and banking the plane, just getting the feel of her. Yep, she was a natural. She pulled back the stick and put her in a steep climb, then she pushed it forward and dove in a spiral, then she pulled it out like a pro. Wow! She was a pro…Then she put it back on course and turned on the auto pilot.

Rosie looked back at me, "Do you want to change places, I want to take a nap?"

As we were changing places, Rosie looked out the window, "What range is that?"

"That's the Medicine Bow Mountains, they lead all of the way up into Wyoming."

Faith asked, "How far are we from your ranch?"

"A couple of more hours, the ranch is in the Big Horn Basin, a little south and west of Ten Sleep. I haven't told them we're coming."

"Why not?" Faith asked.

"I don't know, I thought it would be nice to surprise them."

"I thought you said that you trusted them, these cousins of yours, Red and Daisy?"

"I do, but for some reason, I don't know why, I just want our coming to be a surprise. Okay?"

"No skin off my tush, I was just wondering."

We settled down for the duration. Rosie and Alita were asleep, Faith was nodding off. I was wide awake, I guess because I already had my nap. I got to thinking about why I didn't call ahead, I still could, I had my Satellite Cell Phone. But no, I just had an uncomfortable feeling, something was not right.

Seemed like it was no time at all and I looked down and we were getting close to the Basin. I woke Faith up, Rosie woke up also. I said,

"Just so the both of you know, something is not right. I'm not for sure, but we should be prepared for anything. Faith do you have your weapon handy?" She nodded. I looked back at Rosie, "Why don't you get your Uzi out of your suitcase, or did you put it in the luggage compartment?"

"My suitcase is behind my seat." Rosie said, as she complied.

"Look, I don't know what we're going to get into, but when we land, Rosie I want you to stay in the plane with Alita, duck down out of sight. I know, I know, I'm probably making a fool of myself, but this won't be the last time or the first time, I have."

When I got within sight of the ranch, I dropped down to the deck, just over the tree tops, I hit our runway going a little fast. But was still able to bring her to a stop just outside of our hanger doors.

The door to our main house flew open. Out came two guys with Daisy in between them, they each had one hand in their jacket pocket. I seen the fear on Daisy's face. I didn't have to tell Faith what to do. She opened the door on her side, as I did on mine. We both hit the ground at the same time, with our pistols in our hand.

Those two goons pulled their hands out of their pockets, with Glock 9mm's in their fists. They fired and missed. Faith did a running dive and came up firing. I did something like that, not as pretty though.

Faith's first shot hit her guy between the eyes. Mine got the guy in the shoulder and gut. I had fired twice. Daisy sank to the ground terrified. We started to stand up, when we heard a voice behind us, "Drop em' or you're dead." We froze.

I turned my head, there were two of them. One guy said, "Kill them Eddy, do it now!" The one called Eddy started to raise his AK-47, then I heard the stutter of the Uzi.

Rosie got them both, they didn't know what hit them.

Faith ran over to Rosie and held her close, Rosie was crying, "I didn't mean to kill them, I just wanted to stop them from hurting you guys."

"That's okay, Rosie, that was the only way to stop them, you did the right thing." Faith said, Rosie laid the Uzi on the seat and picked up Alita, who was staring with wide open eyes at the carnage.

I went over and picked Daisy up to her feet, "Where's

Red?" I asked her.

"They have him at the drilling rig, they keep us separated, I guess in order to control us." Daisy said, as she clung to me.

"Drilling rig? What do you mean, they can't drill for oil on this place." I said.

"That's what Red told them when they first stopped and asked about drilling. Red had no more than said that, when they knocked him out. They have the rig about four miles back in the hills where it can't be seen. I don't think they could of heard these shots from there."

"Where are my manners," I said to Daisy, "this is my wife Faith, and our Daughters, Rosie the oldest and Alita our youngest," I said.

"My, you have been busy," then Daisy held her hand out to Faith, "I'm Daisy, cousin to your husband."

"Where are all of the hands?" I asked.

"Working on the rig, the cattle are just fending for themselves. The hands were given a choice, either work or be killed."

"How many of them are there?" I asked.

"There were ten of them, but since you all have killed these four, that makes only six left. Some of the guys who came with them are alright, I think they kidnapped them also."

"Did you try to call the Sheriff?

"They cut the land line, and took all of our cell phones. They've been here about three weeks."

"What in the world did they hope to accomplish. They must of known that sooner or later they would be found out?" Faith said.

"That's a funny thing, I thought of that. But do you know that nature conservancy that you thought you put the ranch in?"

"Thought? So yeah, what about it?" I said.

"One of the two that your little red hair daughter shot, he

was the head honcho of the outfit. I think it was bogus." Daisy said.

"You mean our land is not in the nature conservancy?"

"I do believe it ain't. I heard them talking on how they were going to have to kill all three of you, your Dad and Jake too. As soon as the well came in; they were sort of waiting till then."

"Do you know if they were working on their own, or for somebody else?" Faith asked.

"Come on in the house, I want to show you something." Daisy said.

There was an open briefcase on the table, Daisy shut the case, on the cover was a logo, it was the logo of one of the biggest oil company's in the world, 'Euro-con'. "Of course, we probably can't prove they were involved, but they sure weren't shy about showing this briefcase." Daisy said.

I sat down in a chair, my chair; the one I had sat in at every meal since I was a little guy. "But how could they believe they could get away with it?"

Daisy gave a grisly laugh, "Oh come on, Sonny Boy,(she always called me that, when she thought I was being obtuse.) They started a war and invaded a sovereign country on a pretext. What makes you think they can't take a measly little ranch and get away with it?"

"We have laws in this country." Faith said.

"Laws are only as good as the system behind them. Look how they've twisted the constitution to suit their needs. This administration has packed the supreme court with their stooges. They think their invincible." Daisy said.

"Wow! Sounds like you have given this some thought." I said.

"Yeah, like for over two hundred years. I am surprised you haven't reached that conclusion, you're half Indian yourself."

Daisy said.

"I have Daisy, I have. But there is more to it than that. We fought them till they almost had us wiped out. We have to work within the system. Their own excesses and debauchery will bring them down, as it did the Roman Empire. I think I will call the Sheriff."

I reached in my pocket and got my phone. I had the county sheriff's phone number programmed in. I got the receptionist. "Sheriff's Office, how may I help you?"

"Jean, this is Clay Bronson, is the Sheriff in?"

"Clay! How are you?"

"I'm fine Jean, we seem to have a little mess out here, I need to talk to John."

I heard her say, even though she covered the mouthpiece with her hand, "John, it's Clay Bronson," I heard him say, "What the hell does he want, I haven't got time to baby set every damn Indian in this county?" She answered, "I don't know, he said there was some kind of a mess out there."

He picked up the phone, "Clay, how are you old boy, haven't seen you in a coon's age, what's the problem?"

"John, I just want you to know that I heard everything you said to Jean, now that you know that I heard, I also want you to know if you ever call me a 'damn Indian' again, I'll cut your throat and cram your balls down the hole. Do you understand?"

"Now, Clay, you must of misunderstood," He stammered.

"Can it John, I also want you to know that I'm a 'Special Investigator' for the State of New Mexico, I'm on a special case and it's led me straight here to my ranch. Get your ass out here and bring a bunch of troops with you. Make sure their heavily armed. Also bring the coroner with you, so far there are four bodies, I suppose there will be more." I hung up, then I called Cort to fill him in; Cort asked for the Sheriff's number. I gave it to him....

About forty-five minutes later five cop cars pulled into the yard; three county Sheriff cars and two Highway Patrol cars. A total of ten men. John came toward me with a shit-eating grin on his face. He held his hand out, "I'm sorry Clay for what I said, I was just having a bad day."

I took his hand and shook it, "Just don't let it happen again John. There are four bodies over here, they jumped us as soon as we landed. We shot back. There are six more bad guys out at Coyote Draw, they have an oil rig set up out there, they are holding Red and my hands captive and the way Daisy tells it; they have more captives out there also."

"I thought your Dad put this ranch in the Nature Conservancy?" John said.

"Yeah, so did we. But it turns out one of those dead guys over there is supposed to be the head honcho for the conservancy, he's dead."

"Uh, Clay, your boss speaks rather highly of you, as do we, since you are a war hero and all. Are you going out there with us?"

"Yeah, I am. Otherwise, you'd get your dumb ass shot off." Just then the crime scene guys along with the Coroner showed up. I had Faith stay there and get them lined out. Knowing these local yahoo's, I bet she'd have to do their work too.

"John," I said, "there are horses in the corral; saddle them up. It's almost dark, we'll catch them with their pants down. I'm going to my room and get my Bow. I'll be right back."

When I got back they had half of them saddled. Those Highway Patrol Officers knew more about horses then John's Deputy's did. All of them weren't that swift though.

I saddled my horse with my own saddle. He was glad to see me. I was doing a slow burn, it was like being invaded all over again, we suffered through the first one, I sure wasn't going to take this invasion without fighting to the death.

I tied my bow and quiver to the saddle. That guy that had the AK-47 was still laying there with the gun where it fell, nobody had moved him yet. I walked over and picked up the gun and then took his belt of ammo off him. I liked the idea of using their own weapons against them.

When I had went to my room to get my bow and arrows, I had changed my boots for moccasins. In the same drawer as the moccasins was my old hunting knife, a Texas Bowie, I strapped it on.

Just as we were ready to get in the saddle, Faith came over, "Honey, you be careful, if you get yourself killed, you'd better watch out, I'll follow you and kill you again," Then she kissed me, one of those one's with a promise and a warning.

"You too sweetheart," I said, when I could catch my breath. "The three of you keep your guns handy, I know Daisy has one, make sure she uses it, if any of them show up here."

"Don't worry, if any of them come around, we'll dismantle them limb by limb." My beautiful sexy wife said.

It didn't take us all that long to get to the draw. We could see the rig long before we got there. They were working at least two shifts; I guess they were in a hurry. I stopped on the other side of the hill from the rig. I had the rest of them dismount and wait, I wanted to check things out. I crawled up the hill and peeked over. There were about six guys working on the drilling rig. Some six more were eating. I could tell who the bad guys were; they were the ones with the guns that were lounging around watching the others.

It was all of the way dark; dark like just before the moon comes out and that was good. I lay there thinking. How we could rush them, we'd win, but some of us would get killed along with some of the captives. I didn't want that.

I crawled back down the hill. "I tell you what I want you guys to do. You spread out in a circle all around the rig, stay way back though. I just want you to catch anybody that may run. I don't want you to shoot toward the rig; you might hit innocents. I'm going in there, any of those guys with the guns that come out are your responsibility. But I say again, do not shoot toward the rig."

I unsaddled my horse and took his bridle off, I whispered in his ear, he nodded his head. I took my Bow and Arrows, plus I had my pistol, and my trusty knife. I think I had enough weapons, after all, there was only six of them.

My horse ambled off, stopping to get a bite of grass every now and then. I followed him. We went around the edge of the hill; right toward the rig. My horse continued to graze toward it; while I stayed about fifty feet behind him.

I heard one of the guards say, "Hey, there is something out there; I'm going to see what it is." He came toward us. "It's only a horse, nothing to worry about." He called back. He had his back to me, I stepped on a twig, I must be rusty, he started to turn, my knife sank up to the hilt just under his sternum. He never made a sound as my knife found his heart.

One down, five to go. I wiped my knife on his shirt. My horse turned his head to look at me, then turned back and started to graze toward the rig once more. I could see their faces now. One of the ones that was eating was Red, my cousin. He looked up, a frown on his face. He looked directly at me. He couldn't see me; it was too dark and he was blinded by a floodlight. But I could tell he knew I was there. I seen him pick up a butter knife and stick it under his shirt. He said something to the man that was setting beside him, it was one of our hands, he also slipped a knife under his shirt.

We circled to the side, we got two more. Three left to go. Red and Orville, I had remembered the other hands name. They got up and drifted toward one of them; they got him. Only two left. The last two were on the other side of the rig, one of them called out; "Slim, where are you?" He cradled his gun and started to walk toward where Red was, "Hey, what's going on over there?" He said, raising his AK-47. I had notched an arrow, he took another step, I loosed my arrow, whish, it went home. His gun went off as it fell from his hands. The last guard started shooting, my next arrow went through his throat.

Everyone stood there, as if in shock. Red yelled, "Is that you Clay?"

"Of course it is, who else gives a damn about you?" I called back. Then I whistled, "Hey, you all can come in now."

John came in, "Jesus Clay, you killed all of them."

"I do wish you wouldn't use the Messiah's name in vain, John, He doesn't like it." I said.

"Huh? You are getting on me for that, when you just killed all of these guys?"

"I didn't kill them all, Red and Orville did for one. Besides, it was kill or be killed, besides that they were trespassing."

Red came up to me, "Daisy, is she alright?"

"Sure she is Red, we got all four of those guys back at headquarters. My daughter, Rosie got two of them, she's a whiz. How about these other guys, are they upright?"

"Yes, their wildcatters, they were told it was a legit drill, they didn't know till it was too late, then they had guns in their backs."

"Good, tell them to continue with the drilling, only they will be working for us now. As long as this ranch isn't in the Nature Conservancy, we might as well drill for oil ourselves."

"Yeah, that guy took you for a ride, is he dead too?"

"Yep, sure is, he's one of those that Rosie got."

John came up, again, "Since you killed all of these guys, what do you want us to do?"

"I want you to investigate where these guys are from, I bet it's big oil, do your job. Bring the FBI in if necessary." I turned my back on him and addressed Red;

"Red, I want you and our hands to get back to the ranch, there is a lot of work to do, the place is falling apart. Who's in charge of these wildcatters?"

John was already on the phone with the FBI, I knew he was too lazy to do anything, Oh well, the FBI would do a better job anyway. Red brought the ramrod over.

"Is this the only rig you have?" I asked.

"No, I have another one; their working in Arizona. I don't know what's going on now. They took my phone away."

"Well, good, I have some work in New Mexico, if you're interested. Here you can use my phone and let your family know everyone is Okay." He took it and started to dial, pretty soon he was crying, telling his wife he was alright, she had been frantic.

Red and the hands fired up a truck that was setting near by and left for the ranch. I saddled my horse back up and took my time in getting back. The peace officers had left long before I did.

I did some more thinking as I rode under the starlight. What in the world made these guys think they could get away with a land grab? Were they getting that bold? Did the fact that they got away with breaking the laws of the constitution, make them think that way?

I heard a noise beside me, my horse shied a little bit; a coyote came out of the brush. I pulled up on the reins. The Coyote sat down on his hunch's and just looked at me. "So," I said, "I suppose you're mad at me too?" He shook his head in the negative.

He let a long plaintive howl and then got up and left. I sure wish they could talk.

Everyone was in bed when I got back. I brushed my horse down and gave him a bait of grain. As I was walking toward the house I could see a light in my room. Faith was sitting up in bed reading. "What are you reading?" I asked.

"Well, I see that you have a lot of books, I believe this is one written by a Louis L'Amour. It's pretty good, the hero reminds me of you. There is a sandwich on the nightstand, along with a glass of milk, I thought you would be hungry."

"I am. Did Red tell you all about it?"

"Yep, he said you were hell on wheels. I told him I thought he had the direction wrong, more like heaven than hell."

"Thanks honey, I think I will eat that sandwich. I'm a little tired." I didn't even get all of that ate, before I fell asleep. I woke up the next morning naked next to my wife.

She must of undressed me.

Rosie came into the room carrying Alita. "I fed her, she still wants you." Rosie said, as she handed Alita to Faith. Rosie sat down on the edge of the bed, beside me.

"Dad, can I talk to you?" She said.

"Sure you can, anytime. What's on your mind?" I said, as I sat up a little bit.

"Well, those guys I killed, it bothered me all night. How do you get over it?"

"You don't sweetheart. You'll remember them all of your life, each and everyone. But, it will get where it hurts less." Faith was breast feeding Alita,

"Yes," she said, "that's true sweetheart. It bothers me too. But look at it this way, if you wouldn't of killed them they would of shot us in our backs and then turned and shot you and Alita too."

"I know that. I guess I was just feeling sorry for myself, I'll get over it. Thanks, both of you, I love you both." Then she leaned over and hugged me. I tousled her hair.

"Come on, you guys, Daisy has breakfast saved for you. Oh, yeah, the FBI is down there."

Sitting at the table was a man dressed in a suit, he stood up and held his hand out, when we came in, "My name is Special Agent Harry Silver, from the Cheyenne office."

I shook his hand, "I guess you know who we are." I said.

"Yes, all three of you, and the red haired young lady must be the Uzi expert."

Rosie blushed, "I had to shoot them, they were going to kill my parents."

"Yes, the evidence backs you up on that. You are a hero, young lady." He said.

"Did anybody ever go gather up those bodies at the drilling rig?" I asked.

"Yes, of course, we have a team up there right now. Plus one out here, going over every thing. They tell me there was a briefcase that belonged to one of them here?"

"Yes," Faith said, then she walked to the roll top desk and rolled up the cover, "here it is." Then she handed it to him. He looked at the logo and smiled.

I said, "What's the smile about?"

"Oh, we've been trying to pin something on them for years. They are really good at covering their tracks. Perhaps this time, though." I poured him another cup of coffee.

"How much do you want to bet?" I said.

"On what, may I ask?" He said.

"On how soon you will get stonewalled. I bet it isn't even a week and they will have you reined in."

He took a sip of coffee, then said, "I'm afraid I would lose that bet. I personally think it won't take them 48 hours. You and I both know where this will lead, off the record, we know it's this administration and there's not a damn thing I can do about it. But I will tell you this, I'm going to keep a duplicate copy of everything I find. Perhaps when this administration is gone, then we will see. But really, does anything really change from one administration to the next?"

"No, it hasn't. They all think they can make changes, but when they get in there, it's the same old story, their hands are tied. Then they become just as corrupt as the old ones were. You see, just like the Bible says, it is not up to man to direct his own step. It belongs to God to do that." I said.

"Yes, that's what I'm afraid of; is that God's patience will run out. Well thanks for the coffee, I'll be in touch." Then he got up and left.

I looked at my wife and said, "Well, I suppose I had better call Dad and Felicia and fill them in on the last day or so." Faith said, "Give me the phone, I'll do it. You go and check on your horse, brush him or something."

I handed her the phone. Rosie asked if she could go along, "Sure, why not pumpkin. Would you like to pick out a horse for your own?"

"May I? A horse of my very own?" Rosie said.

"Sure, you may. After all you are a *spirit rider,* aren't you?" I said.

"I don't know what you're really talking about, horses just seem to like me is all." Rosie said, as we let the screen door slam. From the kitchen we heard Daisy call out, "Hey, don't let the screen door slam."

Red and the hands had already saddled up and went to check the cattle. There were still some FBI agents taking pictures and stuff, we ignored them. In the pasture next to the corral were some young fillies and some colts, two year olds. The crew still hadn't started to work them yet. Some of them were still pretty rank.

"How about one of those?" I said, gesturing toward the young stock. As we approached they snorted and ran around, like they were *so* spooked, they were just bad actors.

Rosie sat up on the top corral rail, just looking. Pretty soon they quieted down. Most of them tried to ignore us. But one black colt, was what is called 'proud', meaning they had missed one testicle when they cut him. I could read him like a book, he came running up, snorting and blowing snot.

He slid to a stop right in front of us. Rosie looked at him and said, "Now that was just plain rude, if you're going to be my horse, you're going to have to learn some manners." He hung his head, cowed a little bit you might say, then Rosie said,

"Come here, closer so I can get on." He sidestepped right up to her, she swung a leg over him and they trotted off around the pasture. She brought him back around.

I said, "Is that the one you want?" She nodded. "You know he is what we call 'proud', that means when they cut him to make him a gelding, they missed one of his testicles?"

"Yes, he told me, does that mean he can't father any colts?"

"Well, it's rare, but I guess it's possible, one's better than none." I said. "And just what do you mean, he told you?"

"Oh, I know what their thinking, sort of. They don't speak, but somehow I know their thoughts. I can't really explain it, I just do." Rosie said.

"So do they know yours?" I asked.

"Perhaps, I think they know what I'm feeling, they might understand more. But all horses can pick up on what anybody is feeling, didn't you know that?"

"Yeah, I did. That's what makes them good with the disabled. I had a horse when I was just a young shaver, every time my foot would come out of the stirrup, he would stop, he was a good babysitter."

"Can I take Diablo out of the pasture and pick a stall out for him in the barn?"

"I suppose, but have you asked him if he wants to leave the group?"

Rosie was quiet for a while, then said, "I guess he wants to stay with his friends for awhile, but will you tell the men to leave him alone; he doesn't like them."

"Yep, I can't blame him for not liking them, if someone botched the job like they did, I wouldn't like them either. I'll find out who did that and he won't be allowed to cut anymore colts." I said.

As we walked back to the house, I said, "Why did you name him Diablo?"

"He was just feeling so mean, I told him he was acting just like the Devil. I told him I was going to call him Devil Ray, but he said he liked the Spanish Diablo, better."

"Where did he learn Spanish?" I asked.

"One of the hands speaks Spanish, Diablo says he likes the way it sounds."

I put my arm around Rosie's shoulder and hugged her close, I had one very special daughter here. She hugged me back, we walked into the house that way. Faith was just getting off of the phone. "Well, what are you two so happy about?" Faith asked.

Rosie proceeded to tell her all about Diablo. Then she went to play with Alita. Faith looked at me and said, "How did you know he was 'proud cut'?"

I thought a second, "shoot, I don't really know, it just came to me, must have been how he was acting, I guess."

"Humm, are you sure you're not a little bit like Rosie?"

"Now that you mention it, maybe just a little bit, horses have always liked me."

"Well they're not the only ones; I like you more than a little bit." Then she planted a big wet one on me.

When we came up for air, I asked, "So what did Dad and Felicia have to say?"

"Your Dad was quite upset, he wanted to come up here

right away. But I told him that you had everything under control. I also told him that he would have to oversee the drilling on their place down there. I explained that they would be contacting him. Also that when they did, before he let them on the place, to check credentials."

"Yeah, we're going to have to ask the guys here for some thing that only they would know, like a mole on their ass or something." I said.

"Yes, or something a little bit less embarrassing." Faith said, with her little lopsided grin, which I was learning it meant that I had said something that was gauche.

"I was also wondering Honey; I remember you saying that your caretakers lived in the guest house. How come they are living in the main house?" Faith asked me.

"I don't know, I guess you will have to ask Daisy. Does it bother you?" I said.

"No, I guess not, it was just a small point. You see, I have a good memory and when things don't balance, it bothers me." Faith said.

"Then I would suggest you ask her, I'm sure there's a good reason." I said.

Faith chewed her lip a little bit, I could see the gears going around. Faith headed for the kitchen, where Daisy was making lunch.

I went into the Den and took a book off of the book shelves that lined the walls of the den. Settling into the cowhide leather chair, I started to read. I never even got the first page read, till my wife was back. "I found out why, the hot water heater went out in the guest house. Your Dad didn't leave instructions on what to do, whether to repair or replace. So they just moved up here. Isn't that strange? They can run the ranch, but when a domestic appliance malfunctions, they don't know what to do?"

I laid the book down, I looked at her, "I think I know why. My Mother handled everything to do with the house. I'll call the plumber, have him come out and take care of it. Do you want them to move back to the guest house?"

"Heavens no. I want them to stay here with us. It was just something that was a little off kilter." She started to whistle and bounced off toward the kitchen to help Daisy with lunch. I sat there for a second, thinking. Now some people would of thought that was weird, but not me. I was glad my wife picked up on small details. Who knows her little quirk might save our lives one day.

I called the plumber, I told him to bring a new hot water heater out with him when he came on the morrow. As I hung the phone up, Red and the hands started to come in for lunch. It was a good thing we had a big dinning room table.

At lunch, Rosie asked, "Who cut my horse and missed one testicle?"

Faith choked on the drink of water she was taking, "Rosie! Really, not at the dinner table."

Red laid his fork down and said, "We're sorry Rosie, but we were all doing the branding and cutting, perhaps we got in too big of a hurry. It won't happen again, will it men?"

One of the hands asked, "Which horse was it?"

"The big black," Rosie said, then added, "who speaks Spanish? Diablo likes Spanish."

The same man raised his hand. "Good, you can take care of Diablo when I'm not around, he doesn't like the rest of you." Rosie said, as she took a bite of fry bread. Everyone at the table was staring at her, she just went on eating like they weren't even there. Then she looked up, "I'm sorry, I didn't mean to hurt anyone's feelings, I didn't say that I didn't like all of you. Diablo told me that he didn't, I was just passing on his feelings." Then she went back to eating again. They were still staring at her.

Rosie glanced at me and her mother, I winked at her. She cast her eyes down, but a little smile was building on her lips. She was in complete control of the table and she knew it. I pity the man that she would grow up to marry. That is if she ever did get married.

After we helped with washing and drying the dishes. Rosie asked if we all could go for a ride. Faith and I allowed as we all could, if we only would, which we figured was a good idea. All four of us went to the corrals, Rosie wanted Alita to ride with her. She sat her in front, in between her arms. Their saddle was an A-Fork, where the saddlebow was narrow, so Alita could put her legs on both sides of the pommel comfortably.

Of course they were riding Diablo. I saddled my old horse, Nick, for Faith. I roped one of the working string for myself. He was a Roman Nosed, Strawberry Roan. The first thing he did was try and bite me. I rapped the bit against his teeth and he stopped it. I grabbed his ear and pulled his head down and told him a story, it had an unhappy ending, he didn't like it.

I knew the first chance he got he was going to try and dump me. My old spurs were hanging on the tack room wall. I put them on. I swung aboard, he was a sunfishing devil, I sunk the spurs deep. He came back to the ground and proceeded to try to give me a liver transplant. This went on for a full two minutes. Finally he figured he wasn't going to dust me. So he just up and quit and trotted over to the women, as nice as could be.

Faith said, "What was that all about?"

Rosie answered for me, "Oh, you know how males are, they always have to establish the pecking order."

"Are you alright Clay, your nose is bleeding?" Faith said, as she leaned over and wiped a drop of blood off my chin.

"Yeah, I'm fine, he did ring my chimes for me though, didn't he?"

"That wasn't what I was worried about, I was more worried about the family jewels." Faith said.

"Oh, yeah I think their okay still. Time will tell, won't it?" I said.

"Oh please, will you two stop it," Rosie said, "I know what you're talking about, Dad didn't get hurt any, I read on the internet that they pull back up inside for protection."

"Oh, is that right young lady, perhaps you'd better tell them that. Also, maybe we had better start blocking some of that internet, what do you think about that?" I said.

"I wasn't on any of those sites, this was on the Mayo Clinic site. You don't have to worry about me watching any of those awful web sites. I hate them."

"Well good for you Rosie," Faith said. "We don't like them either."

"Hey," I said, "lets change the subject, it's such a beautiful afternoon, where do you want to go?"

"Well we haven't seen the drilling rig, why don't we ride by there?" Faith said.

"Okay, you did bring your .32, didn't you?" I asked.

"Of course, I never go anywhere without it. What about you?"

"Yeah, mine's in my pocket, what about you Rosie?"

She reached into Alita's diaper bag and pulled her Uzi out. "I have it, one never knows."

I know it seems strange that we'd have to go about armed. After all this wasn't the wild frontier anymore, or was it? In some ways it was more dangerous now then it was back in the nineteenth century. Then you knew what was dangerous and what wasn't, now one just didn't know anymore.

The grass hadn't turned brown, as of yet. Even though it was the middle of summer. This area had been getting rain, for once. We were riding single file, with me bringing up the rear.

Rosie was in front. There was the buzz of a Rattlesnake, Diablo danced to the side. Faith palmed her .32 and blew its head off.

Rosie said, "Oh, what did you kill him for? He was just warning Diablo not to step on him."

Faith said, "I'm sorry Honey, it was just an automatic response, my gun was in my hand before I had even thought about it. When my family is in danger, I react without thinking."

"Your instincts were right Faith," I said. "You see a Rattlesnake also reacts without thinking, he would strike out of instinct also. So you did right. You probably saved one of our horses from getting a venomous snake bite."

"So, am I forgiven Rosie?" Faith asked.

"Yes, it's just sometimes I get overly sentimental, I have to learn to toughen up, I guess. I suppose your quick reaction to danger, was how I felt when those men were shooting at you and Dad."

"Yes, Rosie," I said, "your first reaction was to save us, and you did. Just as Faith's reaction saved our horses."

We could hear the drilling rig working before we came over the last hill. It was still sitting right where it was supposed to be in Coyote Draw, as if it would of moved.

I sure hated them, but I guess it was a necessary evil. The only solace I had was knowing it would all be put back as it should be, the land I mean.

We rode up and ground tied our horses. Yeah, as I stepped off, that Roman Nosed Devil tried to bite me again. He was a funny one, I think he just did it to see if he could get away with it. Then he nickered softly and rubbed up against me, go figure.

Randy Fillmore, the owner of the rig seen us and came our way. (I'm sorry I didn't tell you his name before.) But I guess I had more important things on my mind. He held his hand out to shake, I took it. He said, "I got hold of my cousin Spike in

Arizona, they talked to your Dad and as such they are in the process of moving the rig to his ranch."

"Good, I guess. As you probably can tell, this isn't my favorite activity. If it wasn't for the Oil shortage, I wouldn't do it. The money isn't that important, but anything that decreases our dependence on foreign oil is."

"I'm glad the money isn't that important to you, but I have to feed my family." Randy said.

I looked at him and said, "I'm sorry, I came across as a pompous ass. I just meant that the money wasn't the reason I was doing this, not that I was looking a gift horse in the mouth."

"I understand. I think we should be reaching oil pretty soon; the core samples are looking good. After we get this hole producing I think we can move over a few feet and send out some laterals. That way we won't have to disturb anymore ground."

"Good, that's what I like to hear." Faith said.

"Uh, Mr. Bronson, has any of your men been around here?" Randy asked.

"No, I don't think so, why?"

"Well, just this morning I seen the glint of someone glassing us from the hilltop, over there. It was just a glint and then it was gone." Randy said.

"I'll check it out." I said. Faith and Rosie, with Alita on her hip, had started to pick wildflowers. I walked over to where they were. I told them what Randy had said.

"Who do you think it was?" Faith said.

"I don't know, but who ever it was, was probably up to no good. It'll just take me a few minutes. You guys wait here, Brutus and I will ride up there and scope it out."

"You and who?" Rosie asked.

"My horse, I named him Brutus, just now. Don't you like

125

it?" I said.

"Well it sort of fits him, with his Roman nose and all." Rosie said.

After giving Brutus another rap in the teeth. I mounted up and circled around and came up on the hilltop from the side. No one was there. But I could make out where someone had lain; by the way the grass was bent over. Who ever it was had stepped in a cow pie, I bet he was mad. I could see his footprint very clearly. Whoever it was, was not wearing boots, that was a print from a street shoe or I'm no tracker. Of course that only narrowed it down to about 98 percent of the population, but it got me to thinking.

I followed his tracks, leading my horse. They led back over two more hills. To where an ATV must have been parked, the tracks went back towards the county road. I got my satellite cell phone out of my pocket and called Charles Hester in Montana.

"Hey Charles, this is Clay Bronson, did that Dipper Tick ever show up there?"

"No Clay, he didn't. It's been pretty quite here."

"Oh, another thing Charles, we're starting our own Oil company. Only we're going to do the drilling and recovery in an environmentally safe way. Think about it, if you want in let me know." With that I hung up. Isn't it strange how we still use the expression 'to hang up'? When all you have to do is close the lid to disconnect.

So Dipper Tick didn't go to Montana. I must of really pissed him off. Perhaps he had a vendetta against me and mine now? Who knows, perhaps it's someone else altogether?

I mounted up and sat there, lost in thought, till Brutus reached around and tried to bite my toe. "Okay, okay, let's go, find the women." I said. He turned and headed across the hills, in a straight line, like an Eagle does.

When we found them, they were up Coyote Draw still picking flowers, Diablo and Nick were following along behind them. Alita was sitting on Diablo.

Faith asked, "What did you find?"

"Oh, there was someone up there alright. I found the spot he had lain in and even a shoe print, right in the middle of wet manure. I followed his tracks to where he parked his ATV and seen the tracks where the ATV headed off toward the county road."

"No idea who it was?" Faith asked.

"Not really. Nothing definite anyway. Do you think it could be Dipper Tick?"

"I suppose, he was pretty mad at us. I have a feeling we haven't seen the last of him." Faith said. Then I told her about calling Charles Hester. We had mounted up and was meandering along toward home. When Brutus stepped in a gopher hole and took a little dip, I heard a shot and felt something strike me on the right side of my head, then darkness....

Chapter Eight

I awoke with our whole family seating beside my bed. Dad, Felicia, Jake, Alona and of course Faith, Alita and Rosie. I put my hand up to my head, it was swathed in bandages.

They all started talking at once. "Whoa," I said, "One at a time, what in the hell happened?"

Faith said, "We'll let Rosie tell it, she's the hero." First, Faith leaned forward and gave me a kiss. She whispered in my ear, "If you'd died, I'd kick your ass." Then she kissed me again.

"Well," Rosie said, "it wasn't much, really. But Brutus really saved you. By dropping to his knees, he must of sensed something. Anyway, the shot was meant for your heart. But instead it just cut a furrow in your scalp, it did crack your skull some. But they thought you were dead.

Four of them came roaring down the hill on ATV's. They had the drop on us. They knew Faith had a pistol, they made her drop it. They made us get off of our horses. They said they were going to rape us and then kill us. But Alita was putting up such a howl, crying over you. It unnerved them. They told me to shut her up.

I told them she had a dirty diaper. They told me to change her then. I sat her on the ground and went over to the diaper bag that was on Diablo. It was all over real fast."

"Huh? What happened then?" I asked.

"Oh, you must have forgotten, I had my Uzi in the diaper bag." Rosie said.

"You killed all four of them? Who were they?" I asked.

Faith spoke up. "Some of that same bunch. They had I.D. from California though." Rosie said, "Really I only did for three of them. One of them was still alive, I'd got him in the belly, he was crying and carrying on so, that Faith felt sorry for him, so she put him out of his misery."

"Uh, yeah, but I thought that they had killed you. You had so much blood all over. He might have lived, but you know how it is with being gut shot."

"Yeah, I do know. How did all of you get here so fast?" I said, looking at our family from New Mexico. "And did you call the law? They should be notified."

Dad laughed, "Son, you've been in that hospital bed for three weeks. You started to come out of it yesterday. Till then we've been taking turns setting with you. We have all been by your bed since early this morning."

"When can I go home?" I asked.

"We don't know for sure, they said you had quite the concussion. They said you might have amnesia, but it doesn't appear that way." Jake said, Alona was holding onto to his hand or was it the other was around. Alona leaned forward and gave me a kiss on the cheek.

Felicia said, "You are in the hospital in town. All of us are going to stay in Wyoming for awhile. Red and Daisy have moved back into the guest house. The four of us are going back to the ranch tonight. Your little family is going to stay in this room with you, see the beds on either side?"

"They'll let you do that?" I asked Faith.

"Sure, money talks you know."

Just then a nurse came in, "I'm going to have to ask you all to let him get some rest. Also I need to check his wounds."

Dad said, "That's Okay, the four of us are going to the ranch tonight. We'll be back on the morrow. Is that alright

Clay?"

"Sure, you guys go ahead, I'll be Okay, these two have kept me alive so far, I'll be alright." I said. The nurse said, "Is your wife and daughters going to stay in the room?"

"Sure, why not, I don't have any secrets from them." The nurse looked at me and shrugged her shoulders. She took the head bandages off. "That looks pretty good, I think the stitch's can come out tomorrow. But the Doctor will have to look at it first. Now for the other wound." She started to take the covers down. Faith spoke up:

"What other wound?" She said loudly.

"That's Okay Mom, I know about it, it's not that bad." Rosie said.

The nurse pulled my covers down and pulled up the gown. She reached down and moved my testacies aside. "Oh, yes these stitches can come out tomorrow also." I stared at Faith. She said, "What, how did that get there?"

"I'm sorry Mom, I should of told you. But you were concentrating on the head wound and there was so much blood. And then you went over and gave that man his last rights. I sneaked a look then, I seen the 'family jewels' as you called them were alright, so I just tore off part of his shirt tail and stopped the blood. I'm sorry I should of told you."

"Let me look!" Faith said, as she pushed the nurse aside. "Yes, their alright, wait, there's nick on one of them," she pulled the nurse close, "see there, is that okay?" They both bent over to get a good look. I looked at Rosie and winked at her. She had that small crooked smile on her face. She leaned over and whispered in my ear, "It's just a small nick, nothing serious."

Alita gave a small cry and reached her arms out toward me. I said, "If you two voyeurs are through looking, Alita wants me to hug her." They both snapped upright, their faces bright red.

The nurse hurried out.

"I don't understand," Faith said, "when did that happen?"

Rosie said, "There were two shots, one when Dad was falling out of the saddle. That's when, I guess."

"Rosie, I don't understand how you can be so cool under fire." Faith said. "I was totally terrified. I thought Clay was dead."

"Yes, at first I did also. But then I seen his chest move, that's when I knew he would live. But as to how I can be so cool; I guess growing up in that orphanage makes you that way. Oh, I've got some news for both of you, guess what? My period started yesterday, I'm officially a woman now." She said, proudly.

Faith and I, both said, "That's great Dear." And Faith gave her a hug. I couldn't help but think of the irony of the situation. Here she had just saved both mine and Faith's life, not once, but twice by killing the total of six deadly men. And what she was most proud of, was that she was in puberty. A little late perhaps, because she was not the usual twelve years old, but she had just turned thirteen.

The Doctor came in. She, yes she, said, "So how's my patient this afternoon?"

"Pretty good Doc." I said, "but I feel like I should introduce myself. Being as this is the first time I've met you. Even though you're familiar with me."

"How's your head feel? Any headaches?" She said.

"Well no, I guess not. My head hurts, which I suppose is normal, being they almost put a hole in my head."

"Yes, I think I will pull those stitches out, you heal fast. Set up straight, will you?"

I did. Faith was standing at her elbow, so close she could hardly move. I know it made her nervous. She finished with the stitches on my head, then said, "Now let's see how it's healing down below." She pulled the covers down, my gown was still up. "Oh yes, there ready to come out too." She started to reach down,

Faith said, "Whoa there. I don't mind you handling *my* family jewels, while my husband is unconscious, but when he's awake the only hand that's going to handle those are mine. Here, give me those scissors and the tweezers, I'll do that."

"Alright, do you know how?" The Doc said.

"Yeah she does." I said. "She's stitched me up before. It seems I'm somewhat of a target, but this time they almost did for me." The Doctor stood at her elbow, it didn't bother Faith, at all.

The Doctor noticed that scar in my side, the one that the pickpockets gave me, she poked around on it. "Is this the one she stitched up? It does look pretty good, in time it won't hardly show. You did a good job Faith."

"We'll do an MRI in the morning, just to be safe. If that comes out alright, I think he can go home in the afternoon. But he'll have to take it easy; no knocks on the head and such." Doc said. "Oh yeah," she added, "are you up to having visitors? There's an FBI agent and the Sheriff wants to talk with all of you." I nodded.

I looked at Faith, "They haven't talked to you guys before this?"

"No, they haven't, they came out I guess, anyway that's what Red and Daisy said. Red showed them where they ambushed us. But this will be the first time we've seen them."

John and Harry Silver came in with their hats in their hands. John said, "We hate to bother you so soon after you just come out of your coma, but we have a few questions." Harry said,

"They're not too important; since we investigated the crime scene. The facts bear out what Red told us about how you were ambushed. Was there anybody else there? That you seen anyway?"

"Not me, that's for sure, I haven't asked my women. Did you girls see anybody else out there?

Faith said, "No I didn't."

Rosie cleared her throat, "Uh, no I didn't see anybody else, but I did hear another ATV take off."

"Huh?" Faith said, "I didn't hear anything."

"You were too busy screaming." Rosie said.

"Why do you ask?" I said.

"Well, like Rosie said, there was another set of tracks up there. One that tore away at a high rate of speed." Harry said.

"Did you take casts of the tire prints?" I asked.

"Of course we did, plus also a shoe print that was close to the tire tracks. Funny thing, there were traces of manure in the print."

"One last question," John said, "Did Rosie kill them all?"

Faith spoke up quickly, "No she didn't, I got in one shot, I think I killed one of them."

"Yes, that's what our CSI team said, we were just checking." Harry said, while he was glaring at John. I filed that fact away in the back of my brain. I don't think John and him were seeing eye to eye in this investigation. I think John would like to find some fault with us.

As they were leaving Harry turned and said, "Did they say anything?" Rosie said,

"Yes, they did, they said they were going to rape us and then kill us. And since Alita was crying about Dad, they wanted me to shut her up. I told them she needed her diaper changed. They told me to change her then. My gun was in the diaper bag."

Harry and John stared at her, then they left. I think I seen John shudder a little bit as he went through the door. I asked,

"Do you lady's have your guns with you?"

"Of course we do. By the way, here's yours, you can put it under your pillow." Faith said.

"How did you get them in here? Don't they have metal detectors?" I asked.

"Get real, in a little town like this? Of course not. And that's just why we need them. Anybody can bring a gun in here, so how else are we to protect ourselves?"

Faith and the girls went to the cafeteria for supper, they brought mine. I was pretty hungry, all I had was those intravenous tubes in me. I ate everything they brought, and it was delicious.

I was actually starting to feel pretty good. In my head anyway, my groin was a different story, they ached some. The bullets didn't destroy anything. It felt like I got hit with a baseball bat though.

After they came back from supper, we sat around talking till bed time. Alita and Rosie slept in one bed, Faith on the other side of my bed. The girls went right to sleep, Faith and I held hands from one bed to the other.

My arm was getting tired. "Hey Hon, how about I get in bed with you?" I said.

I'll arrange the pillows on my bed so the nurse can't tell I'm not in there. Don't worry we won't do anything, that's going to have to wait for a day or two." I said.

"Damn, I was hoping you could, it's been three weeks for me, while it's only been a day for you. Since you were in a coma time doesn't count." She said.

I started to get into her bed, then I remembered my gun, I got it and put it under the pillow on my side. It didn't take us long till we were asleep.

We were awoke by gunfire, someone was standing in the doorway firing into my bed, of course I wasn't in it, he shot five times, before Rosie, Faith and I cut loose, we made a rag doll out of him. He had been silhouetted by the light from the hallway. Who ever it was, he knew what bed I was supposed to be in.

All kinds of alarms were going off, Faith and I got out of bed, we told Rosie to stay with Alita. Faith was in her bra and panties, me in my gown that didn't cover anything anyway. We went to the door, just as the so-called security guard got there.

The man, who was dressed in a police uniform of some kind, was laying on his face in the hallway. The guard turned him over, it was John, the Sheriff.

I said, to the guard, "You had better call Harry Silver, the FBI agent. I think he's at the local Motel."

The hallway was crawling with cops, every kind and description. They were all asking questions at once. When Harry got there, he quieted them down. Harry looked at me, "Okay who shot first? Like I didn't know."

"Look at my bed, you'll find five holes in it, I would be dead, all except I was in bed with my wife. Harry, I'm sure getting tired of people trying to kill me. Why would he try and kill me? If I was you I would check his bank account, I bet someone paid him to do it." I said.

The Hospital wanted us out. I guess I wasn't going to get that MRI. Faith and I were still in the same dress mode. I finally noticed that everyone was staring at Faith, well why shouldn't they she was wearing a thong. "Honey, get dressed won't you, did you bring any clothes for me? Do you have a car in the parking lot? She said yes to all questions.

I called Dad and told him what had happened and that we were coming out tonight. They didn't even take me down in a wheel chair, like they do when an ambulatory patient checks out. As we came out of the main door, the press was there, well why not?

I stopped and said, "I tell you what, you come out to the ranch tomorrow and I will answer all of your questions, it's really quite a story." Then we left.

Faith was driving, she looked at me, "Are you alright?" She asked.

"Yeah, sure, I guess. I still hurt and I feel pretty tired. But nothing I won't recover from."

"I'm pissed," Faith said, "the way they kicked us out. I believe it's against the law. I think we have grounds for a malpractice law suit. What do you think?"

"I don't know. I've never been a fan of law suits. But yeah, I think you have a right to be pissed. After all, it wasn't our fault that John tried to kill me. And I'm sure he would of turned his gun on the other two beds. I didn't want to make a bigger scene than what was already going on. When the press comes out in the morning, that will be the time to air our complaints."

Faith's knuckles were white on the steering wheel. Yeah, she was some upset. I can't blame her. If it was her that was injured and they did this to her. I would have been more than pissed. I was a bit sleepy. Faith seen my head nod, she said. "Recline the seat and take a nap, I'll wake you when we get home." I did so. I heard Rosie say, "Is Dad Okay, he's not going to go into a coma again, is he?" That was the last I heard...

The sun was coming in my bedroom window. I was a bit disoriented, was it time to go to school?

Then I heard a voice say, "Well, you're finally awake, I'll call your wife." I looked over at the chair beside my bed. A woman was setting there. She got up and left the room. I moved my arm, there was a tube in it. I followed the tube with my eyes, it lead to a bag hanging from a stand.

There was something else, my hand went down to my crotch, there was tube coming out of it. It was a catheter. I relaxed, trying figure out what was going on. Things were swirling around in my mind. Slowly, they were coming into focus. My name for one thing. I was Clay Bronson.

The woman said she would get my wife. Wife? Oh, yeah, Faith. I smiled, she was one hot babe. How in the world did I deserve such a babe? Then, children, Alita and Rosie, I smiled some more.

I looked around my room, it was more of a hospital room. But I could tell it was my room. Faith burst into the room, followed by Rosie and Alita? They were bigger than I remembered, but Faith was much prettier than she used to be, to me anyway.

"Oh Clay, Sweetheart, you're finally awake," Faith said, with tears running down her cheeks. She fell on her knees beside the bed, kissing me. I ate it up. "How do you feel?" she said.

"I don't know, but you and the kids look wonderful, how have you guys been?"

"Us? Goodness sake, we're fine." Faith said. I tried to set up a little bit, but I could hardly move. "Don't move too fast, you'll have to take it slow." Faith said.

"How come I'm so weak, how long have I been in bed?" I asked. Faith put her hands to her mouth, then Rosie said, looking at her wrist watch.

"Six months, one week, two days, and five hours. So it's going to take you a while to get your muscles up to par." She smiled at me then leaned over and gave me a kiss on the cheek. Alita was standing on her own beside the bed, she tried to crawl on the bed, Rosie lifted her up. She laid down beside me and put her arm around me. I gave her a kiss on the forehead. Tears were running down my cheeks, I don't know why, I wasn't crying, men don't cry.

The woman who was here when I woke up came in the room. "Clay," Faith said, "you remember Dr. Suong Tu?

"Yeah, I remember her, but I didn't know her name. If I'm not mistaken that name is of Vietnamese origin?" I said, as I weakly held out my hand.

"Yes," she said, as she took my hand and checked my pulse. "Hmm, that's good. How are you feeling?" The Doc said.

"Well, there is one thing you can do for me, and that's get that catheter out."

"Do you think you're strong enough to get up to pee?" She said.

"Well, if I'm not, my wife can help me, just get the damn thing out!"

"Alright, if your family would leave the room?" She said, looking at Faith and Rosie.

"They don't have to, I'm sure they have seen me naked before, even Rosie, she stopped the bleeding down there when I got shot." I said.

She flipped back the covers, I didn't have a gown on. I guess it was easier to keep me clean without one. She proceeded to pull it out. Now if you've never had a catheter in, it's hard to explain how it feels coming out, put it this way, I didn't like it.

"What about these feeding tubes, can you take them out?" I asked. They were a little easier coming out, they only bled a little bit, when she pulled the needles out of my veins.

She said, "I hope you're not getting, how you say, 'the buggy ahead of the Donkey'?"

"That's the 'cart ahead of the horse.' How come you're here?" I asked, rather bluntly.

"Behave yourself Clay," Faith said. "Dr. Tu has been very

helpful, she's on the company payroll now."

"Huh? What payroll?"

"The Spanish Bit Oil Company. There have been a lot of changes in the last six months. One of them I'm sure you will like, Rosie is now officially a Bronson. The adoption papers went through last month."

"Good, but how can that be, I thought I would have to sign some kind of papers?"

"Don't worry, I have your signature down pat, you've signed oodles of papers since you went back into a coma." Faith said, "In fact even Rosie has mastered your scrawl."

"Why does the Company need a Doctor?" I asked.

"Well, someone is always getting hurt someway. But we owed it to her. You see, the next morning after you left the Hospital, she came out to check on you. She's been here ever since. Also she testified on our behalf when we sued the Hospital."

"Oh? What grounds did you use?"

"Several, from malpractice, to failure to provide proper security. It was sort of their fault that John ever got there to shoot into that empty bed. And then when they kicked you out, that was really a no-no."

"Did you win?" I asked.

"We settled out of court, for three million, they were glad to pay it."

"Well, you've turned into a regular money bags, haven't you? But where is the rest of our family?"

"Oh, they went home a long time ago, they have to run the Oil company in New Mexico. They have been calling every day. As soon as you feel better, you can call them.

And I'm not the money bags, we are. You, me and Rosie, plus Alita. Of course, in the Oil Company, Dad, Felicia, Jake and Alona. All eight of us really."

Dr. Tu spoke up, "I think we ought to let him rest for a little while, you can fill him in on everything that has happened later."

"I want Faith to stay." I said. Rosie took Alita, and the three of them filed out.

"So," I said, "Just who has been giving me baths, during all of those months?"

"Now who do you think? Me of course. But I will sure be glad when you can take your own."

"I'm sorry Honey, for all of the trouble I've put the family through. Not only the work of taking care of me, but the heartache of it. It must have been hard on all of you."

"Well yes, but its been worth it, now that you're awake again. This time you had better stay that way. We did get you that MRI, there is no permanent damage, but that bullet sure did rattle your brains."

"How soon do you think I can get up?" I asked.

"Well, why don't we play that by ear. First we had better see if you can hold down solid food. We have to get your digestive system working again. We know your kidneys work fine, as many times as I had to empty that bag."

That took a week, before I could get out of bed and stand on my own. And another week, before I could get down stairs. I had been out for six months, missed winter. That I didn't mind, but now spring was in full blossom. That I was determined not to miss.

Rosie had started going back to school. They gave her a placement test, she qualified for the 11th grade, she was a Junior in High School. The Bus picked her up right at our gate on the county road. She drove one of the ranch pickups there each morning. She made sure she locked it up tight. She didn't need a driver's license to drive on our own property.

Being a thirteen year old in with seventeen year olds was a test on one's patience. It wasn't the boy's that gave her problems, but the other girls. You know how girls run in packs, just like wolves.

Anyway, they tried to beat her up, just because she was smarter than they were. Big mistake. There were six of them, they cornered her in the Gym. Rosie was a great one for learning things off of the internet. She could see it done, then translate that image into action. She had been watching a video on street fighting.

We had to pay for the Doctor bills, they couldn't press charge's since they started it. I guess we could of fought it, but I felt sorry for them, it wasn't their fault that they were saddled with a 'stupid gene' in their makeup.

I was setting on the porch whittling, when Rosie drove in the yard, It was the first week in May.

She came up and set beside me. "Dad, can I have some money for my graduation ring and the gown and stuff?"

"Huh? Graduation? You don't graduate till next year, do you?" I said.

"No, it's this year, I have been doing double work."

"Why in the world did you want to do that for?" I asked.

"It wasn't my idea. The principal came up to me last fall, he told me they'd make all the arrangements, if I would do extra work. So I figured, why not?"

"You don't have to ask for money. You can have what you want anytime, you know that. Is that why those girls tried to beat you up? Do they think you're a nerd?"

"Not anymore. Their all scared of me now, even the boys. Plus also they've all heard the stories about our family. They say we shoot first and ask questions later."

"Well, that's certainly not the truth, we've never shot first." I said.

"Yeah, really I think they're just jealous, they think we're rich." Rosie said, then, "I'm going to get some cookies and milk, do you want some?"

"Yes, please." I said, as I laid my whittling aside, thinking back to what Faith had told me about our late Sheriff. The morning after the shootout in the Hospital, Harry Silver had checked John's bank account. Just that day he had tried to kill us, someone had deposited five hundred thousand dollars in his bank account.

The FBI could of froze his account, but he had children and a wife. Faith had talked Harry into letting his family have it. It wasn't their fault he was an idiot. Faith had told me how she met her one time in the grocery store. His wife started to call us killers. Faith took her aside and explained things to her. Now they were the best of friends.

There was still some unfinished business; Dipper Tick. I was sure it was his bunch that paid John to kill us. We hadn't heard anymore about him and we didn't have any more trouble. But how long can one go in this world without having any trouble?

Rosie came out of the house with milk and cookies, Faith came out behind her, carrying Alita. I said, "Alita, how come you're not walking? Making your decrepit old mother carry you, shame on you."

She just giggled and reached down to me, I took her and sat her on my lap, we shared the milk and cookies. Faith twisted my ear, "Just who is decrepit? I think it's time you started pulling your weight around here. The men need help in the spring roundup and branding. I told Red that you and Rosie would help them."

"Sure, do you know how to rope Rosie?"

"Some, I've watched the men. But I would like you to teach me, the men missed about half of the time."

"Sure thing, Sweetheart, we'll start the lessons this evening. Have you been riding Diablo? And how has Brutus been?" I asked.

"Mom and I have been riding. We take turns in riding Brutus, he gets mad when we ride Diablo and Nick, he doesn't like to be left back."

"Did you have any trouble with him?"

"At first, but when I told him you were hurt, he quieted right down." Rosie said.

Then she got up and took Alita, "We're going to check on the horses." As she walked away I noticed how she was growing into her bones. I suppose I'd have to put up a fence around her pretty soon.

Faith noticed me watching, "Yes, she is becoming quite the young lady. The last time we went to the movie in town, I noticed all the boys looking at her. Don't worry though, she has a level head on her shoulders."

"You've been going to the movies?" I said.

"Of course, you've had all of those sexy dreams for the last six months, while we had to pay for ours." She said, as she sat down in my lap and gave a little wiggle.

Dreams? She was right, I did have some. Not sexy ones, but weird ones. Funny thing, I could remember each and every one of them. Which is unusual, most dreams you forget as soon as you wake up. I was still trying to figure them out.

I was feeling a lot better. Faith gave another wiggle. It dawned on me, she had been without for over six months. I said, "Come on Honey, I think we have time." She said, "You mean?" I picked her up off of my lap and carried her into the house, "Yes, that's exactly what I mean.".......

143

Chapter Nine

After supper Rosie and I went to the Tack Shed and got our ropes. First we practiced on the fiberglass steer head. She caught it every time. So we saddled Diablo. I wasn't sure how he would react to the rope twirling around his head and flanks.

We had some bucket calves in the barn. So I turned them out in the corral. Rosie took Diablo in the far gate. The calves spooked and ran. Diablo was right on them, Rosie's loop fell true. I said, "That's the easy part, now catch their heels."

The only thing was, Diablo wanted to cut them, not heel them. Rosie had to talk to him. Then he got behind them and Rosie caught both heels. She shook her loop loose and said, "Is that all there is to it?"

"Yep, but the trick is, can you keep it up all day?"

"Sure, why not? I'm not an invalid." She said, then she roped a few more, catching both heels every time. She kept it up, till I told her that was enough, the calves were tired. Besides, I was starting to fade. I knew I wasn't up to my old self, yet....

Leaning on the corral rail was Dr. Tu. She came over. "Let me look into your eyes." Which she did. "Okay, you all right."

I said, "Hold on a minute, what was that? 'you all right', you know better than to talk that way, why did you do it?"

"Okay, yes I know better, I can talk English, probably better than most of your hands on the ranch. But when they see an Asian, they expect us to talk that way. So sometimes, I just do it on purpose, I'm sorry."

"Alright Doctor, don't ever talk down to your heritage." I said.

I helped Rosie hang her saddle in the tack room, then we both walked back to the house. The sun was setting and its rays highlighted Rosie's red hair. Only thing it wasn't as red as it used to be, it had gotten darker, it was now a deep auburn. Faith and Alita met us on the porch with some hot chocolate. In the spring, in Wyoming the nights were still chilly.

I was sipping mine, looking at my wife. Her hair was still black, but she had cut it in a pageboy cut, it reminded me of what the flapper's from the 1920's looked like. She was so cute, it hurt to look at her....

Alita was setting on my lap as I rocked back and forth, pretty soon she dozed off. It was one of those evenings when everything is perfect in one's own small world. Rosie's head was nodding, Faith said, as she took Alita from my lap. "Come on Rosie, it's bed time," then she looked at me, "are you coming?" she asked.

"Sure, for some reason, I'm wiped out tonight." I said.

"Boy you have a short memory, did you forget what we did this afternoon?"

"No, but that didn't use to tire me out." I said.

"Well, you're not quite up to snuff yet, but you couldn't tell that by this afternoon." Faith said as she put her off arm around me and the three of went into the house.

The next day dawned bright and clear; the weather was anyway. I don't think I was. You know how on your computer 'spam' keeps popping up? Well anyway that was how those dreams were that I had while I was on my six months vacation.

They would pop up, randomly. Sometimes in the middle of the night or even briefly when I was awake. Very annoying.

It was after breakfast, I took my cup of coffee and went to sit on the front porch. I sat there sipping it, listening to the birds.

"Clay, Clay, are you alright?" Faith was calling me from somewhere far away, so was Rosie, "Daddy, Daddy, please wake up," she said, with tears in her voice. Why was she crying? Also, Alita was crying from some where.

"What's wrong with Alita?" I heard myself say.

Faith said, "Thank heavens you're back. Are you alright?

"Of course, why are you all crying and having such a fit?" I asked.

Dr. Tu came into my line of vision. "Can you see how many fingers I am holding up?" She said. When I said the proper number, she said, "Follow my finger with your eyes, don't turn your head." I did so, she gave a sigh of relief and said, "He's back; how long was he this way before you called me?"

Faith said, "I don't know for sure; Rosie and I were doing the dishes. Clay had come out here to drink his coffee, maybe an hour or less. But we've been trying to wake him for over a half hour, since we found him."

"He hasn't been asleep, he's been somewhere else, where were you Clay?" Dr. Tu asked.

"Well, my body has been sitting right here, but, I guess you could say that my mind or something like it has been into the future. Yeah, I know, that's a bunch of crap. But if I wasn't actually there; I was having hallucinations or maybe even a vision. Cause it was more than a dream. How do I know? Because I can remember every little detail. Even to how many pubic hairs my wife has."

"What? You don't even know that; how could you?" Faith said.

"Well this particular vision, or whatever, was way in the future; like thousands of years. I've had others that were closer to our time, but this one was way out there. Nobody wore

146

clothes. And there was no shame attached. We were all there."

"Oh, I don't believe that." Dr. Tu said. "Me without clothes, I would die of shame."

"Tell me Suong, do you have a tattoo?" I said.

"Yes, I do." She said.

"What would you say, if I told you what it was and where it was?"

"I would say that was impossible, no one has ever seen it, including my mother."

"You have a tattoo of a small dragon, on your left buttocks." I said.

"How did you know that? Have you been spying on me?" She gasped.

"You know better than that. I would never do that. You were very proud of that tattoo. It had something to do with your family's heritage. It was part of your family's heraldry. When you had it put on, you couldn't tell your family, because they would of considered it to be some sort of sacrilege. Anyway that's what you were telling everyone."

"No one knows that, except me. I'll be damned," Dr. Suong Tu said, as she sat down on the top step. Her face was turning red from embarrassment.

"Don't be embarrassed. In that future, no one is. I wasn't." I said. "But more important, are the ramifications of me knowing that you, or anyone else has a mole or some other hidden blemish. It means that the vision I had was true!"

"Are you sure Honey that it wasn't just a fluke?" Faith said.

"No, it wasn't, it was so clear, just as I'm talking to all of you right now; it was that clear. But more upsetting to me is the other's. They weren't all so happy. I don't even want to think about them."

"Don't then." Faith said, then to Dr. Tu, "Are you sure this isn't just some malfunction in his brain wiring?"

"How could that be? He knows things that no one else knows. No there's more to this than some physiology quirk. It's more metaphysical, wouldn't you agree?" Suong said.

Rosie cleared her throat, "I would agree with that assumption. I know for sure that things happen and there is no rational explanation for their coming to light. For example, me being a *spirit rider*, who can explain that?"

"A 'spirit rider', what in the world is that?" Suong asked. Rosie told her the full story. Rosie then turned her inquisitive mind, my way.

"Dad, are you going to tell us the rest of your visions?"

"No, not at this time. I think I'll use that old saw, that the military uses, 'the need to know basis'." I said.

"That's not fair, Dad."

"I know it Rosie, but believe me you're better off not knowing. Wouldn't you agree, that the animals are happier not knowing their fate, just living in the moment?"

"I guess so, but Dad, we're not animals."

"Yes, but we all have the same eventuality, don't we?" I said.

"Yes, at the present time, we all do die in the end." Rosie said, rather glumly.

"Yes, but even that is not set in stone, I will tell you that much."

"Clay, will you stop playing word games?" Faith said.

"Yeah, sure sweetheart, but I've got some arranging to do. I have to get them categorized in order of importance and chronologically. It may take some time. It's like I said though, you are probably happier not knowing."

Red was coming across the yard, "Hey," he said, "I thought you and Rosie was going to help with the roundup and branding?"

"Sure," I said, glad of the respite of getting back to the present. Too bad I wasn't an animal....they live in the present....

Rosie and I missed lunch, we had a big breakfast anyway. We spent the rest of the morning and the afternoon brush popping strays out of the timbered draws. When we got back, Faith and Alita met us at the corral. "How come you didn't ask me to go, I can ride you know?"

"Uh, didn't know you wanted to go, and yes I know you can ride, beautifully too." I said.

"Well, I really didn't say that I wanted to, I guess I just wanted to be asked. I'm sorry if I came across as a bitchy wife. Besides I didn't have anyone to watch Alita. Daisy was busy, cooking for the roundup crew. And Suong had to go the drilling rig; someone hurt his arm. I guess I was just feeling left out." Faith said, as I picked her and Alita up and gave them both a kiss.

"Say," I said, "what about the drilling, how's it going?"

"Pretty good, we're already having one well producing. They hope to have another one on line within a week. Since Red has been busy with the ranch; I've sort of been overseeing the drilling. Do you want to take over that?"

"No, no way. Since you have it well in hand, you keep on, keeping on."

"Well, I do like the way they whistle at me." Faith said. I seen the twinkle in her eye and knew she was just funning me.

"You know, I would be very disappointed if they didn't whistle at you, you're the prettiest thing in Wyoming." I said.

"Oh? Only in Wyoming?" Faith said.

"Nope, in the whole universe, and I should know." I said.

"There you go teasing again." Rosie said, "When are you going to tell us more?"

"I don't know, some of the things I seen I don't like to

149

think about. But soon, Okay? Do we have time to take a shower before supper?"

"Yes, Alita and I will get it on the table," Faith said, "you and Rosie can get cleaned up."

The hot water felt good, as it washed away the dust and grim, and soothed the bruise's and small cuts, that the brush gave me. Even though I wore chaps. I was glad we had installed a commercial grade hot water heater, I took my time.

The shower door opened, Faith stood there, "Hey, I didn't say take all night, get your butt out of that shower; the food is getting cold."

I wanted to pull her in with me, but that could wait. I turned the water off and got out. She handed me a towel. She licked her lips, she was thinking the same thing I was, but she had to wait also. Rosie tapped on the door and said, "Come on, you two, no shenanigans now."

After supper, Rosie took Alita into the den to read to her. I cleaned off the table and then dried the dishes as Faith washed. We had a dishwasher, but at times we liked to do them by hand. When married couples shared domestic chores; it brought them closer together. And closer was always better, right?

After we finished the dishes, Faith and I went into the den. We snuggled up on the couch and each of us picked up a book to read. My hand fell on George Orwell's- '1984'.

I read the first chapter. It was disturbingly close to one of those visions that I had. But not that close, his was fiction. I was pretty sure what I had seen wasn't fiction.

Faith was calling, "Clay, Clay, come on now, you're not going to drift off again are you?"

"Uh, no. I'm alright. You both wanted to know about those visions that I had?

Well, this book made me think about one. This one that I

am going to tell you about, has to do with religion. Or the fall of it, anyway. Have either of you ever heard of 'Babylon the Great?"

Faith nodded, but Rosie spoke up, "Oh, I have. Isn't it the world empire of false religion?"

"Yes, you might say that. I don't know whether you know it or not, but religion has been responsible for most of the blood shed in the world. But before I tell you anymore each of you get a Bible and read Revelations the 18th chapter." They did.

"As you know the Apostle John wrote Revelations. Anyway, did you notice how true Christians were told to get out of her, so as not to share in her sins? Because, did you pick up on the reason? And that was because she was going to be destroyed? Well that is what one of my vision was about. The fall of Babylon the Great and her final destruction." I paused, then Rosie said,

"Well finish it, what did you see?"

"I seen how the world's governments got tired of her adulteress fornications with and interference in their affairs. You know how the so called fundamentalist's interfere in the politics of our government. Plus also the jihads of those other religions. Well they got together and outlawed religion. I seen the sacking of all of the church's and temples all across the whole world. Those priests and monks and such were executed outright, if they resisted. Of course religion only got what they had been dishing out for thousands of years, ever since the time of Nimrod.

Now that's not to say that the governments were in the right, as you can see by the Bible, there in Revelations. They were only the tools God used to destroy false religion. So I guess that's the end of one of my visions."

"Okay," Faith said, "that was the end of false religion, does that mean that was the end of religion in the world?"

"Well, in a way, yes. But not the end of the true worship of Jehovah God. That's another vision, you'll have to wait to hear that one. Did you know that God had a name?" I said.

"Yes, I did," Rosie said. "I found it in the Bible, at Psalms 83:18. Of course false religion has removed his name from most of their translations, but I found it in the King James version."

"Good for you Rosie. I'm afraid I didn't know all of this till I had my coma for six months. You are way ahead of me."

"You didn't tell us many of the details, just generally what happened." Faith said.

"You really don't want the details, do you?" I said.

"No, I guess not. But when does this happen?" Faith asked.

"I can't tell you that. Because, it happens in the time line leading up to the battle of Armageddon. And the Bible says that no man will know the day or the hour, only Jehovah God knows that. Jesus his son, doesn't even know the day or hour."

"Well, it must be getting close." Rosie said, "Because look at what a mess the world is in."

"Yes Rosie, Jesus said at Matt. 24:32,33. That for us to take an illustration from the fig tree. 'as soon as it puts forth its new branches we know that the summer is getting near, likewise when all the prophecies start to occur, you know that he is near at the door'." I said, not knowing myself where all of these things I was saying were coming from, I had never read the Bible that much before.

Faith said, "What are you, some kind of prophet or something now?"

"No, I don't think so, I think I'm what's called an eavesdropper. In all of these visions, I was sort of standing in the shadows, no one knew I was there. At times I was sort of like an Eagle, flying high and just observing. In fact most of the time I was high in the sky, just looking on, sometimes I would swoop down for a closer look."

"I've had dreams like that," Rosie said, "I dream I'm flying, it's very exhilarating."

"Yes," Faith said, "Me too, you're flying and you can see everything. But I didn't see anything important. Of course I wasn't an Eagle, I was just me." Then she stuck her tongue out at me. I carefully laid my book on the coffee table, then I grabbed her and kissed her, long and hard. I heard Rosie say, "You know you two have a room." Then she picked Alita up and said, "We're going to bed." Then she stomped out. We never did make it to bed, till much later....

The next morning all three of us saddled up to work the cattle. One of Daisy's niece's was visiting Daisy, we corralled her to baby sit. I showed Faith how to heel, she would catch every other throw, which really isn't bad. I've known some old cattle men who didn't do much better. I left Faith and Daisy to drag the calves to the fire. I went looking for some strays, that the guys on the oil rig said they saw. (said they saw, was that proper English?) You know when you go to read a story, don't get caught up in the mechanics of it, just enjoy the story being told.

You see that is what I'm trying to do, is recount the happenings leading up to the end. And being that I'm not an English professor, but a warrior, you will find some grammatical errors. Enjoy them. After all doesn't it make you feel superior?

Brutus and I, cantered for a ways, then cut back to a walk, just enjoying the ride. I had a 30-30 stuck in a sheath, under my left stirrup, plus my pistol in a shoulder holster. Even though we were lollygagging along, we both were alert to our surroundings. I didn't want to be drygulched again.

I had just kicked Brutus up to a trot, when I seen Old Man

Coyote sitting in the middle of the trail and by his side sat the biggest Bald Eagle that I had ever seen.

Brutus came right up to them and stopped on his own. "Well, what do you want Old Man?" I said, expecting no answer. I got no audible one, but I heard his voice in my mind.

"Want? I want the Buffalo back, I want the Elk, the Grizzly Bear. I want things as they used to be before the white man came, that's what I want, but both you and I know that it is up the Great Spirit to do that. But right at this minute, Eagle and I have come to warn you of danger. It's too bad you didn't listen the last time I seen you.

But now, I know that you can hear me. They are back. Eagle says there are three of them. They are on top of the ridge in back of the oil drilling rig. They want to kill you, but if you don't show up by sundown, they will kill some of your drilling rig crew."

"Why do they want to kill me, I'm just a small cog in the wheel around here?"

"It's not what you are now. Oh, they think it is, but it's what you will accomplish in the future. The Dark one wants you dead. He is one of the reason's that we can warn you. He being a supernatural being, you deserve some supernatural help, us...."

"Why can I hear you now and not before, when you gave that long mournful howl?" I said.

"That bullet you took to the head, scrambled some of your circuits, the Great Spirit just took advantage of that and rewired a few connections, so to speak. Our job is to keep you alive till you can develop some of your new God given skills."

"What do you want me to do about those guys?" I asked.

"What do we want you to do? It's not up to us, you do what you have to do. We'll help you in anyway we can. Eagle will go ahead of you and pinpoint their exact location. If I was you I would circle back around and come up on them from behind."

"Okay, say did you guys see my strays?" I asked.

"Yes, they are waiting for you. They are two draws to the west." Eagle said.

With that Eagle flew off, Coyote got up and said, "Follow me, I'll show you the best way to surprise them."

Brutus followed in Old Man Coyote's footsteps, or as close as a hoof print can follow a paw print. We stayed in the timber. They were on the ridge line above the drilling rig. They were having some kind of a heated discussion. There were three of them alright. And guess who one of them was? That's right, Dipper Tick.

Coyote said, "I'll go closer so you can hear what they are saying."

"Huh? How am I going to hear if you go closer?" I said.

"How are you hearing me now? That was a rhetorical question, don't answer. I'll simply pipe what I am hearing directly into your brain, like I'm doing now." With that being said, he started to work his way close to them without being seen.

I got off of my horse and my hand fell on my old saddlebags. They had been on my saddle before I left for the Navy. I don't know why I hadn't looked into them since we came back to the ranch. I opened the flap on the off side bag. The first thing I saw was my old sheath knife.

I used to practice with it all of the time, I was pretty good, if I remember right. It was still in its sheath, the one that I hung around my neck, with knife and sheath down my back. The strap had a beaded medallion in the front, so it looked like I was wearing a rawhide necklace. That was no one knew that I was carrying a knife back there.

I had just put it on and adjusted it, so I could grab it

without delay, when I heard what Coyote was feeding me.

"Look!" Dipper Tick was saying, "You guys said that you would back my play, you both said that you were killers for hire." I could see them pretty clearly, the two guys looked young, both dressed western, like they were local Cowboys.

"Yeah, that's right, that's what we said, but you ain't too bright, we would of told you anything just to keep you buying our drinks." The oldest looking one of the two said.

The other one piped up, "Yep, haven't you ever fed a broad a line to get in her pants?

That's what we were doing, in essence, to just get in your wallet."

The other one came back, "Yeah, and just what did you put in our drinks, I don't even remember anything about getting out here. This looks like the Bronson spread. Now you say you want us to help kill Clay Bronson, and if that fails, to kill some of those roughnecks down there! Well you can go straight to hell, we ain't going to kill anybody."

All of the while this was going on I was creeping closer. Dipper reached on his hip, where he was wearing a holster, the same kind some of the cops I've seen wear. He said, "You are, or I'm going to kill the two of you." He caught them flat footed. They weren't wearing any guns; there were two rifles laying up against an old stump close by. But they couldn't reach them.

I was carrying my 30-30, plus also my pistol in my shoulder holster. I could kill him right now, but for some reason I waited. I said, "Dipper, Dipper, Old Man, now you don't want to kill those two Cowboys." He turned sharply to face me, his face going ashen, "Whoa, now," I said, "don't do anything foolish, I have this here rifle pointed right where your heart is supposed to be and I can't miss, even if you get a shot off, I'll still kill you."

"I tell you what, Dipper Old Man, I'll give you a fair shake though, you just put that gun of yours back in your holster and I'll lay my rifle down on the ground. You see I'm wearing a shoulder holster gun. Then we'll let one of these puncher's count to three and we'll draw, how's that?"

"Yeah, but you're faster than me?" He said, his voice cracking.

"Now why would you say that?"

"I seen the video of you killing those men on the highway down in New Mexico; I've never seen anybody shoot like that?"

"Alright, I'll tell you what, I'll put my hands behind my head, you know like the cops make you do when they arrest you? You can keep your hands at your side, that way you will have the advantage, Okay?"

He smiled, I could see his mind working, "Alright, what about these two, are they going to interfere?" Dipper said.

"Nope, we ain't going to lift a hand, Clay don't need no help, his rep precedes him." The oldest looking one said. Seems they knew me, I hadn't placed them, guess I had other things on my mind.

We were only standing about fifteen feet apart, he was really smiling now; he figured he could beat me with time to spare. My right hand was only inches from my knife, it was a special made one, by a traveling tinker, when I was just a kid.

You know how sometimes in times of crisis how every-thing seems to play out in slow motion? That's how this was. He signaled by his eyes before he made his play. I waited till his hand was on his gun butt; he had it almost level when my knife reached him. The razor sharp tungsten steel blade entered his forearm right back of his wrist, it cut the tendons to his hand, the gun fell to the ground. The blade lodged in the bone of his arm. He fell to the ground screaming.

"Damn, I ain't never seen nothing like that, man that was fast." The youngest puncher said. I said, "Well, you had better take that rag you have around your neck and make a tourniquet or he'll bleed to death. Then the two of you pick him up and take him down to the drilling rig; there's a Doctor down there. I'm going to call the FBI, then I'll get my horse and come on down. Oh yeah, leave that blade in there, don't pull it out, let the Doctor do that." I said.

Old Man Coyote said, "Why didn't you kill him?"

"Don't rightly know, must have been some reason, right at the last second I changed my mind. I was going to put it right through his throat. I'm going to turn him over to Harry Silver, he can play around with him." I went over to Brutus and tightened the cinch that I had loosened when I got off. He reached around and playfully nipped me in the butt, I absent mindedly switched him on the nose with ends of the reins. Then I mounted up and was going to round up the strays two draws over, when Old Man Coyote said, "Are you just going to leave those two rifles and that pistol laying on the ground?"

"I don't know, why don't you do something with them?" I said, as I rode off. I heard him say, "You know I don't have opposable thumbs, don't you?"

I put my cell phone back in my pocket, Harry said he would be right out. I had told him he should probably send an ambulance. He wanted to know if Dipper was going to live. I told him 'yeah, if I didn't change my mind and cut his throat'.

There were thirty head grazing in belly deep grass. I couldn't blame them for wanting to stay here. I told them it wouldn't be long and there probably wouldn't be any men around to bug them. That cheered them up considerably.

I drove them by the drilling rig, then told them to keep moseying on down toward the ranch, they did, grazing as they went.

Randy Fillmore came out of the location shack as I rode up. "The Doc is with him now, those two punchers are in the cook shack eating, the way they're putting it away I would say they hadn't ate in a week." Randy said.

"Yeah? They're just probably taking advantage of the free chuck and loading up. I would do the same thing in their place. Did Suong get my knife out of his arm?"

"Yes," Randy said, "here it is. I have never seen one like it. Where did you get it?"

"Oh, an itinerant tinker came by when I was in my early teens, he made it for me."

"What's it made of?"

"I believe he said it was made from a new metal called tungsten. It keeps a good edge." I said as I took it from him and put it in the saddlebag. I didn't want anyone to see where I kept it, even though those two punchers had seen the whole thing. I suppose I had better go and talk to them.

"How's the new well coming?" I asked Randy.

"Good, we hope to bring it in within the next few days, didn't Faith tell you?" Randy said.

"Yeah, sure, must of slipped my mind." I said, as I my eyes locked with his, he broke first. I can be pretty mean at times, poor Randy's face had turned pale. He knew he had goofed when he used her first name. I shuffled off toward the cook shake.

As I came through the door, both of them were still shoveling it down. It was lunch time and some of the roughnecks were still eating also. I sat down between the two brothers, cause brothers is what they were, I could tell.

"Well boys," I said, "you just about got your tail in the wringer this time didn't you?" They kept eating with downcast eyes. "It seems that I should know you two, you look right down familiar. Where do you hail from?"

The cook brought me a plate of food and a cup of coffee, I looked up at her. I recognized her, she used to cook for a greasy spoon in town. "Thanks Kate." I said.

I turned my attention back to the almost miscreants sitting beside me. "So, spill the beans," I said.

"We're the Hoeffer brothers, Chip and Dale, I'm Chip," The older one said.

"Chip and Dale? You're shitting me, I mean, Chip and Dale? Is your Dad, Doug Hoeffer? From over Powell way?' I said.

"No, we're not shitting you, we get that all of the time, although I have never figured out why people think it's so funny. And yes our Dad's name is Doug."

"Why aren't the two of you punching cattle for him?" I asked.

"He done committed the sin that we can't forgive." Dale said.

"And just what might that be?" I asked.

"He turned the place into a Dude Ranch, he wanted us to wrangle them dudes. We said, no Sir, we weren't going to do that; he told us to light a shuck then, we did." Dale said.

"Well there's a sight more money in wrangling dudes, then cattle now days." I said, "I can't really blame your father. But I also know how it offends a Buckaroo's sensibilities. Where's your Saddles and Tack?"

"In our hotel room in town." Chip said.

"Well, if you want a job, I'll have one of Randy's crew run you to town to get your plunder, then he can drop you off at the ranch. You tell Red I said to put you on the payroll. Oh, by the way, how old are the two of you?"

"I'm twenty-one," Chip said, "Dale here is twenty."

"Did the two of you graduate High School?" I asked.

"Didn't seem to be any point in it, we weren't learning

anything." Dale said.

I had another wild thought, "Just what bar were you guys drinking in last night?"

"The Double O, it's a new bar run by some guy from the east." Chip said.

"Alright, finish eating, when you get done stuffing your jeans, Randy will have someone to take you to town." I said, as I finished my plate and downed my coffee.

As I came out of the cook shack, Harry Silver's helicopter was just landing. We must be some important, him coming in a copter and all. As I was walking to meet him, I was thinking about those two boys.

They needed an education, high school anyway. I wonder how many of my ranch hands had a high school diploma? We'd have to do something about that.

I took Harry into where Suong was still operating on Dipper's arm. She had given him some kind of drug to knock him out. She said to me, "Why didn't you just kill him, it would of saved me a lot of work." It wasn't a question, it was just her needling me.

I said, "You're the second person today to ask me that question, are you going to be the third," I said to Harry.

"No, I'm glad you didn't. I have a lot of question's I want to ask this guy. Do you want to fill me in on the details?" I did so.

"Were those two guys mixed up in any of his shenanigans?"

"Nope, they were just duped, or doped I guess you could say, I've put them on my payroll." Randy was standing there, I told him to take the boys to town to get their stuff. He didn't like it much; me telling him what to do. He started to say something, then he clamped his jaw shut and stomped out.

"What's eating him?" Harry asked.

"Oh, he's got the hots for my wife. She's been overseeing the oil stuff while I have been under the weather. I hope I don't have to break his jaw." I said. Suong looked up, "You don't have to worry about Faith messing around on you, she loves you all of the way." She said.

"I know that, I haven't the slightest bit of doubt about her. I guess I can't blame guys for going bug eyed over her. I know I still am." I heard the ambulance coming. I said my goodbyes and went out where Brutus was grazing, as I tightened my cinch, he tried to nip me again. I mounted up and we headed for home.

As I rode up to the branding fire, Faith came over, "I thought I heard an ambulance in the distance, I was worried." She said while holding onto my stirrup.

"Yep, you did." I said, as I dismounted and both of us led Brutus to the barn. Rosie came riding up. "What happened?" she asked.

I told them the whole story, all except Randy's infatuation. I would tell Faith about that when we were alone. I didn't want Rosie kicking his ass.

Before I hung my saddle on the tack room wall, I took my knife back out of the saddlebag. Rosie and Faith both looked at me as I put it back in the sheath down the back of my neck. Rosie said,

"Will you teach me how to throw a knife?"

"Sure thing Rosie, no problem. That comes in right down handy at times." I said, as I put one arm around each of them and walked back to the house. Rosie said, "I'll be in pretty soon, I forgot to unsaddle Diablo. Then I'm going over to Daisy's after Alita."

"Those boys you hired, you think they're on the up and up?" Faith asked.

"Yeah, I do, I know their Dad, we worked a few roundups

together. He's pretty stiff necked, but he's on the level. Those boys just have some growing up to do."

Chapter Ten

Faith and I were both dirty and dusty from our day's work, so we decided to take a bath. Our room had an oversized tub in it, along with a big shower stall. We used the tub this time. While we were soaking our aches and pains away. Faith asked me, "Just why didn't you kill Dipper Tick, you know he's just going to keep trying?

"It's going to be pretty hard from a prison cell." I said.

"Oh, you know better than that, he will either make bail or hire someone else to do it." Faith said as she turned around and laid up against me. "You know it doesn't do any good to just take a Rattlesnake's rattle, you have to cut the head off and bury it." Faith said.

"Sure, I know that. But just at the last minute, the thought hit me; who am I to be judge, jury and executioner? Oh, I know I've been rather quick on the trigger in the past. And I don't have any qualms about killing someone to save a life, either mine, or my family's. Or even some stranger, but why not let the legal system of Satan's world take care of it?"

"Satan's world? What in the world are you talking about?" Faith said, as she wiggled a little tighter against me.

"Well, as you know the Devil is the God of this system of things, or didn't you know that?"

"Well, I often thought as much, but never really gave it much credence. How do you know he is?"

"Do you believe in the Bible? Okay then, at 2 Corinthians 4:4 and 1John 5:19, it says how he's the God of this world, and

164

even at Revelations 12:9 it says how he was hurled out of heaven and down to earth to mislead the entire inhabited earth."

"How do you know what the Bible says? I have never even seen you read it."

"I don't know, these things just pop into my mind, at the most opportune times, I might say."

"Well, what does it say about making love to your wife in the tub?"

"Okay, at Proverbs 5:19, it says and I quote, 'let her own breasts intoxicate you at all times. With her love may you be in an ecstasy constantly.' So let's get it on!"

As we were drying off, I said, "Oh, by the way, did you know Randy Fillmore had a thing for you?"

"Does he?" Faith said, as she got the last spot dry on her tush. "I have suspected as much, he's sweet, the way he fawns all over me. But you don't have to worry, he's not my type."

"Oh? And just what is your *type*?"

"Big, dumb and ugly, didn't you know that?" Faith said, I rolled my towel and popped her on her luscious derriere. She of course retaliated, we ran out of the bathroom popping our towels at each other.

Of course setting on our bed was Rosie and Alita, I hurriedly covered myself, Faith didn't bother.

"Well, if you two are done playing around, I need a bath myself, you can watch Alita." Rosie said, with the proper disdain, as she got up and walked primly out of our bedroom.

"Do you think she seen me?" I said to Faith. She turned to look at me as she picked up Alita, "Well of course she seen you, you're not invisible." Faith said.

"I mean, you know what?" I said, as I put my shorts on.

"Well of course she did, does that bother you?"

"Yeah, it does, it embarrasses' me. She's my daughter." I

said.

"Don't worry about it, I bet she's seen a lot of them at the orphanage. Maybe not that big though." Faith said giggling.

"Well, alright, but how am I going to face her at the supper table?"

"Will you stop it, it's no big deal. In a family situation, things like that can't be helped at times. I realize that you didn't have any sisters, but I had brother's, believe me I've seen theirs plenty of times. And beside that, who do you think took turns bathing you, while you were in that coma? That's right, we both did. She probably knows your dingus better than you do."

"Well, be that as it may, it makes me uncomfortable. So next time I'll check before I run out of the bathroom." I said.

"I'll just never understand you, you don't mind if I run around naked, but then when it comes to you it's a no-no." Faith said.

"Yep, that's right. You don't have to understand, it's just the way I am. A grown man just doesn't run around naked in front of children. Even with Alita, I know she's just a baby, but it won't be long till I'll have to watch it around her." I said, as I finished getting dressed.

Faith and I, along with Alita, went down to the kitchen and started supper. We usually shared the chores. We had it ready by the time Rosie came down. Rosie said, as we sat down to eat. "You know, you two aren't the best cooks in the world, not that I'm complaining. But have you given any thought to hiring a cook? I know we have enough money. And I bet there's someone out there who needs a job."

"Okay, Miss Smart Alec, if you want a cook, or whatever, you have to find one and interview them, it's all up to you. Your Mother and I delegate it to you…"

"Good, I know of a family that needs help. There's a girl

that Graduate's this spring with me. They don't have a father, he was killed in a mining accident. There are three children. Their mother works in a small Café in town. They pay her peanuts. Do I have free rein on how much to pay?"

"Sure, as long as you use common horse sense." I said.

"Good, one other point, can they live here with us?"

"I suppose, this is a big house. But one thing, none of them smoke, do they?"

"I know Tiffany doesn't, I don't think her mother does either."

"How old are the children?" Faith asked.

"Well Tiff is 17, her brother is 14, and then the youngest girl is 12." Rosie said.

"They must be a handful for the mother. What are their names?" Faith said.

"Her mother's name is Hope Friday, the boy's name is Hank, the girl is Popular, they call her Poppy." Rosie said.

"Alright, it's up to you, have you talked to them about this?"

"Of course not, not yet, I wouldn't do that till I asked the both of you. Oh, one other thing, their black. Is that a problem?"

"No, why should it be?" I said.

"I didn't think it was. But why is it, when someone is half black and half white, they always call them black?" Rosie asked.

"I take it their half white. But to answer your question, I don't know. They do that to me also, I'm half white, but people around here consider me to be Indian. I don't mind of course, I'm proud of it. And I bet they are also." I said.

Faith said, "If you do hire them, they can take over the west wing. That way they will have privacy and so will we. But of course we'll all eat together and such. When do you graduate?"

"The 22nd of May, it's only a week away. I'll talk to Tiff tomorrow, it's Monday."

"You know it's funny," I said, "I don't seem to be able to keep track of the day of the week anymore. One day is pretty much as another to me."

"Well, that's the way it is, when you're a lazy ass." Faith said, as she poked me in the ribs, letting me know her jib and jab was just in fun.

Faith said, "Rosie is there going to be a graduation party?"

"Yeah, the school has one planned. It will be in the gym, it starts at ten that night, and they don't let the kids out till the next morning, it's one big slumber party, sort of. There will be games, and the kids can win gifts and such. They say it's a lot of fun, but I'm glad you brought that up. They need more chaperons, will you be one Mother?"

"You bet I will, do you think I would let you go without me?" Faith said. Then she turned to me, "Since you're feeling better, are you going to take over the drilling oversight?"

"Yes, do you think I want Randy ogling you?" I said, acting jealous, even though Faith knew I wasn't. (like so much, I wasn't).

The next morning I helped with the cattle for awhile, then rode out to the drilling rig. Randy wasn't too happy to see me, he was expecting Faith. But he recovered quick enough. That was the way the rest of the week went. The Friday family accepted Rosie's offer of employment. Hope gave the Café a weeks notice to find someone else. They planned on moving out right after Graduation.

Graduation day came. Of course the three of us were in attendance. We got to meet the Friday family. Like Rosie said, Hope was half black, she was a good looking woman of 37. Hank and Poppy were quite protective of their Mother. Their father was evidently white, cause they were of lighter complexion than their mother.

There were a lot of men giving Hope the eye, but Hank and Poppy were running interference. Their father had only been dead for six months. Time would heal their hurt.

When Rosie introduced them, Hope said, "Are you sure you want us to come and work for you?"

Faith said, "Of course we are. Rosie has excellent judgment, we trust her completely. Has she explained everything to you?"

"I think so, but the youngest children still have two weeks of school left, I know they can ride the bus, but how will they get to the bus stop, Rosie said, it's about a mile from the house to your fence line?"

"Don't worry," I said, "we'll find a way. Rosie has been driving to the bus stop. Does Hank know how to drive?"

"I don't know, Dave used to let him drive once in awhile, I suppose he could."

"Okay, like I said, don't worry about details, they always work themselves out."

Tiffany now, was a knockout. As I was introduced to her, I looked into her eyes. And staring back was a level headed girl who had not let her looks influence her outlook. I was satisfied that she would do. She said, rather directly, "Why do you want to help us?"

"I don't. Rosie does. Not that I'm opposed to it, but it was Rosie's idea. Don't worry, you'll all earn your keep, if that's what's bothering you."

"It is, I don't like to accept charity. I believe in working for what we get."

"Well then, I guess it's a done deal, because I bet Rosie can find things for all of you to do, and get paid for it." I said.

Hope said, rather embarrassedly, "Tiff can be rather direct

at times, but what she said goes for me also. We've always worked, Dave never liked something for nothing."

"That's good to know," Faith said.

That evening Faith and Rosie went to the school sponsored party. This was the first time that I had to do without my wife since we got married. I mean, we had to sleep alone when I was in that coma, but this was different. I missed her very much.

The next morning I got up and fixed my own breakfast and then rode out to the drilling rig. Randy was getting used to me. I had got the latest price on the world market for crude, it was selling for over a hundred and thirty-two dollars a barrel. But we were only getting eighty for our domestic crude. The big oil company's were making windfall profits. The general public didn't know that domestic crude was cheaper, they thought all crude cost the same.

"Randy, old boy, what would you say if we built our own oil refinery?"

"What? That would cost a fortune. I know you don't have that much money."

"No, we don't. But I bet we could raise it. You just keep drilling and bringing in the wells. I bet we could sell gas for half of what the oil company's are getting and still make a big profit."

"Beyond a doubt, but where would you build it?"

"Right here on the ranch. There's a spot that's all alkali, that would be a good place to build. It wouldn't hurt anything. We'd just have to get the proper permits from the state. At the price of gas closing in on five dollars a gallon, I bet they would be easy to work with." I left him thinking about it. Not that I needed his approval, I didn't, he worked for me.

When I got back to the house, Faith was sound asleep. Alita was still over at Daisy's. I looked into Rosie room, she was sound asleep also, they must have had some night.

I called Dad in New Mexico, and told him my idea. He said he would talk to all of the Spanish Land Grant people down there. Then I called Charles Hester, he was all for it. He would start rounding up support in Montana. The game was afoot....

Later that afternoon when the women woke up. I told them my idea, they were all agog over it. Faith said, "Uh, honey, there's only one thing. I don't like saying it, but you're not the man to see this through to the end. You've not fully recovered, there's times that you blank out, did you know that?"

"I suspected as much. Sometimes I have to play catch up to know what's going on. These visions just show up, I don't know when they're coming." I said.

Rosie said, "I don't have anything to do right now, I can help to organize the whole thing, that is if you want me to?"

"Why I think that would be a great idea. I've got the ball rolling. Maybe you could just keep it going. Things like this tend to snowball, all you have to do is direct it."

"Alright, would you mind if Tiff helped me, she's pretty smart and good with people? Are we still going to call it the 'Spanish Bit Oil Company?" Rosie said, then added, "I'm going to call Tiffany right now."

I looked at Faith and winked, "I think we just turned a Tasmanian Devil loose on the world, what do you think?"......

I never did hear her answer, cause I woke up in bed. It was dark, Faith was sleeping with her one arm over me. I turned to face her, I kissed her gently on the lips, her eyes opened. "Oh, so there you are, where have you been this time?"

"Been? Right here beside you." I said.

"I know your body has been, but you haven't. Clay, it's been three days. You blanked out, three days ago, I walked you to bed, like a zombie."

"Aiieee, I remember now. You don't want to know where

I've been, it wasn't pretty. Oh, the land was pretty, everything nice and green, that was after the tribulation was over. The blood was bridle deep, it was terrible."'

"What do you mean the tribulation?" Faith asked.

"Do you remember what I said about Babylon the Great, the world empire of false religion? And how she fell. Well it was right after that, the tribulation started. People were killing each other, for no reason. I heard a voice calling the birds of heaven to the great feast of the almighty God, Jehovah. All the scavengers of the earth were to feed upon the dead."

"When is this supposed to take place?" Faith asked.

"I don't know, they didn't tell me. I was scared shitless. I didn't see all of it. What I did see was enough, I woke up just as the four Angels were coming to finish it. Why are they tormenting me with these visions?"

"I don't know sweetheart, all I know is, that I'm glad to have you back." Faith said, as she helped me up, I had to go pee. As I did, Faith turned on the shower. We got in together....

While I was incognito for three days, Rosie had been busy. She had called Dad again, they were all aboard. She had also been in contact with Charles Hester, they were solidly in place also.

Rosie had filed articles of incorporation for the Spanish Bit Oil Co. With each of the family members as officers of the corp. I really wasn't too interested. Faith was though. She told me not to worry, that she would keep track of everything.

Hank and Poppy drove one of the old pickups to the school bus stop. Hank was a very conservative driver. I don't believe he broke over 20 miles an hour all the way there.

That's the way the next two weeks went. Slow and no inconsistency. I spent the time working with the horses.

I took one of the stock trucks to town, to the horse sale. I bought ten more head. When I got back, Red met me. "Just what are you going to do with all of these horses? He asked me.

I thought for a second, then said, "Damned if I know, I just figured we needed more horses." Red shook his head and walked off talking to himself. I turned the new horses into the corral. I leaned on the corral rails looking at them.

I was racking my brain, trying to figure out why I bought them, then it came to me…in the last vision I had, someone or something told me how many horses we would need. I couldn't pull up who it was that told me that though.

Faith came up and gave me a kiss. "So, you bought more horses, Red thinks your crazy, literally. I don't though, eccentric, but not crazy."

"He may be closer to the truth than you. At times I think I'm not quite right myself." Faith pulled me close and said, "Hey, you're not crazy, anybody would act a little weird, if it was them that got a bullet to the head."

"Maybe, but I think it's more than that. Why would *they*; whoever they are, tell me these things, I'm nobody special?"

"To me you are, very special. You're my whole world, aren't I to you?" Faith said.

"Well of course you are, you know that, why else do I tell you I love you about a million times a day?" I said.

"I know you do, I was just being facetious. I also know that those visions you are getting are *visions* and not hallucinations. I didn't tell you this, but the last one you had you talked in your so called sleep. It scared me to death. And I know why you bought those horses, even if you don't."

"Why?" I said.

"Because we will need them, when all of the mechanical things don't work anymore. Anyway that's what you said."

"Did I say when we would need these horses?"

"No, you didn't. But it is always good to be prepared, isn't it?"

"Yes, sweetheart, it is." I said, "Do you have panties on?"

"Why do you ask? Don't answer, I know of course. But really my wearing panties or not, would that make a difference to what you have in mind?"

"I reckon not, but it's just the idea. You know how anticipation is half of the pleasure." I said, holding her close.

"Yes, I certainly do, so you can just anticipate till bedtime. And by the way, I'm not!" She said as she danced easily out of my arms. My eyes followed her all of the way to the house. Damn, but she was fine...

I turned my attention back to the new horses that I had just purchased. Most of the time I would have never purchased any mares for ranch work. But these weren't for just ranch work. In the ten of them, eight were three year old mares. The other two were Morgan Stallions. Breeding stock, for the future.

But now, what I needed was some pack animals, Mules. Where would I get them?

Where could I buy good pack Mules? Why from some outfitter, for sure. Cause right now with the economy the way it was, there were less and less people able to afford to hire an outfitter to go hunting.

Where was there an abundance of outfitters that were down on their luck? Where else but Gardiner, Montana. Why? Not only the economy, but also due to the depredations of the Wolves on the Elk herds that used to come out of the Yellowstone National Park in the winter time.

I went to the barn and crawled up the ladder to the loft, and tossed some hay out of the loft door into the corral for my new brood horses. When I got back to the house, Faith called out as she heard the screen door slam, "Don't slam the screen door, wash up, then you can set the table, supper is almost ready."

I set eight places at the table. The whole family helped with all of the chores. That is all except Alita, but she wanted to, she just couldn't quite get the job done yet. I put Alita in her high chair and took the tray off, then slid her up to the table, she would set between Faith and I.

Hank and Poppy had just got home from school. Faith and Hope were bringing the food to the table, Rosie and Tiff, came down from their upstairs office and sat down.

I waited till everyone was settled, then I said the prayer, after all, I was the head of the family, my wife told me I was...

After everyone was eating I asked Rosie how things were going. "Fine, but I think we should just have one refinery, not two. I was thinking that it would be better in New Mexico. We could just truck our crude down there. What do you think?"

"What do I think? I think the better question is, what does the family in New Mexico think? But to answer, I think we should have two refineries."

"Grandpa and Grandma are all for it, they have the sight all ready picked out. In fact I think they are due to break ground tomorrow." Rosie said.

"Then what did you bother asking me for?"

"Well, Tiff and I didn't want you to feel left out, and all..." Rosie said, her face getting red.

"Are you going to have to go down there?" I asked

"Well, not right away. It turns out that Jake and Alona are more than a little interested in this oil business. Along with Grandpa and Grandma, they're going to handle that end of the business. But of course Tiff and I are going to keep a handle on things."

"Good," I said, "are they okay with that?"

"Yes, we have discussed everything." Tiff said. I looked at her, she glanced down at the table, embarrassed.

The only thing I could say was, "Good, keep up the good

work. Seemed like when it came to my family, I was using the word *good* a lot...

I had another thought, "Are you getting legal counsel on all of this?"

"Sure, that's the first thing we did, was hire a legal firm, one out of Cheyenne. Don't worry, we're following all of the laws." Rosie said, with just a hint of chagrin in her voice.

"Don't pay any attention to Dad, he's a day late and a dollar short, but he's trying." Faith said.

I thought to myself, yes, I probably was not keeping up with what they were doing when it came to material possessions. Because to me, that was not the most important thing. What was?

Survival, that was...the most important. Why was I in favor of what they were doing? Because, it would help the environment and lower gas prices. We had to live till the end came, since no man will know the day or the hour, we had to keep, keeping on.

"One more question, if you girls don't mind?" I said, they nodded. "What impact is this refinery going to have on the land and air?"

"We have been doing an environmental impact survey, plus all of the latest pollution abatement devices will be incorporated into the building of the refinery." Tiff said.

"Well, I guess I can put my mind at ease then. I'm sorry to question you, it's just my stupidity, I guess." I said.

"Dad!, you're not stupid! Don't you ever say anything like that again." Rosie said.

Faith spoke up, "Yes Honey, you're not stupid, and you have my permission to tell people that, also." She said, with a giggle.

Hank cleared his throat, "Uh, we get out of school at the end of the week, what am I going to do then?"

"You can help me, we need to not only help with cattle, but I've just bought ten new horses. Plus, I'm going to buy some pack Mules, you can help with that. In fact you can go to Gardiner with me. I think we can pick up a pack string pretty cheap."

"This is the first I've heard about buying mules, what for?" Faith said.

"I thought we would take some pack trips this summer, don't you want to?"

"Sure, I guess so, who? All of us?"

"Anybody that wants to go, that's up to them." I said.

Alita gurgled and pointing to herself, said, "Me, me want to go." We all looked at her, this was her first sentence, beside Mom and DaDa. Faith said to her, "The proper word is 'I' want to go, not 'me' want to go." Alita nodded then said, "I want to go." I sat there dumb founded. From that time on, we couldn't shut her up.

Rosie said, "I don't know whether Tiff and I will have time, we might be pretty busy."

"I'm sure you'll have time to take a break, all work and no play makes Jane, uh, makes Jane, I forgot the rest. Sometimes, the most common saying escapes me." I said.

"That's Okay Dad, we know what you mean, Tiff and I will make it a point to go with you." Rosie said.

"This Pack Trip, have you picked out where to go?" Faith asked.

"Yeah, I think so. When I was a youngster, I went on vision quest. I went east into the Big Horn Mountains. There was a stream, with a waterfall, where I camped. It's still located on our land. But it gets pretty rough going, nobody has been there, as far as I know, since I was. But just the other day, I had a dream about it. It wasn't a vision, at least I don't think it was."

"So just how far is it?" Hope asked.

"About twenty or thirty miles, as I remember, a good days ride, with a pack string. Now when I said it was on our land, I might have misled you. It's on our Forest Service grazing lease land. In fact as soon as we get all the branding done, we'll be moving the cattle that way. Not as far as the waterfall, but within two miles of it, we'll just kick them on lease land and let them wander."

"Do the cattle go as far as the waterfall?" Hank asked.

"Not usually, it's pretty steep and rough there." I said. "Besides, there is no reason for them to, the grazing is better down stream from the waterfall."

"Then why do we want to go there?" Faith asked, "If the grazing isn't good, what will our horses and mules eat?"

"I said it wasn't as good, they'll have plenty to eat. So don't worry, they won't starve." I said, "Trust me."

"Haven't we always," Faith said. "And I plan on continuing to do so."

Alita banged her spoon on her plate and said, "Me done." Faith turned to her, "How many times do I have to tell you, it's 'I am done'. Not 'me done'. Alita looked at her, "I am sorry Mother, I will try to do better next time."

Rosie started laughing like mad, "I taught her that, I knew it would drive you crazy, when she said 'me' instead of 'I'."

"What? Do you mean to say that she can talk like that all of the time?" Faith said.

"Sure, she's been able to talk for a month now." Rosie said. "Haven't you noticed?"

"I guess not, I've been sort of busy, with everything. You know...." Faith said.

"Yes Mother, we know and we don't blame you for not noticing. It was something we thought we would surprise you with. I think Alita is some kind of prodigy or something." Rosie said.

Alita held her arms out to me and said, "Daddy, will you read me a story?"

"Yeah, sure, that is unless Mommy wants to?" I said, looking at Faith. Faith said, while taking Alita out of her high chair, "Yes, Mommy wants to read to you, Daddy can clear the dishes from the table." Faith leaned toward my ear and said, "It appears I have been neglecting one child while taking care of another one." Then she nipped my ear with her teeth. Ahhh, Mommy lion is pissed.

After the dishes were done, I went into the den and sat down next to Faith and Alita. Faith said, "I'm sorry, it wasn't your fault. I guess I had to take it out on someone, and deep down I knew you wouldn't get mad at me."

"That's alright, I knew you weren't mad at me. We have been under a lot of pressure lately. I have an idea, let's just let Rosie and Tiff handle all of this oil stuff. You concentrate on the family for awhile."

"Maybe just for a little while, till I catch up. You say that you are going after mules, can Alita and I go with you?"

"Sure, I'll have Hank work with the horses that I just bought, that'll keep him busy, while we go to Gardiner." Just then, Rosie came in the room,

"Mom, are you mad at me? I didn't mean to make you mad, I'm sorry." Rosie stood there, sort of wringing her hands. Faith stood up and took Rosie into her arms,

"Rosie, Honey, I'm not mad, well maybe just a little bit-mad at me, not you. My inattention was all my fault, not yours. Dad and I and Alita are going to go to Montana to buy some mules. Can you and Tiff handle everything here?"

"Sure, no problem. But you both be careful, I heard that they let that Dipper Tick out on bail; while waiting for his trial." Rosie said…

Chapter Eleven

The next morning I took Hank and Poppy out to the corrals and introduced them to the ten new horses. The two Morgan stallions danced around some, just to show who was in charge. But the lead mare nipped them and they settled down.

The lead mare took a 'like' to Poppy. The feeling, I could tell was mutual. I left them to get acquainted and went and seen to the 12 horse gooseneck trailer that we would take to Gardiner. The ranch had just bought a new Diesel 4 door, 1 ton pickup to pull it with. I filled it with fuel from our storage tank. Red seen me, and came over.

"So where are you going now?" He said, a bit truculently.

"Whoa, there old pard," I said, "by the tone of your voice, you're getting just a bit out of line. Would you like to tone it down a little?" I said…He swallowed, I could see the gears turning over in his head, he said.

"I'm sorry Clay, it's just that we have been working our butts off, I guess I'm tired."

"Right, I understand, if you need more hands, feel free to hire them. How are the Hoeffer boys working out?"

"Good, but I have to keep them separate, they argue so much with each other, that when they work together, it upsets the other hands." Red said.

"Well, you know how sibling rivalry is. Anyway to answer your question, Faith and I are going to Gardiner, I'm going to buy some pack mules." I said as I looked at Red, I could see those gears turning over again, he started to say something, but shut his mouth and walked away. I made a mental note to talk to Daisy. You see Daisy was my mother's cousin, Red was just her husband. Blood is as blood does though....

I hitched the trailer to the pickup and drove over to the house. I went in the house to help with the packing. Faith already had most of it done, she was in our bedroom getting dressed.

She was standing there in her Bra and Panties. She was fixing a holster to her thigh to hold her small pistol. The holster had a sheath for a knife also, the knife was a stiletto. "Where did you get that?" I asked.

"From my Grandmother, when I was a little girl." She said.

"A stiletto, that's some what unusual, isn't it? I haven't seen it before."

"I guess, to some it could be. But you see, my Grandmother came from Germany, she was, or is, I guess you could say, a Sinti Gypsy. She taught me how to use it."

"How are you going to reach them through your jeans?" I asked.

"I'm not, I'm going to put on a skirt and blouse, I don't need jeans to ride in the truck do I? Can't I dress frilly once in awhile?" She said, as she put some long Gypsy ear rings in her ears. The skirt was colorful, along with a plain white blouse, she was a knockout.

"I didn't know you were a Gypsy, but I like it. What's Alita going to wear?"

"Jeans and tee shirt, what else? Plus Daisy made some moccasins for her, they're cute. Do you mind changing her big girl diaper, then get her dressed will you? I have some sandwiches in the kitchen, that I want to put in the cooler."

Alita was standing in her crib, watching us. I went over and took her out and laid her on the bed, I said, "When are you going to start using the potty?"

"Well," She said back, "when are you going to help me do so. I can anytime you know. Everyone has been so busy, they don't have time for me."

I just couldn't get used to her talking like a grown up, "Okay, young lady, how about right now, I'll take you, and when you want to go from now on, just pull those pants down and go, how's that?"

"Alright Daddy, but you have to set me on the toilet, I'm too small to get up there on my own, that is unless you make a step or something for me?"

"Yes, I can do that, when we get home from Montana."

"Daddy, when are you going to get me a gun like Mommy's?"

"Oh, I don't think for awhile yet, you're not even two years old yet, are you?"

"No, but soon. Will you get me one then?"

"We'll see, I'll have to ask Mommy, she's the boss you know." I said.

"No she's not, well over me she is. But you're the boss Daddy, you know that, don't you?"

"Sweetheart, you just keep believing that, but I do have mommy's permission to say that I am." I said, as I lifted her off of the toilet.

Faith came back into the room, "What's the hold up, you don't even have her dressed." She said.

"Alita says that she wants to use the toilet from now on, but that we have to start paying more attention to her, since she can't get up there by herself." I said.

"Yes, Daddy, and don't forget to ask Mommy if I can have a gun like hers." Alita said.

"What's this, you want a gun like mine?" Well, not for awhile yet, but I do have a small stiletto like mine, but you have to be careful with it, it's very sharp. And it's only to be used as a last resort, to save a life." Then Faith went to a drawer and took a small knife and sheath out, "I'll put it in your diaper bag for now. When we get home I'll spend some time showing you how to use it."

"Mommy, I'm not going to need the diaper bag anymore, didn't you hear, I want to use the toilet from now on."

"Well, be that as it may, we'll just take it along anyway, Okay?" Faith said.

"Alright, I'll play like it's my purse and keep my private things in there. Just like you do your purse." Alita said.

"Honey, my purse isn't all that private."

"I heard Daddy say it was, he said that it was against the laws of nature for a man to get in a woman's purse."

"When did Daddy say that?"

"One time when we were still at Grandma's house." Alita said.

"Do you remember everything from long ago?" Faith asked.

"Yes, what do you want to know?" Alita said.

"Nothing right now, you just don't tell other people, besides Mommy and Daddy anything that you may remember or see or hear, they are family secrets, Okay?" Faith said.

"What about Rosie, can I tell her?"

"Yes, Rosie is your sister, she is family." I said.

"Alright, come you two, Rosie and Tiff have everything in the truck." Faith said. We went downstairs. Rosie was a little misty eyed, she hadn't been away from us since we first got her. I told her, "don't worry, we won't be gone long. I'm going to have the Hoeffer boys keep a close watch on the house, so if they seem to be hanging around a lot, that's what their supposed to do. Don't kill them, Okay?"

"Alright, as long as they know their place, I don't want them peeking in our windows." Rosie said.

It was almost lunch time, most of the hands were just coming in for lunch, I went over to the cook shack. I corralled Chip and Dale and told them what I wanted them to do. They were more than happy to do so. Turns out they had been eyeing Tiff, I told them to watch out for them, not to get too familiar. That Rosie might take exception and shoot their ears off. Dale said, "Yeah, that Rosie, she's a pistol, sometimes I get a chill, when she levels her eyes at a person. We know our place, don't worry."

I pulled Red aside and told him as much, told him to give the boys chores close to home, so they could keep an eye on the house. "You mean I'm going to lose two more hands from the branding?"

"Yep, I guess so. Why don't you go to town and hire some temporary hands, I am sure there are some cowboys who would like some day work. Pay them over the going wage. But make sure you know them, don't hire any strangers, okay?" He said he would.

Rosie told us later when we got home, that they couldn't go anywhere without those two brothers right on their heels. Even when they rode out to the drilling rigs, the boys would saddle their horses for them and never let them out of their sight. When she got on them about it, they told her that they were more scared of me, than her.

We finally got underway about one that afternoon. We headed over to Basin and then over to Cody, went north from there, till we got to the Sunlight Basin road, then up through the mountains to the Cooke City highway. Then into the Park, we always called Yellowstone National Park, just the Park. Then over to Mammoth and then the few miles out the North Gate to Gardiner. We got a room at the Best Western, they had a place we could park our horse trailer. From there we went to the Town Café for supper. A lot of the locals ate there. Didn't take me long to find out about some mules; turns out one of the Outfitters up the North Fork, out of Jardine, had some mules for sale. I got his cell phone number and gave him a call. Told him I would buy twelve of them if he had that many. He did, I made arrangements to meet him there in the morning.

I had got the Honeymoon sweet at the Best Western, it had a heart shaped hot tub and a heart shaped bed. But what I liked best, it had a separate room for Alita. Alita liked that hot tub. We didn't let her stay in it very long, about five minutes. It's not too good for little kids. The hot water made her sleepy though, she went right to sleep when we put her to bed. You can bet that Faith and I did not go right to sleep though....

The next morning it was raining a light mist, the clouds were hanging low. We went to the restaurant right here at the Motel. There were a few tourists already eating. We sat by the wood fireplace, the warmth felt good.

While we were waiting for our food, I used my cell phone to call the Brand Inspector and a local vet. When you hauled stock over the state line, you had to have a current brand inspection and a clean bill of health for the livestock. I made arrangements to meet them both at the local fair grounds after I got down the road from Jardine.

Faith had hiked her skirt up a little bit, to let the heat in better. The bottom part of her holster was showing, just a tad bit. There was a little girl of eight or ten watching us. She had leaned over to her mother and whispered something, the woman looked at Faith and got up and came over to our table.

"Would you mind pulling your skirt down just a little, your gun holster is showing, my daughter was wondering what it was. I'm a Detective from Los Angeles, I knew what it was. I also seen the tip of the stiletto, I am a Gypsy also, I knew right away you were one too. My name is Mary Jane Hunter." She said, as she held her hand out to Faith. Faith took it and shook it. Faith told her our names. While they were talking Faith had pulled her skirt down to cover her thighs.

Anyway, they hit it off. Her and her daughter were traveling alone. We pulled up a couple of more chairs so they could set with us.

"So Mary Jane," I said, "are you on vacation or what?"

"Well, sort of. My husband was a police officer and he got killed in a shoot out."

"Oh, we're so sorry!" Faith said, holding her hands.

I was looking into her past, she glanced up sharply, looking at me. "You, you're one of them aren't you?" She said to me.

Faith said, "One of whom, my dear?" as she glanced back and forth between Mary Jane and me.

"Your husband, he's been there and back hasn't he?"

"Been where?" Faith asked.

"He's been dead and then came back, he can see places that most people cannot. I know, because so have I."

"Well, he's been shot and in a coma for six months. Plus he blanks out every now and then. So I guess you could say that he's been there and back. You say that you've been there also?"

"Yes, three years ago, I was shot in the head, but my coma only lasted for three months and I don't blank out, I'm fine now. But for awhile I was having all kinds of hallucinations. Did you have them?"

I looked at Faith, she nodded, "Yes, but mine are more than figments of my imagination. They are just as real as we are talking right now. What were yours about," I asked.

"The future mostly, ghastly stuff, I don't even like to think about them. Yours, what were they about?" She asked.

"Some of the same. What's your daughter's name again, I'm afraid I didn't quite catch it?" I said, just to change the subject.

"Iris, I've always liked Iris's, so when she came along I named her that. Hunter is my maiden name, I went back to it, when John got killed. I hate LA, we sold everything, including our old car, we just rented this one. We are just sort of driving aimlessly, just stopping here and there." She said, still looking at me.

Damn, I could get right in her mind, but she couldn't quite get in mine. They were like lost souls, hunting for a home. Alita looked at me, then said, "Mary Jane, can Iris take me over to the curio shop, I would like to look at the souvenirs."

Mary Jane gasped, "What? What was that?" Faith spoke up, "Oh, I'm sorry, she's somewhat of a prodigy. She surprises us also."

Mary Jane said, "Let me take her over there, Iris can come too, I want to talk to her some more." Mary Jane picked Alita up and the three of them went to the curio counter.

I said to Faith, "I can get in her mind. They are sort of lost souls, what do you say, do you want to help them?"

"Help them, how?"

"Well, they could come with us, being that she is a Gypsy too, she didn't say what kind, Sinti or Roma though did she?" I said.

"How do you know there are two different kinds?" Faith said.

"You told me, didn't you?"

"No, have you been in my mind?"

"Well, aren't I always, we are one flesh, you know."

"Yes, I want to help them, while you go get your mules, I'll talk to them." Faith said. With that, they came back to the table.

"My but Alita is smart, did you know she knows her alphabet?" Mary Jane said.

"No, not really, but it doesn't surprise me, our other

daughter Rosie, has been teaching her all kinds of things. I wouldn't be surprised if she knew how to read." Faith said.

"She does, she knows how to read," Iris said. "she was reading labels to me."

"Well, that's good, Iris." I said, "Since we are done eating, I'm going to go get some mules that I have bought. Perhaps, Mary Jane, you and Iris would like to go back to our room, where you and Faith can get better acquainted?"

"Yes, I would like that. Being that we are both Sinti Gypsy's." Mary Jane said. "How did you know I was a Sinti?" Faith said.

"Oh, I'm sorry. Didn't you tell me? Or did I just assume as much?"

"It seems that all of us have more in common than we realize." I said.

When I went out to my truck, I heard a rustling in the back, my pistol came into my hand of its own volition. Sticking its head out from under the tool box was a Border Collie pup, about six months old. He whined at me. "Well boy, where did you come from? Are you hungry?" I knew he was, I remembered that lunch that Faith had packed, we hadn't eaten any of it, it was in the cooler in the back seat. I reached in and got a couple of liverwurst sandwiches, they were a favorite of mine, the dog liked them too. He was a little wet, so I got some rags out of the toolbox, and dried him off, then I let him jump in the front seat with me. Of course he smelled like a wet dog, but that was Okay with me.

The road up to Jardine was paved, I was glad of that, cause the first part of it was sort of steep. The town of Jardine used to be an old gold mine, the buildings were right up to the road. The outfitters place was about a mile further, at the end of the road. He met me at the gate.

I asked him how things were going, he said, "How do you think? Those damn wolves are going to bankrupt me. I have about thirty head of mules, I don't need that many anymore. How many did you say you needed?"

"Twelve, that's all. Can I take my pick?"

"Sure, I saved the ones I'm going to keep, they're in a different corral. Just take your pick out of the bunch over there." He said, gesturing to a corral with a stream running through it.

Dog and I, ambled over to it. The mules turned to face me. The outfitter called after me, "Watch out, some of them are right down mean." I crawled through the rails, they watched me with their ears in the alert position. I walked among them, silently talking to them, "so who wants to go with me, it'll be an easy life," I said. I got a question in return, "how many do you want?" they asked.

"Twelve," I said. They put their heads together, then twelve of them walked toward me. That left two of them. I heard another question, "are you sure you can't take all of us?"

"Well," I said, "yeah, probably could, it might be a little tight, is that okay with all of you?" They nodded their heads. "Okay then, just follow Dog and me, we'll load you up, we have to stop at the brand inspector and the vet has to check you over." I said, silently....

"I thought you wanted twelve, not fourteen?" The outfitter said. "Do you have a certified check?" He asked.

"How about cash, is that good enough?" I said. I counted out 57,000 in cash, "three thousand apiece, is that right?" I said. He was licking his lips, "I'll need a bill of sale on each one." I said.

"Sure," come to the house, I have them all made out, all I have to do is sign them."

"Why don't you go get them as Dog and I load them up, how's that?" He went to get them.

As they got in the trailer, I assessed their overall health, I asked each one how they were as they jumped in. They were all fine, except for a few aches and pains and scratches. When he got back I took the papers and looked them over, then handed him the money.

As we headed down the mountain, I asked Dog, "did any of them seem mean to you?"

He went "Arf, Arf," I said, "you're going to have to speak English, I don't speak dog." He gave me a big smile. "Well Okay then, we'll work on that." I said.

I drove to the fair grounds, it was small, but they had a good Rodeo every spring, it was big enough. The Brand Inspector and the Vet, met me there. All I had to do was open the trailer rear door and they backed out on their own. I paid extra for a permanent brand inspection on all fourteen head. They all checked out, vet wise. I paid the vet his fee. "Can I leave them here till I get my family, we might want to stay another day, would that be Okay?" I asked the Brand Inspector.

"Sure, they'll be alright here, there's hay and water, we won't even charge you for it."

I went around to all of the mules, telling them to just rest and take it easy, that we'll leave in the morning. Dog followed my every step. When I got back to the Motel, they were all gathered in our room.

Faith and Mary Jane were setting there sipping coffee in their bras and panties. "Uh, what's going on?" I said.

"We were comparing our sheaths, you know for our stilettos. Look at the bra Mary Jane gave me." Faith stood up and walked over to me. There were two handles sticking out each side of the bra, where the under wire should be. "Isn't it neat, now I can carry them even when I wear jeans."

"Uh, yeah, but what about?" I gestured to the neither regions. "Oh, we were trying on each other's thigh holsters. Clothes just get in the way."

"You don't mind that Mary Jane is standing there in a thong. Do you?" Faith said.

"No, I don't, that is if you don't?" I said.

"Honey, we're both Sinti Gypsy's, we're sisters in the hood, you might say. We look at nudity different than some people."

"Yeah, I can see that." I said, Mary Jane spoke up, "If it makes you uncomfortable, we can put clothes on?"

"Well perhaps. But no, don't. I'm not so shallow that lack of clothes will turn me into a raving sex maniac." I said, as I did my best not to look at Mary Jane. "But to get back to what's important, did you two talk?"

"Yes, we did. Mary Jane and Iris do not want to go back to LA, they would like to go with us. Did you get the Mules alright?"

"Yes, they're at the fair grounds, uh, there is someone else I'd like to introduce you guys to." I opened the door, Dog came into the room and sat looking at everybody. He gave a small bark, Iris and Alita were in the other bedroom, they came running. All four of them were gushing all over him.

"What's his name?" Iris asked. "I haven't given him one. How would you and Alita like to pick one together? You two talk it over and come to one mind, then tell us what it will be."

They and Dog went into the other bedroom. I said, "Well then, what about your rental car, can you turn it in here?"

"I think they have a rental office at the Hotel in Mammoth. I can turn it in there." Mary Jane said.

"Good, that's on our way. We have enough room in our truck for everyone and their luggage. It's almost lunch time, we have enough lunch in our cooler that we forgot about, I'll go get the cooler and we can eat lunch right here." I said. I went to do just that. When I got back, the women were in the hot tub. I took some lunch into the children and the dog.

"Are you going to join us Honey?" Faith said. I looked at them. "I will if I can leave my shorts on." I said.

"I guess so, it's usually not done, but for you we'll make an exception." Faith said.

I skinned out of my clothes and made sure I kept Faith between Mary Jane and me. As I settled into the water, I noticed that both Faith and Mary Jane were equally endowed, as they endowments were floating on top of the water.

I said, "This really doesn't bother you two, being naked in front of me?"

"No, of course not. Like I told you, we both think a little differently than you. We were raised that way." Faith said.

"Alright, I won't mention it again. Mary Jane, you said that your husband was killed, how did that happen?"

"He was one of a team who was investigating a porn film outfit, that was somehow connected to the price fixing in the oil industry. He was killed from ambush by a single rifle shot, they never did find out who did it. But I think I know who was behind it." Mary Jane said.

I looked at Faith, she made a sharp intake of her breath. Mary Jane said, "What? Did that ring a bell or something?"

"Yes," I said, "have you ever heard of a man named Dipper Tick?"

It was her turn to be surprised, "Yes, how did you know about him?"

"It was him that was behind Clay getting shot and spending six months in a coma. Plus we had run ins with him in New Mexico. Clay could of killed him just a week or so ago. Instead he just broke his arm and severed some tendons in his right arm with his knife. We just heard he made bail while waiting for trial."

"Damn, I was sure he was behind me getting shot, also." Mary Jane said, with great agitation, she stood up and stepping out she started pacing around the room. "Where is he? I would enjoy killing him slowly."

I jerked my head toward Mary Jane, signaling Faith, Faith stood up and grabbed a towel and put it around Mary Jane's shoulders. I said, "That doesn't help much, it's her bottom I was talking about." Faith stuck her tongue out at me, and took the towel from Mary Jane's shoulder. Then she gave me a look that said, how do you like that now?

Crap, I couldn't win for losing. I stood up. What I didn't know was those new silk boxer shorts that Faith had bought me, were clingers. I got up and went and got me a beer from the fridge. I turned to look at them, they were both staring at me. "What?" I said.

"Those white silk boxers, leave nothing to the imagination, you might just as well take them off." Faith said.

I looked down, I bent and took them off and threw them at my wife, they landed on her head. Then I ran for the bathroom. I heard them laughing like mad. I got in the shower, just to cool off.

When I came out of the bathroom, they were both dressed, Mary Jane said, "We're sorry for teasing you, are you mad at us?"

"No, of course not. I'm just not used to your openness. Don't worry about me, I'll get used to it. I love my wife very much and would never cheat on her." I said.

"And you had better not, or you will get shot somewhere else, a lot lower." Faith said. I finished getting dressed. I showed Mary Jane my knife, she had never seen one like it. I told her about the Tinker. She said, "I wonder if he was a Gypsy?"

"I don't know, could have been. He was dressed funny. He sure knew his business. Say, does Iris have knives also?"

"Yes, of course. I taught her a long time ago. She's pretty good." Mary Jane said.

"Faith just gave Alita her first ones, they're in her diaper bag."

"I wondered why she always kept it closed, she's going to be a good one." Mary Jane said.

"One what?" I asked.

"A Gypsy, of course."

"Oh, I thought you meant like an assassin." I said.

"We can all do that, but that isn't what we are." Faith said.

I went to the cooler and got some sandwiches out, then to the fridge and got three beers out and opened them. We three sat around the table and ate lunch. The kids and the dog came out and joined us.

"Have you seen any of the park yet?" I asked Mary Jane.

"No, we just got here this morning we didn't even get a room yet."

"Well now you don't need to, you can stay with us." Faith said, then turning to me she said, "And as far as the Park goes, I've only seen it from the Cooke City gate to here. Can we go in the Park this afternoon?"

"Yeah, of course we can. We have to turn in Mary Jane's car at Mammoth anyway. It won't hurt us to play tourist for awhile." I said.

We all trooped out to the truck, Mary Jane got in the back seat with Alita in her car seat in the middle of the back seat and Iris on the other side. Dog got in the front seat between Faith and I. I said to the kids in the back, "have you thought of a name for the dog yet?"

"No," Iris said, "we want it to be a good one, not just a run of the mill name like Rover or something."

"Alright, you both keep thinking. He answers to Dog, in the meantime."

Mary Jane spoke up, "Oh, we almost forgot, my car, we have to take it to Mammoth. It's setting in the upper parking lot by the Café." I started the truck and pulled into the other lot. Mary Jane got out with her keys in her hand. She was about to open the door, when I yelled at her- "Stop! Don't touch the car!" She stopped in mid-stride.

I got out and went around the truck, the hood on her car wasn't quite closed all of the way. I told Mary Jane to get back in the truck and said to Faith, "Pull the truck away from here." "What are you doing?" Faith said.

"The hood's not closed all of the way, either someone swiped the battery or something else is going on. Just in case, pull over there a ways." She did so....

I opened the hood, slowly. The first place I looked was the battery. There was a wire running from the positive post down under the firewall and disappeared under the car. And it wasn't original equipment on this model. I got down and looked under the car. Sure enough, there was a home made explosive device strapped to the frame. It had another wire going up through the body under the dash. I bet it was hooked to the ignition switch. I stood back up and disconnected the wire from the battery.

I stood there thinking, that hood being cracked open like that was a mistake only an amateur would make. Now if I was doing it, that's what I would do, leave a glaring clue, so a dummy would think he had it disarmed. In this case, whoever did this thought I was the dummy. They weren't necessarily after Mary Jane, they were after me.

They must be watching right now, they knew I would spot it. And when I thought it was disarmed and got in the car, maybe just opening the door would set it off? I didn't know for sure. I wasn't a demolition expert.

I took out my cell phone and called the Brand Inspector, I bet he would know if there was a bomb expert around here. Turned out a friend of his had just got back from Iraq. He had spent his time over there defusing road side bombs. He was here in ten minutes.

He said as he stepped out of his jeep. "Having a problem are we?"

"Yeah, somewhat. Someone either wants Mary Jane dead or me dead, I think it was me." He looked everything over.

"Yep, it was set to kill whoever thought they had it disarmed." He jerked a few wires loose here and there, then slid under the edge of the car and took the bomb out. He laid it on the hood and took the outside wrapping off, "Wow! C-4, this is really uptown stuff. They were professionals alright."

"Yeah, I suspected as much. How much do I owe you for saving my life?"

"Nothing, I suppose I had better tell the FBI about this, maybe even Home Land Security. Are you staying here at the Motel?"

"Yeah, do you think we can turn this car in to the rental agency?"

"Nope, I wouldn't even touch it; anymore than we have. They'll probably go over it with a fine tooth comb. I'll call them for you, what's your name?"

"Clay Bronson, the woman who rented this car is Mary Jane Hunter, from LA. We're all staying in room 204. But we're going to the Park this afternoon, we'll be back before dark." He shook my hand and said, "My names Pete Frank, I was raised around here, see you when you get back."

I got back in the truck and told the women, "Looks like we'll probably have to stay not only tonight, but maybe longer. Pete Frank, the guy who dismantled the bomb, said he'd have to call the FBI. So let's just play the tourist and enjoy ourselves, Okay?"

Mary Jane looked over her shoulder at Pete, "He's cute, did he say whether he's married or not?"

"Nope, he didn't. But he said he would see us when we got back. If you can contain yourself that long." I said. She looked at me and stuck her tongue at me. Then she added, "I want to thank you Clay for saving our lives. We could have been killed if you hadn't noticed that hood."

"Oh, they weren't after you per se, they were after me, I'm pretty sure it was Dipper Tick."

"What makes you think he doesn't want me dead too?" Mary Jane said.

"Why? You're not working that case anymore, but he has a score to settle with me. No, I'm pretty sure you would have been just collateral damage. He left that hood cracked on purpose, he knew I would see it."

We had been driving while we were talking, I pulled up to the entrance gate and showed them the annual pass that I had purchased at the North East gate. They waved us on thru. We stopped at the General Store at Mammoth and got some ice cream cones. Then drove up the hill toward Norris. At Mammoth there must have been 50 or 60 head of Elk grazing on the lawns. Alita said, "Can we ride them like Horses?"

"No sweetheart, we can't." Faith said, "They are wild, not tame like horses."

"Not even if we asked them?" Alita said.

"No, not even then. Why don't you count the number of Bison and Elk that you see along the road?

"Alright Daddy, how many are there?" Alita said.

"Well, I don't know for sure, but I will after you count them." I said. We spent the rest of the day just sight seeing. This was the first time either one of the women had been to the park. Of course I spent a lot of time here as a kid.

When we got back to the Motel, guess who was waiting for us? That's right Harry Silver, my personal FBI agent. They were still processing the rental car when we pulled up. Pete Frank was still there.

I got out of the pickup, "Well Harry, how did you get here so fast?"

"They have a small airport here, I brought a helicopter. Who do you think did this?" He said.

"Well, the car belongs to Mary Jane Hunter, turns out she has had run-ins with our old friend Dipper Tick, but I suppose Pete here has told you how I think it was a trap for me. And if it didn't get me, at least it would get Mary Jane. Mary Jane had come over and was listening. Harry looked at her and said, "Is that right Miss?"

"Yes, pretty much. If it wasn't for Clay being very observant, me and my daughter would be part of the scenery around here."

"Harry has any of your agents asked around, did anybody see who messed with this car?" I asked.

"Yes, of course. Turns out a couple of guys were seen, one of them had his right arm in a sling. I have an APB out on Dipper. Even if he was just here and didn't do anything, he has violated his bail, he was supposed to stay away from you."

"Well, I've always given a rattler an opportunity to pull in his fangs and run. But I guess next time, I won't." I said.

"I didn't hear that. It seems the older I get, the less I hear." Harry said.

All of this time Pete Frank and Mary Jane had been giving sideways glances at each other. "Well," I said, "it's supper time. Do you want to join us for dinner, Harry?"

"No, I've got some calls to make, maybe later." He said. I turned to Pete, "Well Pete, I guess that leaves you, I owe you the biggest steak that you can hold. How about it?"

"Sure, I would be glad to." He said, talking to me but looking at Mary Jane. She smiled at him. That made him beam. They both walked into the restaurant, together. Faith was standing there with Alita on her hip, and Iris holding her hand on the other side. I took Alita. Iris looked up at Faith and said, "Mom forgot me."

"No she didn't, she knew you was with us, don't worry." Faith said, as she still held Iris' hand as they walked in the Café, in front of Alita and I.

They found a table for us that would seat six. I made sure that Mary Jane and Pete didn't set beside each other. They both gave me a dirty look. Why did I do that? Maybe because Mary Jane did walk off without thinking about Iris? Or maybe just because I was ornery at times. Faith had told me that at times I had a mean streak. I didn't think I did, but just maybe I do.

Faith kicked me under the table. She jerked her head toward Mary Jane. I knew what she meant. "Okay, okay. Trade seats with me Pete. It seems my wife wants to let you set beside Mary Jane. She thinks I'm some kind of big meanie, or something."

Iris cleared her throat and said, "I don't think you are, Uncle Clay, I think you're nice." Then she looked at her mother....

Mary Jane looked at Pete, then said, "I don't know what everybody is so upset about. Yes, I was, or am, interested in Pete. As I can see that he is in me. We seem to be attracted to each other. But we're not going to fall all over each other. I have a Master's Degree, and I think I'm smart enough to control my feelings."

"Being smart, Mother, has nothing to do with feelings. Anyway that was what you told me last year." Iris said. Mary Jane looked down at her hands, than sideways at Pete, then she said, "Yes Dear, I did tell you that, and you're right.

Sometimes the smartest people are quite dumb. Thank you, for bringing me down to the ground."

"Look Mary Jane, there is nothing wrong in love at first sight, that was how Faith and I fell in love. She was sound asleep in bed when I first seen her. I knew right away that this was the one. I was just being a jerk." I said.

Pete took Mary Jane's hand, "I felt the same the second I seen you, but I know we have to get to know each other. And also Iris and I need to get acquainted. I live here, but you don't. Are you going home, or what are your plans?"

Mary Jane looked at Faith and I. Faith spoke up, "They are going with us, to the Big Horn Basin. Are you working here, or what?" She said to Pete.

"No, I just got back last month, I've sort of been just hanging loose, spending my mustering out money." Pete said.

"Then you're completely out of the service?" I said.

"Yep, footloose and fancy free, that's me."

"Well then, perhaps you would like a job? I know that Dipper Tick won't stop till one of us is dead, you might come in pretty handy."

"Sure, what would I be doing?"

"Can you ride? Do you know cattle? Can you fix fence? How are you with a hammer and saw? In other words are you a hand?" I said.

"Yes, I'm pretty handy, I'd do most anything to stay close to Mary Jane and Iris."

"Okay then, you're hired. The first thing I want you to do is, after supper, go over to the fair grounds and check on the mules, make sure they have feed and water. Okay?"

"Sure, no problem. When do you plan on leaving for home?"

"I don't know for sure, but hopefully tomorrow or the next day, can you get your affairs in order that quick?"

"I don't know for sure, but I'll try." Pete said. While talking to me, but looking at Mary Jane.

We got our food and the conversation lapsed, first things first, you know. We were just finishing up when Harry Silver came in. He wanted to talk to me. I paid our bill and left a generous tip, after all it's no easy task waiting on a table of six people. Pete left to check on the mules, said he would see us in the morning. The women went to our room. Harry and I, went outside, where we could talk without anyone hearing.

"Clay, we finished up on the car, like I told you. But I also wanted to let you know that I did a quick background check on Pete Frank and Mary Jane Hunter. And before you split a gut, it's just routine in a national security case, like any bomb related cases are anymore. But anyway, Pete checks out alright, *so far* he is what he says he is. As to Mary Jane, she also is. But have you ever heard of the Carmel Foundation?"

"Yeah, I think I have. It's some kind of a philanthropist organization, they give scholarships and stuff don't they?"

"Yes, and a lot more. Their net worth is probably more than the U.S. Government. They have bases all over the world on every continent. They are top secret conclaves. The founder of them is one 'Wolf Hunter'. That's his name, plus maybe his vocation. He's in his late eighties now. His wife's maiden name was Carmel. She was a Sinti Gypsy. They met in Germany at the end of world war two. The rumor is that they found Hitler's hidden wealth. That's just the rumor, no one has ever known for sure. But I'm getting away from my point. Mary Jane Hunter, is a Great Grand Daughter to them. Now I'm going to tell you one more thing, I'm not prying it just came up on the research on Mary Jane. Your wife, she is a cousin to Mary Jane. Did you know that?"

"No, I did not. I don't think Faith did either. They aren't in any kind of trouble are they?" I said.

"No, heavens no. I just wanted you to know. Even if they were, we have a hands off policy on the Carmel Foundation. They help us out all of the time. If the FBI needs anything and we can't get it from our government, the foundation helps us." Harry said.

"You say they have bases all over, where is the closest one?"

"In Central Montana, up close to Lewistown. On Hunter's ancestral ranch."

"Fine, so we can return that car tomorrow?" Harry nodded, then left.

Chapter Twelve

I stood there staring at the starry night, thinking. The wonders of creation always quieted the turmoil of life, as it became more and more complicated. They say that the only thing that remained constant was change. But that wasn't quite true, God, he always remained the same.

When I was growing up, my Indian relatives always called the Almighty God Jehovah, the Great Spirit. And he certainly was that, Great. I seen a shooting star, some space rock or debris as it fell to earth and burnt itself up. Made me think of how brief our life here on earth was, just like a shooting star, bright but brief.

I shook myself and went to our room. I opened the door, it was unlocked. Faith and Mary Jane was in the hot tub. I said, "You really should keep the door locked, anybody could come in."

"Yes, anybody did," Faith said with a giggle. "Seriously though, you're right, but we left it open for you. Would you mind tucking the girls in, they said they wanted you to tuck them in."

"Sure, no problem." I went in the bedroom, they were reading a book together. "What are you reading?" I asked.

"Huckleberry Finn, have you ever read it?" Iris asked.

"Of course, it's one of my favorite books. Are you girls ready for bed?"

"Yes, Daddy." Alita said, "Daddy do we have to put pajama's on?"

"Why, don't you want to?"

"Well, Mommy and Aunt Mary Jane don't wear clothes, they took theirs off as soon as they got in the room. Why does everyone wear clothes?"

That was a stumper. I sat there for a few seconds thinking. Just why do we wear clothes? Oh, I know to keep us warm and to prevent sunburn. But why does society think nudity is shameful? Why do I get embarrassed when people see me naked?

"Well why do you two think we wear clothes?" I asked them.

Iris said, "I know in the Bible, Adam and Eve didn't."

"Well yes, at first they didn't. But do you know why they started to?"

"Uh, because they were bad?" Iris said.

"Alright, let's think about that. When they were first created, they didn't wear clothes, and they weren't ashamed of it. Do you remember what they did wrong in God's eyes?

"Yes, I think so." Iris said, "They ate an apple off of a tree that God said not to eat from. I learned that in Sunday school."

"Right, well let's read that account." I said, as I reached into the bedside stand and took the Bible out. I turned to that story in Genesis the third chapter. "You see how the serpent lied, of course it wasn't the snake, it was Satan talking. He said, 'is it really so that God said that you cannot eat from every tree of the garden?'

And Eve answered and said, 'of the fruit of the trees from the garden we may eat. But from the tree that is in the middle of the garden we may not eat. God said, 'you must not eat from it, no, you must not touch it, that you do not die.'

And how the serpent lied and said, 'you positively will not die. For God knows that from the very day of your eating from it, your eyes are bound to be opened and you are bound to be like God, knowing good and bad'."

"And it goes on to say how Eve ate of the apple and then took it to Adam and he ate too. And it says down here in verse seven, 'how the eyes of both of them became opened and they began to realize that they were naked. And hence they sewed fig leaves together and made loin covering for themselves'."

"So is that why we were clothes?" Alita asked.

"Yes, I guess so, we now know good from bad."

"But," Iris said, "they didn't die in that day, like God said they would."

"Yes, they did. You see the Bible also says that one day with Jehovah God is like a thousand years. They both died within that thousand year day. Adam was 939 years old when he died. And that is also why the earth wasn't created in a literal earth six day period. It was created in six thousand years." I said. Where was I getting all of this? I had never read the Bible, it was just coming to me. Must be those visions. Alita and Iris were quite, they were thinking.

Alita said, "What would of happened if they hadn't disobeyed God? Would we still be wearing clothes?"

"Well, there are some things to consider on that. But yes, if the whole earth had been made into a Garden of Eden, then we would not be wearing clothes. Because the moisture laden atmosphere that the Garden of Eden had would of continued to protect us from the sun's ultra violet rays."

Iris asked, "What happened to all of that moisture in the air?"

"Where do you think all of the water came from that flooded the earth in Noah's day? That's right, from that thick swaddling band that used to encircle the earth."

"Uncle Clay, how do you know all of this?" Iris asked.

"Uh, from the Bible of course. Anything more you want to know, before you go to sleep?"

"Yes Daddy, do we have to wear pajamas?" Alita asked, as before.

"No, it's up to the both of you. If you both want to sleep in the altogether you can, but you both have to agree, if one doesn't want to, then you can't, Okay?"

They nodded, as I left the room and turned their lights down low. The women were just getting out of the hot tub. "What took you so long?" Faith asked.

"They had a lot of questions. Prompted I might say, on your libertine ways, the both of you. What have you guys been talking about?" I asked.

"Oh, just about everything. Including you." Faith said.

"Well, let me ask you both this question, do you know who you are?"

"What in the world kind of question was that?" Mary Jane said, as she dried off and then handed the towel to Faith. Then Faith finished drying off, using the same towel.

"For instance, what you two just done, using the same towel to dry off, why did you do that?"

They looked at each other, Faith said, "I don't know, I've never done that before."

"So is it safe to say, that you two have some connection or bond, that just seems to be there?"

Again, they just looked at each other. "But you don't know what that is, do you? I see that you don't. Then I will tell you, you guys are cousins."

"How do you know?" Mary Jane asked.

"Harry Silver, he did a quick background check. You Mary Jane are a Hunter, related to 'Wolf Hunter', the founder of the Carmel Foundation. And you sweetheart are a Carmel, a great granddaughter of one Edith Carmel. Who was married to Wolf Hunter's wife, Sharon's brother."

"Harry told you all of this?" Faith said.

"No, in fact he didn't. He told me some of it, one thing that you two were cousins. The rest of it, just popped up into this jumble I call a brain. So you two have a lot to talk about. I'm going to bed." I looked at them as they sat down on the couch, without putting anything on. After you knew they were related, it was apparent. Their bodies were almost identical. Even down to the blackness of their pubic hairs. I shook my head and went to bed.

I awoke in the middle of the night, I was in the middle, they were both wrapped around me. I tried to crawl over my wife and get on the far side of her. As soon as I moved they both tightened their grip on me, I gave up and went back to sleep.

I awoke again, just before dawn. I slipped down the bed, coming out at the foot, they didn't wake up. I took a shower. Then shaved. They were still asleep, they must of talked a long time last night.

I put my knife on down the backside of my neck, and my pistol in the standard issue holster on my belt. After all I was still an agent of the New Mexico State Police. I found my badge in my suitcase and put it on under my overall jacket, so no one could see it. I shut the door quietly, making sure it was locked.

I walked to my truck, I didn't open the door right away, I walked around it, then I looked under the frame. I couldn't find anything. Maybe due to the FBI all over the place, it scared them off for awhile. I should have killed him when I had a chance. But I believed in the innate goodness of man. Was I that far off base in letting him live?

I sat down on the curb, still thinking. If I was a bomber, where would I hide a bomb? I didn't know, because I wasn't a bomber. But I sure would like to tamp one up Dipper Tick's ass. Up his ass? Tailpipe? Yeah, sure, up the tailpipe. I went around to the back of the pickup. I looked up the pipe, couldn't see anything, it was too dark. I had an LED penlight in my jacket pocket. I looked up the pipe again, yep, there it was. I found a piece of bailing wire in the back of the truck. I made a hook, and slowly pulled it out.

I looked it over, some more C4, but this had a heat sensitive fuse on the upstream end. The heat of the exhaust would of tripped it. The cooler was still in the back end, I had put it back in there when we had taken all of the food out of it. I put the C4 in there, then went to the Café and got some ice. I packed it around it.

I got in the cab and started it up, holding my breath. I let my breath out slowly, I was still alive. I put the truck in gear and drove to the fair grounds to check on the mules. They were glad to see me. I tossed them some more hay and checked their water. I went around to all fourteen of them, giving a word of encouragement and a pat to each one of them. They gathered around me, wanting to know where we were going. I told them. I got the same reaction from all of them, glad to be out of the dude business.

Mules are very intelligent animals, a lot smarter than most of their handlers. A mule will not go somewhere that is dangerous. A horse on the other hand wants to please a man so much that he'll jump off a cliff. Both of them have their place in the scheme of things.

When I got back to the room, the two women were just waking up. "Good morning sleepy heads." I said

"Where did you go?" Faith asked, as she padded to the toilet. Mary Jane laid there and stretched.

"I went to check on the mules, they're fine. They wanted to know where we were going. They were happy that they didn't have to deal with dudes anymore." I said.

Mary Jane said, "They told you this huh?"

"In their own way they did. I just listen better than most

people." Faith came back and Mary Jane ran for the bathroom. Faith came and sat on my lap and gave me a kiss. "I missed you last night."

"What do you mean, you missed me. I was right there in bed with you." I said.

"You know what I mean." Faith said, kissing me again.

"Well that is going to have to wait for awhile, isn't it? In the mean time, why don't you two get dressed, I'll wake up the girls, then we can go get something to eat."

I woke the girls up, they didn't have any pajama's on. "Come on kids, get dressed and come on out so we can go get something to eat. And yes, you have to wear clothes." I went back out to the main room. They were just getting dressed.

"You two are a bad influence on the kids, they don't want to wear clothes now, since you two run around naked." I said. "But I made them."

We went into the Café, after we were seated, I said, "Order for me too, will you Honey? I want to make a phone call." I went back outside with the cell phone. I called Harry Silver's cell phone number. "Hello," he answered, "Yeah Harry, it's me Clay, are you guys still here?"

"Yes, I was just coming over to get something to eat."

"Good, is your forensic team still here also?"

"Yes, they were going to fly out with me this morning. Why?"

"Well, I have a something I want them to check for fingerprints, Okay?"

"Sure, where are you now?" Harry asked.

"I'm standing outside the Café, I'll meet you by my truck."

I went over beside the truck and waited for Harry. He came out of his room, with one of his forensic team, she was the only female on the team. She looked to be about Harry's age. Well anyway, Harry was getting some, he should be in a good mood.

"So what do you have that's so important?" Harry said.

I lifted the cooler to the back tail gate. I opened it and showed them what I had packed in ice."

The woman said, "Wow! Is that what I think it is? A heat sensitive fuse on that C4?"

"I think so, I found it in my tail pipe. Do you think you can check it for prints?"

"Sure, my kit is in the room, I'll take this in and dust it, then I can use my lap top and hook into the FBI's main frame and see whose prints they are." She said. Then she took the whole cooler with her.

"Harry, when you first told me about doing a background check on Pete Frank, you said he was clean, *so far*, what did you mean by saying so far?"

"Just that, it was a preliminary check, he was in the Army in Iraq. But for some reason his whole record wasn't there."

"Harry, don't you think it is quite the coincidence, that an explosive expert was so handy, when such a sophisticated bomb showed up?"

"Well, yes and no, there are a lot more people trained in explosives since this damn Iraq war. But yes, you may have a point. It won't take Karen long to get those prints and have the results, we'll join you in the Café with the results."

The food was there by the time I rejoined my family. Mary Jane said, "I was sort of expecting Pete to join us for breakfast, you haven't seen him have you?"

I looked at her and spoke rather bluntly, "Mary Jane, I know you're starting to have a slight crush on Pete. But do me a favor, in your mind go back over everything he said and done since you met him and analyze your results."

"Huh? That's rather a clinical approach to matters of the heart, don't you think?"

"Yes, but in today's world, 'the heart is a lonely hunter', to borrow a cliché, the heart at times can't be trusted, it has to be backed up by the mind. So just think about it, and let me know what you come up with."

Faith asked, "Who did you call?"

"Harry Silver, I had a little task for him."

"Well, are you going to tell me about it?"

"Yes, but not right now, let's see how that task turns out first."

The waitress came over, "So how's the food?" Of course we all said 'fine', then she asked me, "Was that enough ice that I gave you this morning, or do you need more?"

"No, that was plenty, thank you." I said, Faith turned a bit in her chair and said, "What Ice?"

"Uh, I borrowed some ice for the cooler, I had to keep something cold, that something was a bomb that I took out of our tailpipe. Harry and his woman are checking it over right now for prints." I never could lie, worth a damn, especially to the woman that I love.

"Does this have anything to do with you asking me to analyze my feelings for Pete?" Mary Jane said.

"I don't know for sure, why don't we wait till Harry gets the results, he said it wouldn't take long, not with today's technology. Does anybody need more butter on their hotcakes?" I asked.

"I won't ask how come you knew it was in the tailpipe, I'm just glad you found it. It could of killed all of us." Faith said.

Mary Jane's complexion turned a little sallow, I could just see the gears going around in her head. Then I heard her whisper under her breath, "Damn, damn it to hell."

Harry was right, it didn't take long, both he and his woman, Karen came in and sat down with us, after they had ordered, I asked. "Well, whose prints were they?"

Harry said, "Was Pete with you when you found this, did he handle it?"

"Well, I guess, we have our answer, No he was not. I'm the only one who touched it." I said. Mary Jane gasped.

"The only prints we found, beside yours, were those of Pete Frank. I've told the main office to do an extensive background check on Pete. In the meantime, I would say that he is armed and dangerous. And Oh yes, by the way, the District Office has approved of assigning you as a special agent, they have been in touch with New Mexico, they seem to like your work. They told me to get you a badge and I.D. Will you be staying here longer, or are you going home?"

"We plan on leaving this morning. On Pete Frank, when I guy goes bad there is usually a reason, what do you think his was?" I asked.

"I don't know, but I've already been in touch with Home Land Security; they are looking into it. They think it might have something to do with 9-11."

"Oh, I hope not. I hope it's just something mundane, like money." I said.

"It would be a lot simpler that way, wouldn't it?" Karen said. I hadn't paid too much attention to her, but now I looked her over. She was a typical pant suited FBI agent. All business, well maybe not all, but mostly I bet.

"Yes, money addiction is a lot simpler to deal with, than religious fanaticism. But what if it's both, what then?" Mary Jane said. I looked at her, she seemed to be over her slight crush on Pete. I knew if she was anything like her cousin, my wife, that she would land on her feet.

"Nothing," I said, "as long as he stays away from us, if he doesn't he will reap what he sows."

"Harry," I said, "this decision to make me a special agent, didn't have anything to do with Faith and Mary Jane, being that they have connections to the Carmel Foundation, did it?"

"No, I don't think so. Not on my account anyway. Hard to say the motive behind it though. I'm just a small cog on a big flywheel. I just do what I'm told."

"Why in the world would that have anything to do with it?" Faith said.

"Well, it just seems funny, right after they found out who you both are, they offer me a position in the FBI. Maybe they are hoping that we can do a little spying for them." I said.

"Goodness why, all they have to do is ask Great Grandfather and I'm sure he would tell them anything they needed to know." Mary Jane said. "If anything, I'm sure they're just trying to get on his good side."

"Oh yeah, Harry, would you and Karen make sure that Mary Jane's rental car gets returned?" I said.

"Sure, we would be glad to, don't worry we'll take care of it."

"Good then, I guess we'll pack up our stuff and go get the mules and be on our way." I said, looking at the women for confirmation. They both nodded their approval. It didn't take us long and we had everything in the truck.

When we got to the fair grounds, the mules were waiting for us. They came over to the fence, visibly upset. I walked over, "What's wrong boys?" I went to each one and gave them a little rub behind their ears. "Okay, I think I understand, don't worry, I'll take care of it."

Faith came over, "What's wrong?"

"They tell me someone has been messing with the trailer, now I wonder who that was?"

"What did they see?"

"Who ever it was did something under the trailer; you all go on the other side of the arena. I'll see what they did under there."

"You be careful, I lost one husband and I don't want to lose another, I want to live till we're old and simple; together."

"Well we've already accomplished one of those things, the simple part." I said, as I gave her a kiss.

I scooted under the trailer, yep, it was easy to find, when you knew it was there. Someone had rigged another C4 charge to the floor boards. It was wired into the electric brake circuit, the first time I would have applied the brakes, BAM, no more us or the mules. This Bomb was the biggest yet. As big as any of those road side IED's in Iraq.

Now I could sort of forgive Pete for trying to kill me, but not for trying to kill my family or mules. People that were cruel to animals were beyond forgiveness, in my book. I disconnected the wires and carefully un taped the bundle. Sliding out, I held the bomb up for them to see.

I heard a car coming, I glanced over my shoulder. What the hell, it was Pete Frank in his jeep. My family was still standing on the other side of the arena. He got out of his Jeep, he said, "Hi, sorry I'm late, but I had a few things to do at home before I could leave." He looked at the women and children standing over there staring at him. Then back at me, holding the bomb in the air. "Where did you get that?" He said.

"You don't know? I bet it has your fingerprints all over it."

"Could be, but where did you get it?"

"From under my stock trailer, like you didn't know!" I said, gritting my teeth.

"Whoa, I didn't plant that there. I recognize it, because I made it."

"What about the tailpipe bomb I got out of my tailpipe this morning, it had your fingerprints all over it?"

"Shit!, look I sold them to some guys last week. I know, I know, I shouldn't of done it, but I needed the money. I just sold them the C4, there weren't any fuse's attached."

"Where did you get the C4?"

"It's easy to get on the black market. There's a link on the internet. They already had some, they said they needed more, they were doing some mining in a remote area in the Big Horns."

"Weren't you the least bit suspicious about what they wanted it for?"

"Sure, but like I said, I needed the money. That C4 in Mary Jane's car must have been some of what they already had, it wasn't some of what I sold them."

The women had come over and were listening. Iris had stayed over there with Alita. Mary Jane said, "Yeah but it had your fingerprints all over it."

"Of course, I diffused it. When I sold them the C4, they were wearing gloves, so they didn't leave any prints. On the stuff I sold them, my prints were all over that stuff."

"Well, his explanation sounds plausible, what do you think Clay?" Faith said.

"Well, I want him to be guilty, so I can slit his throat, but I think the only thing he is guilty of, is extreme stupidity. Plus being super naïve." I said. I pulled out my cell phone and called Harry. It didn't take them long to get here.

He told Harry the same story. Of course they had to take him into custody, till they could get to the bottom of everything. Mary Jane had taken him aside and they were talking.

"Harry," I said, "I think he is telling the truth. I want you to give him the benefit of the doubt. Plus of course follow through and get a handle on who he sold the stuff to, that might be a good lead on finding these guys. And above all, don't turn him over to Home Land Security, you know how crazy them guys can be. They would probably send him to Cuba."

"Sure, I agree with you. I'll do the best I can. You watch yourselves, Okay?"

"Yes, Harry, we'll be alright, you take good care of the boy, you hear?" I said. I think he got my point. They took him away. Mary Jane and Faith, along with the children came over.

"He's telling the truth," Mary Jane said, "he wanted the money for his Mother, she needed an operation. She just got out of the hospital yesterday. Will he be alright?"

Now I knew how things worked, I wasn't sure. I knew Homeland Security, trumped the FBI. "I'm not sure Mary Jane." I said. She took out her cell phone and dialed while she walked away, a little bit. She talked for about five minutes.

"It's all taken care of, I called Wolf. He'll retrieve him if they are going to let Homeland Sec. get him."

"He can do that?" I asked.

Faith said, "Yes Clay, he can do that. I don't know how, but he can."

"Well then, let's load the mules up and get our act on the road, Okay?"

Chapter Thirteen

I had Iris hold the horse trailer rear gate open. I opened the gate to the corral, they trooped out and headed for the horse trailer. One of the mules stopped beside Iris, he nuzzled her, she patted him on the nose. The rest of them got in the trailer, one by one. The one by Iris was the last to get in.

Iris said, as she swung the tail gate toward me, "His name is Luke, I think he likes me."

"Oh, he told you his name, did he?" Mary Jane said.

"Well, not exactly, I asked him if his name was Luke, he nodded his head yes. Isn't that the same as telling me?"

"Sure it is, how would you like him to be your Mule, no one else's, just yours?" I said.

"Yes, Oh yes. You're not kidding me are you?" Iris said, jumping up and down.

'Nope, he's yours." I said. Alita was squirming in Faith's arms, "Me, me too. I want my own mule, also."

"Alright, when we get home, you can pick one out for yourself, it'll be just yours. Okay?" I said. Alita held out her arms to me, I took her and she gave me a big kiss. Iris pulled at my elbow, wanting me to bend down, she gave me a kiss also, "Thank you, Uncle Clay." She said.

"Well," I said, "I got kisses from two of the females, how about the other two?"

Faith came up on one side and Mary Jane on the other, they each gave me a peck on the cheek. Faith said, "That'll have to do, till we get home." Mary Jane said, "That'll have to do, period." I stuck my tongue out at her. It was going to be fun having her around.

It was just a little after nine when we finally got on the road. We went back in the Park, to Mammoth and made a left toward Roosevelt Junction, where one road went toward Tower and the other through the Lamar Valley, beside the Lamar River, to Silver Gate and Cooke city. This road stayed open year around, it was the only way to get to Cooke City in the winter time.

We took our time. There were a lot of Bison that used the Lamar Valley year round. Alita was busy counting them. We did see a couple of Wolves, just hanging around biding their time.

"Now I was never a fan of them restocking our range with Wolves. But it was over and done with now. I was of the mind when somebody shovels shit in your yard, use it for fertilizer. In other words make the best of a bad thing.

We stopped in Cooke City for lunch. Then proceeded toward Red Lodge, but we turned on the Sunlight Basin road, the same route we came by. It used to be just a trail across there, toward Cody. But now it was a paved road, with all kinds of houses, that didn't make me none to happy either.

It was just after seven that night that we arrived home. There were still a couple of hours of daylight left. The first one to meet us was Rosie, with Tiff at her heals, with Hank and Poppy right behind them. Hope stood in the kitchen doorway, shading her eyes at the late afternoon sunset.

Faith opened the truck door, Dog jumped out. Rosie reached in and took Alita, Alita fastened her arms around Rosie's neck. Rosie looked at Mary Jane and Iris, "Who do we have here? My, but Faith, she looks just like you, is she your sister or what?"

"Not quite, she's my cousin, Rosie this is Mary Jane, and

the little one is Iris, her daughter." Then, "Mary Jane and Iris, this is our daughter, Rosie. And standing beside her is Hank and Poppy, they're family too, and that's Hope standing in the doorway, their Mother." Dog ran around checking everything out. I think he liked his new home.

As they all jabbered at each other, I jerked my head at Hank, then indicated the horse trailer. He followed me to the back. "Hank, why don't you open the corral gate, I'll let these guys out, just whistle and they will follow you." It went pretty much that way, all except for Luke, Iris' mule, and one other. They came and stood close to the talking women. Hank said, "What about those two?"

"That's Okay, leave them alone, the big one there belongs to Iris. And I guess the other one must belong to Alita." I walked over and took Alita, the smaller Mule came over, "Well Alita, I guess you didn't get to choose, it looks like he choose you, is that Okay?"

"Yes, Daddy, I like him, can I sit on him?" Alita asked.

"Sure," I put her up on his back, she grabbed his mane, and kicked him in the ribs, he walked around the yard, with her talking a mile a minute to him. Iris had me lift her up on Luke, they joined the other two, with Dog right on their heels.

Hope called from the doorway, "I have supper ready, it was a good thing Faith called and said how many there would be." They all went in the house, I called to Iris and Alita, "Hey come on in, supper's ready." They rode over, Alita said, "Daddy, can Matthew and Luke stay in the old coal shed outside the back kitchen door. There is nothing in there now, can they please Daddy?"

I looked at her, "How did you know about that old shed?"

"I seen it out there before, Rosie told me what it used to be used for. They said they wanted to stay close, incase we needed them."

"Oh, they did, did they? Well alright, I can't see that it would hurt anything. There's an old tub that Iris can fill with water for them. I'll get them a bale of hay after supper."

Alita never ceased to amaze me. She noticed everything. I helped them down, Iris led Alita into the house. I said to the mules, "well go around back, I'll run you some water and get you a bale of hay." I went to the hay stack beside the barn and grabbed a hundred pound bale of alfalfa. I cut the bale open and then filled an old wash tub that was hanging on the side of the shed. They seemed quite content.

I went in the house, they had saved a place for me, someone had filled my plate. That was nice of them, I wasn't a picky eater, I cleaned the whole plate full up, and then held out my plate for more.

Hope said, after noticing the mules out the back kitchen window. "Are they going to be alright there?"

"Yeah, I reckon, I can't think of better watch dogs, than mules. A lot better than Guinea Hens, the hens might make more noise in case of intruders, but mules will kick the shit out of them."

Faith said, "Please Sweetheart, your language, the children, you don't want them to use that word, do you?"

"Well no, I guess not. You're right, I'll try to do better." Mary Jane gave me a wink, she knew I would backslide.

As to sleeping arrangements it was decided, by Alita and Iris, that Mary Jane would take Alita's old room. There was an extra room off of the kitchen that hadn't been used in years. Iris and Alita wanted to share that room, so they could be closer to the mules. And of course Dog would sleep in there also.

The only thing I wasn't too happy about, was that Alita's old room had a door opening into ours. I wasn't sure the lock worked on that door. All of the bedrooms upstairs were full up now. Well really all of the bedrooms were, since the one off of the kitchen was now occupied. Nothing like a full house.

Hank had finished eating, I asked him, "Well, how are those horses coming, do you have them all broke yet?"

"Funny thing, I don't have to do much, their pretty much training themselves. Seems they are very anxious to please." Hank said.

"Well now, that's good to hear. Tomorrow you can start on the mules, I don't expect they'll give you any trouble, they've been used in a dude string, packing supplies in and out of the mountains. Mules are a bit different than horses. If they take a liking to you, they will do most anything for you." I said.

"What about those two outside of the kitchen window?" Hank asked.

"Leave them to me, they belong to Iris and Alita, I don't expect them to take too much training."

The whole family turned to on the dishes. All but Hank and I, we went out to check on how the mules were getting along with the horses. I guess we didn't have to worry much, they seemed to be getting along pretty good.

Red came out while we were there, filling me in on the branding and such. "How's the count coming; did we lose many over the last winter?" I asked.

"Just a few head; I found about five carcasses bunched up in a dead end coulee. That last blizzard we had probably drifted them in there."

"Didn't lose any to rustlers though huh?"

"No, not us. But the outfit next door did, they seemed to think it was funny that we didn't. I sort of got the impression they thought we might be branding a few that weren't ours." Red said.

"Who said that, Old Man Dithers?" I asked.

"No, they sold out to an outfit from back east, some rich

bastard, I didn't like him none." Red said, as he spit tobacco juice into the dust.

"When are you going to stop that chewing Red. It's going to give you cancer, sure enough if you don't?" I didn't wait for an answer, cause I knew he wouldn't, "What's that ranny's name?" I asked.

"Joe Cummins, anyway that's what he told me. He stands about six foot four, looks to weigh in a shade under two eighty. If you asks me, he's a big bag of shit." Red said.

"My, I guess you sure don't like him none. I'll ride over there tomorrow and let him vent his ire on me." I said.

"Well, watch your back if you do, some of his hands look like they came from the back alleys of New York. They can't rope worth a damn, but I bet they can shoot you in the back." Red said.

We went back to the house, Hank went in, I stopped to talk to Luke and Matthew. I scratched them behind their ears. "Well boy's," I said, "you two are the official watchmen, if anyone comes around, just Hee Haw really loud, I'll hear you." I went in, everyone was already in bed, I tiptoed up the stairs.

Faith and Mary Jane were setting on our bed. For once they both had PJ's on. I told them about what Red had said about our new neighbor. Faith said, "I don't think you should go over there alone, Mary Jane and I will go with you. No, don't argue, it's settled."

"I wasn't going to argue, I know you both have your knives, but does Mary Jane have a gun?"

"No I don't. But, being an ex-cop, I know how to shoot, that is if you have an extra gun." Mary Jane said.

"I have one, I took it from the closet in hallway at home, just before we left. I thought we might need an extra one." Faith said, then she went to her suit case that was in the closet. She put it on the bed and opened a false bottom on it. She not only had this ten shot .41 caliber auto, but ammo for it, and her little .32 Mag. Plus about ten more stiletto's,

Mary Jane took the .41, pulled the receiver back and checked to make sure it was loaded, which it was. Then snapped it home. I could tell she knew what she was doing. "Is that an extra clip for it?" She said, Faith handed her two extra clips. Mary Jane smiled. I looked back and forth between the two of them, I sure wouldn't want to get on their bad side.

Mary Jane said, "Well, I'm going to bed. You two hold it down when you make love, I don't need to hear it, I haven't had any for ages." As she went through her bedroom doorway, she pulled her teddy off over her head and wiggled her naked butt at us. Then she shut the door. That I was glad of....

The next morning I was the first one up, I went downstairs and put the coffee on. Hope heard me clanking around and came down in her robe and curlers in her hair. I looked at her, "You still wear curlers at night, I thought that went out with the 60's?"

"Yes I do. My mother always did, and I just got in the habit. Don't you like curlers?"

"I ain't got nothing against them, just surprised some is all." I said.

"Do you want breakfast now, or do you want to wait for the rest of the family?" Hope said.

"I can wait, I just wanted to get the coffee started. I'm going out and check the stock. Do you want me to the feed the chickens, or are you going to?" I said.

"You can, while you're at it, gather the eggs too, will you?"

"Sure, no problem, it's sure nice to have you and your kids with us, Hope. How are you liking it so far?" I said.

"It's a dream come true for us. I always wanted a big family, now I have one."

"The same goes for us, it's nice to have the house full. It's what I always wanted too." I said.

I stopped and fed Luke and Matthew, then went to the barn and checked horses and mules. I was some glad that we didn't have milk cows, they tied you down morning and night. Then I went to the chicken coop, it and the chicken yard was all fenced in with chicken wire. When I was a kid, we let the chickens free range, but now it was simpler to keep them in one spot. Safer for the chickens also. I tossed them some cracked corn and then gathered the eggs.

I stopped again at the mules, I noticed that there was no manure around where they were standing. "Where are you guys going to the bathroom? I asked them. They sort of tossed their heads toward the garden. I looked over there. Sure enough they were placing it in a nice pile close to the garden. All we'd have to do is shovel it where we needed it. Now how did they know to do that? Well at least there would be no stinking mess beside the kitchen door.

As I went through the kitchen door, Hope said, "You're just in time with those eggs, wash some of them off for me, then crack them in that bowl, would you?"

I did as instructed. We had both white and brown eggs. Now I always favored brown ones. Now most people can't tell the difference, but I could. Mom always said that I was nuts, but I knew better.

By the time we was done, we had platters of sausage, potatoes and eggs, along with hotcakes. "Hope said, "I sure wish we had a milk cow, I always liked home churned butter. Plus the cream is always better. I like buttermilk, homemade. Can we get a milk cow?"

I had just counted my blessing that we didn't have one, but I said, "Sure, no problem, do you know how to milk?"

"Yes, I learned when I was a little girl, these kids need to know how to milk and churn butter, don't you think?"

"Yeah, sure, shouldn't everybody?" I said.

"I'm glad you agree with me, if we get one, I'll make up a milking schedule. That way it won't be a burden on any one of us." Hope said. Then she added. "I see that there is a separator in the pantry, it looks like it hasn't been used in years though."

"It hasn't, but it's all there, I'm sure. It's still the old hand turned one. But I guess I could rig up an electric motor to it." I said.

"No need to, the cranking will be good for everybody." Hope said.

Everyone trooped in at the same time, I said, "I bet you've all been just waiting till we got breakfast on the table, to show up, haven't you?"

Mary Jane said, "I don't know about everyone else, but Faith and I were."

"Okay, just for that, you Mary Jane can say the prayer this morning." I said.

"Are you sure, I thought the man of the house had to do it?" She said.

I grabbed up a tea towel and tossed it to her, "put that on your head, the Bible just says that when a woman prays in the congregation that she has to have her head covered, so there." I said. She wrapped the towel around her head and gave a prayer that made mine sound juvenile. She even used Jehovah's name and closed in Jesus' name.

"Where did you learn to pray like that?" I asked.

"My Uncle, he was sent to Siberia in the 80's, he never came back."

"I'm sorry, that must have been just before the Berlin wall went down." I said.

"Something like that, I don't know for sure. Pass the pancakes will you?"

All of the kids kicked in to clean the table off and do the

dishes, even Alita helped. Hope said that she would keep an eye on Alita and Iris. I told Hope that she could put them up on the back of their mules, that they could baby set for awhile.

The three of us went out to the barn and we saddled up Brutus, Nick and Diablo. Rosie said that Mary Jane could ride him. Mary Jane knew how to ride, as I suppose all Sinti Gypsy did. The horses were raring to go, Brutus and Nick hadn't been rode for awhile. Of course Rosie had been riding Diablo almost every day. Tiff had been riding one of the new ones that Hank had been working with. Dog stayed with Hank.

I made sure we left the saddle guns at home, I didn't want it to look like we were hunting trouble. We had enough fire power anyway.

We let the horses run, that is after they got warmed up a little bit. It was about ten miles over to Old Man Dithers place. They were still branding. They were gathered in a flat about a mile from the house. I could see them working as we rode up. Well not all of them were working, just the old hands that used to ride for Dithers. There were six hands just lounging around doing nothing. I could pick out that Joe Cummins, and one other man that I recognized right away, that made eight that were packing guns. The one I recognized? It was that lawyer that was with Dipper Tick, the one that I knocked out before. I think his name was, Delbert Westinghouse. Faith recognized him also.

I reined in watching Joe Cummins, I could tell by just looking at him, that he was just a front man. He was both arrogant and stupid. Stupid because I knew by the expression on his face that he was going to try and kill me, and that this day would be his last. He was leering at the women. Delbert said something to him, he shook off his advice.

I said, "I hear that you think that we're responsible for some losses that you say you've experienced." I figured we might as well get right to the point.

"Yeah, that's damn right. You're a thief, get down off that horse, I'm going to beat you to death and then I'm going to screw your women." Brutus danced around, I just let him, making it look like I couldn't control him. Brutus knew what he was doing, his rump came around about three feet from Joe Cummins, he kicked out, catching him right in the face. Blood and snot flew all over the place. He was down like a pole axed steer.

A bullet bounced off of my saddle horn. I dropped from the saddle, my gun in my hand. Mary Jane and Faith were both down on their knees firing. Six of those thugs were firing at us, I guess their leader going down in blood and gore unnerved them, because they were missing a lot.

But not for long, because they were falling like fall leaves in a blizzard. I only got one of the six. Old Man Dithers hands were standing there with their hands in the air, we ignored them. Delbert was couched down on the ground with his arms over his head. He was screaming "don't kill me, don't kill me, I'll tell you everything."

I walked over to Delbert, I clubbed him over the head, I sure hated the sound of his voice. Next I went over to Joe Cummins. I knelt and felt his neck for a pulse, there was none. I checked him over, no bullet holes, well chalk up one for Brutus.

Faith and Mary Jane were checking the other six, they looked at me and shook their heads. "They all dead?" I asked. They just nodded, reloading their clips. I looked at the Cowboys. There were eight of them. I said, "You guys Okay with this?"

One of the cowboys was an old fellow that I knew from when I was just a little shaver, we called him Yankton, cause he was a Sioux from the Yankton reservation in South Dakota.

He came over, "Well Clay, it took you long enough. I sent up a prayer weeks ago."

"I'm sorry Grandfather, for being so slow. I haven't completely recovered from the coma I was in for six months. I will do better next time." He wasn't my Grandfather, calling an elder Indian Grandfather was a sign of respect.

"Is Old Man Dithers alright? Red said that they bought him out, is that right and that he left the country?"

"He is locked in the basement. The land never changed hands. I think they just wanted to lure you in, so they could kill you, they hate you real bad." Yankton said.

"Why do they hate you so much?" He added.

"I don't know Grandfather, perhaps it's not me, perhaps it's the Great Spirit that they hate so much."

"How did you train your horse to do that?" Yankton asked.

"I didn't Grandfather, Brutus has a mind of his own, I think the Great Spirit sent him to me. Just as he did my wife Faith and her cousin Mary Jane." They both came over and held out there hands to shake, instead Yankton hugged them both. The rest of the hands hadn't moved, I think they were still in shock.

I got in my saddle bag and got my cell phone, I called Harry Silver, yet again. "How many? He yelled. "Take it easy Harry, they started it, I have Delbert Washington, he's still alive, he said he would tell us everything, that is when he wakes up." I said.

I turned back to Yankton, "Why don't you send in one of your hands to free Old Man Dithers, he must be getting right down tired of that basement." I said. I could hear Harry's helicopter coming by the time I heard Old Man Dithers coming, they both got there at the same time.

Dithers came up to me, "Clay thank you so much, I thought they were going to kill me. Yankton thinks that God sent you."

"As to that, we're all just tools of his aren't we?" I said.

Then Harry started in, I just walked away, saying back over my shoulder, "talk to all of them, they seen it. Delbert's waking up, put the screws to him."

"You just wait a minute young man, I want to talk to you." He said running after me. I stopped, "Okay, okay, what do you want?"

"What do you know about the disappearance of Pete Frank?"

"What the hell do you mean? You're the one who has him in custody." I said.

"Not anymore, he was supposed to be picked up by Homeland Security this morning, we went to his cell to get him and he was gone, with the cell door still locked. How did you do it?"

"Really Harry, how in the hell could I do that. There must have been someone on the inside who helped him escape."

"No, no one was there. The camera was trained on him all of the while, one second he was there the next he was gone." Harry said.

"Well maybe you're like Yankton over there, he thinks the Great Spirit sent me, maybe God took him." I said. Harry went away cussing, then he turned back, "Here," he said, "is your badge and I.D. You're now a special agent of the FBI, why in God's name they made you one is beyond me." He said, stomping away.

Mary Jane and Faith had been right there all of the time we were talking, Mary Jane was smiling, I said, "I suppose that was your Great Grandfather's work, right? Freeing Pete?"

"You got that right, don't ask me how he does it, I don't know." Mary Jane said.

Faith said, "So now you're not only an agent for New Mexico, but now the FBI? What do they want you to do?"

"I haven't the slightest idea, nothing I hope. I sure don't

know what's going on."

"All I know is, that it has been one wild roller coaster ride since I met you. And I like it." She said, jumping up and putting both of her legs around me, kissing me like there was no tomorrow. Well maybe there wasn't.

Mary Jane said, "You two aren't going to do it right here, are you?" Faith let loose, "No, but I sure could, have you ever felt like that?" she asked Mary Jane.

"Yeah, at times, with my husband. I sure miss him." Mary Jane said.

We walked back over by Harry Silver, he had calmed down. "Well, what did Delbert tell you?" I asked.

"It's that damn Dipper Tick again. But Delbert said that the orders came from someone higher up, he doesn't know who. But he wants protection, he's say's he will give us all the details. All I know is that the body count is getting way too high."

"It's not my fault, if they keep trying to kill me, maybe I should just let them do it, how would you like that?" I said.

"Don't tempt me, cause I just might do it myself." Harry said.

We mounted up and rode off. Mary Jane said, "Isn't it strange that they keep giving you these badges and stuff and don't want you to do anything?"

Faith said, "Yes, I find it more than strange, weird even. And I don't like it, it's like they are setting you up for a fall."

I looked at my wife, she just could be right. But I was slowly preparing for it. The fall, not them precipitating it. Who knows what Satan has in mind.

Chapter Fourteen

"Clay, Clay, wake up! Shit, he's winked out again," I heard Faith saying, as through a fog. Mary Jane said, "How often does he do this?"

"It's been over a month since the last one. And that one only lasted for a few minutes. He's been quite for at least fifteen minutes, I thought he was reading, then I looked over and he was just staring straight ahead.

"Does he often read in bed?" Mary Jane said.

"Yes, of course, when we aren't doing something else." Faith said.

I could see them, like through a mist, tho. Then their images started to clear up. "Mary Jane, are you naked again?" I asked, although I could see that she was.

Faith said, "Well where were you this time?" I looked at her, she was dressed just like Mary Jane, "How come your outfit is prettier than Mary Jane's?" I said.

"It is not," Mary Jane said, "we've both had the same number of children, I defy you to find any differences in our bodies."

"I'm sorry Mary Jane, you're right, but you see Faith is my wife, as such, she could be an ugly old witch, and she would still be prettier to me, than you." Faith hit me over the head with the book that she had been reading.

"Hit him again for me." Mary Jane said. "But he is right, and that is how it should be. I hope my future husband is as nice as this lazy lout is." Mary Jane said, then added, "Scoot over, I want to hear where he has been." Then she got in bed beside Faith.

They both looked at me like I was going to reveal all of the secrets of the universe.

"It's not where, but more of a time. I seen more of the way things will be in the so called time of the end. It was not pretty. What I don't understand is why they keep doing this to me?"

"It must have something to do with that hole in your head, it must give them easy access to your pea sized brain." Mary Jane said.

"Mary Jane, if that's all you can do, is make fun of my husband, you can just wiggle that tail out of here." Faith said, with a giggle.

"Seriously Honey, we don't know why, but there must be a reason. So do you have any details?"

"I don't know if I should share them with you, are you sure you want to hear a few?" I said, as I got up and padded to the bathroom. As I was standing there turning the water yellow, Mary Jane said, "Do you need any help?"

"No he doesn't, besides that job belongs to me." Faith said, as she got out of bed and came in. "Put something on, a towel even. You know she hasn't had any sex since her husband died." Then she handed me a bath towel.

"What about you two running around naked?" I asked as I wrapped the towel around me.

"Oh, that's alright, I keep you satisfied, that's right, isn't it?" She said with a tone that I had better agree with. "Yes, dear it is." I said. We went back in.

"Alright I'll tell you a little bit. It has to do with the economy. At least it starts out that way. You remember reading about the crash of 29, don't you?" They nodded, I went on. "Well that was nothing, a little blip compared to what's going to happen, world wide.

First the stock market completely falls apart. Can you imagine what would happen if it did? I see by the expression on your faces, that you do.

You know, I think that's all I'm going to tell you, it's enough, and believe me anything that you can imagine will be tame to what really happens. So just read between the furrows in your brain and multiply that by the freckles on your butts and you'll be pretty close."

"But you really didn't tell us anything." Mary Jane said.

"Yes I did. Even though the freckles on your derriere have nothing to do with it, I just thought they were cute. You see, if the world's economy tanks, everything breaks down, everything. I don't like to think about it, but now you two can be just as miserable as I am. That's why I don't like to talk about it."

"By the way, is it morning or night?" I asked.

"It's night Honey, are you tired?"

"Yeah, I think I am." I looked at Mary Jane, "Is she going to stay here or what? If she does, she sleeps on the other side of you." I said, as I turned out the lamp beside my side of the bed.

"May I," Mary Jane said, "thinking about what he said, makes me depressed."

"Sure," Faith said. I said, "I told you that you didn't want to hear it."

When I woke up the next morning, I was in bed alone. I looked at the bedside clock, it was six in the morning. I got up and got dressed, going downstairs, I could hear everyone already eating breakfast.

"Good Morning, sleepyhead," My beautiful wife said. "We saved some food for you." I filled my plate, for some reason they always saved the place at the head of the table for me.

Hank was setting beside me. "Hank, how are you coming with the horses and mules?" I know I asked him that before, but I had more of a pressing reason. "Why don't I come out after breakfast and we'll talk some more?" He nodded.

Hank was already leaning on the corral rails, waiting for me. Dog was setting beside him. Hank and the Dog had become buddies. We were all watching the mules eat.

"Do you see how there is a pecking order? Some of them are what you'd call Dominant?

"Yes, of course, everyone knows that?" Hank said.

"Yes, but the order of animals in a pack string will either make for a harmonious trip or a feuding pack. I know you've been with these guys for awhile, so you know each one of their so called, social status, don't you?" He nodded again, not quite sure where I was going with this.

"Okay, there are four things I want to talk about, #1. Dominant animals. #2. Herd mates. #3. Caboose, or the rear of the string. #4. Horse among Mules.

"Why are you telling me this? Hank said.

"Did you notice any other men at the breakfast table, but you and me? No, you didn't. Look Hank, there may be times that I won't be around, you'll have to take the lead in the family, especially if we're out in the wilderness."

"Uh, sure, Uncle Clay." He said, not quite understanding, but he would.

"Okay, Dominant, animals in the top of the pecking order won't tolerate being placed behind a socially inferior animal. Instead, you place the Dominant horse or mule in front. Then there comes Herd mates, you pair them together in a string, but make sure you put the dominant herd mate in front of the other one. Next, the rear, or caboose you could say. If you have one that is a kicker and he can't be broke, he goes last, then you also tie a red ribbon on his tail, that will tell everyone that he is a kicker. Now lastly, mules have a naturally tendency to follow a horse, keep a veteran pack horse in the string and locate him wherever a calming effect is needed.

And also, always send out a lead rider to clear the trail for hazards, and if that can't be done, the lead packer must be attentive and recognize hazards from his saddle."

"Alright Uncle Clay, you sound pretty serious, what's going on?"

"Oh, in the world today, it pays to be prepared, remember that, think ahead Hank, you may not get a second chance." I said, as I left him to his charges.

As I walked back toward the house, my mind swirled around the things I had seen. Could they have been hallucinations? No, no way, they were real. What worried me was all of the death and destruction, what about my loved ones. What did we have to do to be prepared. They say to be forewarned is to be forearmed. But what I had seen, how could you be prepared for that?

The destruction of Jerusalem in 70 AD came to mind. All of them didn't have to die, cause the Roman army pulled back for awhile. Jesus warned them that they had a window to escape, but most of them didn't listen, only the devout Christians did. But this was the whole world, where can everyone escape to?

I shook my head to dislodge the disquieting thoughts. They say worry is nothing but a circle of inefficient thoughts whirling around a point of fear. If you are unable to remove the point of fear, the next best thing is get your thoughts in order, do something, quit pissing into the wind, be like the cattle turn your butt to the wind and drift with it.

I dropped by Red and Daisy's house. They were just finishing breakfast. They invited me to set down and have some coffee with them. I did. "Daisy, you're my Mother's cousin, as such I feel I have to warn you both about what is going to happen."

"What do you mean?"

"As you both have heard I have been having 'visions', no there not hallucinations. The world is in store for a fall, that they will not be able to recover from. The only thing I can think to do about it, is return to our old ways. The ways of our forefathers. I have already started to make some changes. You both think about it. And oh yes, can you find a milk cow or two? Hope wants a milk cow." I drained my coffee cup and got up to leave. They were both staring at me. I touched my hat brim and left.

Shit, now they really thought I was crazy, but I had to warn them. What else?

What else indeed. Life must go on, must'en it? He really wouldn't wipe out all life would he? Naw, in the flood, eight people lived through that. A small voice from somewhere said, 'no stupid', just those that don't listen'. Listen, listen to who?

"Clay, where are you going, get back here, what were you doing walking off toward the mountains?" Faith's voice brought me back to earth.

"I'm sorry, I was just thinking. I told Red and Daisy about how the world's due to flush itself down the John, they looked at me like I was crazy. You don't think I'm crazy do you?"

"No honey, I don't think you are, but I can see how others might. I don't think you should go around telling people." Faith said, taking my hand and tugging me toward the house.

"But, if I didn't tell people, would I be responsible if they got killed?"

"I don't know, you're not your brother's keeper, are you?"

"That's what Cain said, after he killed Abel, we just might be, you know." I said.

"Okay, I'll give you that, people should be warned, but why don't we start with our loved ones in New Mexico. Rosie said that she needs to go down there and correlate details. Tiff will stay here and keep things running. Have you checked the plane lately?"

"No, but what about Mary Jane and Iris?" I said.

"Wolf Hunter called her this morning, he's sending a helicopter for them."

"Really? Well, that's only logical, if Pete Frank is up there, I get it. When are they leaving?"

"It's supposed to be here in about a half hour."

"How can that be, if he just called, it would take longer than that for one to get here." I said.

"I don't know sweetheart, but I hear they have all kinds of stuff that the governments of the world would like to get a hold of. Perhaps it's some kind of new one or something."

We went in the house, Alita and Iris were setting on the couch talking. Alita didn't want Iris to go. Faith went up to help Mary Jane with her packing. I sat down by the girls. Alita crawled into my lap and hugged me. "It'll be Okay," I said, "we have to go down to see Grandma and Grandpa anyway, that way Iris won't be lonely. Iris, did you say goodbye to Luke, you had better explain things to him." Iris got off of the couch and went out the back kitchen door.

Rosie came in, followed by Faith. "You don't have to check the plane. Rosie has been doing that." Faith said.

"Yes Dad. It's fully functional." Rosie said.

"How do you know?" I asked.

"Well, I haven't told you this, but while you were in that six month coma, I have been taking the plane out and practicing my take off's and landings. I was taking navigation and flying lessons from the internet. Are you mad?"

"No, I'm not mad, relieved I guess, to have another pilot in the family. But I take it, that you don't have a license?"

"No, I haven't got around to taking their test yet. Should I be worried?" Rosie said, with a lopsided grin.

"No, not really. I don't think it will be too long and there won't be any need for one." I said.

"What do *you* mean?" Rosie asked.

"Well, what will you need a license for when the governments no longer exist?" I said.

"I get your point, but till then, I suppose I had better get one. Since we really don't know how long this system of things will last." Rosie said.

Faith changed the subject, I think all of the talk about things going down the toilet makes her uncomfortable. "Suong will be staying here with Hope and the children while we are gone. She's getting tired of living out there at the rigs. She's finally got them more safety conscious, they aren't hurting themselves so much."

"Good, I'm afraid I haven't been paying too much attention to everything like I should. In fact I haven't seen Poppy very much, what has she been doing?"

"She's been keeping herself busy helping Hank with the horses and mules, she's rather good at it. You know how much young girls love horses." Faith said.

"Good, that talent will come in handy in the near future." I said.

"There you go again, you're always looking on the dark side of things." Faith said.

"I'm sorry Honey, Suong isn't thinking about leaving us, is she?"

"No, of course not, she likes it out here. And besides, we are paying her rather handsomely. But I don't think it's the money, the reason she wants to stay. She sort of talks like you, she thinks something is going to happen, also." Faith said.

"Well, it's not hard to see the hand writing on the wall. Shoot, there I go again. I guess I should write a song, 'there you go again', or has it already been done?"

"I don't know, that phrase does sound familiar." Rosie said.

"So," I said, "how soon are we to leave for New Mexico?" Knowing it wasn't up to me to decide. Since it was Rosie who wanted to conduct some business down there. I just wanted to see everybody, so did Faith.

"How about the day after tomorrow, I want to have some fresh fuel delivered for the plane. Boy, aviation fuel is sure expensive now, it's up to ten dollars a gallon. Those clowns in the present administration sure have a lot to answer for. History is going to paint them black, that's for sure." Rosie said.

"What about getting fuel from our own company?" I said.

"Dad, you really haven't been paying much attention, our refineries aren't on line yet. When they do come on line, it's going to shake up prices good, I mean we'll sell for a lot less than the oil company's do." Rosie said.

I sat there thinking about what Rosie just said. I looked at Faith, I think she was reading my mind. "Rosie, have you beefed up security at the refinery sights, as well as our wells?"

"No, not all that much, we do have security guards and all, but just the usual. Why do you think they'll try to blow things up?

"Yes, of course, do you think they'll take the loss of their billon dollar profits without a fight? I think you ought to call down to New Mexico and put them on alert and then hire more guards up here." I said.

Just then Mary Jane and Iris came down all packed, "I just got a phone call from the helicopter, they'll be here in three minutes." Mary Jane said.

"Wow! I wish I had a plane that would fly that fast." I said.

We all got up, I took a couple of their suit cases, I was going to miss them both, even with Mary Jane running around without any clothes on. We went out in the yard, by the time we got there, a big copter was settling down. Now when I said big, I wasn't kidding. It was about the size of an old DC-3. It had copter blades on top, but they weren't going around. Something else was powering this beast.

It settled down on its wheels, but then they sucked back up inside of it, and it settled on its belly. A door slide open with a whoosh, and a walkup ramp slid out. No one came out. A voice said, "I'm Elizabeth, Oh, there you are Mary Jane, and I see Iris with you. Are you ready to embark?"

I said, "Who are you? Where are you at? Can't you come out, or do you need to stay at the controls?"

"Oh, I'm sorry, I'm being impolite." A holographic image appeared standing in the door way. "I'm afraid that's the best I can do. You see that is just the image of what I would like myself to look like, you see *I am* the machine that you are looking at."

We all looked at each other, "Why isn't the image wearing clothes?" Faith asked.

"Again, I'm sorry, have I offended you? You see where I was created, humans do not wear clothes, do you want me to put some on?"

"No, no need, we're rather liberal around here anyway. Are all of the women where you come from that pretty?" Mary Jane asked.

"Well yes, as a matter of fact, they are. But I'm afraid that I don't have the time or the permission to explain everything to you, perhaps next time we meet, would that be alright?" Elizabeth said. The holograph held out her hand to Mary Jane and Iris. They went ahead with us following with the luggage. The inside was luxurious, with chairs and couch's and tables. Of course I didn't have time to look at everything.

Elizabeth showed them where to store their stuff. I had a chance to look at the image. She was standing right next to me.

I reached out a hand and touched her, she turned to look at me. I touched her again. "You feel like a real human, not an image?" I said.

"Yes, it is rather nice, isn't it. But it's only inside here that it is that way, if I step outside, it goes back to a regular holograph."

"I get it, nothing like this was made on this planet, you come from another planet, don't you?"

"Well, yes and no, but that can wait till later, we have to get underway." She took us by the hand and escorted us out. Her hand even felt warm. But not before we gave Iris and Mary Jane a good bye kiss.

Just before I went down the gangway, I said, "Do you mind if I give them a feel?" Pointing to her breasts. I wasn't trying to be a letch, but I just wanted to see if they felt real also. She smiled at me and indicated to go ahead. Yep, they were sure enough real.

As we were standing in the yard, Faith said, "Well, were they real?"

I said, "I don't know, let me feel yours." She kicked me in the shins.

The gangway slid back in and the hatch closed with the aforementioned whoosh. There was no noise and the blades didn't turn, it just lifted straight up and then it started to cloak itself and disappeared. The blades must have just been for looks.

Rosie said, "Dad, sometimes I just don't know about you, asking to feel her boobs."

Faith said, "Well from now on, just stick to the real things, mine for instance." Then she kicked me again. It was a good thing I was wearing cowboy boots.

Alita leaned over to her mother's ear and said, "What are boobs?" "Never you mind Dear, you'll find out soon enough."

Faith said.

Then Alita said, "Are they what Daddy was feeling on Elizabeth?"

"Now see what you started?" Faith said to me, as she kicked me once again.

I couldn't believe how feeling an holographic image could get me in so much trouble. "For goodness sake, she wasn't real people, get a life." I said. Don't you hate it when your teenagers tell you to 'get a life', I know I sure do.

"That's Okay," Rosie said, "I shouldn't have said anything, I was really wondering myself. Anyway, I had better make that call to Grandpa and Grandma. Then where would you suggest that we hire more guards?" Rosie said looking at both of us.

"I guess, we could check with the National Guard, or such. Maybe some of their returning Vets would like a job?" I said.

"Good, then I'm giving you that job." Rosie said to me. "Who and where do I tell them to report to?" I said.

"Give them my cell phone number, I'll take care of it." Rosie said. I looked at Faith, "Do you suppose that Hope could watch Alita, then you and I could go into town and see what we can round up, then perhaps we could eat out and have a few cocktails?"

"Sure, it would be nice to have a night out, sort of a date night, right?" Faith said.

When we left after lunch we were wearing our regular ranch clothes, but we had changed to clean and pressed jeans and shirts. We had been having cool weather, so we both had our overall jackets on, and of course our weapons. We never went anywhere without them. But we did pack an overnight bag, Faith had put a dress in there. One never knew, we might want to go dancing.

I don't know whether I had told you or not, but where that bullet had grazed my skull, the hair that grew back was white and it looked like a lightning bolt. Faith said that it gave me a rather sinister look. I just thought it looked silly.

When we got to town, we went by the recruiting office. Faith stayed in the pickup, I went in, there was a female staff sergeant setting at the desk. She looked at me, "Want to sign up?" She said.

"Nope, I've did my time. I was looking to hire some security guards. I thought maybe you might know of some Vets that needed a job?" She got up and sat on the corner of her desk, looking at me. "Well now, I just might," then she said, "are you married?" I guess there's nothing like being direct.

"Yep, sure am, my wife is waiting in the truck, so?" I said.

"Damn, all of the good looking ones are. But as to the help you want. Their having a drill at the Armory this afternoon. Some of those week end warriors might need some extra money." She said as she stood up right on top of me. I thanked her and got out of there, if I had of stayed longer, I'm afraid she would have thrown me down on her desk and had at it.

I got back in the truck and said, "Whew, that was one horny woman in there, next time you're going wherever I go, Okay?"

"What's the matter, can't my big brave boy defend himself?" Faith said, mockingly.

"Not from her, I should of known that she was in heat, I was lucky to escape with my pants on."

"Alright, next time I'll go in with you." Faith said, scooting closer to me.

We went over a few blocks to the Armory. We went in together. This time there was a male at the front desk. I didn't mind him giving my wife the once over, after all she was a knockout. I explained what we wanted. He said, "Give me your phone number, I'll post this up on the bulletin board. I'm sure you'll be getting some calls. I know a lot of them are out of work right now."

So that task being taken care of, we went to the fanciest Hotel in town. It was a brand new one, with eighteen floors, with a restaurant and dancing on the top floor. You could eat, get drunk and dance till you dropped and your room was within crawling distance. Mighty convenient. Oh yeah, it also had a Casino, which we didn't pander to, since I hated gambling.

We made reservations at the restaurant at the same time we checked in. The room was nice, with one of those tubs that had air jets. It was a while before it was time to go eat, so we laid on the bed and turned the idiot box on. They had cable of some kind. The previous room occupant's had left the TV on a racy channel. We were some surprised by all of the moaning and groining going on. We hurried and changed the channel. Not that we were against sex, which we weren't, we just didn't need to watch other people doing it. We stopped on the Disney channel.

We watched a movie, then it was time to change for dinner. Not me, but Faith, she had brought a nice little black dress. That was just long enough to cover the stilettos that she had strapped to her thigh. Plus of course, that Bra that held two of them. Shoot, you couldn't even get to second base with all of that steel she had on. I mentioned as much, she said that was just the way she wanted it.

We were seated at a window that overlooked the whole town, what there was of it. I hadn't notice it before, but it was Saturday night. The place was filling up fast, I guess it was a good thing we had made that reservation. Isn't it strange, I had to ask my wife what day of the week it was. I didn't even know what day of the calendar it was.

A waiter with a fake French accent appeared at my elbow. He asked what we would like to drink, I had him bring us a bottle of wine. I wasn't in to it much, but Faith liked wine. He had rattled off some fancy French name for the wine, I told him sure to bring what was the best. Turned out the best went for two hundred dollars a bottle, but what the hell. We didn't go out that much. He poured a splash in the bottom of my glass. I wasn't a complete red neck, I knew what I was supposed to do, so I done it. Then he poured our glasses to the proper level.

After we ordered Steak and Lobster, he went on his way and we could look around us. Every table was full. Some of the men were dressed like me, local ranchers. But some had some pretty expensive suits on. Them I marked in my mind.

Seated at the next table was two such, with two women dressed somewhat like my wife. Those two guys, I knew the type right away. I looked over at my wife, she had seen them also. She nodded.

Now if you will remember, I am from this neck of the woods. Those two women, I knew them. From my single days, they were hookers, nice girls, but hookers never the less, I had went to high school with them. They were trying to be unobtrusive, but I could tell they knew I had seen them.

I leaned over and gave my wife a peck on the cheek, whispering to her, she looked at them, then nodded to me. The girls at the next table got up to go to the bathroom. Faith got up and followed them.

The two men were in close conversation, they'd glance at me when they thought I wasn't looking. I could tell by the small bulges in their suit jackets that they were packing. Now in Wyoming it was legal to pack, but not if you concealed it. Of course I had a permit for my gun, being that I was now an FBI agent.

In Wyoming prostitution was illegal, the johns could be arrested as well as the girls. Faith came back, the two girls came back a few seconds later. The music started up, Faith and I got up and danced.

Faith said, as she laid her head on my shoulder. "They just picked the girls up an hour or so ago. The girls work for an escort service. It was supposed to be a no sex call. But when they got to their room, the first thing they did was throw them on the bed and rape them. So I guess you could arrest them for rape. By the way, they say they know you."

"Yes, I went to High School with them, they were nice girls at that time. Well I guess they still are. No body deserves to be raped. What else did they have to say?"

"Well their scared for their lives, those guys said that they would kill them unless they did everything they told them to."

We twirled around the dance floor a couple of times, I made eye contact with the girls, and nodded to them. I could see the relief in their eyes. I whispered into Faiths ear, "Those girls are as good as dead unless we help them, there is no way they are going to let them loose to yell rape. Plus of course, I know they are here to kill us. And if they killed us, they would surely kill those girls."

"How do you know they are here to kill us?" Faith said.

"I just do, don't ask me how. There is this little voice, yes literally, telling me so."

"Sometimes, you're down right spooky, you know that?" Faith said, as the music came to an end. We went back to our table. The food hadn't come yet.

One of the guys had Angelina by the arm and was twisting it. The other girls name was Patty, if I remembered right. Faith looked directly at the man and he dropped her arm. Faith's eyes were blazing with fury. I laid my hand on her arm, "Take it easy honey, we can't kill them here, unless they try and kill us first."

"Like so much I can't, if he does that again, I'm going to." Faith said.

I got up and went over to their table, "Well as I live and

breath," I said, "Patty and Angelina, I haven't seen you two since high school, I told my wife I went to school with you two, she wants to meet you, go over and say hello."

The two goons eyes were wary, the girls got up and went over to my table. I sat down in one of their chairs. "Well boys, your ride is about over, your ticket's have been punched. All that remains, is how you want to go out." I said, with a big smile on my face. When I had sat down, I palmed my pistol, it was pointed at them.

"I guess you know, you're ruining my night out with my wife. This is such a nice carpet on this floor, I sure hate to ruin it with your blood. Say boys, who's paying you anyway?" I gave them another toothy grin.

One of them said, "I guess you can't count, there's two of us and only one of you."

"I guess your math is just as fuzzy as the president's is," I said, "you see I have a .44 Mag pointed at your guts right now. And if I miss, my Wife will have cold steel sticking out of your necks in under a second." With that I flicked open my jacket a bit so they could see my FBI badge. They seen it, and they got a little more white around the gills. I continued on, "so you see boys, you're dead meat either way, you might just as well spill your guts, that is before I spill them."

"Will you let us go if we tell you?" The goon on my left asked.

"Well now, I didn't say that, but what I will do is not kill you, how's that?"

"You're an FBI agent, you wouldn't kill us anyway."

I gave them a low sinister laugh, "Boy's, you don't understand who you are dealing with. You see I'm also a New Mexico State Ranger, them and the FBI hired me because I'm an assassin. I don't have to take any prisoners. Now shall we try this again, who paid you to kill us?"

They looked at each other, licked their lips and then one of them said, "We don't know for sure, but the guy was named Jeff Strong, he's a Porno actor for Fantasizes Inc. out of LA. That's all we know, really?"

"How much did they pay you?"

"Twenty Thousand down and another twenty when it's done."

"Well at least I'm not cheap. Okay, put your guns on the table and empty your pockets. Everything on the table." Guns, extra clips, brass knuckles, strangulation wire, small bag of crack, switch blade knives. Billfolds, crammed with money. One thing that was missing, no rubbers. I looked at them, "you didn't use any protection when you raped those girls?" They turned a little more pale.

"Shit, I should kill you right now. But I'm not going to. Just leave everything on the table and get out of here."

"You're not going to give us any money?"

"Nope, I'm giving it all to Angelina and Patty. You're fortunate you're getting away with your lives, now get out of here before I change my mind." They got.

I took a large cloth napkin and put all of their stuff in it and tied it like a Hobo's bundle. I went to our table and sat the bundle under my chair. The waiter came over, "Have the gentlemen left?" He said.

"Yep, they sure did, just bring their food to our table, we'll pay for it." He gave me a snide look and started to say something, I flicked back the edge of my coat. He slammed his jaw closed.

He not only seen my badge, but also my gun. Faith said, "You let them go again, how many times are you going to let the Rattle Snakes get away?"

"I didn't want my food to get cold, I'm hungry, aren't you?" I said, smiling at the girls. "After we eat, you girls have an appointment with the emergency room, I want them to run a rape kit on both of you, take a few tests for STD's and the like, okay?"

We not only had the orders that Faith and I ordered, but also all four of the other table, we split the food the two goons ordered between the four of us. People were looking at us, I smiled at them and gave them the thumbs up, they looked away. After we ate, the two girls got up to go to the bathroom, they stood there waiting for Faith. Faith bent down and said, "Why did you let them get away?"

"They didn't get away, their going to try and kill us when we leave the Hotel tonight." I said. Faith asked: "How do you know that?"

"I told you about my little voice, don't you remember. One of them had an extra key hid in his shoe, it's to their car, they have more guns and money in there. Really I didn't want to get blood all over this white carpet. The management would never forgive me."

"Oh you, you make no sense at all." Faith said, then followed the girls to the bathroom. I paid our bill and left the waiter a hundred dollar tip, when he seen it, he smiled, for the first time. I really didn't like male waiters. I guess I was a sexist about some things, I just didn't like men waiting on me.

I picked up the bundle from under my chair and met the women when they came out of the bathroom. We went to our room. I undid the bindle stiff, and counted out the money, there was eighteen thousand dollars altogether. I laid it on the bed, and checked over one of the pistols. I put it in my jacket pocket. It held fifteen shots, that should be enough. Faith was watching me. I looked at her, "are you ready?" I asked.

"No, I want to change clothes, it'll just take a second. She pulled off her dress over her head, she was standing there in her Bra and Thong panties. I lost my train of thought. She quickly undid her knives and slipped on her jeans and shirt and overall jacket. She put her stiletto's in her jacket pocket, the other jacket pocket held her .32 Mag. The two girls were standing there watching us. Patty asked, "What are you people?" I answered, "Survivalists."

Chapter Fifteen

We took the down elevator to the side door of the Hotel; we stopped just inside of the door. "Clay, Clay, wake up, you're doing it again." I heard Faith calling me. "I'm Okay, they're out there." I said, as I got one gun out of my pocket and my .44 out of my holster. "You all just stay inside, I'll take care of this; I know just where they are. No, Faith it's Okay, I'll take care of it, it's my responsibility." I said, "You just hold this door, it opens to the inside."

Faith held it open for me, I did a roll and tuck, it was a good thing, because they must have had an Uzi or something, cause there sure were a lot bullet's coming my way. I had a pistol in each hand. On my left about 30 feet away stood one of them and on my right at the same distance was the other one. They were still firing, I put one through the right eye of the guy on my left and one through the left eye of the guy on my right. They fell over like cord wood.

It was quite, abnormally so; till we heard the sound of a siren coming our way. I turned to Faith, "take the truck and take the girls to the hospital, will you. I'll be there in a few minutes. Don't worry, it'll be alright."

A city police cruiser pulled up, an officer jumped out. "What's going on here?"

I indicated the two dead men, "They tried to kill me, they missed, I didn't."

"Alright, give me your guns." He said. I looked down, I still had them in my hands. The officer had pulled his. "Drop the guns and get your hands up." He yelled. He was getting excited. "Calm down man," I said. "I'm an FBI agent, just take it easy."

"I don't care who you say you are, drop your guns or I'm going to shoot." He yelled frantically. Shit, I tilted my right hand gun and shot his pistol out of his hand.

I walked over to him, he was holding his wrist, "You're okay, the numbness will go away pretty soon," I said as I showed him my badge and I.D.

"How long have you been on the force?" I asked him.

"Two months," he said, looking at me with fear.

"And they let you on the street by yourself. You almost got yourself killed tonight. You lost your cool, that could cost you your life next time," I said. Another cop car pulled up. I told them the story and left them to clean up the mess.

But how was I going to get to the Hospital? I tapped the cop that I had shot the gun out of his hand, on the shoulder. "I'm taking your cruiser, you can pick it up at the Hospital." He nodded his head. I started to turn away, then turned back, "You had better not tell them that I stole your car." "No, no, you can take it, it'll be all right." He said backing up.

When I got to the Hospital, Faith was waiting for me. "They are both in there, getting examined now. We can wait over here, do you want a cup of coffee?"

About twenty minute's later a Doctor came out. "We took both rape kits, we found enough fluid to get good DNA out of them. We took samples to test for STD's also. They are getting dressed now. So you can take them home." He had no more than left, than guess who showed up, that's right, Harry Silver.

"Well it didn't take you long to get here." I said.

"The second I heard, I knew it was you. Nobody else can shoot their eyes out at 50 feet. So who were they?"

"I didn't take time to get their names, but their I.D's are in our room. They raped two girls, earlier tonight. Who are you going to have do the autopsies?"

"I suppose the local M.E. can handle it. Then we'll have to send the DNA samples to either the State lab or our lab. As soon as I hear anything, I'll let you know." Harry said.

"Yeah, you can call me on my cell phone, we're going to New Mexico for awhile. Rosie has some business to wrap up down there." I said.

"So, you guys are building two new oil refineries huh?"

"Yeah, I guess so, maybe only one. Rosie is handling it."

"Well watch your backs, I have already heard rumblings from Washington. The present administration, they don't like the competition. I can't wait till November." Harry said, shaking his head as he walked away. Then he turned back around, "Oh yeah, if I was you I'd keep a close eye on those girls, they might want them dead too."

I looked at Faith, then said, "I guess we don't get to have sex on our date night."

"I think there is an adjoining room right next to ours, I noticed a locked door anyway. We'll stop at the desk when we get back and rent it too." Faith said. I leaned over and kissed her. Just then the girls came out.

"Where do you guys live?" Faith asked them. They said that they had a little house on the outskirts of town.

I said, "I suppose every low life in town knows where you live?"

"Clay, behave yourself, that was unkind." Faith said.

"The reason I asked was that the head FBI agent thinks they might still want to kill you. I don't really know why he thinks that, but it behooves us to take precautions." Faith said.

"Can we go by and get some clean clothes?" Angelina asked.

"No," I said, "they might be watching your house."

"Clay, I remember you from High School, why are you being so mean? You used to be so nice." Patty said.

"Pay no attention to him, he's just a little out of sorts. He thinks he isn't going to get any nooky tonight. Come on let's go back to the Hotel." I followed along behind them. I remembered them well. I remember that I asked Angelina out, but she was a *popular girl*, I was a nobody, just a breed kid. How the mighty have fallen. Angelina turned around and looked at me, a little tear ran down her cheek.

I got behind the wheel, still feeling out of sorts. You know how it is, when memories from High School come flooding back, especially if those memories weren't the greatest.

I started up and looked to the rear, when a bullet came ripping through my side rear view mirror. I jerked open the door and rolled out, both guns in my hand. I heard the squealing of tires coming toward me. I stood firmly in the street with my feet braced, firing both pistols. The windshield of the car was shattered in a million pieces. The guys behind the window, weren't in much better shape. Their car careened into a parked car right behind my truck. I stood there, reloading my guns. The wail of sirens started up again. I was sure getting tired of this.

The city police were coming to get the cruiser that I had borrowed. That was why they were there so fast. They got out of their car, "Well if it isn't the one man crime wave." One cop said. He made the mistake of saying that while he was within arm length of me. I knocked him cold. Faith got out and took me back into the Hospital. The next thing I knew was when I woke up back in my own bed at the ranch.

Faith was setting beside the bed, reading. I looked at her and said, "I didn't get any nooky, did I?"

She turned and jumped on the bed, "Oh, you're back. I was so worried. How do you feel?" She said, feeling my head.

"How long was I out this time?"

"Thirty days."

"I'm sorry. But I guess we can go to New Mexico when I get out of bed."

"No need. Rosie took the plane, the Hoeffer boys went with her, as body guards."

"But she doesn't have a license."

"Yeah, I know. But she went anyway. They're due back in three days. Rosie said the boys are doing okay. They make good body guards. They can shoot right on target, she taught them how to use a knife. They'll be alright."

"I didn't even know that she knew them, how did this all come about?"

"Everybody on the ranch knows everyone. Rosie told me that she had been noticing that they were doing a good job. That was why she picked them."

"Which one is she sweet on, Chip or Dale?"

"I don't think she is sweet on either one. But I think Tiff likes one of them, I don't know which one."

"What ever happened to Patty and Angelina?" I asked.

"They're living with Red and Daisy. We hired them on as ranch hands. They're doing pretty good. Not great, but they are trying."

"Are they causing any ruckus, like you know, sex wise with the male hands?"

"No silly. They don't do that anymore."

"Well that's a relief." I said, just as Suong came in the door.

"So, how's my patient doing today? Is that head wound healing alright?" She said, looking at Faith.

"I was just going to take the bandage off and look at it, when he woke up." Faith said, reaching for my head. I put my hand up there instead.

"When did I get this?" I asked my beautiful wife.

"Do you remember what happened when we came out of the Hospital? I see that you do. Anyway, the bullet hit your door jam and split up, part of it broke your outside rearview mirror. The other piece hit you on the left temple. Blood was streaming down your face, but you didn't seem to notice. I at first thought it was just a scratch. But it put another hole in your head, just like you needed more. Anyway it sort of match's the other side now. I think it's also going to turn your hair white; I hope it leaves a lighting bolt pattern, just like the one on your right, that'll be neat, won't it?"

Suong, came over and started to take the bandage off. She poked around a little bit, then said. "I think we can leave the bandage off now. Let it get some air, he's a quick healer." I have to go to the oil well and also the Refinery sight. You can get him up, if you want to. He should have a real bath, instead of those sponge baths."

"So, who's been bathing me this time?"

"Me, mostly. But Tiff and Hope have helped out."

"Oh? That makes me a little bit embarrassed." I said.

"Don't worry about it, they didn't. Yours isn't the only Tally Whacker they've every seen, you know."

"Okay, are you going to help me out of bed? I feel a little weak, laying here for thirty days."

Faith helped me sit up, then I swung my feet to the floor. Faith said, "Just set there awhile, I'm going to run you a hot bath." I was a little dizzy, not bad, it passed quickly. I called to Faith, "When did you take the I.V's out, I see the marks where they were?"

"Oh, we did that yesterday, Suong said that you would wake up today. She was right. Just a minute and I'll help you in, the baths almost ready." Faith came in, just as naked as I was. She said, "I thought I might as well take one with you, kill two birds with one stone, you might say."

It was a good thing our tub was a big one. It also had those water jets. I sat at one end, Faith got in and laid back up against me. The water was nice and hot, I dozed off.

"Hey, wake up, you've slept enough. It's time to get back in the swing of things." We did….

As we were getting dressed, I asked, "So who were those guys?"

"The same as the others. Harry Silver seemed to be glad that you were in another coma, he said, 'perhaps now I can get some rest.' isn't that funny?"

"No, it's not. He seems to think that this is all my fault. I still can't figure out why they want me dead so bad. What did I ever do to them?"

"I don't think it's you so much, I think it's what you represent."

"Well, what do I represent, I'm just trying to take care of my family, that's all. And perhaps do the right thing. I'm certainly not a do-gooder, that's for sure."

"You know, something else is different, you remember that old movie, 'the night of the walking dead, or something like that, how these zombie's came walking with one purpose? Well, Harry said that they seemed driven, like they have a one track mind, 'Kill Clay Bronson, Kill Clay Bronson. Do you think there is something else, besides a mundane reason, like money, that they are trying to kill you? Like maybe something supernatural?" Faith said.

"Oh Yeah, 'the Devil wants me dead.' I can't be that important, he wants us all dead, not just me."

"Well, you're important to me and the rest of the family. Say, that looks pretty neat, the way your hair has grown back over the bullet scars, they look like two lightning bolts. Hey! You could be a superhero, like from one of those comic books." Faith said, as she came over and taking my head in her hands, gave me a long kiss.

"Come on, let's go downstairs, the kids want to see you." Faith said, taking my arm as we went downstairs. Setting in the front room, was Tiff, Hank and Poppy, with Alita setting beside her. Alita hopped off the couch and ran toward me, I swooped her up in my arms, she fastened her arms around my neck and wouldn't let go. The rest of them grouped around me, hugging where they could.

Hope came in with a cup of coffee for me. "I saved some breakfast for the two of you, the kids have already ate."

Everyone trouped into the kitchen with us. Alita wouldn't let go of my neck, which I didn't mind it in the least. She sat on my lap as I ate. I fed her some of my hotcake. She liked it with plenty of butter and syrup. The rest of the children sat down and had some, although they had just eaten.

I looked at Tiff, she was a beauty, "So Tiff, how's the oil business going?"

"Good, they're right on schedule. The second well came in while you were sleeping. And we are starting a distillation process, since Diesel comes off lower on the tower, we are actually making some product. We haven't got the Cat Cracker on line yet. But things are looking up."

"Where are you selling the Diesel that you have?" I asked.

"We opened one of the closed stations in town. You know, the one that was a Casino, we took all of the machines out and turned it into a family restaurant. We have two Diesel pumps. We're selling it for a dollar a gallon. There is a line all of the time. The Big Oil stations are madder than a wet hen."

"Well have they brought their prices down any?" I asked.

"Some, but they say they can't. Which I suppose is true, since they get their supply from Big Oil Refinery's. They keep pressuring us to raise our prices. I am getting a little worried about what Big Oil might do. Do you think we should hire more security?"

"You do what ever you think is necessary. More guards might make them think twice, before they start a war with us." I said.

I turned my attention to Hank and Poppy next. "So guys, how are the training of the Horses and Mules coming?"

"Good, we don't have to do too much, they seem to be training us. But we need more saddles and pack saddles with panniers."

"Alright, you guys just buy what you need. I'll call an open an account with the Saddle Shop in town. Hope can drive you in anytime you want." I said.

I looked back at Tiff, "Say, has the EPA given you guys any trouble?"

"Some, they are there all of the time, if they want something done, we just do it. We follow all of their guide lines."

"I bet that pisses them off?" I said.

"At first it did, I think they were looking for an excuse to shut us down. But now I think they are pretty happy about how accommodating we are."

"What about down in New Mexico, how are things going down there?"

"I just talked to Rosie this morning, their right on track. Rosie said that she would be back in a couple of days."

We talked for awhile longer. Then everyone went about their chores. Alita went with Poppy, they were going to ride Matthew and Luke. Poppy had been riding Luke, since Iris wasn't here. They were both standing right outside the kitchen door. If you weren't careful to shut the door, Hope told me, those two mules would be right in the kitchen.

Seeing Luke, Iris's mule, made me think of Mary Jane and

Iris. As Faith and I were cleaning off the table, I asked, "Have you heard from Mary Jane?"

"Sure, we talk almost everyday. You wouldn't believe the layout they have up there. She couldn't tell me everything, top secret you know. But she did say that the Helicopter that picked them up; it can go into outer space, way out, not just forty of fifty miles. She said that Earth was sure pretty from the Moon."

"No? You're kidding, right?"

"Nope, Elizabeth took her up there, before they went to the Ranch. But she did say that they miss us. I told her that we missed them also. And oh yeah, she did say that they have been seeing a lot of Pete Frank. Mary Jane said that Pete had been through some kind of reconditioning."

"Reconditioning? What do you mean, physical?"

"No mental. Wolf told her that they went through his brain and removed any harmful tendencies."

"I don't think I like the sound of that. Smacks of brainwashing to me." I said.

"No, nothing like that, I asked her. She said that they just put his brain back in perfect working order."

"Perfect? How can that be, there hasn't been any brain that has been perfect since Adam and Eve, then they lost that for us."

"I don't know, that's just what she told me. But, I sort of like your Devilish little mind, especially in bed. I don't think it would be as much fun if you were perfect."

"Oh, you can never tell, it might be better." I said as I reached for her and gave her a kiss and squeeze. When we came up for air, I said, "Do you want to go for a ride, we can saddle Brutus and Nick up?"

"Sure, I haven't been riding either, been setting beside you mostly. But we had better get our weapons. We didn't put them on when we came downstairs. From now on, I think we had better put them on anytime we leave our room."

"Isn't it the pits, to have the forces of evil so pissed at you, that you have to go armed." I said.

"Isn't that pretty melodramatic, 'forces of evil'?" Faith said, as I walked behind her up the stairs.

"Huh? Oh yeah, I sort of got lost in your get-a-long there, I can't believe one woman can be as beautiful as you." I said.

"Well, you had better believe it, Buster, because I think it's ditto." Faith said as she pulled off her top and bra, to put her special bra on, the one with knives built in. "Fasten that for me, will you sweetheart?" She said. I did so with trembling hands....

On our way through the kitchen, Faith knocked together a little lunch for us, something easy that would fit in our saddlebags. Hope said, "When will you be back?"

"Should be before dark, can you watch Alita? Faith said.

"Sure, her Mule watch's her most of the time, I have to talk like a Dutch Uncle to get her off him. Don't worry, if you're a little bit late, her and Poppy can sleep in that bedroom by the kitchen anyway."

"We have our Satellite Cell phone, we'll call if we're going to be late, Okay?" I said.

"Yes, you two have a good time. Are you sure you're feeling up to a long ride?"

"Yeah, Suong must have put some hi powered stuff in my I.V.'s". I said."

While we were saddling up, Alita and Poppy came into the barn yard. "Where are you going Momma?"

"Daddy and I are going for a ride, why do you want to come?"

"Yes, can Poppy come too?"

"Do you want to go for a long ride Poppy?" I asked.

"Yes, but I would have to ask Mom, I'll run and ask her now, okay?"

"Perhaps you had better go with her Faith, should probably pack more food and water." I said. All three went back to the house. I went to the gun locker that was in the tack room and took out two Winchester Saddle Guns, .44 Mags. The same size as the revolver that I was carrying. I also tied a camp ax and shovel behind the Cantle on top of the bedroll's, one never knew.

I checked the saddle's on Luke and Matthew, rearranged them a little, then tied bedrolls behind their saddles also. Why was I doing this, when we were going to be home before dark? I didn't know, perhaps who ever was pulling my strings, maybe they knew.

The women came back with more food tied in a canvas bag. The children had changed to shirts and jeans with hats. They also brought jackets. At night in the mountains it gets cold. Now why did 'night in the mountains' come up in my mind?

I glanced over at Alita, she wasn't even bouncing in the saddle. Matthew sure had a smooth trot. We went by the oil rig, waved at them and kept on going. We came to a small spring, that I used to water my horse at when I was a kid. It was still cold and pure.

We had a bite to eat, just enough to keep hunger pangs away, made sure our canteens were full of the spring water. The animals cropped grass and then drank their fill from the spring. We didn't have to hobble them, they wouldn't go anywhere. Why? Because they were where they wanted to be, with us.

I didn't realize it, but we were making a bee line for one particular spot, that waterfall I told you about earlier. Faith pulled Nick up and said, "What's the hurry, Honey? Where are we going?"

I looked around at the hills and the towering mountains. "Uh, right up in that cut over there into those beautiful green hills, right close to the mountains." I said.

"Did you know that before I asked you?"

"No, I didn't."

"I thought as much, lead on McDuff." She said, as she gave Nick his head. I followed along in the rear, riding drag was my thing. Although I was in the rear, I could still see way ahead of everyone else.

We followed the stream back into the hills, till we came to a small valley with the waterfall at the other end. We rode up within 50 yards of the waterfall. Dismounted, loosened the cinches' and let the mounts graze. We walked around easing our legs and backs. After all it had been awhile since we rode.

Alita was over two years old now and she was in better shape than us old ones. If 28 was old. She walked over close to the falls, I went after her. And took her hand, "Daddy, there is a cave behind the falls."

"Huh? There is?" I said, as we walked closer. Why hadn't I noticed that before?

Maybe because, when I was here before, it was in the spring time, when the streams ran high. We got closer still. It was the last part of August and the stream flow was down. We had a dry summer, with little rain.

I picked Alita up, Faith was right behind me, with Poppy behind her. I walked into the waterfall. The cave, if it was a cave. Was about eight foot tall and about the same wide. Funny thing, there was no debris laying around. Then I felt a breeze, not from where we just walked under the falling water, but from the depths of the cave?

You would expect it to be dark; the further in we went. But it was as if the stone walls were giving off a soft reflected light.

The breeze smelled like spring time. You know when the dew is heavy on the grass and flowers in the early morn.

I heard the clip-clop of hoofs, I glanced back over my shoulder, our steeds were following us. I should of expected it, they wouldn't be left behind.

The light was getting brighter, we had went about fifty yards, I expect. I really wasn't counting. I hesitated, why? Maybe it was the unknown, or just my natural caution at a new experience. I got no feeling of dread, it wasn't that.

Alita leaned close to my ear, "It's Okay Daddy, there's nothing there to hurt us."

"Oh, and how do you know Missy?" I said, kissing her on the cheek. Faith and Poppy were hanging onto my coattails, so to speak. We all felt it, the feeling that our life was going to change, somehow.

We stepped out into a beautiful light, soft diffused light, but sunlight, never the less. There was a valley, ringed by the mountains. Running down the middle, toward us was a nice crystal clear stream, it disappeared into the ground a short distance away.

Where did the water come from that caused the waterfall that we just walked through? It couldn't be from this stream that ran back underground, it had to come from someplace higher. I bet this would be a geologist's dream.

The valley ran on for at least a mile, I would bet. We could see fruit trees, Apple, Pear, I don't know what all. The grass was belly high to a tall horse. A Doe and Fawn bounded away, they didn't go far, just stood there looking at us. We stared back. The Doe stomped her hoof, snorted and tossed her head. Alita said, "Daddy, I think she wants us to follow her."

There was a trail of sorts, we followed them as they started off at a slow walk, with both Doe and Fawn looking back to make sure we were following along. Bees were busy at the many flowers growing everywhere.

Setting beside the trail was a Coyote, chewing on a raw carrot, that he was holding in his paws. No, I'm not kidding. He was sitting on his haunch's holding this carrot, using his dew claws like thumbs.

We stopped, with jaws agape. "What are you looking at? Haven't you ever seen a Coyote before?" He said, at least that was what I heard, whether it was through my ears or was it just in my mind?

Alita clapped her hands in delight. Poppy was almost jumping up and down, giggling. "Daddy, can we keep him?"

"Keep me? Young Lady, I'll have you know that I'm not a pet. I'm a free individual the same as yourself." Alita squirmed to get down, I sat her on the ground. She walked over to him. "Would you like a bite of my carrot?" He said, holding it out to her, Alita took a bite and then handed it back to him. All before we could protest.

He was almost as tall as Alita, setting on his haunch's, Alita put her arm around his shoulders. "Oh Daddy, isn't he just wonderful?"

"I reckon he is, Honey." I said, then to the Coyote. "Well you've got us here, what's next?"

"What do you mean, I've got you here? You all came of your own freewill. But there is more that I would like to show you. If you will follow us." He got up and dropped in behind the deer.

We followed in a daze. I did look up at the sky. The sun was filtering through what looked like water vapor. So that was why I had never seen this place from the sky, when I had flown over. I know I've covered every inch of these mountains by plane.

Thinking back, I've often wondered why clouds always hung around this one spot.

As we walked, there was about every species known to this climate, running around. A Grizzly bear that was overturning rocks for grubs, stopped what he was doing and waved at us as we passed. I glanced back at our animals, they never even turned a hair at the bear. Most of the time horses and mules would do most anything to get away from a bear.

We came to a clearing, setting in it, was a long stone building. The roof was also made of stone, slabs cut about two inch's thick, overlaid like clay tiles. You could tell that it had been there for hundreds of years, moss was growing on what must have been the north side.

There were more fruit trees, plus what looked like a garden spot. Coyote seen me looking at the garden. "Oh, that's our garden, we tend it now. We even store food in the root cellar over there." He pointed.

"Who built this?" I asked.

"I don't know for sure, but there's some kind of writing on the walls in places, Norse, I believe." He said.

Faith spoke for the first time, "Vikings? Really? It must be well over a thousand years old then."

"I suppose it is. There's a few graves over near that hill, I'll show you when you have time." Coyote said. "Would you like to see inside the house, we've been keeping it clean, waiting for you?"

"Huh? Waiting for us, how could you know we would come?"

"So many questions, only normal though, they will be answered in time, come." Coyote said as he went toward the house.

There were four doors, one on each side, and one on each end. They were made out of some kind of isinglass, as were the seven windows per side, as well as two windows on each end of the house. As such, we were well surprised at the light being reflected inside.

On one side was what could be called the kitchen, with basins or sinks, that had cold spring water running into one and out again. The other sink had hot spring water running in and out. The house was at least a hundred feet long. With bedrooms. I looked into one, a stone bedstead. And what could pass for a toilet, it had running water continuously running by, just like aboard some of the older ships. They also had stone bathtubs, with hot and cold running spring water, mixing together. Who ever built this house was some kind of a genius.

A few birds had followed us in, they were singing and chirping as they followed along as we looked at everything.

I looked at Faith, she was staring around like a little kid at Disney Land. "Honey," She said, "Do you remember that old movie, 'Shangri-La', doesn't this remind you of that?"

"More like Disney Land, but yeah, with Shangri-La thrown in. I don't know about you, but this makes everything that has happened to us in the past, seem normal. And now, this sure isn't normal, is it?"

Coyote said, "Normal is, as normal becomes."

I looked at my pocket watch, since it was pretty hard to tell the time by the sun, you know with the vapor haze covering the valley. Almost five, no wonder my stomach was growling. I looked at my wife as she was bending over sniffing a flower, I would never get used to how comely she was, especially from this angle. "Sweetheart, we won't be able to make it back tonight, I suppose I had better call Hope and let her know."

Coyote looked at me, "There isn't any reception for your phone from here, normally, but I will ask them to clear the airways so you can make your call."

"Ask who?"

"Them. You know," he said, pointing up with his paw. He sat there for a few moments, then said, "It's Okay, go ahead and make your call.

"Hope? Yes, well, we aren't going to be able to make it back tonight. Is everything alright there?---Good, Okay then we'll see you tomorrow, I guess. If you try to call and we don't answer, just leave a message, we'll get back to you." I closed the lid.

"So, where do we put our bedrolls?" I asked Coyote.

"You had better put them in the Stone House, this valley is watered by the falling dew during the night time hours. You would get pretty wet, if you slept outside. Feel free in helping yourself from the food in the root cellar. Of course you won't find any meat, we are all vegetarians in this valley."

Faith and Poppy went to the root cellar, they came back with fresh fruit and vegetables. I had unsaddled the stock and took our stuff into the Stone House. Faith and Poppy were listening as Coyote was telling them how to prepare steamed vegetables over the hot spring water.

I was surprised that I didn't even miss meat for supper. It was late enough in the fall, so that sunset was around seven. By the time the sun went down the horses and mules had finished grazing and were standing close by the Stone House, under a covered area just off the lee side of the house, so they wouldn't get too wet. Cause the dew was heavy.

I knew the sun went down, but the light had dimmed, to what looked like a full moon. You could still see. I went back inside, the light was the same inside, reflected through the isinglass door's and window's. I was somewhat confused.

I asked Coyote, "Where is all of this light coming from?"

"The face of the mountains round-about, is made of fifty percent glass, just like the moon. Only since they are closer than the moon, they reflect the moons light into the valley, better."

"You mean, they do more than reflect, they enhance?" I

said.

"Yes, that's right, you aren't as dumb as you look." Coyote quipped.

"Well, it's pretty light in this house, too light to sleep, what do you do about that?"

"Rub your hand across the face of the windows, they will darken, where you rub. When you want more light, just rub again."

I thought a minute, "There's one thing I do know, is that the Vikings did not invent that, so who did?" I asked.

"Really Clay, there you are going dumb on me again, you know who."

"Yeah, right, like hell I do, I might suspect, but I don't know!"

"Clay, behave yourself! You know what he's talking about, in fact you've told me some of what is going to happen, from your time in coma's." Faith said.

I looked down at the clean stone floor, "I'm sorry Coyote, it's just that you sound so smug and self-righteous. But I suppose you have a right. By the way, do you have a name?"

"Of course I do, it's 'Clancy.'"

"An Irish Coyote? I don't believe it. Those Irish get around don't they?"

"Faith and Begorra, tis true, Irish I be, but don't worry, I don't drink." Clancy said, with a Coyote laugh, which sounded more of a whisky brogue, than Coyote. He may not drink now, but sometime in his past, I bet he did. Whatever he used to be......

"I know what you're thinking Clay. You do know that there is no such thing as reincarnation, don't you? Of course you do. You were wondering where I got the name of 'Clancy'? Well wonder no longer, I will tell you." Coyote said, with one of those toothy grins, where you're not sure if he's laughing or growling.

"It was when they were putting the trans-continental railroad through. It was close to Cheyenne, I was just a pup. An orphan I was. I hung around, begging food. The Irish Gandy Dancers sort of adopted me. They were the ones who named me Clancy."

"That's a bunch of Irish blarney, if I ever heard it." I said. "And I'll tell you why, that railroad went through in the 1860's. That would make you way over 140 years old. So what do you have to say about that?" I said.

"Yes, you're right. I should of died a long time ago, shouldn't I of? I would have too, but for this place. It seems it ad's years to your life. Must be all of the clean living."

I started to open my mouth, Faith interrupted me, "That's enough Clay, can't you see that he's telling the truth?"

"No, not all of it, they were just partial truths, that's what browns me off. Can't I be petulant once in awhile?"

"Yes, but not childish. So if you have that out of your system, get our bedrolls and put them on the stone beds."

Alita was watching me and trying to help carry the bedrolls, Poppy was strong enough to carry them on her own. There were separate sleeping areas. Alita and Poppy were whispering to each other. Alita said, "Daddy, Poppy and I don't want to sleep alone, we want to sleep with you and Mommy?"

Clancy was listening. "There's one bed that's big enough to hold all four of you. Down at the end. It must of have been the Segundo's room. It has a Isinglass door, with a name engraved in it. Come see."

On the door, was a name, 'Harald Hardrada' and the year '1043'. "Who is that?" I asked. Faith was right behind me. "I know. He was a Viking. He was King Olaf II's youngest half brother. He did a lot of exploring."

"How do you know all of that?" I asked.

"I paid attention in school, besides', I was really fascinated by the Vikings. They always reminded me of us, you know Americans."

I opened the door, and put all four bedrolls on the oversized stone bed. On each side of the bed were cherry wood night stands with drawers. I pulled the top drawer out. It jingled, there were some kind of old coins tossed loosely in there. I picked one up, it was thin, made of silver and had some kind of Arabic writing on it, with the year 893 stamped on it. I handed it to Faith, she said, "Oh, I didn't think I would ever see one of these. Their 'dirhams'. They were minted in Baghdad, between the years 750 to 950. The Vikings did a lot of trading for them."

"Is there anything you don't know?" I asked her.

"Yes, a lot, but like I told you, Vikings fascinated me in school."

I opened the drawer again and tossed the coins back in. The Cherry wood nightstand was hand made, and made without any modern tools. Nice job...

Clancy had came in with us, he said, "Will you people be alright here tonight?

I thought I would go howl at the moon, so to speak." He said.

"Yes, I think so," Faith said. "I don't suppose there are any Viking ghosts hanging around, are there?"

"No, I don't believe in Ghosts, do you?" Clancy said.

"No, I don't think so. But you know how the old boogeyman in the closet thing, when we were just tykes. Our older siblings always tried to scare us with them." Faith said. Poppy edged closer to us. Alita said, "What are you talking about? Of course there are no ghosts or boogeymen either. But,

I might add, there are Demons, they try to make you think they're ghosts."

"Where did you get all of that?" Faith asked her.

"Really Mother, if there are Angels, of course there are Demons. Demons were the fallen Angels that came down to have relations with the women in Adams day. Didn't you know that Mother?"

"Well, yeah, I guess so. Just never gave it much thought." Faith said. Clancy was staring at Alita. "Smart girl," he said as he turned and padded away.

Chapter Sixteen

"Mommy, can we take a bath in the indoor pool?" Alita asked, "We're pretty dusty from the trail."

"Sure, I don't know why not. But first you had better let me check the temperature, it might be too hot." Faith went over and touched it with the back of her hand. She used the back of her hand, that way the normal reaction would be to pull the hand back toward you. "Feels alright, but let me test it with my elbow, that's the best way." She said. As she dipped her elbow in.

"It's fine, I think I'll take one with you girls, are you going to take one with us Clay?" With that they all three started pulling clothes off.

"Uh, no I'm not." I said.

"Why not Daddy, you're dirty too?" Alita said.

"That's a good question Alita, and I'll tell you why. You see Daddies don't take baths with their daughters, or even with any young girl, like Poppy. It just isn't done."

"But then, who are you going to take a bath with?"

"Well, I thought I'd go for a ride. I know the sun has gone down, but with that reflected, enhanced moonlight, filtering through the mist. I will be able to see alright, plus I guess the mist will act like a shower, won't it?"

"I don't know Clay," Faith said, "are you sure it will be okay? I mean we haven't scouted everything out, you really don't know what's out there."

"Oh, I'm sure it will be okay, I'll ride Brutus, plus I bet the rest of them will want to go along." The two girls had got in the tub while we were talking, Faith came over in her altogether and gave me a kiss, "Be careful Honey," she said, pinching my butt.

I went outside, it was a pretty sight, the mist swirling and twisting around the moonbeams reflected from the glass like mountains. I went to the shelter where the animals were standing, I took my clothes off, down to my shorts and hung them on a wooden peg.

I grabbed a hand full of Brutus' mane, and swung up. I was right, the rest of them followed along. It wasn't long before we were dripping wet. Funny thing though, it wasn't cold, like you thought a heavy mist would be. I felt a little like Goldie Locks, when she tasted the little bear's porridge, it was just right.

I followed the stream back up the valley. It wasn't too deep, we crossed it several times. There were holes where the horses had to swim, that was fun, they enjoyed it too.

As I had mentioned before, about every animal native to the area resided in this valley. They'd come out of their dens, tall grass, everywhere they slept to watch us go by. None of them were scared by the scent of man.

At the end of the valley, was a large mountain, out of which came the stream we were following. I looked up, the mountain disappeared into the heaving cloud mass that hid it's far away peak.

I heard the screech of an Eagle, and coming down out of the clouds was a Bald Eagle. It lit on a tree branch, about two feet from my head. It sat there looking at me and Brutus. Brutus looked at it, and blew snot from his nose. The Eagle spoke...

"Now that was down right insulting. Haven't you taught your horse better manners than that Clay?" The Eagle said.

Brutus snorted again. "Him, teach me? Shoot, I have to do

all of the teaching around here. Oh not them three 'R's, but you know, stuff that requires horse sense." Brutus said, or at least I thought it was coming out of him.

"Was I talking to you? I thought I directed my question at Clay." Eagle said.

Brutus snorted and stamped his hooves. "Whoa, there Brutus, he's just trying to get your goat." I said. "Anyway, Mr. Eagle, what can I do for you?" I said, patting Brutus' neck, to calm him down.

The rest of our mounts had gathered around to listen. Eagle spoke, "It's not what you can do for me, but more exact, it's what I can do for you and your loved ones."

"Well, just what can you do for me and mine?" I said.

"Save your lives, that's what. That is if you want to be saved. Some people don't, they like the way the world is, but I hope you are sighing and crying over the deplorable conditions rampant in the world today."

"Well yeah, I don't like them none. In fact I downright hate them, but what can I do about it?" I said. "And yeah, we sort of would like to go on living, just like I suppose most every creature on this earth would."

"Alright then, when the time is right, you all can come on back and I'll open the gate for you." Eagle said.

"Two questions," I said, "number one, when is the right time to come back? And number two, what gate?"

"You'll know when the time is right. As to the gate, you came through it on your way here, the tunnel under the waterfall. And no, it isn't always open, I opened it for you, just before you got there. When you were a young boy, you didn't just fail to see it, because it wasn't there for you to see, I had closed it."

"So what's your name, I suppose the 'gate keeper'?"

"No, it's not, my name is Gabe, and don't be facetious, this is serious business." Gabe said with a frown. Have you ever seen an Eagle frown? Believe me you don't want to. Then his face broke into a smile, "I was just joking, and you're right, I guess I could be called the 'gate keeper'. But my name is Gabe. So Clay, stay for a few days, then go back and handle life as it comes, you and your beautiful wife Faith, and all of your children."

"I actually don't have any children of my own," I said.

"You don't? But of course you do, all of those that are of your household are your children. Rosie, Tiff, Hank, Hope, do you want me to go on, or do you understand? You see even the ranch hands are your children. Even Mary Jane and Iris. And oh yes, they will be coming back, you're going to have to add on to your house, will that be a problem?" Gabe said.

"No, no problem. But what about Dad and Felicia, and those in New Mexico?"

"Yes, they too will have to be taken care of. But you see this isn't the only sanctuary. There are many around the world. Don't worry, the ones from the stars will be saved." Gabe said, then flew up and disappeared into the mountains mist.

'From the stars'? All of us stood there and watched him go. Matthew said, "There is more to him than meets the eye. He's just not an Eagle."

Luke said, "No kidding Einstein, what ever gave you that idea?" Matthew took a playful kick at him.

"Come on you two, you might miss and hit one of us, let's go home." I said, as Brutus turned to go. We took our time, we stopped and went swimming some more.

Before I went into the stone building, I took off my shorts and wrung the water out of them. I hung them on the back of a chair in the bedroom. The two girls were sleeping on the other side of Faith. They had spread the bedrolls out to make one big bed. Alita was sleeping in between Poppy and Faith. I crawled in front beside Faith, and snuggled up close to her. She felt warm and inviting. She moaned a little as I held her close. Funny thing, you'd think the stone bed would be hard, but it wasn't. It must of taken me a whole ten seconds to fall asleep.

The next morning, when I awoke, I was alone. I could hear them in the kitchen making breakfast. I stretched and yawned. Then footsteps, Faith came in.

"Are you ready for breakfast?" She said. I looked at her and smiled.

"Sure, if you are." I said. She glanced down at herself.

"Oh you! Not that kind of breakfast. Just because I didn't put any clothes on, don't get any ideas."

"What about the girls, they had better be wearing clothes?" I said, with a question in my voice.

"Yes, they have underwear on. So I guess you had better put your shorts on." She said as she picked them off of the back of the chair, and threw them at me. I was surprised, they were completely dry. I jumped into them and followed her out, why hadn't she put any clothes on?

I asked her that very question. "Why? You've seen me naked thousands of times. And as far as the girls go, we're all girls. If you were one too, we wouldn't have to wear any clothes." She sort of sounded like she was sorry I wasn't a girl...

Faith looked over her shoulder, "No I'm not, I'm glad you're a man!"

"How'd you know what I was thinking? I didn't say that out loud." I said.

"Didn't you? Must be this place, seems like the girls and I have been talking without words since we got here."

We sat down and I said a prayer. When I glanced up, Poppy was setting across from me. "Uh, Faith, I think Poppy needs something on top also. I hadn't noticed before, but she's becoming a young woman."

Faith looked, "Yes, perhaps, but will you stop being such a prude. Leave the girl alone, if you don't like it, don't look at her." Faith stuck her tongue out at me. Perhaps I was being somewhat of a prude. I guess it's all in how you look at it. I sat there thinking as I chewed my food. Yes, Faith was right, I could remember those self-righteous hypocrites in church, when I was a kid, they could make anything seem shameful. It's all in the eye of the beholder... After all Adam and Eve didn't wear clothes, that is till the biggest hypocrite of all came along...Satan.

After I finished eating. I stood up and took off my shorts and hung them on the back of my chair. I cleared the table off and then left the room, with all eyes on me. It was the hardest thing that I had ever done. No pun intended.

At the door, I turned, "When we leave here, it's all clothes back on and that's final." I went out to the animals. They looked at me. Nick cleared his throat, "Uh, doesn't that pull back up?"

"What do you mean?"

"You know like us, we can let it down or pull it back up inside."

"No, I'm afraid it's like this all of the time." I said.

"That seems awful dangerous, it could get caught on a thorn bush or something, that would be really painful." Luke said.

"Yes, well, you see most of the time we wear clothes, they protect it. But the women, they think I should go without clothes when we are here. But I told them when we leave here, its clothes back on."

Faith came out of the house. One of the horses nickered. It sounded like a whistle. I looked around, "who did that?" I asked. They all laughed. "Okay, I don't blame you, she is a knockout, isn't she?"

We spent the next couple of days just taking things easy, swimming etc. Gabe and Clancy came by, occasionally. You might say we got a peak at what paradise could be like. But noting lasts forever. The animals were getting sleek and fat. It was sort of their idea to leave, they were getting restless, just laying around. Of course they were right, man and animal were made to work. Without a purpose, there was no purpose. Was that redundant?

So we packed up and put our clothes back on, they seemed heavy and itchy, after going without them for days. One thing for sure, we all had a nice even tan, without burning, since all of the sun's harmful rays were blocked by the mists that covered the valley from stem to stern.

When we put our rifles back in their scabbards and strapped on our other weapons, they seemed gross. Would there ever come a time when we wouldn't need them?

Gabe and Clancy showed up as we were just mounting up. Gabe said, "Keep an Eagle eye out, they still want you dead."

"Who does?" I said.

"The one who roams about like a roaring Lion, seeking to devour everyone, since he knows that his time is short." Gabe said.

"Yeah, but why is he picking on me? I'm nobody special."

"Aren't you? He must think you are, so that makes you special. A target anyway." Clancy said.

"Yeah, I know that, these white blazes in my hair are evidence of that. Why does he always aim at my head?"

"Cut off the head of a snake and he dies, cut off his tail and he lives on." Clancy said.

"Thanks a lot, now you're calling me a snake, huh?"

"It's all relative to who wants who dead. To him, you're as dangerous as a Rattlesnake. To us, it's him that's the snake."

Gabe said.

"Alright, enough of this reverse philosophy, we're heading out, see you guys later." I said, as Nick stepped out in the lead, with Matthew and Luke following him. I followed along in the rear, as usual.

Just after we got clear of the waterfall, I looked back, no tunnel, just solid rock! What the hell? "Hey Faith, look under the waterfall." I yelled. She turned Nick and rode back. We looked at each other, not saying anything, then we lined out again for home.

We got home mid-afternoon, Hope came out of the house, "You guys weren't gone very long, just over night, I thought you said you was going to stay a few days?"

"Huh? We were gone for four days, what do you mean overnight?" Faith said.

"Well, you just called last night and said you were going to stay for a few days, now here you are." Hope said, then added, "Where did you get your tans, you look great."

"Mom," Poppy said, "we were gone for four days, we were in a wonderful valley with all kinds of animals that spoke English, can you believe that?"

"No, I can't, cause you were only gone overnight. Check the date on your cell phone Clay, what does it say?" Hope said. I looked at my cell phone. She was right.

"I can see the date, but we were gone for four days, no matter what it says. I can't explain it, but it happened." I said.

Hope lifted Alita from her saddle, "My but aren't you as brown as a berry, all over too. What did you do run around naked?" Hope said.

"Yes, we all did. We even swam naked. It was so much fun. Even Daddy did, after Mommy told him to, he didn't want to, but he did."

"Well, you all have your story's straight, so I guess you are telling the truth, but after you take care of your horses, come in the house and tell me all about it. And also, Rosie's back."

"Yeah, I seen the nose of the plane sticking out of the hanger. Where is she now?"

"Her and Tiff are in the office working, what else? That's about all they do."

"Yes," Faith said, "that does worry me. They both need to have some fun, they work too hard."

I led the stock to the barn and unsaddled them. Then went to the oat bin and gave them each a generous helping. The oats were getting low in the bin. I went to the silo, where we kept the grain. It was empty. I guess I would have to take a truck to town for some more.

When I got back to the house, everyone was gathered around the dinning room table, including Rosie and Tiff. Faith was telling them about our adventure. I sat down and listened.

Rosie was asking all sorts of in-depth questions about the valley. She said, "You know, Jake and Alona was telling me about another place on the Chama that sounded a lot like your valley, I thought they were just funning me, but I guess not."

"So Rosie, how did the business trip or your sojourn go?" I asked.

"Fine, we are making in roads in the supply of low cost gas. The big oil company's are getting nervous. It worry's me a little bit." Rosie said.

"How so?" Faith asked.

"Well, they've tried to get the courts to shut us down, but that's failed, so-I don't know, they may try sabotage. But I've beefed up our security, both here and down there, so I don't think there is much danger from that. But I did hear, that they think, you Dad, are the one who is running the show. So watch your back, huh?"

"I've been their target for quite awhile now. What I'm

scared of is, that they might miss me and hit one of my loved ones. They've tried to blow my brains out twice now and it hasn't worked."

Faith had a twinkle in her eyes as she said, "Well you have to have some brains before they can blow them out." Then she giggled some more.

"HaHa, very funny Dear. But you might be right, I always come back for more…That, I guess does show like of smarts." I said.

"Oh fiddle, you know better than that, you're one of the smartest men that I know. So, don't belittle yourself sweetheart. You're the backbone of this family." Faith said.

"Yes Dad, without you, none of us would be here, lord only knows where we would be, dead probably." Rosie said.

Hope spoke up, "So who's going to help me with supper?"

Everyone, but me, said they would, then they got up to do so. I stopped Rosie,

"Rosie, stay a bit, I want to talk." She sat back down.

"So, did you have any trouble? How did the Hoeffer boys do?"

"They did alright, Dale was always calling Tiff, but otherwise they did a good job."

"Do you think they are capable enough to take on more responsibility?"

"I guess so, I trained them some on self defense. They can shoot pretty straight now. They're not too good with knives, but passably so."

"Good, I need to go to town tomorrow and get a load of oats. I thought I would have them go with me." I said.

"Are you expecting trouble?" Rosie asked with a heavy note of concern in her voice.

"I'm always expecting trouble. That way I won't be surprised. You can go help the women now, if you want, I'm not trying to tell you what to do." I said.

"I know you're not Dad. I do have to make a few phone calls, so I think I will do that. You don't think Mom will be mad if I don't help with supper?"

"No of course, not. Besides I think I will set the table, that don't require any brains." I said with a smile....

That night when I gave Faith a kiss goodnight, I said, "Oh, by the way, I thought I would go to town tomorrow and get a load of oats. Thought I would take the Hoeffer boys with me."

"Oh? Alright, but I'm going with you."

"You don't have to if you don't want to." I said.

"I want to, do you actually think I would let you out of my sight?"

"Swell, no problem, but don't forget your weapons."

"Of course I won't, do we ever go anywhere without them?" Faith said.

"No, I guess that's why we're still alive." I turned over to go to sleep.

"Hey Mister, you do know it's been four days without any lovemaking?"

"No, according to Hope, it's only been overnight." I said.

"Well not according to my clock, it's been four days, so turn over here mister and get busy." I did as I was told....

At the breakfast table the next morning, I asked Rosie if she would watch her sister for the day. She said she would be pleased to watch her. Said she would start teaching her the oil business. At first I thought she was joking, but looking at her, I could see that she wasn't.

I went over to Red's place to see the Hoeffer boys. They were just heading to work when I stopped them.

"Chip and Dale, I need you to get the one ton duelly and

fuel it up. We need to get some oats for the horses and mules. We'll get just get enough to last till we can get a semi load for the silo."

"Sure no problem, you had better tell Red though, he wanted us to check the stock up by the oil drilling today."

"Sure, you guys go ahead and get the truck ready, Faith and I will be going with you." I walked over to Red and Daisy's house. Some of the hands were just finishing breakfast. I went into the dinning room. Red turned around with a sour look on his face.

"So, what do you want now?" He said.

I looked around at the hands that were just getting up, I hooked my thumb toward the door, they took the hint. Daisy was clearing the dishes from the table, she looked at me…her face turned pale and she hurried from the room.

I walked over to Red and jerked him out of his chair. Holding him at arms length, with his toes an inch from the floor. My hand was slowing tightening around his throat. My vision cleared and I sat him back down.

"Red," I said, as he coughed and tried to get his breath, "now you know better that to talk to me like that, it gets my German up. I just wanted to tell you that I'm taking Chip and Dale with us to town to get some oats. How come you let them get so low?" Then I turned and left the room.

Daisy had gone out the kitchen door and around to the dinning room door, she met me. "I'm sorry Clay, he's been so surly lately. I don't know what's getting into him. Please don't kill him."

I stood there a minute and then said, "Kill him? Why in the world would I do that? He's your husband and you're my mother's cousin. He's family isn't he?" Then I walked away…

Kill him? Why would Daisy think I would kill Red. Was Red into something that I didn't know about? I guess I would have to put Rosie on to that, she could find out if anybody could.

Faith wasn't quite ready so I went into the office where Rosie and Alita were. "Rosie, would you do me a favor? Red has been up to something, would you nose around and see what's going on?"

"What do you mean Dad? What do you think he's been up to?"

"I don't know, I've noticed right along that he don't seem to like me, but it's all been under the surface, well no more, he was just down right disrespectful. I'm afraid I lost my cool and grabbed him out of his chair. Daisy thought I was going to kill him. Why would she think that?"

"I don't know Dad, but I will put out some feelers. I have a lot of contacts, not only with the hands and the oil workers. But people in town also. I'll find out what's going on."

I leaned over and gave Alita a kiss and then hugged Rosie, then kissed her on the cheek. I held her for a couple of seconds. "Dad, are you alright?"

"Yes, of course, it's just that I love my girls and I'm afraid I haven't told the two of you that, very much."

Rosie had a quizzical look in her eyes as she nodded and gave me a peck on the cheek. I turned and met Faith at the foot of the stairs. I told her all about it, as we walked to the truck shed.

"What do you think his problem is?" Faith asked.

"I don't know. But Rosie is looking into it. If anybody can get to the bottom of it, she can."

Chip and Dale had the truck setting there idling. I got behind the wheel, with Faith in the front seat with me. Chip and Dale got in the back seat. The truck was a Diesel, four door long box, 1 ton. It would hold enough sacks of oats to tide us over till we could get a semi load in.

I got out on the county road and set the cruise control to seventy. It was a long straight stretch to town. I had went but a few miles till I seen a flashing light in my rearview mirror, it was county deputy. I pulled over...

I got out and met him, "What's the problem officer?" I asked.

"You were going over the speed limit, you were going seventy and the limit is sixty-five. I'm afraid I will have to take you in." He said with his hand on the handle of his revolver. I looked at him, he was a new one....

"Uh, just give me the ticket, I'll take it to the Judge in town."

"No afraid I can't do that, you have to go to jail." He pulled out his gun, I reached forward and grabbing his hand I bent it back till I heard the bones snap.

He was screaming in pain, I backhanded him across the face, he was out like a light. Faith had jumped out and was running up. "What the hell did you do that for?" She snapped at me.

"He wanted to take me to jail for exceeding the speed limit, five miles over he said. He pulled his gun. Right then I knew he wasn't a real cop, check his I.D. if you don't believe me." I said, as I kicked his prone body in the ribs and then I walked over to his cruiser and yanked the door open.

I was right, there was no two way radio or anything. I yanked the clove box open and pulled the registration out; it was registered in the state of New York, but the plates were from a county vehicle, probably stolen.

I walked back to where he was laying, he was just waking up. I grabbed him by his collar and lifted him to his feet. "Who are you and why did you almost commit suicide?"

He was holding his mangled wrist and whining. "Oh knock it off, that pain tells you that you are still alive, be thankful."

He didn't pay me no mind. Faith said, "His I.D. says he's from Washington D.C., he's on the White House staff."

I whistled, "Oh boy, you do have your problems, don't you? You know of course, that they will kill you. You failed in your mission, they won't let you live, I'll tell you what, you get back in that car and head north through Montana and get your ass into Canada; that's the only chance you have, even there they might find you, but you'll have a chance anyway."

I took his gun, he whimpered all of the way to his car, he backed it around and headed north, I guess he knew the deep shit that he was in.

Chip and Dale were standing there taking it all in. Dale said, "Rosie said that you were hell on wheels, I sure can see that she was right."

"You didn't know that before?" I asked.

Chip said, "Oh we knew alright, you forget you grew up around you, we know alright." They both got back in the truck.....

"You guys drive, Faith and I will set in back." they crawled over the seat. They held it to the speed limit. I put my arm around my wife, I could feel her weapons under her clothes, she felt me, then she smiled. She could feel hardware (guns, just the guns).

I put the bogus cop's gun in the back seat pocket in front of me. Who knows it might come in handy sometime. We came into town at the crawl, I think the boys were afraid to attract attention to us.

We pulled up at the feed store, all four of us went in. The same people were still there from when I was a boy. They were glad to see me. I ordered the oats, they said it would take a week or so for the semi load, but they had plenty of sacks, so they loaded the truck up.

It was coming on to lunch time when we were done. So we

went to lunch. The place that we usually went was under new management. That's what the sign said anyway. It was combination bar/casino. The place was mostly full, we found a table and sat down. The waitress was busy, but she seemed to be ignoring us.

I went up to the bar and caught the bartender's attention. He sort of sneered and came over. "We don't serve Indians in here, hit the road redskin."

I stood there for a second, digesting that. There were some hard cases setting at the bar. They turned on the stools and said, "Yeah, get out of here you stinking Indian, and take that Indian loving slut with you."

I just stood there. Four of them got off of their stools and came toward me. I seen Faith get up and adjust her skirt, she was making easy access to her weapons. They grouped around me. Two more of them headed toward Faith.

Now I can take a lot of shit, but threaten my wife and you had better start singing your death song. The room had taken on a red haze. I smiled and stretched raising my arms up beside my head, I laid my hand on the shaft of my Bowie Knife.

Those four thought that they had easy pickin's. One of them had brass knuckles, one had a knife, the other two had guns. I glanced over at Faith, those two had reached her, she stuck a stiletto through one of their throats. The other one lost his balls to one fell swoop of her razor sharp stiletto. I could see all of this going on as I sidestepped a lunge by the one who had the knife, just as the one with the brass knuckles took a swing at me.

My Bowie knife was very sharp, it cut the hand clean off the one with the knife, my swing continued on to the ribs of the one who had the knuckles. The other two were surprised, therefore it hampered their reflex's. I was on them before they could raise their guns. I jammed the hilt of my bowie down one of their throats. The other one was holding his insides in, blood was dripping down his hands.

I heard the bang of a gun, I turned in time to see the bartender shooting at me, I staggered back, I seen a black hole appear in the forehead of the bartender. I looked toward my wife, her gun was held fast in her two hands, still smoking.....

Chapter Seventeen

Clay sat down on the nearest chair, staring straight ahead, I ran over to him, Chip and Dale on my heels. I felt his neck, he was still alive. He had a furrow down the center of his head, damn another head shot. Couldn't they just shoot him in the shoulder or something. I tried to take the knife from his hand, he wouldn't let go of it.

I turned and checked the room, "If anybody has any ideas, you had better forget it, or I will plant you just a sure as looking at you." Then I said to Chip and Dale, "Pick Clay up, let's get out of here." They picked him up, his legs still worked, Clay walked along between them. I glanced around the room, there was a man standing in the office door in the back, he raised a pistol, I shot him through the head.

I got to the door and turned around, "You all seen what happened, they started it. Is there anyone here who thinks otherwise?" I said. No one said a word.

Chip mumbled to Dale, "Eight of them, did you see that, they killed eight of them."

"I don't think the one who got his hand cut will die, I least I don't think so." Dale whispered back.

Chip and Dale lifted Clay into the back seat. He sat there staring straight ahead. There was a siren coming down the street. It was the local law. The same guy who we had dealings with last time.

His car slid to a stop beside me. "What happened? I got a call that someone was killing everybody?"

"Not someone, us. They jumped us, we just defended ourselves, tell him Chip and Dale." They told him what happened.

I asked him, "Do you know any of those people who bought the bar?"

"No, well, just by name, they're from back east somewhere. There were eight of them, hard cases, they looked like to me."

Chip said, "Not anymore, their pretty limp." Then he giggled. I looked at him, nerves, I guess.

"If you're done, I have to get Clay to the Hospital, they hit him in the head again."

I got in the back seat with Clay. I pulled out my phone and called Suong. I told her to beat her butt to the Hospital. "No, don't take him there, if he's stable bring him home, we can keep him safe here. In the Hospital we can't."

She was right, I don't know what I was thinking. It didn't take us half as long to get home, they put the pedal to the metal. Everyone was there waiting for us, well not everyone, Red wasn't. I opened the door, Hank jumped in with Rosie right behind him, Tiff was holding Alita.

Suong was right there as they lifted Clay down. They hustled him into the house. Daisy was standing there, "Where's Red?" I asked. "He's at the house, he's been drinking, you know how us Indians are, we can't handle alcohol very good." I turned and walked over to Daisy's house, Red was setting at the table with a bottle of whiskey, he stood up when he seen me, I kicked him right in the balls. He bent over, I took the bottle and hit him over the head. Then I left.

Daisy was coming, I stopped her and said, "Tell him he stays sober, or he's history. Also he had better talk with respect when he talks to Clay, or I will cut his tongue out."

I went into the room where they had Clay hooked up to

I.V.'s and such. "How is he?" I asked Suong.

"He's stable, he's in a light coma. The bullet didn't penetrate the skull, but he has a concussion again. He sure has a hard head."

Daisy was at the door, "Uh, Suong will you come look at Red. He hasn't woken up yet." Suong went with her.

I sat down with Alita on my lap, Alita was holding Clay's hand. "Is Daddy going to be alright?"

"Sure Honey, he's just in another coma, he'll be alright."

Suong came back, "You hit him pretty hard, but it wasn't that, that was the problem, he was dead drunk."

"Well, that's good, I guess. I shouldn't have hit him with that bottle, but the kick in the nuts, I don't regret. Sometimes men get to thinking that their so superior, it just makes me so mad."

"Yeah, I know. But Clay was never one of those, was he?" Suong said.

"Nope, or I wouldn't have married him. My first husband had that tendency, but he got killed before I could correct his attitude." Suong left the room. I continued to rock Alita. I heard someone coming down the hall, it was Rosie.

"Mom, Harry Silver called, he wanted to talk to you. But I told him you were busy. He said that he talked to the rest of the patrons in the Bar and that they backed up what you told the local law. He wanted to know how Dad was, I told him he was in another coma, he said he was sorry to hear that, but a coma was better than being dead. Then he laughed, I hung up on him."

"Yes, he has a weird sense of humor, but I think he means well. How are the Hoeffer boys? I hope they weren't too traumatized?"

"No, I don't think so, all they said was, 'Boy, you're Mother is one bad dude.' They know how bad Dad is, they expected it out of him, but I think they'll make a wide circle around you from now on." Rosie said, with a crooked little smile.

"Which one of them is sweet on Tiff? Or are they both?" I asked.

"To tell you the truth, I think they both are, but of course Tiff can't have both of them, or can she?"

I rocked on for a few seconds, "No, of course not, it wouldn't be fair to them, would it?"

"No, it wouldn't. But I bet Tiff would have a ball." Rosie said, as she left the room laughing.

I checked Clay, he was breathing easy, Alita had went to sleep so I laid her beside him. Then I sat back down and picked up a magazine. I absently read some of it. I heard a flapping at the open window, Gabe settled himself on the window sill. I now heard a tapping on the hallway floor, Clancy came in the room....

"Well, you guys are a 'day late and a dollar short', aren't you?" I said.

"Could be," Gabe said, "but you two are pretty hard to keep up with. Contrary to what some people might think, we can't be everywhere, every minute of the day. Isn't that right Clancy?"

"Well me, anyway, I don't have wings. But the truth be told, Gabe was just funning you. We can be everywhere, if we need to be."

"You didn't think you needed to be there, we almost got killed." I said.

"No you didn't. Haven't you ever wondered how come Clay never dies from these head wounds?"

"Well, I just thought it was chance and circumstance, wasn't it?" I said.

"No, we won't let them kill him. Oh they want to, but he's

something like Job, they can only go so far. But unlike Job, we won't let them kill his family either. So you don't have to worry about you or the children being killed by them. You can have an accident that's unrelated to them and kick the bucket. So you had better make sure you fasten your seatbelts." Gabe said.

"Why haven't you told Clay this?" I queried.

"We have, didn't he tell you?" Clancy said. "No, I don't suppose he did, it is all a little far fetched, isn't it?"

"Yes and No. It's not really, given what's been happening to us. I would believe almost anything at this point."

"Momma, who are you talking to? I don't see anybody." Alita said, setting up and looking around.

"Gabe and Clancy was just here, they just wanted to see how your Daddy was. They said he was going to be fine."

"Why didn't they stay? I would like to talk to them." Alita said, as she crawled out of bed and came and sat on my lap.

"Perhaps next time they come for a visit, they'll stay longer." I said.

"They had better, or I'll be mad. They're my friends too." Alita said. Clay stirred a little in bed, I went over to him. His fever had went down, he was sleeping comfortably, I don't think he was in a coma, I think he was just sleeping now. Or anyway, I hoped so…

"Mom?" Rosie came in, "are you ready for supper? Come on Alita, I'll help you wash up for supper." She lifted Alita up and put her on one hip and left the room. I bent over and gave Clay a kiss on the cheek, smoothing his hair back from his eyes, I gave him a better kiss, he stirred a little bit with that one. Well at least *that* wasn't in a coma…

Chapter Eighteen

I was dreaming about my wife, we were making love. "Come on Clay, wake up, you don't get to lay around this time." The voice sounded like Clancy. I opened one eye. Yep, it was him, with Gabe standing on the window sill, Clancy was setting on the chair, with his tongue lolling out.

"How are you feeling?" Gabe asked.

"Surprisingly, pretty good." I said, as I raised my hand and felt my head. It was all bandaged up. "So, they got me in the head again, huh?"

"Yes, you have a very hard head, if they hit you anywhere else, it would probably kill you." Clancy said.

"Do you think I can get up?" I asked, as if they were Doctor's.

"We can't see any reason that you can't, that is if you take all of those tubes out of yourself." Gabe said.

I shut off the I.V. clips, then pulled the needles out of my arm. There were some band-aids beside the bed, I put one over where I took the needle out of my vein. I sat up. I wasn't even dizzy. I sat there a while longer.

"Say, did I get them all? I can't remember."

"You only got four of them, Faith did for the other four, by the way she saved your life. The bartender was going to finish you off, after he bounced a bullet off of your head. Faith got him as well as the one that came out of the office, plus the two that came her way, when those other four jumped you." Clancy said.

"Who were they? Did you find out?"

"Their identities doesn't matter, they were some of the Evil Ones crowd. They were just some of his tools." Gabe said.

"Alright, I guess I can get up now." I said.

"Maybe you had better wait a few more minutes, for that swelling to go down." Clancy said.

"Huh? What swelling?" Clancy inclined his head. "Oh, I hadn't even noticed it. I was dreaming about my wife." I said.

"We know." Gabe said. "You humans are so fortunate, you can make love anytime you want to, we have to wait till our preprogram kicks in."

"Yeah, I guess you're right, I hadn't thought of it. So what's next, what are we supposed to do?" I asked.

"Do? You do what you always do. Everything humans do is all vanity anyway. But I suppose you're talking about what to do in this time of the end. Do onto others, as you would have them do unto you, but you already do that. That's one of the reasons that your ancestors came here. You will be guided, when it is needed." Gabe said, then he looked at Clancy, "It's time for us to go." He flew away, Clancy jumped down from the chair and jumped out of the window, even though we were on the second floor.

'My ancestors came here?' What that meant I didn't know. My clothes were laying on the chest at the foot of the bed, they were clean. I suppose the ones I was wearing were all covered with blood. I got dressed, I could hear the family talking from the dinning room downstairs. That's where I headed, I was hungry.

Alita was the first one to see me, "Daddy," she shouted, holding out her arms. I picked her up, she gave me a big kiss. Faith and Rosie were all over me. "Are you alright?" Faith said, taking Alita.

"Sure, but I'm hungry, what's for supper?" I asked as I sat

down.

"The usual, fried Chicken, meatloaf, corn on the cob, green beans, carrots, mashed potatoes. Everything you like." Faith said.

"Good, load my plate up. Were Gabe and Clancy there, before you left?"

Hope looked at me, "Who's Gabe and Clancy?"

"Uh…Friends of ours, you remember we told you about the Valley. Well they came to visit." I said.

"Uh-huh, hallucinations more than likely." Hope said. I just let it go. Faith said, "Yes, honey they were. But Alita was asleep, she was disappointed that she didn't get to see them."

Suong was eating with us. She said. "Why didn't you call me to take the needles out? You could of bled."

"Yeah, I suppose, but Gabe and Clancy said it would be alright." I said. Suong just rolled her eyes. "But I tell you what, you can take these bandages off after supper, if that would be alright?"

"You shouldn't take them off yet, you haven't even started to heal, it's only been a few hours since you got shot."

"I don't know, it itch's, I think it's healing, it wouldn't hurt to check, would it?" I said.

"I suppose not, I could check the stitch's anyway." Suong said.

"Okay, before bedtime, I want to check the stock after supper." I said.

"My, but you must be feeling pretty good." Faith said, with a thoughtful look.

"Yep, I do." I said, giving her a leer." She said, "Just as I thought, that'll have to wait, till your head gets better." I leaned close and whispered, "Which one?" She kicked me under the table.

Rosie was setting across from us, tapping her fingers on the table, she said, "Will you two act your age?" Faith stuck her tongue out at her. I winked at Rosie, "We are." I said. Faith giggled.

After Suong took the bandages off, she exclaimed, "I don't believe it, they're already healed!"

"What's healed?" I asked.

"Well you had two grooves in your head, when that bullet hit you, it split in two, making two grooves, on either side of your crown. I stitched them up, but now I can take the stitch's out, cause they're healed." Then she giggled.

"What's so funny?" I asked.

"Well, you have those two white lighting strips at your temples from the previous hits, but now you're going to have two more going back on each side of your crown. We're going to have to think up some kind of a nickname for you." She laughed, as she was taking out the stitches.

After the last stitch was out, I said, "Come on Faith, let's check the stock together." I took my hat off of the peg by the door and clamped it on solid. "Me too, me too." Alita said. Rosie said, "I guess I will come along also."

The four of us walked out into the moonlit yard. The yard light had come on automatically. We skirted around its edge of light, no use tempting fate. We went over to the barnyard where the horses and mules were standing hipshot. They picked up their heads as we approached. They came over, wanting us to pet them. We each picked up a curry comb and brushed them down, one by one.

It was calming on our part, and I guess on theirs too, this task. After we were done, we leaned against the corral rails and talked. I picked Alita up and sat her on the top rail.

"Well Rosie, what's your thoughts on all of this?" I asked.

"All of this what?" she said.

"Everything, the oil business, the ranch, your hopes, your

desires?"

"I really haven't given it much thought, I've been too busy."

"Well then, let me ask you this, are you happy?" Faith asked her.

She looked at the moon and glanced around the barnyard. "Yes, I'm happy, who wouldn't be. I have everything that I've ever dreamed about. A loving family, mostly. All of the material things do not matter that much. Oh, they're nice, but I could live in a cave and still be happy, as long as I still had the three of you."

I pulled her close and hugged her. "Us too, Rosie. That's how I feel and I'm sure Faith does also." We had a group hug, Alita had crawled on my shoulders, so she wouldn't miss out.

"But Dad, I don't understand, why do they keep trying to kill you and not us?"

"Well, they did try to kill your Mother this time, maybe they're branching out. But it could be they figure to kill the head and the rest would die. But they don't know the three of you like I do. I know if I was to kick the bucket, you three would carry on.

But don't ask me who they are and why they want us dead, I don't know. But I think it has something to do with what's coming upon this world, they think I have something to do with it. What, I haven't the slightest idea."

Faith said, "On your trip to New Mexico, those Hoeffer boys didn't try anything did they, like hitting on you?"

"No. Chip is sweet on Tiff. And would you believe Dale was always asking questions about Hope?"

"Hope? She must be ten years older than he is, if she's a day." I said.

"That doesn't make any difference," Faith said, "just because she's a woman. If it were the other way around, if he was older than she, no one would even raise an eyebrow."

"Yeah, you're right, I'm sorry. Besides Hope is a looker, I guess your can't blame Dale for trying. Has he said anything to her?"

"Not much, every time he tries, he gets lockjaw. But I think Hope suspects he likes her. At times I see her get a soft look in her eyes when she talks to him."

"You know, I never did understand why people pussyfoot around, if they like someone, just tell them and get it over with." I said.

"I think their afraid of rejection." Faith said.

"Balderdash, life is too short, you have to grab it by the horns." I said.

"Balderdash? Where in the world did you get that word? This isn't the 1920's you know." Rosie said.

"I don't know, it just came into my mind, I must of read it somewhere when I was a kid." I heard steps on the gravel, I turned, it was Hank.

"Mom wants to know if you all would like some ice cream before bedtime?"

Alita said, "Ice Cream. I want some, can we Mom?"

"Sure, we'll be right in, that sounds good."

Sitting around the table was Hope, Tiff and the Hoeffer boys. Why I called them boys, I don't know, except that they were brothers, that were always together. When we came in, Hope stood up, her cheeks putting on a little color. That is more than her ethnic color usually was.

One thing I guess I will never understand, why is it if a person has some Black or Indian in them, why are they called Black or Indian? Take me for instance, I'm half Indian, so therefore I'm an Indian. And Hope, she was half white, but was called Black. Now Tiff, her Dad must have been half white, because she wasn't any darker than me.

I guess I got off track a little bit. Anyway, both Chip and Dale stood up when we came in.

Chip said, "Good evening Sir, Mam," I detected a little fear in his demeanor, as well as Dale's.

"What's this Sir and Mam Bit?" I asked.

That really shook them up. They started to stammer, I said, "Forget it, just call us by our names. We haven't changed, have you?"

"Uh, no sir, I mean Clay." Dale said.

"Where's that Ice Cream." I said. Tiff jumped up, "I'll get it, sit down."

When we all had our bowls full and were chowing down, I had time to assess their feelings. Hope and Dale were covertly eyeing each other. Tiff and Chip weren't being coy about their interest in each other. I winked at Rosie and inclined my head toward the four of them. She nodded.

I went back to giving my bowl the attention it deserved. But I was still thinking about Chip and Dale and their reaction to Faith and I. I guess I couldn't blame them for being a little apprehensive about the two of us. They probably thought that we were dyed in the wool killers. Which we weren't. We had never killed anybody, that weren't trying to kill us at the time. But I guess at times we were a little zealous at defending ourselves.

But really, can a person ever be too zealous about that?

Poppy and Hank finished their bowls and went off to bed. Alita's eyes were drooping also. Rosie and Alita slept in the bedroom that was off of the kitchen, Rosie picked Alita up and they went to bed. Suong excused herself, said she had a big day tomorrow. It was time for the Oil workers surprise drug tests.

That just left the six of us. I got up and collected the empty bowls and took them to the kitchen. Hope said, "You don't have to do that, I will do it."

"No, I'm Okay. In fact a feel just fine. Besides, you guys haven't finished mooning over each other, it's pretty obvious that you're going to have to get married pretty soon, or there is going to be a whole lot of fornicating going on."

All four of them sat there with a shocked expression on their faces. Faith said, "Clay, you behave yourself. But yes it is pretty evident that the four of you like each other. But it is up to the four of you, if you want to get married or not."

"Well, well, Uh," Hope stammered, Dale spoke up, "Yes, I do want to marry Hope, that is if she will have me." I guess he got over that case of lockjaw. Chip wasn't to be left out. "That goes for me also! I mean, not marry Hope, but Tiffany, if she will have me."

Both Mother and Daughter, said in unison, "Yes, we will."

Well sir, that's the way it went. A week later we had a double wedding in our living room. We hired an outfit from town to set up a reception tent in the pasture off of the kitchen, just about the whole town showed up. Chip and Dale had relatives up a gum stump.

Our wedding present was a honeymoon trip to Hawaii, they were to be gone two weeks. While they were gone I arraigned for two wings to be added to the house, on either side. Told them money was no object, as long as they had them completed in two weeks.

Red was a changed man, he no longer drank. And he was downright respectful. I had him oversee the construction. The rest of us, including Rosie, Hank and Poppy, saddled up and headed for our Viking Valley, as I was prone to call it.

Gabe and Clancy met us at the waterfall. The stone that was behind the falls was an optical illusion. When we got close we could see the opening of the passage way to the valley. Hank and Rosie were the only ones that hadn't been here with us. Poppy was overjoyed to get back. We had no more than cleared the passageway, than her and Alita started to pull their clothes off.

Rosie said, "What are you doing? Leave your clothes on."

Faith said, "That's Okay Rosie, they can take them off, we all went that way last time. But you don't have to, till you want to, that goes for you too, Hank."

Hank said, turning as red as me, "I think I will leave mine on, if you don't mind." Like I told you about Tiff, Hank's and her color was on the light side, so you could tell when they were embarrassed, of course so was Poppy's, but she wasn't the least embarrassed.

"Won't they get sunburned?" Rosie said, looking at Alita and Poppy.

"No," I said, then I explained about the water vapor in the air filtering out the harmful rays. Plus everything else as we rode along toward the Viking house.

Rosie said, "Well maybe I will pull these jeans off, I have underwear on." Then she stood up in the saddle like a trick rider and pulled her jeans down, then standing on one leg then the other one, she pulled her jeans off. Hank made sure he was looking the other way. Rosie sat back down in the saddle and tied the legs of her jeans around the saddle horn.

Faith said, "I can do that, watch." She stood up in the saddle and did the same thing. Of course I watched with interest. Hank was getting more miserable by the minute. I couldn't blame him, almost fifteen years old, this was pure torture for him.

The only thing different between Rosie and Faith was that Rosie had regular panties on, Faith had thong panties on.

"Come on Hank, I'll show you the swimming hole," I said, as we spurred ahead, leaving the women to go on to the Viking House. We got to the pool in short order, "Now you can take your clothes off, there are no women around. The water is just the right temperature." I said, as I stripped, Hank did also.

We were sunning ourselves beside the pool when the women arrived about a half hour later. Of course by this time they were all naked. Hank dove in the pool. Couldn't blame him, the second he seen the women, he started to swell. The curse of being a teenager. I guess we should of left him to help Red. Well shoot, he'll have to start learning to control it, sooner or later.

About an hour later, the women got their things together to leave, Faith said, "We had better go so Hank can get out of the water, before he turns into a prune."

Rosie said, "I feel sorry for him, does it hurt when it stays like that for a long time?"

"No, just his ego, he won't be able to look you guys in the eye for a long time. Don't worry about him, we guys all have to go through that when we're teenagers."

"It just gets like that for no reason?" Rosie asked.

"No, believe me there's a reason, and you guys are the reason. Don't worry we'll be along in short order."

Faith giggled, "In 'short order', huh?"

"Go on, get out of here, let the poor guy get out of the water." I said.

"I thought they would never leave." Hank said as he climbed on the rock I was setting on. "Well Hank, you do have a problem. And it's not going to get any better. It doesn't' bother you when you look at your sister, does it?"

"No, she's my sister."

"Well, I'll tell you what, just pretend that Rosie is your sister, which I guess you could say she is. And then just pretend that Faith is your Mother, again in effect she is. Then you won't have the problem. Every time you feel it start, just close your eyes and think of your mother or your sister."

He closed his eyes, "Yep, that should work. What do you

think about when you look at Faith?"

"I try not to think, if I dwelled on it, I would have the same problem that you do. That's just the way the Creator made us, to propagate the species."

"Do women have the same problem?" Hank said.

"Yep, but it doesn't show, aren't they the fortunate ones?"

"Yeah, I would say so. But it helps knowing they have the same problem." Hank said. He perked up quite considerable, with that last thought.

We picked up our clothes and tied them behind our saddle, then we rode slowly back to the Viking House. Hank was smiling by the time we got there.

We unsaddled and stowed the gear in the tack shed. Then we went into the house. Hank walked right in, smiling. Rosie and Faith turned as we came in, Hank said, "Hi, I'm feeling much better, Clay explained a few things to me, I understand now. Do you need any help with supper?"

Rosie said, "Yeah, you could get in some wood, there's a stack beside the door."

After Hank went outside, Rosie said, "What did you tell him?"

"Simple, I told him that women have the same problem, only it doesn't show."

Faith said, "Oh, we do, do we?"

I looked at her with a small smile, "Yes, you do." Both her and Rosie looked down at the floor. They both had small smiles on their faces.

"Alright, it's a push, man and woman, are more alike than they like to admit. Just don't make a big deal out of it." Faith said.

"Deal." I said, as Hank came back, in complete control. He smiled at Rosie. Rosie stuck her tongue out at him.

"What? What did I do?" Hank said.

"Nothing Hank," I said, "you're just a man, that's all."

Alita and Poppy came in from outside, with some Raspberry's, they each had a hatful. "These are really good, much better than the ones at home." Poppy said. She looked at her brother, "You alright now?"

"Yes, thanks for asking." Hank said, without any embarrassment.

The supper that night was delicious. And one good thing about it, we didn't have to worry if we spilled something on ourselves. We could always just take a bath. Of course we had to be really careful not to spill hot stuff in our laps. Seems like every good thing has its drawbacks.

Clancy and Gabe were the fortunate ones, they didn't need clothes, because the creator had provided them with the needed covering. After supper that night we sat around and talked. Hank didn't want to sleep in the house. So Clancy said that he could sleep outside with them and the saddle stock.

Hank thought that was a good idea. Cause he had been sleeping in the barn a lot of the time back at the ranch. Also he was relieved that he didn't have to sleep in the same house with naked women. He had a ways to go to conquer the teenage curse.

The three girls had picked out a room that they liked and were going to sleep together. I was overjoyed to hear that, as well as Faith was. Oh come on, you know why, I don't have to tell you.

This Viking House was versatile, it seemed to change to meet the needs of its occupants. I do believe at times I could hear it breathing, of course it wasn't, was it?

"No, of course it isn't, does your head hurt, Honey?" Was Faith's answer to my musings.

"No it doesn't. Just that everything seems so convenient here, do you think that's how it was in the Garden Of Eden?" I asked.

"Yes, I do. Look, if you want some fruit, all you have to do is just go pick some. Seems like there is always some kind of fruit just right for picking. And the vegetables in the garden, did you notice there are no weeds?" Faith said.

"Yes, I did notice, do you think it's like this year around?" I asked, as we walked to our bedroom. The diffused moonlight that was coming in through the windows put a romantic light over everything. Including my wife….

Faith never did get around to answering my question. I had no more than asked it, then I forgot about it myself…

Alita woke us up the next morning by jumping into bed with us, Rosie followed her in.

"Breakfast is ready, that is if you guys are?" Rosie said. As we detangled ourselves.

"Sure," Faith said, "but first I think we need a shower."

"Yeah, I suspect that you do. We already had ours, when you're ready, the foods on the table." Rosie said, as she picked up Alita and left the room.

I looked at Faith, "Do you think she's a little miffed at something?"

"Yes, I think so, I think she is just a little jealous of us. She is starting to wish she had a man, herself." Faith said.

"What? She couldn't be thinking that, she's not old enough." I said.

"Yes, she is, she's going to be sixteen her next birthday. Plus she's, say, like in her twenty's when it comes to life experiences."

"Yeah, I guess you're right, have you talked to her about it?"

"It? You mean sex?" Faith said.

"I don't know, I guess maybe, hell I don't know. About life in general, I guess."

307

Faith gave me a sideways look as she brushed at her hair, why I don't know, brush her hair I mean, not the look, cause we hadn't taken a shower yet, am I rambling?

She laid the brush down,

"What do you think of Rosie?" She said.

"What do you mean? I like her of course, she's our daughter."

"You know what I mean, do you like her as a woman?"

"I think she is a fine woman. If you mean am I interested in her as a woman? I am not! She is my daughter, that's all, period. How could you even ask me such a question?"

"Alright, alright, don't get in a snit. I'm just a wife, that's all, strange things pop into our minds every now and then. Forget I even asked you that, okay?"

I picked her up by the shoulders and pulled her close and kissed her hard, "You are the only one that turns me on, so don't ever get jealous of any other woman, ever."

Rosie stuck her head in, "Hey, come on, didn't you guys get enough last night, we're all waiting for you!"

"Alright, give us a minute," I said, as Faith and I got in the shower, together.

We spent the next two weeks in a paradisiacal haze. We all got the best tans of our lives, without any skin damage. Due to the misty haze that covered the valley that screened out any harmful rays from the sun. I think I told you about this before, didn't I?

Hank and Poppy were a little anxious to get back and see their Mother and Tiffany. But at the same time were hesitant to leave this Garden of Eden. Now Rosie was a different story, she had no hesitation either way, she knew what she wanted to do. We were setting around the breakfast table, when Rosie said,

"It's time to go home." It was a flat statement, with no indecision. She sat there with a firm set to her jaw, like I would disagree with her. She had blossomed in the last two weeks, her female assist's were more pronounced, as in fact all of the women's did. I hadn't paid much attention, but looking at them now, they were more than beautiful. I cleared my throat,

"Uh, yes, I suppose you're right, so I guess we had better find our clothes. I haven't seen mine in awhile, but I suppose there around here somewhere."

Faith said, "I washed all of our clothes, they are in the closets. I tried mine on the other day, it seems in places they are a little tight, not in the waist, but you know, up here."

Rosie and Poppy turned a little pink, Poppy said, "Yes, mine have been getting bigger also, so has Rosie's too." Hank and I, kept our mouths shut, it seems our minds worked a little better now, enough to know not to comment on the size of the girls breasts.

Alita was following all of the conversation. She put her hands up to her chest, "Mommy, where are mine, it's not fair, you three have big one's, why don't I?"

Hank and I, got up, "We're going to get the saddle stock ready, there's too much female talk in here this morning." I said. Clancy was setting beside the tack shed, eating a turnip.

"So you're leaving this morning." It was a statement not a question. "I want to warn you, things have changed a little bit."

"What do you mean, changed a little bit?" I asked. "It's only been two weeks, how much could they have changed?"

"Hmm, two weeks? Yes, in here it has been two weeks, but never mind, just be ready." Clancy said, then swallowed the last of his turnip and walked away.

I didn't like it, reading between the lines, I was sure there was a lot more to his 'Hmm' then he let on. I glanced up to the sky, Gabe was making big circles, riding the air currents.

Faith came out where we were working with the stock, "Honey, I just tried the Satellite Phone, the battery is still alright, but there's no signal, how can that be?"

"There's no signal from here." I took the phone and poked in a diagnostic code, nothing happened, "Yep, like I said, no signal" I said as I handed it back. I looked at her, "Did you forget your top?" She had put on jeans and boots, but no top.

"No I didn't forget, not only will my bra not fit, but my blouse is way too tight, I'll have to borrow one of your shirts, is that okay?"

"Sure, what's mine is yours anyway, or did you forget that we are one flesh?"

"No, I didn't forget. My jeans are just a little tight, how do they look?"

I looked, wow! How jeans could improve over being naked, I had no idea, but they did. "Uh, honey, they look just fine, just fine. Are the girls getting ready?" I had to change the subject, if I kept looking at my wife, we wouldn't get underway this morning.

Faith went back into the house, "Hank, be sure we don't forget anything, especially any of our weapons. I have a feeling we might need them."

"Why do you say that? Has Clancy and Gabe said anything?" Hank said.

"Some, nothing concrete, Clancy is being less than efficacious."

"Huh? What the heck is efficacious?"

"Oh, sorry, I simply meant that his words were not producing the desired effect that I was hoping for."

Hank looked at me funny, "Where in the world did you get that word?"

"I don't know, it just popped into my brain, things have been doing that lately. But to get back to the point, we have to be prepared for almost anything. Clancy said that things have changed some out there. I don't see how they could change all that much, it's only been two weeks."

"I sometimes think that he likes being a drama queen." Hank said.

"I don't think so, most times he understates things." I said.

Chapter Nineteen

The women came out of the house with all of our stuff. I packed it on the pack horses. Some we tied behind the cantle of our saddles. I looked at Faith and Rosie, "Do you have your weapons? I see you have your rifles, but your hideouts, knives and pistols?"

"Yes, there a little uncomfortable, since we have been running around with nothing on, now we not only have these cumbersome clothes, but these weapons chafe a little bit." Rosie said.

"Well, be that as it may, I'm sure a little chafing is better than being dead." I said.

"That's easy for you to say, you don't have these stilettos strapped to your inner thighs." Faith said.

"No, but I have my Bowie down the back of my neck. It itches at times."

"Oh, boohoo, it itches, big deal. Let me put these blades next to your testicles, then tell me how they feel." Faith said.

"Mom, Dad, you're both being infantile, here we just had an ideal two weeks, lets don't spoil it. I'm sorry I said that they chafed." Rosie said.

She was right, "I'm sorry Faith, I think were both being a little apprehensive about leaving here," I took her in my arms and gave her a kiss that I wished I could follow up on. She returned it with a promise.

"So," I said, when we came up for air, "Faith you take the lead, put Alita on her mule, Matthew, Poppy of course will ride

Iris's mule, Luke. Hank will be right behind you, with Alita and Poppy behind him, I'll ride drag, of course. The Pack horses will follow behind me."

Hank said, "How come I don't have any hide out pistol, just this knife."

"You have your 30-30, don't you?" I said.

"Of course, but Rosie is better armed than I am. I'm a man, she's just a girl."

"Oh, Hank, how young you are. Rosie is so much more than just a girl, you notice I didn't tell her where to ride, you see she is better used when she's free to ride where she's needed. Someday, you'll understand just who she is." I said.

Faith whispered in my ear, "Just who is she?" "Salvation," I whispered back.

"You say the weirdest things at times, 'salvation' indeed. You just forgot to tell her where to ride is all." Faith said.

"Could be there was a reason I forgot, did you ever think about that? You know I don't always know what I'm talking about."

"Huh? I don't even know what the hell you're talking about right now. Are you feeling okay?" Faith said, as she felt my forehead.

"Yeah, I'm alright. I guess, it's just that I have this feeling that everything is changing. What we knew, we don't anymore. When we ride out under that waterfall, we had better be ready for just about anything." I said, as I tied off the pack on the last pack horse.

Rosie swung into her saddle and looked down at me, "You didn't tell me where to ride in this string?"

"Faith said I just forgot to tell you, but you can pick where you want to ride. You remember what you were called, Espiritu Jinete? Or Spirit Rider?

"Yes, I do. I don't feel much like a spirit though. I think I will fall in behind all of the Pack Horses, if that's Okay?"

"Sure, you know best, just look where it ain't." I said.

Faith spoke up, "I don't think he's himself this morning, 'look where it ain't' doesn't make any sense."

"Alright, I'll explain. It simple means to use your peripheral vision. I mean if you think you seen something, instead of looking directly at it, look where it isn't, then your peripheral vision will pick it up quicker."

"Balderdash, I never heard of such a thing. Are you sure you're feeling fine?" Faith said, as she felt my forehead again.

"No, that makes sense, I think I've read about it before." Rosie said, as I picked my wife up and put her in her saddle, Alita and Poppy were already setting in theirs'.

"Just try it sweetheart, you too Hank, you both will see that it works." I said, as I swung onto Brutus' back, he was dancing around, impatient to get going. He didn't like the idea of where we were going to ride, he wanted to be in the front. I pulled him up sharp then leaned forward and whispered in his ear, he quieted down.

Just before we rode into the tunnel, I turned in my saddle and looked back. The valley seemed to be saying to come back soon. I don't know whether I told you much about this tunnel before, but I probably didn't, I forget things at times.

Anyway, it was imbedded with crystals. They glowed, giving a blue effervescent light that one hated to leave for the harsh sunshine that awaited us.

Faith pulled up at the mouth of the tunnel, looking through the mist of the waterfall. I rode up beside her, "What's wrong?" I asked.

"I don't know, I just have a bad feeling. Like our lives are about to change, do we have to leave here?"

"Yes, I'm afraid so. We have family out there, we just can't hide in a Rabbit hole. We have to face whatever lies in wait for us. Drop back behind the girls, I'll go first." I said, as I leaned over and gave her a kiss, her lips were cold, I held the kiss till I could feel them start to warm up.

I rode through the water, the wet clothes felt good as we rode out into the bright sun of our future. The sun was just short of high noon. The sound track of that old Gary Cooper movie was running through my mind. I shook my head, clearing the cobwebs out.

We sort of grouped up a bit after we came out. Faith pulled the Satellite phone from her saddle bags. "There still is no signal, how can that be?" She said.

"I don't know, but never mind, I think I did hear of a time when there were no cell phones, telephones, telegraph, or regular mail service. I guess they had drums and smoke signals and bet they were considered right up town." I said.

"Very funny, but I'm worried, something is really wrong." Faith said, looking around at the sky. I nudged my horse close to hers. "Honey, cool it. You're going to scare Poppy and Hank." Alita was close by, she said, "Yes Mommy, I think Poppy is missing her mother, don't scare her."

Rosie said, "I think I'm going to scout around a little bit, you guys stay in the timber line, don't skyline yourselves. Just drift toward home, slowly. I'll be back within the hour." She whirled her horse and headed off, staying in the timber herself. I did notice Gabe circling around, he followed her.

We lined out, I took the lead. That didn't last long, Faith was up beside me. I had never seen her so nervous. "Faith, just keep to the timber, I'll drop back behind the kids."

Alita pulled her Mule up beside Faith, "Mommy, it's alright, I'll ride with you, don't worry." Faith gave her a relieved smile, "Thanks Honey, but Mommy is okay, but you can ride with me if you want to."

Riding drag, I could watch over everybody, that gave me a

sense of relief. I guess I was a control freak. The pack horses were close behind me, I looked back, "Hey, don't run over me, what's wrong with you guys?" They were sure jumpy.

Why was it, that the loss of our cell phone service, sent us into a dither? We would probably really feel silly when it turned out to be some sort of glitch. I kept telling myself this platitude. Of course the fact that Clancy and Gabe warned us that things had changed, did that mean anything?

With all of my musings, I almost missed the flash of something bright up ahead, out in the valley. I took my own advice and looked to just one side of where I seen the flash. Yep, there it was again, just a flash, like a shinning peace of metal in the sun.

I spurred ahead, I waved our crew deeper into the timber. I stopped them a little ways in. "You guys stay here," I said, as I stepped down. "I'm going to injun up on that flash I seen out in the valley." I pulled off my boots and got my moccasins out of my saddle bags. I pulled my rifle out of its scabbard. "Just stay here, I'll be back directly."

"Honey, be careful, I don't know what we'd do if something happened to you."

"You know I will be. Rosie should be back pretty quick, tell her not to follow me, to stay with you guys." I said, as I disappeared into the tall grass. The sun felt unusually hot, that is after we had spent time in the Viking Valley. The flash was erratic, like the breeze was blowing something around.

The grass was also unusually tall, like our cattle hadn't grazed it for awhile. I could crouch down and stay hidden. It only took me about ten minutes to get close to where I thought the flash was coming from.

I bellied down, and snaked forward, pushing the grass apart as I went. What did I see? I seen my plane, the twin engine Cessna. Some asshole had tried to land and flipped it over on its top. The flash was caused by a piece of broken glass flapping in the breeze, where the front wind screen used to be.

I didn't stand up, but finished the crawl on my belly. No use taking any chances.

I didn't have to worry though, no one alive was there.

But there was a Skelton half in and half out of the smashed window. I stood up and looked closer. There were the remnants of his clothes still hanging from his bones. And in what used to be a pair of jeans, was a billfold.

I pulled it out and dug out a Wyoming Drivers License. Damn, it was Red, you know, Daisy's husband. What the hell was he doing flying my plane, he didn't know how. Duh, that was pretty evident.

I stood there for a full minute anyway, thinking. Now that was work…cause nothing added up. We had only been gone for two weeks, and it sure took longer than that for a body to deteriorate down to bare bone. Heck, it didn't even smell anymore.

I looked toward where I left the rest of my family. There was a flash, someone was glassing me. I stood up on the belly of the plane and waved at them, motioning them to come over to me.

Rosie was with them when they got to me. I didn't say anything, I just tossed the Drivers License to Faith. She looked at it then tossed it to Rosie. I gave them a few minutes to take it all in. "Well, what do you make of it?" I said to them all.

Rosie said, "It doesn't make any sense. You'd think he had been dead for a least a year. And we have only been gone for two weeks. But, Clancy did say things weren't what they seemed anymore."

Faith had got herself together, she was back to her old self. "Yeah, but they never have been. But just like the first time we were in the Valley, our sense of time, didn't match the time elapsed outside of it. What else is in the plane, did you look?"

"Nope, I sure didn't, probably should though, huh?" I said.

"Yes, you should, Hank hop down and help Clay." Faith said, in charge again as usual.

I opened the door that was ajar a little further so I could crawl in. The first thing I found was a bag. I opened it, it was full of money, I zipped it back up and tossed it to Hank, he tossed it to Faith.

What I hoped was still in the plane, was. I always carried survival gear stowed in the tail section. I crawled back there. Yep, it was still here, no one had taken it out. "Hank come on back here and help me get this gear." There was a tent, shovel, axe, and so forth, plus dried food that would keep for years. We shouldn't need this stuff, but one never knew.

I distributed the stuff among the pack horses, so no one would have too heavy of a load. After all these horses were volunteers, they were free to leave anytime they wanted.

Faith had looked in the bag that Hank had tossed her. "Where did he get all of this money?" She asked, as if I would know.

"I don't know, but one thing, knowing Red's personality, it wasn't his. It probably belonged to the ranch. Too bad he didn't gas the plane up before he took off, it was the death of him."

"How long were we in the Valley?" Poppy asked. I hadn't noticed but Clancy had come up while I was inside of the plane. He spoke up.

"Two years and a few days. A lot has changed." He said.

Poppy said, "Is Mom and Tiff alright?"

"Yes, but their not at the ranch anymore, Elizabeth came and got them. Mary Jane and Iris were worried about the lot of you. They came with Elizabeth, you know the helicopter? Anyway they picked up Daisy and your Dog. Of course Chip and Dale, went along. It wouldn't have been right to leave your Mom and Sister's new husbands to fend for themselves. They also took Dr. Suong." Clancy told her.

"So what about our Ranch?" I asked.

"Oh, it's not yours anymore, Eminent Domain, is what they used to take it."

"How in the world could they justify that? Isn't it supposed to be for the good of the public? And then of course, there's supposed to be just compensation!" I said.

"Ho-Ho, you're really naïve, aren't you? This administration has been flaunting the constitution right from the start. They have made it nothing but a scrap of paper." Clancy said.

"Well if the government took it, what are they doing with it?" Faith asked.

"They have installed their man to run it. They did the same with your Dad and Felicity's Ranch in New Mexico."

"So, who's on the Ranch? And what about everyone in New Mexico, where are they?" I asked.

"Harry Silver is on the ranch up here, and a Dipper Tick in New Mexico. Your family is still there at the ranch in New Mexico." Clancy said.

"Harry Silver and Dipper Tick, you're kidding me?"

"No, they have been deep in this since the beginning. This administration has been just biding it's time to declare a modified version of martial law. It's sort of a cross between communism and a dictatorship. They have been doing this eminent domain thing all across the country. The only one's they can't overcome is the Carmel Foundation's property. Every time they send troops against them, the troops just disappear, no one knows what happens to them."

"Well what does our loved one's think happened to us?" Faith asked.

"Oh, they think you're all dead, even the foundation thinks so."

"What? Why didn't you tell them the truth?" I said.

"What is the truth? How do you know that you aren't dead?" Clancy said, with a lopsided grin.

"Oh, I know we're not, and so do you. Why were we kept in the Viking Valley for two years anyway?" I said.

"They would of killed all of you for sure. But when you disappeared they just took over your ranch with no more bloodshed. So we just slowed down your sense of time, to think you were only in there for two weeks."

"Why couldn't of we just went to the Carmel Foundation as the rest of our loved ones did?"

"That was not to be your purpose."

"What the hell is our purpose?" I said.

"You don't know? You've been doing it all of your life. It's to fight injustice! And no you're not some superhero. You all are just flesh and blood, you are human. As such you know right and wrong. Oh, how simple it would have been if they had never ate from that apple. There would have been no such thing as wrong, right would of reigned.

But, no use crying over spilt milk. You have to run the race to the finish."

"Fight injustice and right the wrongs, isn't that God's job?" Faith asked.

"Make no mistake about it, his day of vengeance will come, but no man or beast knows the day or the hour. But the season is late and well along to its finish. Until that day comes, it's up to the honest hearted doer of right things, to carry the load. Of which you all just happen to fit that bill. It's not to say that you're supposed to overthrow any government on earth, that's still God's job. But there are still the poor and weak individuals that need help to survive, could you perhaps be of help there?"

"Haven't we been?" Faith said.

"Yes, you all have. But even stout hearted ones like yourselves, need help now and then. That's what Gabe and I have been sent to do. Lend a hand when you get your tit in a wringer."

"That wasn't a nice thing to say. I know they've got bigger, but I can still handle them." Faith said.

"I'm sorry, I didn't mean it in that way, I was just using a metaphor, it was in bad taste." Clancy said.

Poppy and Hank were whispering. Hank spoke up, "What about us, Poppy and me? Are we part of this stout hearted bunch?" Clancy turned to look at him, "Do you want to be?"

"I don't know, Poppy and I, we just want to see Mom and Tiffany. Can't we just do that?"

"Yes, we were a little apprehensive when the two of you went with the others. But it couldn't be helped. You were just in the wrong place at the right time. I do suppose that you could be taken to the Carmel Foundation in the Judith Basin. That is if Clay and the rest of you will take them?"

Rosie said, "Sure, I know how it is to miss your parents. We will take them, won't we Mom, Dad, Alita?"

I noticed that she included Alita in that question. Why? Maybe because she was mentally equal to the rest of us, almost anyway.

I said, "It's Okay with me, as long as Faith and Alita agree." They both nodded.

"But why can't they just pick them up with Elizabeth, like they did the rest?" I said.

"Because they don't know that you are alive. And also they don't know that we have taken a hand in this difficulty. You have been the only ones that we have communicated with. Well, that is outside of the livestock, we always talk to them."

"What? Do you mean you have always talked to the animals?" I said.

"Of course, they have committed no sin." Clancy said.

"Alright, while we're being so open and honest, the Carmel Foundation, you mean you haven't helped them?" I said.

"No, we haven't. Besides, they have had help from a different source, a different branch of the heavenly organization."

"I suppose that's none of our business either?" I said.

"That's right, it's on a need to know, and you don't need to know."

"Well you slammed that door in our face, but you're right, we don't want to know, I do believe in this case that ignorance is bliss."

"You're heavy into metaphors and clichés aren't you? But never mind, it's what makes the English language colorful and interesting. Have you ever thought how boring it would be, if everyone always stuck to the rules of language that is taught in schools?

Besides that, some arbitrary rules are meant to be broke, why else were they made? I just love talking in English, it's so ambiguous." Clancy said.

Alita spoke up, "I think that both you and Daddy like to run off at the mouth, to use a colorful metaphor, I think we had better head back for the timber, we have been in the open long enough." Out of the mouth of babes, comes wisdom, I thought to myself as swung a leg over the back of Brutus.

Damn, I thought to myself, couldn't I even talk anymore without using a metaphor, cliché or colloquialism (to use the word erroneously), when I should of said, localism or regionalism. (For you readers with a Masters Degree in English).

I was watching Alita on her Mule, Matthew. She had

grown at least eight to ten inches while we were in the Valley. That should have given us the hint as to the passage of time. But maybe not, strange things had been happening to us right along. Alita sat her saddle like she had been riding for a decade. She reminded me of Rosie. Perhaps they were both Espiritu Jinete. Faith and I, both sat a good saddle, but nothing like our two girls.

We got back in the timber and circled around back of the drilling rig, there were still people working it. They didn't see us. We stayed in the timber line all the way back toward the ranch house. We had to pass it, to go north. We got off our mounts and bellied up to the crest of the ridge. We had field glasses. We didn't see any stock any where around. I guess it was too much work for them to take care of them. They probably just turned them all loose. Lazy Bastards.

"I know what you're thinking." Faith said as she crawled up beside me. "And you can forget it."

"Why? Just one bullet through the brain and he would be fertilizer."

"It's not up to us, let the higher powers take care of it. We only kill in self- defense." Faith said as one of her breasts pressed up against my side. I promptly forgot all about Harry Silver. I rolled over on my back and pulled her close and kissed her.

"Hey, knock that off, there is a time and place for that stuff." Rosie said. Alita was standing beside her, giggling. Poppy and Hank were with the stock.

"Yeah, of course you're right," I said as we both scooted back from the crest. "But, your Mom is quite the dish, did you know that?"

"Yeah, yeah, you just have an out of control libido, that's all." Rosie said. Alita just giggled some more.

We joined Hank and Poppy. I glanced around at our

animals. Looked like we had gained some more. "Where did they come from?" I asked Hank.

"They just showed up, they're some of the mules and horses that I had been working with, you know from that last bunch you bought. It's alright that they go with us, isn't it?"

"Sure, the more the merrier." There I go again. Is that all I am, is one big metaphor? Or maybe it's just one little simile?

"Did you see many people down there?" I asked the women. "I know I didn't, I was just wondering what you guys seen?"

"No, I didn't." Rosie said. "Why? What do you have in mind?"

"Well, I thought if we waited till tonight, we could go down and get some more tack, you know for the extra stock. Also, some oats. Maybe even get in the root cellar and get some canned goods for us. What do the rest of you think?"

"Yes, they belong to us anyway," Faith said. "I didn't see much of anybody down there. I don't think they think they have anything to worry about. I didn't even see any of our ranch dogs down there. Maybe, Elizabeth picked them up when she got our people?"

"Let's hope so anyway. Otherwise those jerks probably would of shot them." I said.

Faith and Rosie had their heads together. They said, "Do you think any of our clothes are still there?"

"I don't know sweetheart, it's been two years. I would suspect that they were got rid of." I said.

"Well, while Rosie, Alita, Hank and Poppy get the extra tack and canned goods, let's you and me, sneak in the house and see?"

"Oh, I thought you only wanted to kill in self-defense?"

"Well yes, of course."

"What about if we surprise someone in the house, I might

have to slit their throats?"

"Well, only if they try and kill us, okay?" Faith said. Faith had planned our recovery intrusion well. I told you she was back to her old self. But that was alright with me, I loved her.

We waited till full dark and an hour besides. The kids went toward the barn, with Matthew and Luke following them. I wouldn't want to mess with those two mules. We went to the kitchen door, it wasn't locked. There was a small light burning over the kitchen range, enough to see the kitchen was a mess. Just like a bachelor would leave it.

One thing all of those shots to the head had given me was a good sense of hearing. At each bedroom I stopped to listen, if there was anybody in them, I could hear them breathing. So far they were all empty. Till I got to our old bedroom.

I motioned for Faith to run on quiet. The bedroom door was ajar. I could hear two people breathing. We moved over by the bed, we stood there. We could see two people in bed. Due to the warmness of the night they were laying there with no covers and no clothes.

The man was Harry Silver, the woman we couldn't tell. Did he have a wife? We didn't know. There seemed to be a lot that we didn't know....Faith moved to the side of the bed that she was sleeping on. We both laid the points of our knives against their throats.

Harry opened his eyes, "Is that you Clay?" He said, "Yep, are you surprised?" I said.

"No, I knew you weren't dead, I was expecting you. "I know you have at least nine lives, or hell maybe more. That was why I took this job. Of course I didn't have much choice, they thought I was a friend of yours. If I hadn't of took this job, they would of killed me."

I didn't know if he was telling the truth or not, so I decided to find out, I took my knife away from his throat and laid the point against the base of his penis. He gasped. The woman next to him had woke up. Faith increased the pressure of her knife point, the woman whimpered. I said.

"Is that the truth Harry, and make sure of your answer." I put a little more pressure on the point of my knife. It turned out he was telling the truth. "Who's the woman?" I asked.

"She was put here to watch me, you can kill her if you want, she's a lousy screw anyway." He said.

Faith said, "Why Harry, that's cold, maybe you just don't turn her on." I looked over at her. She was in her middle twenty's. I looked again, hell, it was Patty. You remember, I told you about Patty and Angelina. I had went to school with them.

"Patty, what the hell are you doing here?" I said.

"It's not my fault Clay, they beat us up, Angelina is still in the hospital. It was either do this or they said they would put us in a whore house. And Faith was right, he doesn't' turn me on."

"Alright Patty, get up and get in the shower, is there anyone else in the house?"

"No, it's just us. You aren't going to leave me here are you?"

"No, I guess not, ask my wife." I said. As I left Faith to see if anything of ours was still in the bedroom. I went to my gun closet and took what weapons I wanted. Harry was padding along after me.

"Harry, for craps sake, go get dressed, no one wants to see your scrawny body."

"What about me, you can't leave me here, they will kill me for sure?" He whined.

"I tell you what, you apologize to Patty and if she agrees, you can come with us."

We went back into the bedroom, Patty was just getting out

of the shower, after Harry apologized, she said, "Alright, but if we ever have any sex again, you're going to do exactly what I tell you to do. I'm not the lousy lay, you are. Have you ever had any sex with any other woman besides me?"

He nodded his head. "Alright, I said. Now if you two will get traveling clothes on. Plus any extra's that you might need, we'll go see how the kids are doing."

Faith said, "Uh, honey, would you give me a few minutes, I would like to take a quick shower, okay?"

"Sure, just wait till they get out of the room, I don't want Harry to see you naked." As soon as they were dressed, I hustled them out of the room. Faith was already naked before they got out of the door. She had found some of our clothes, so she had clean ones to change to.

"Come on you two. You are going with me to the barn." We went to the barn, I kept a close eye on them, they would have to earn my trust. The kids already had everything loaded on the pack horses.

I said to the girls, "There is no one else in the house, you three can go find anything you need, Mom is taking a shower, you girls might like one also." They beat a path for the house. Hank said, "Can I go to my old room, I would like a shower too."

"Yeah, I'll go along. Matthew and Luke can watch these two." I motioned to the mules, they came over and gave Harry and Patty the evil eye.

Patty said, "Very funny Clay, you know me, and I'm not scared of these two mules."

"I know you Patty, but you might have changed a bit, and as far as these two mules go, you had better be afraid of them." I turned and went back to the house, Faith was just getting out of the shower, I was already naked as I passed her and got in the shower. The hot water felt good.

Faith had clean clothes laid out for me. It was well past midnight when we left.

Harry and Patty were still verbally jabbing each other. Now I don't know about you, but when two people act like they were acting, they usually had some affection. I turned in my saddle, "Shut up you two, or I'll have Luke kick your lights out." They shut up.

Chapter Twenty

The moon was shining bright, it made our way easy to see. I wanted to get miles away before daylight. I had a place in mind, one with both water and enough cover so we couldn't be seen from the air.

I was riding drag, as usual, with Rosie and Faith in the lead. Their horses knew the spot I was thinking about, so all they had to do was just enjoy the ride. How did they know? Easy, I had talked to them and told them.

Harry and Patty were quiet, except for a few muttered curses about the bumpy ride. Now it wouldn't be bumpy, if they knew how to ride. But they both were bouncing up and down like dummy's made of rubber. Harry dropped back, he had the typical cop personality. He said, "So, where were the lot of you for two years?"

"Around, really, it wasn't a place so much as a time. But you wouldn't believe me anyway, so I'm not going to waste my energy. I have a question for you, what's the economy, infrastructure and such in the world like?"

"The world? I don't know, but my guess is, that's it a lot better than ours." He said.

"Well then, how about inflation?" I asked.

"Oh there is none, the government strictly controls prices, as well as everything else. You remember what Communism used to be like, it's pretty much like that."

"Is the whole world like that?"

"No, well really, I don't know. I think most of them are

into Capitalism, ironic isn't it?" Harry said, with a sigh.

"That really doesn't surprise me too much, when this administration started bending the constitution, you could see the hand writing on the wall. I suppose that they have banned the general public from owning guns?"

"Of course, that was the first thing to go. Would you believe it was the Republican's that pushed that? Again, ironic." Harry said.

"And all of this happened in just two years? The country that was known for hundreds of years for freedom, now has turned despotic!" I said.

"I'm afraid so. Tragic, just tragic." Harry said, as he rejoined Patty.

I glanced back at all of our packhorses, they were right where they were supposed to be. Plus about fifty head of loose stock followed along. I guess they didn't like the powers that be any better than we did.

There were cattle scattered everywhere. I could see that it wouldn't take long till they were like the Longhorns of Texas used to be after the Civil War. When there was no incentive to work, besides a form of slavery, people didn't. And that was what communism was, just a subtle form of slavery.

We reached our camping spot just before dawn. A nice clear little stream ran through it. Large Fir trees provided cover. We unsaddled our horses and took the packs off of the others. I told them to fan out and graze, just be back at twilight for the next leg on our journey.

Harry and Patty weren't much use, they were so pooped. They spread their bedrolls and were fast asleep. We had to wake them to eat. The rest of us inventoried our supplies, before laying down to sleep.

I woke up about two hours before sunset. I gathered dry wood for a smokeless fire. I got some food going before I woke the rest of them. The horses and mules had already gathered around. I gave them each a small bait of oats. Just a small treat, for there were so many of them.

Faith, Rosie and Alita, sat up and rubbed their eyes, they stood up and took their clothes off and headed for the stream. Harry and Patty, I had to go kick them out of the sack. Patty seen the women in the stream and went to join them.

Poppy was standing there, trying to make up her mind, "Poppy, get your clothes off and take a bath, we have a long ride ahead of us tonight." I said. Then I looked at Hank and Harry, "You two, go downstream to take your bath's, I'll have food ready after everybody is finished, then I'll go take mine." That's what I did.

I used the same hole that the women did. I floated around on my back, just enjoying the water. It was cold, but not that bad. Faith and Patty came down with the dishes. Faith looked at me, "Looks like the water is cold, by the looks of you." She said.

I said back, "Yeah, just because you don't have a visible thermometer like I do, no need to get snippy." Patty giggled, "It's still better than Harry's, even in cold water." I stuck my tongue out at them.

Faith tossed me a bar of soap, "Wash your beard, you had food in it. Your hair needs cut, probably in the morning I'll cut it, when I trim your beard." She said. I looked at them both, "Hey, you two, don't forget to get dressed yourselves, you're upsetting Harry, or didn't you notice?"

"Oh, we noticed, it's just fun seeing him try to hide it." Patty said, as they did their *woman walk* back to camp. Well, they had it, they might as well flaunt it.

Hank had the horses all saddled when I got back, I helped put the pack saddles on, then we both loaded them. I knew the country pretty good, plus of course Clancy and Gabe were still around.

Clancy had made himself scarce all last night, but tonight he showed up. Harry seen him, "Hey, there's a Coyote over there, he's not rabid is he?"

"Rabid? Why you poor excuse for a human being, it's me that should be asking that about you." Clancy said.

Harry took a couple of steps back, "Huh? What the hell, he can talk!" He said.

"Yes I talk, better than you, I would surmise. Why did you bring those two along?" Clancy said, looking at me.

"Well, they said if we didn't they would have been killed."

"So, what's the big deal? Oh well, I suppose you have to be kind to dumb animals." Clancy said, turning his back on Harry. "But she isn't too bad, looks a little dumb though." He added looking at Patty.

"Clay are you going to let that Old Man Coyote talk to me like that?" Patty said, with a smile, as she bent to pet Clancy. Clancy shook his head, as if it annoyed him. Patty didn't know it, but she just made a friend.

Gabe came down from the tree tops, landing on a low branch close to us. "You will have to travel quiet tonight, there are a few of the People's Patrol's out. They make camp at night, drink too much and then sleep pretty solid. But you still have to be careful.

Just keep skirting the west side of the Big Horns, but stay on the east side of the Dinosaur Beds. You will find a good little stream to camp by, much like this camp spot. The next night, just at the foot of the Medicine Wheel, there is a deep spring, both cold and warm. Camp there."

"Spring? Beside the Medicine Wheel? I didn't know there was one there." I said.

"It's new, just this week, after all it is the Medicine Wheel." Gabe said. "And you are an Indian."

"Half, you know that. Who made that wheel anyway?" I asked.

"The Ancient Ones. The ones who came before." Gabe said.

"What was it for?" Faith asked.

"They thought they needed a star map to reach the Great Spirit, they didn't. All they had to do was pray to him out of a pure heart. When he told them that, they just left the wheel there, makes a good mystery though, doesn't it?"

"Yeah, I would say so." Faith said, then she added, "Why are you and Clancy helping us?"

"Why? Because you are descendants of the Ancient Ones, among other reasons. And their prayers are still in the Great Spirit's memory. Their pure hearts are still working for you."

"But, I'm not an Indian," Faith said, "like Clay is."

"Aren't you? You and Clay both are descendants of the Other Ones. You were meant to be together, your children, both Rosie and Alita are Spirit Riders, why wouldn't we help you?" Gabe said, then flew off into the night.

"Do you know what he was talking about?" Faith asked me.

"No, not all of it. I have heard of the Ancient Ones, but the Other Ones? As far as being descendants of them, I wouldn't know. But like I've said before about the two girls being Espiritu Jinete or Spirit Riders. We sort of knew that."

Rosie cleared her throat, "Dad, it's full dark, I think we had better hit the trail."

That we did. Clancy jumped up behind Alita, with his paws on her shoulders. I came up beside them.

"Clancy, why are there patrols out in this wilderness, what are they looking for?"

"Looking for? Basically you. But they'll *devil* anybody they come across."

"Why are they looking for us?" I said.

"You guys are like a small sliver in the Evil ones foot, hurts just enough to be annoying. He'll swat you like a fly, if he gets the chance."

It was about an hour before dawn when we came to that small stream Gabe told us to camp by. It was a good spot, with plenty of good grass for the stock as well as plenty of tree cover for us to spread our bedrolls under.

We ate a cold breakfast, or was it Supper? It didn't matter, we were plenty pooped. Rosie, Alita and Poppy spread theirs close to each other under a big fir tree that spread its lower branches out like a mother hen spreads its wings for her chicks.

Hank spread his under another tree, but close enough to the girls. He was in those teenage years where he wanted to be tough and independent, but not that much, to get out of sight of the girls.

Now Harry and Patty spread theirs about a hundred yards away from the rest of us. Which I was glad of, I didn't want to hear any of their nonsense. Faith and I, we stayed close to the kids. We didn't feel very amorous anyway. I don't know where Clancy went, some secret mission I suppose.

I never sleep that hard, especially when danger might be near. About an hour after we went to sleep, Faith and I were awakened by noise coming from Harry and Patty's sleeping area. "What the hell is that?" Faith said.

"Go back to sleep, Patty was always a screamer, as I remember from High School." Faith punched me. "How do you know that?" Faith said

"That's what my buddies told me, so don't hit me. I never messed around with her. I hope it didn't wake the kids up." I lifted up a bit and looked at the kids, Rosie was looking at me. I signaled her to go back to sleep, she smiled and nodded.

We woke up about two that afternoon. The kids were

already in the swimming hole. Faith and I joined them. Harry and Patty were still asleep. As we had spent time in Viking Valley running around naked, it didn't bother any of us to skinny dip. That is as long as Harry and Patty were still asleep.

Faith had crawled out and was standing in a shaft of sunlight drying herself, she said. "What are we going to do about those two, I don't trust them." She was turning slowing, letting the sun reach every drop of water. I was floating on my back watching her. She was sure a sight. I glanced over at the kids, they were diving for a colored rock or something, paying no attention to us oldsters.

"What do you mean you don't trust them?"

"Just that, something just doesn't ring true." She made a few more turns, then said, "Do you think I'm getting fat?" I let myself slowly sink to the bottom.

After we got dressed, I went over to where Harry and Patty were, they were still asleep, spread out over each other, naked of course. I sat down on a rock and watched them sleep. Funny thing, staring at a sleeping person can wake them faster then kicking them in the ribs. Harry opened his eyes and looked at me.

"You had quite a time, didn't you Harry?" I said. I looked around their clothes were scattered all over. They must have been in a hurry when they got undressed, cause some of Harry's buttons were torn off of his shirt. I picked the shirt up, one button was just hanging by a thread. I looked at it.

"Well Harry, either you're as dumb as a tick on a fence post, or you're soon going to be dead." I said.

"What? What's wrong, what did I do?" I plucked the button off of his shirt. Patty had woken up. "Patty let go of his tally-whacker and go take a bath in the stream." She hopped up and ran for the creek. She heard the tone in my voice and knew when to shut up and run.

I flipped the button to Harry, he caught it. Looking at it, his face turned ashen. "Clay, I didn't know it was there, I swear." He started to get dressed.

"No, don't put those on, gather all of your clothes and Patty's and go toss them in the fire, everything that you brought with you, everything." He scrambled around on his knees, with his naked butt in the air, gathering stuff up, then he ran for the fire.

Watching him, he reminded me of that character Ichabod Crane from The Legend of Sleepy Hollow, with the Headless Horseman chasing him. Everyone of us stopped to stare at him.

I walked over and tossed Faith the so called button. She caught it, looking up at me with a question in her eyes. "It's a tracking device." I said, as I took it from her and dropped it on the ground and crushed it under my boot heel. "Faith, give Patty something to wear. I had Harry burn all of their clothes. Will any of mine fit Ichabod?"

"Ichabod? Who's he?"

"Harry, I gave him a new nickname."

"Oh, I get it, Ichabod Crane. Cute. And I suppose you're the headless horseman?"

"Well sometimes I feel that way, headless that is." I turned to Hank, "Hank, would you go over all of the tack that we took from the Ranch last night, look for anything unusual. We're looking for bugs, electronic bugs. And Oh yes, check all of the horses hoofs, even the horse shoe nails." I might as well be headless, for not thinking of the obvious.

"Uh, Faith, when Patty gets out of the pool, check her breasts for lumps, will you?" I said. Then I went to help Hank. It took us about two hours, we came back with thirty of them. When I got back to where Faith was setting with Patty, Faith tossed me one, just about the same size as the button on Ichabods' shirt.

"It was under her left breast, it didn't bleed very much, I only had to put two stitches in it. What about down below, should we check that?" Faith said.

"No, if she had one there, old Ichabod would of found that last night." I said, Faith giggled, "That or broken it, for sure." Faith said.

"Patty, what's the story, did you know that you had that bug in your breast?"

"No, I swear, I had a boob job six months ago, it was free, a guy I was banging paid for them. Then he dumped me, I never knew why he would pay thousands of dollars and then never stick around to enjoy them."

Faith started to laugh and fell off of the rock she was setting on. I looked at her, "That's not funny." I said.

"Yes, it was. Didn't you see, she said that with a straight face, she has a better delivery than Joan Rivers, even better than Gracie Allen. Maybe as good as Jack Benny."

Rosie was standing there listening, "Who's Joan Rivers, Gracie Allen and Jack Benny?" She said.

"They were comedians, famous for their laid back style." I said. "They lived in the twentieth century. Rivers might have lived on into the twenty first, I don't know for sure."

Alita spoke up, "Why are we setting here discussing dead people, when they might be closing in on us as we speak?" I looked at her, out of the mouth of babes, comes common sense.

"You're right sweetheart," I said. "We should be moving. Come on everyone, let's pack up, we'll be moving, come the twilight of dusk."

Rosie fell back beside me, "What I don't understand, is, why did they put those bugs on those two and on all of the tack?" She said.

"Well," I stopped and thought for a few hoof beats, "that is something that I haven't given much thought to, I see what you mean though. As far as everyone knew, we had dropped off the face of the earth, so were they put there on account of us? Maybe not. Doesn't really matter, cause maybe they were just covering all of their bases. It could be they just wanted to keep track of Harry."

"That doesn't make any sense Dad. They already had him by his short hairs. No, I think it was still us they were after. I think the God of this system of things, Satan, knew we were still alive. And I think he knows right where we are anyway. But his dumb servants, don't. That's the reason for the bugs."

"Do you mean to say that he can't communicate directly with his servants?" I said.

"Yes, that's what I think. I think the Great Spirit is going to give us a fighting chance. I think the Evil One, is going to have to work through his earthly servants. Even his Demons, can't interfere with us." Rosie said.

"Do you mean to say that, the playing field is more or less even?" I asked Rosie.

"No, of course not. It's the fight between good and evil. You know in the end, good always wins." Rosie said, then kicked her horse up to go scout ahead. I thought a minute about her last statement. I certainly hoped that was true. But I knew evil sure had won a lot of battles, but *the war* was yet to be fought.

I sort of let Brutus do his own thing, as I sat a looked at the stars. They had been up there for God only knows how long. Yep, God only knew. I got to thinking about his patience with us. Then this thought popped to mind: Could Patience be only a mild form of Despair, disguised as a Virtue?

Well one thing I did know, was that expectation postponed makes the heart sick. I think that is in the Bible. So I suppose that if patience was long in drought, then it could be a form of despair. I don't know, a Philosopher I ain't. But I do hope that

God doesn't despair over us too long, he might get tired and lose his temper.

Faith dropped back beside me, "What are you day dreaming about?"

"Oh, I don't know, snakes and spiders and puppy dog tails, I guess."

"Posh! I don't believe that, you're probably thinking about sex, isn't that what men usually dream about?" Faith said.

"Yeah, you're right sweetheart. But why dream about it, when you're setting not two feet from me?" I said, as I leaned over and picked her out of her saddle and sat her down facing me across my lap. Ah, expectation fulfilled!

Well not quite, cause Rosie came riding back. She reined up beside us, "What are you two doing? Never mind, I seen a campfire up ahead, do you want to go around it or what?"

I sat Faith back in her own saddle, "Yeah, I want you all to give it a wide berth, I'm going to Injun up on it and see who it is."

"Do you really think that you should, sweetheart?" Faith said, as she adjusted her clothing. Rosie had watched me as I sat her Mother back in her saddle.

"I didn't realize that you were that strong Dad. Mom must weigh a hundred and twenty and you lifted her like she was the same weight as Alita."

"Yeah, I do seem to be able to do certain things, that I didn't use to." I said.

"A hundred and twenty, my goodness! Rosie, I bet I don't weigh over a hundred and fifteen." Faith said. I left them debating the five pounds. As I left the group, Clancy fell in behind me.

"I know who they are." He said.

"I know you do, but I want to see them for myself. Nothing like eyeballing them to get the sense of their intentions."

"I can also tell you what their intentions are, but you go ahead and look for yourself, you know curiosity killed the cat?"

"Well only one thing wrong about that old saying, I ain't no cat." I said, as we slowed to a walk. I dismounted, taking my boots off, I fished my moccasins out of my saddle bags, tying my bootstraps together, I hung them over the saddle horn.

As I slipped my moccasins on, years of the white man's ways fell off of my shoulders. I became what I truly was. I took my 30-30 out of its scabbard. I loosened my knife in its sheath. My senses sharpened. I could smell every little whisp, even a dung beetle as it did it's work on a pile of horse manure, breaking it down to nourish the plants of the earth.

The stars seemed like flood lights to my eyes. Of course they weren't, they were normal, but my vision was as sharp as my hearing and smell was.

Clancy and I, made our way towards the raucous sounds coming from their camp. We made sure we didn't starlight ourselves. The moon was just hanging over the horizon. Sort of like it didn't want to be there at all. I couldn't blame him any, it must have been a long time since I seen him smile.

We stood in the dark shadows of the timber. There must have been thirty of them. Dressed in combat fatigues. They were getting liquored up. Some of the revelers were women, dressed as the men were and acting much the same. We, Clancy and I, stood there as if we were invisible, which to them we were.

At the edge of their firelight we could see five or six, I couldn't quite tell, trussed captives. They had their hands and feet tied. We were only about fifty yards away, just a good stones throw. I reached in my pocket and got my sling out. I squatted down and picked up some suitable stones, six in number. Looking at them, I kept thinking 666. The Devils spawn, they surely were.

I looked around for Horses, there were none. But there were five Military type Hummers, parked haphazardly. They had Wyoming National Guard stenciled on their sides. But I bet they used to belong to the Guard, but now?

I really couldn't tell the sex of the captives, since they were lying on the ground, dressed much alike they were, jeans and such. I looked at Clancy, "Well, what should I do? Kill the lot of them, or just walk away?"

"Have you ever thought of a course in-between those two alternatives?"

"Well, you're the smart one, but yes. It's not going to take long for that bunch to get so drunk, they won't be able to function, let's hope so anyway. When they do I'll just walk in and release those yahoo's that are tied up over there."

"Good plan, but what if they don't all get soused?"

"Well then, I'll just have to deal with that, won't I?" I said.

"Yes, well, let's just wait a spell and see, you might just as well set down." Clancy said, as he made the canines usual circle turns to pick just the right spot to lie down.

"Why do you do that? I've often wanted to know. Why don't you just lie down?"

"Well, when you make your bed, you have to lie in it. So therefore I want to be comfortable." He said, finally settling down to earth.

One by one, they were passing out. All except two of them, that I had noticed were not drinking as hard as the rest, one of them was a woman. At least I think she is a woman, looked like one of those Russian wrestlers. Built like a brick shit house, literally.

When all except those two were conked out. They both got up and headed for the captives. I woke Clancy. "Look there, I think they're up to no good, wouldn't you say?"

"Yes. I know what they are thinking. You have my permission to take them out, that is if you can do so without waking the whole bunch of them."

"Oh, I have your permission, do I? What makes you think I need your permission?"

"Quit being childish, look!" Clancy said, indicating the Cossack's. They had reached the captives. The big woman, bent over and picked up one of captives, when she did, I could see that this captive was a young girl.

She had put her hand over the girl's mouth, and with the other one was tearing her clothes off. I fitted a stone into my sling. I got her right between the eyes. Goliath went down with a hiss. The same thing was happening to a young boy, the man had put his hand over his mouth and was trying to undo the boy's belt. My stone caught him in the back of his head. I looked around, no one had noticed.

I put my sling and extra stones in my pocket and picking up my 30-30, Clancy and I walked over. I hated perverts. Just to make sure, I slit both of their throats, then I took their belts off and hung them upside down from a low tree branch. Clancy was watching me. "What? You think I shouldn't of done that?"

"No, you're supposed to bleed dumb animals, when you kill them, and they're the dumbest of the lot. But I'm not the only one watching, those children seen also."

I looked at them, there were six of them, those two children and four young women in their twenties. I went over, "Who belongs to those two children?" I asked the prone women.

Of course they couldn't answer, they were gagged. I pulled their gags out. They still couldn't talk, they had been gagged for I don't know how long. I went over and found a canteen, I smelled it to make sure it was water. Then I gave each of them a drink.

One of the women, the oldest looking one said, "Their

mine, Jessica and Peter. Thank you so much, I thought we would all be raped and killed, which we would of if you hadn't of come along. They picked us up early yesterday morning. They killed my husband and oldest son. They already had these other four, but I suppose their story is about the same as mine. My name is Seven Tosh." She looked at me as if expecting me to answer. I did,

"My name is Clay, Clay Bronson, we have a Ranch a few days south of here, well did anyway. Can you move? Good, if all of you would get ready we have to leave here before they wake up." Clancy got a few strange looks from them. I said, "That's Clancy, he's a friend of mine. Well I guess more than a friend, he's over three hundred years old. And yes he's supernatural."

"How are we going to go, walk?" Seven said. I looked at Clancy, he said, "The horses are waiting over in the timber, Gabe sent them."

Seven sucked her breath in, "What? He talks?"

"I told you he was supernatural."

"Yes, but I thought you were kidding." She said, then helping her children put their clothes back together, she got ready. I checked on the other four. They were in sad shape. Most had their clothes in disarray. And they were in a little bit of shock, not at what I did, but what happened to them and their families.

I poured some water on a rag and cleaned them up as best as I could. One of the women had most of her blouse torn off. I tried to fix it, stuffing her breast back in, but it kept falling out. So I went over to one of the Hummers and found a suit case, I took out some fatigue shirts, five of them, one for each of the grown women. At least it would cover them up. I didn't try to get their names, I figured Faith could do that when we caught up with them.

343

I got them sat firmly in the saddles, then I said, "Just follow Clancy, well really you don't have to day anything, just hang onto the saddle horn, the horses will take you to our camp." To Clancy I said. "You know of course I can't leave anybody alive back there?"

"Yes, I know. Catch up when you can." Then they all headed off north into the darkness. I walked Brutus over to their camp. I found a case of Antifreeze in back of one of the hummers. Good, it was the old kind, pure poison. I took a bottle out and opened it up. Then I went to each passed out drunk, opening their mouths I poured a goodly amount down their throats. They didn't even stir. As I came up to the last one, she jumped up, "I'm not with them, they captured me two weeks ago, I played along, or I would have been dead, I wanted to live."

I looked at her, she was about in her mid-thirties. Her face turned red, "Don't say it, I know what you're thinking, death before dishonor, well that's a bunch of bullshit, when push comes to shove, I wanted to live."

"Why didn't you do something when they started to molest those children?" I asked. She started to cry, "I wanted to, really I did, but they would of killed me too."

I thought a minute. Hell, if I wasn't who I was, but just a pencil pusher, I might of did the same. "Alright, get yourself some clean clothes and come along, you can jump up behind me, you stink, you know that?"

"Yes, I need a bath, but I thought if I could repel them just a little, they wouldn't rape me so much."

"I know of a stream close by, we'll stop so you can take a bath." I said. She got up behind me. I said to her as she settled behind me. "Who did this bunch report to?"

"Nobody. They just did whatever they wanted to."

"So I suppose they won't be missed then, huh?"

"No, I don't think so, do you think anyone will find them?"

"Well, when they start stinking, someone might come see what smells so much. But maybe not, I think the vultures and such will take care of most of it." We rode on in the dark of the night. I stopped at a small stream, it was just breaking light in the east.

"Hop off and skinny out of those stinking clothes, crap, you have me smelling also. I'm going to have to wash my clothes. She wasted no time in disrobing. At least she wasn't shy. I got a bar of soap out of my saddlebags and tossed it to her. "Use this, but not all of it, I want to wash my clothes as well as myself." I said. As I also got undressed.

The water was bracing, to say the least. She was a redhead, all the way. Reminded me a little bit of Rosie. She soaped down and tossed the soap back to me. I washed my clothes on a rock, she had just tossed her dirty ones in the stream and let them float away.

We both got out and let the morning breeze dry us off. She looked at me. "Nice," she said, "but I suppose you're married?"

"Of course, her name is Faith, we'll catch up with them pretty soon." She went to the horse, where I had tied her clean clothes on back of the cantle. She untied them and walked back to me. "There wasn't any underwear, do you think your wife will have some I can borrow?"

My clothes were damp, but wearable, they would finish drying on me. She was a little disappointed when I got dressed. "Look, whatever your name is, what did you do for a living before they got you, you seem pretty brazen?" I said.

"I was an exotic dancer, I wasn't a hooker though. I played it straight. And my name is Lacy O'Claire."

"O'Claire? I've heard that name before. Anyway, let's hit the trail, my wife will be getting worried." She hopped up behind me, I mean hopped! She was standing flat footed and just jumped. She put her arms around me and pressed her breasts into my back. I ignored them. At least she smelled better now.

We got up with them about ten that morning, they were camped near the Medicine Wheel. There were two springs, one warm and one cold. With plenty of tree cover. Clancy and the other ones had caught up with them at dawn.

Lacy jumped off and lit beside Faith, who was standing there tapping her foot.

"You must be Faith, do you have any clean underwear I can borrow?" Lacy asked.

"Uh, yes, of course. Who are you?" Faith asked.

"I'm Lacy O'Claire, your husband rescued me, isn't he just a darling?"

"O'Claire? Where are you from Lacy?"

"Southern California, but that was sometime ago. I was dancing in Cheyenne when the shit hit the fan." She said, then Faith and her walked off toward the rest of the women. I was dismissed, I guess.

I walked over to where our bedrolls were already stretched out. Clancy was curled up sleeping not far away. He opened his eyes, "Well, how did you do it?"

"Antifreeze."

"Good choice, they won't be found for a long time anyway. So there won't be much left of them. When they are, they will just think they killed those two you hung up and then drank themselves to death. I see you found one of Rosie's relatives."

Huh? You mean Lacy O'Claire?"

"Sure, she's a cousin of Rosie's. Didn't you notice the red hair?"

"Yes, but a lot of women have red hair."

"With the name of O'Claire?"

"Okay, but she's so different. Rosie is so refined. Lacy is a roustabout. But she does resemble Rosie to some extent."

"Oh, come on, didn't you notice her breasts, they're just like Rosie's."

"I don't make it a habit of looking at my daughter's breasts. I did see Lacy's and they do some what look alike, I guess. But don't tell Faith I said so." Then I laid down and went right to sleep.

I awoke to the sounds of laughing and giggling. I turned toward the cackling. There sat Faith, Rosie and Lacy playing some kind of card game. They were setting cross legged around a blanket. They were in different stages of dress. I watched them for awhile. Didn't take me long to figure out what card game they were playing: Strip Poker.

I got up, quite like, and skulked away. Maybe skulked is the wrong word, crept might better describe my leaving. I wasn't about to go anywhere near that.

Most of the women and children I had rescued, were still sleeping. I went over to the warm spring. Hank and Poppy had just got out. I asked Poppy, "How are those new people doing? Are they fairly healthy?"

"Yes, but they were sure dirty. It's a good thing this warm spring has a good turnover in water. Who is that woman you brought with you?" She asked me.

"Her name is Lacy O'Claire, Clancy said she is a cousin to Rosie, but I wouldn't know. She's an extrovert, it looks like." I said, glancing their way. Lacy was completely nude. While Rosie and Faith had most of their clothes on. Now how can one person be so unlucky in cards? That is unless she purposely lost? I didn't mind nudity any, but I don't like to flaunt it.

I turned my back and jumped into the warm pool. It must have some kind of minerals in here, it sure felt relaxing. Hank went off to tend to the horses. Poppy went along to help him.

"Dad?" It was Rosie. She stood on the bank.

"What Sweetie?" I said. Looking at her, she was fully dressed.

"Did you know that Lacy has the same last name as mine?"

"Yes, I did, well not really, your last name is Bronson, don't you remember we adopted you?"

"Yes, of course. Do you think she is any relation to me. She sort of resembles me. Even her, you know, down here, is not only red, but the same pattern."

"I wouldn't know about that Honey. I don't make it a habit of looking, you know down there. But I will tell you this, Clancy said that she was a cousin of yours. I hope it's a distant cousin." I said.

"Don't you like her? I know she is sort of brash. But I think she could grow on a person." Rosie said, while looking over where Faith and Lacy were setting, they were cutting for high card.

"Yeah, I suppose, she told me she was an exotic dancer. She's in pretty good shape. I guess all of that dancing is the reason. But she still has a ways to go, to catch up to you and Faith."

"Does she know that she is a cousin of yours?" I asked Rosie.

"I don't think so, you just told me that yourself."

"Yeah, stupid of me. You can tell everybody that we will be spending a couple of days here. Those women and children need the time to rest and recuperate. Besides I'm tired of traveling at night. Tell them to make lean-to's. Cover them with boughs from the trees, we need to cover the supplies up. We might make sort of a base camp here. I haven't decided."

"Shouldn't we put that to a vote?" Rosie said.

"Nope, this is not a democracy. I'm the patriarch. You all are my responsibility. Do you want that responsibility?"

"No, no way, Dad. You can have it."

"But, I'm open to any input. Anytime anyone has a suggestion, feel free to tell me. I'm the patriarch, not a dictator. And I have my wife's permission to say so."

"Oh Dad, if I didn't know you, a person would think that you're a wuss. But of course you're not."

"Well Rosie, that's what marriage is all about; is the two becoming one. I wouldn't dream about making a big decision without talking it over with Faith. But the decision to stay a couple of days, isn't a big one. There is something that you and Hank and Poppy can do. Those new people, after they get rested, they need to start doing their share."

"What do you mean, their share?"

"Well, taking care of the stock. They need to learn how to do that, you know load pack saddles and such. Also KP."

"What's KP?"

"Kitchen Police. They need to learn how to cook and clean. Also we need to set a lookout schedule, you know routine stuff. Do you think the three of you can take on the task of teaching them?"

"Sure Dad, what if they balk?"

"I don't think they will, what choice do they have?"

'Yeah, you're right. None of us have much choice, if we want to survive. And that's what it has come down to, isn't it?"

"Yes, Sweetheart, it has. It feels like things have been pushed back hundreds of years. All except now there is technology that makes killing each other easier. Oh, and don't forget Lacy, she needs the same schooling as the rest, so go pry her away from what they are doing. Tell Faith I want to see her down by the warm pool."

I went and sat on a rock watching the water cleaning itself. Faith came up and sat down beside me. She was carrying her clothes. I looked at her. "Don't you think you should put them on?"

"Nope, I haven't had a bath yet, you coming in?" She said, as she laid the clothes down and stepped into the water. Of course I was.

We floated around, "What were you and Lacy talking about?" I asked my beautiful black haired wife.

"Mainly woman talk. But I did learn that she was raised in So-Cal. You know southern California. She's definitely some relation to Rosie. I know, Clancy said that she was a cousin to Rosie. I think she's basically a nice person. She's just had some bad breaks."

"Well, yeah. But so did Rosie. If we hadn't of come along, I don't know what would of happened to her. Where's Alita?"

"She's with Jessica, they seem to be getting along pretty well. You never did tell me the full story of what went on back there?"

"Not much to tell, but they were all captives of those so called Militia. Jessica and Peter were about to be molested, when I killed the perverts. The rest of them were dead drunk, so I just finished them off, I poured anti-freeze down them. Clancy said it would be a long time before they were found."

"What about the family's of the captives?"

"They told me that their families were all killed when they were taken. I sort of imagine that sort of thing is going on all over, you know survival of the fittest, or at least survival of the ruthless. I wonder if there is going to be any meek left to inherit the earth?"

"What precipitated all of this?" Faith asked, after she came up from diving to the bottom to get a pretty stone.

"Well, the way Clancy told it, it started with the collapse of the financial market's world wide. It just snowballed from there."

"Yeah, I knew it would. That last administration ruined not

only our economy, but the world's as well. Since all the world's markets are so tied together. More or less like Dominos, I bet." Faith said.

"Yes, I suppose so. We don't know for sure, since we have been gone for two years. But we can see the results, anarchy for one." I said. There came a voice heard over our splashing.

"Hey, is it alright if I get in with you guys?" It was Seven. She was already pulling her clothes off. One thing about the present, there was no room for false modesty.

She was in her middle thirties somewhere. She had two children. But she was fit, no fat anywhere. In fact all of the women and children didn't have any fat on them. Why would they? They had barely been getting enough food to survive on. "Well, is it?" She said, standing there.

Faith said, "Of course it is. If all of us are to survive, at times we're going to have to forget about the old taboos."

Seven dived in. Then came up and swam over by us, where we were standing in about four feet of water. She had brought a washrag with her. She was washing herself. She said, "How long are we going to stay here?"

Faith answered, "Well, I thought at least a couple of days. I haven't talked it over with Clay yet." She looked at me.

"Yeah, that sounds good, do you think we should stay longer or not?" I said.

Seven spoke up, "You're damned right. I was talking to Rosie, not only do we all need training in the basics, but weapons would also be nice. I see in your packs that you have plenty of them. Believe me, I have been out there, we're going to have to know how to defend ourselves."

I looked at my wife, she nodded. "Yeah, Okay, we'll set up a program, Faith and Rosie will be in charge, their both experts. I'm going to scout around for a couple of days. I'll have Gabe look out after all of you, Clancy can come with me." I said.

"Hold on there, this is the first I've heard about this. You're just going to go off by yourself?" Faith said.

"No, I told you, Clancy will come with me. Gabe will watch out here."

"Where do you think you're going?"

"Well, we are heading for the Judith Basin in Montana. So I thought I would go overland from here to Fort Smith in Montana. Pick the best trail, so we can travel in the daylight when we all leave here. But don't worry, I'm going to travel at night, and I have a pair of night vision goggles that I liberated from that bunch."

"I'm not worrying about you, you big lug. I'm more worried that you're leaving a bunch of women to fend for themselves." Faith said.

"I'm not worried, you all can beat ten times your number. Besides, as to all women, what about Harry Silver, he used to be an FBI agent, he should be good for something."

"Oh yeah, sure. Maybe, if he and Patty weren't off banging each other all of the time. I swear, I've never seen two people go at it like them." Faith said.

"Seen? You mean you watch?" I said with a laugh.

"No, silly, that was just a figure of speech, but I have heard them. I think maybe I'll have to throw a bucket of water on them, they must be stuck together." Faith said with a straight face. Seven broke out in a fit of laughing. She almost drowned she was laughing so hard. That was good to hear, her laughing. Showed that she was a survivor anyway. Anytime someone could laugh, they were going to be alright.

We all got out and stood in the sun to dry. One thing I did notice about the ones we just liberated. They didn't have any fat on them, like I said before. Seven seen me looking, she said, "I used to have stretch marks on my belly and varicose veins, but now my tummy is flat and muscled and the varicose veins are gone. I guess there is something to be said for not having the amount of food we used to have. Also in doing a lot of walking and work."

"Yes," Faith said, "they say riding horseback is the second best exercise, just short of playing tennis. Look at my muscles." She said turning in the sun.

Seven was looking at my hair, "What's with those white lightning strips in your hair, one on each side and two down the middle?"

"I'll answer that," Faith said, "he's always making himself a target. One time he was in a coma for six months. Of course sometimes I still think he is in one." She said as she plastered herself against me, kissing like there was no tomorrow.

"Whoa, you guys had better cool it, you're both starting to steam." Seven said. She was right, I had to turn a little so no one could see just how steamy I was.

"Yeah, I want to get things ready to leave, I have to talk to both Clancy and Gabe. Faith, why don't you explain to the rest of our party about staying here for awhile. After I talk to Clancy and Gabe, we'll go for a walk. I wasn't going to leave till after dark."

Clancy thought scouting out the trail ahead of time was a good idea. But Gabe didn't see the need, since he could always see what was ahead from his place in the sky. He knew though that I didn't feel like setting around while the women rested. So he agreed to stay and watch over them.

Of course, the walk that Faith and I took wasn't for exercise. Well not exactly, we needed to be alone, it was pretty hard to make love with everyone so close around. We weren't like Harry and Patty.

Afterward, with Faith laying beside me, she said, "How

come I haven't gotten pregnant? We certainly do it enough."

"Yeah, but maybe it's due to the stress level. We've been on a roller coaster ever since we got married. It'll happen when the time is right."

"I suppose you're right. It's really not a good time to bring a child into this world." Faith stood up and picked up her Stilettos and strapped them back to her leg. I was sure glad she had taken them off. She even swam with them on, everyone sort of looked at her askance when she did though. But she wasn't the only one, Rosie and Alita did also, that is swim with their knives on. All three of them could hit a rabbit on the run with them.

I don't know why I am telling you this, like it was something unusual, I swam with my Bowie on also. Faith had started to wear a short buckskin skirt and vest, with her black hair tied back in a ponytail, she looked more Indian than me. Especially since I hadn't shaved in a coon's age. I did keep my beard trimmed though.

As she put her skirt on, I said, "I notice that you don't wear panties anymore."

"Oh they just get in the way. Except when it's my time of the month, then I do. I need something to hold the moss."

"Moss? I thought you used female napkins?"

"Now do you see a store anywhere around here? I could use rags and wash them out, but it's less trouble to use moss and then burn it or throw it away."

I guess you're right. I do remember Mom said something about moss one time, but I didn't understand what she meant." I said, as she tied her vest in place, then I added, "What about the rest of the women, what do they use?"

"I don't know, do you want to ask them? What's with all of this interest all of a sudden?"

"No, I don't want to ask them. I never thought of it before, but when you mentioned it, with all of these women around, I was just curios, I guess. If I run across a store, I'll be sure and bring some back."

Chapter Twenty One

Clancy and I left right after it got dark. Of course I rode Brutus, but a couple of the other horses followed along. Since they wanted to go, I put pack saddles on them. Who knows what I might want to bring back.

I had two rifle scabbards, one on each side. Of course my old standby 30-30, plus a .50 caliber Sharps, that would hit a target at nine hundred yards. I always liked to ride with boots on, must be the white side of me. But my moccasins were in my saddle bags. Those night vision goggles hung from my saddle horn.

Between Brutus and Clancy, I let them pick the trail. They could see in the dark better then the goggles could. Besides the moon was full and the stars were extraordinarily bright. Must be that with most of the electrical grids down, you could finally see the stars as you should.

In the moonlight I could see the Big Horn Lake Reservoir in the distance. It ran between the Pryor Mountains and the Big Horn Mountains. I stayed east of it. The land was more level and hilly. We made good time, better than usual. As it started to get dawn, I was on a hill top and in the distance I could see Yellowtail Dam, and the town of Fort Smith.

Fort Smith had electricity, the Dam must still be generating power. As I watched the yard lights were blinking out, one by one. I was watching through a set of hi-powered Binoculars that I had taken from those Hummers.

Talking about Hummers, there were a lot of them down

there. The National Guard must be protecting the Dam. I heard Revelry played. A whole platoon of troops came out of their barracks and stood at attention. That was good to see, there must still be some sort of discipline left. I was going to give them a wide berth though. One never knew where their loyalty lay, they could be ran by a despot.

I adjusted the glasses, so I could get a better look. Yep, a lot of them were glassy eyed and hung over. The officer strutting back and forth in front of them was dressed like a peacock. No these weren't regular troops.

We went back down the hill to a little spring. There was graze for the horses and shade for Clancy and I to sleep under. Clancy said, "Their Mercenary's, hired by a regional war lord." Then he curled up and went to sleep. Of course he would of known, I didn't have to speculate. I suppose electricity was a high end item, and not everyone could afford it anymore.

I laid myself down under the shade of a stunted Juniper. It didn't take me long to go to sleep, I had a clear conscious. You're probably thinking how could I have a clear conscious, with all of the blood I had spilled? Well, they deserved it. And there is a precedence, King David killed a lot of people and he wasn't condemned. Now you say, yes, but he had God on his side. Well, maybe I do too, just maybe....

My dreams started as soon as I closed my eyes. I seen a tribulation coming upon the earth, one like had never been seen before. There were four Angels, holding back the wind for an appointed time. I tried to wheedle the day and hour out of them, but they just looked at me....

There was total anarchy, people were killing each other for no apparent reason. All except one group of people who were residing in the mountains. I asked the Angels who they were, they said, simply...the Meek. That was when I woke up.

The sun was hanging low over the Pryor Mountains. It was

about a half hour till sunset. I got up and washed my face then got some dried Pemmican out of my saddle bags and Clancy and I sat down and ate.

"Did you see my dreams?" I asked Clancy.

"Sure, that's nothing new, that prophecy has been in the Bible for thousands of years. But the harvest is now much nearer."

"What about those people down there, do you think any of them are part of the *meek*?" I asked, as I stripped out of my clothes and sat down in the little pool at the outlet of the spring.

"Funny you should ask. There's two down there, but of the meek, they're not. You know them. This little scouting trip of yours, wasn't your idea. Do you remember Mary Jane and Iris?"

"Well of course I do. Are you saying that they are down there?"

"Yes, they wanted to do a little riding. They got too far away from the compound and got turned around. A detail, something like the one's we ran across the other day, got them. They haven't been hurt, yet." Clancy said, as he scratched himself behind his ear.

"But I don't understand, how come the Carmel Foundation didn't just go get them?"

"They could have, but you were getting close, so it was decided to let you rescue them."

"Who decided?" I asked. Clancy just looked at the north star, that was becoming brighter in the night sky. "Yeah, I thought so. Supernatural again."

"Don't worry, they've had protection. One bad ass Wolverine is with them. He's a friend of mine."

"So where are they? And what about the horses they were riding?" I asked as I got out of the pool and shook myself somewhat dry.

"In a storage room at the store. The horses are waiting for us. 'Tas', that's the Wolverine's name, has chewed through their picket ropes."

"What did that bunch intend to do with them? Mary Jane and Iris, I mean."

"That 'Warlord' has been kidnapping women and children for his pleasure, they were next in line. He's down there, in the end cabin at what used to be a Motel. We're supposed to take him out, that is if you feel like it."

"If I feel like it, huh? Of course I do. I hate people like that. But I still don't understand, why doesn't the foundation just wipe them all out?"

"They are not supposed to interfere; with the normal order of things. But we are free to do what we want, that is as long as it's justified."

"Why are we different than the Carmel Foundation?" I asked.

"Because we are, sort of, part of this earth, they are not."

"What the hell do you mean, they're not?"

"Just that. They are under a *prime directive*, which they've stretched to the limit."

"What do you mean, stretched to the limit?"

"Well, they have been given some leniency, as long as the help was beneficial. But in this time of the end, they have been told to keep their hands off."

"But, it seems like that's all I say is 'but', anyway, then what about Mary Jane, I thought she was a Hunter, related to the man who started the Foundation, Wolf Hunter?"

"Yes, they are both part Earthlings. As are most of the people in their compounds. It's hard to explain, so I don't think I am going to. You don't need to know anyway."

"Well, you don't need to be rude about it. I always thought

there were a lot of ET's running around this earth, anyway. But never mind, it sounds like a party is going on down there." I said, as I got out my night vision goggles.

There was. Debauchery at it's best. I put my glasses on the store. Everyone was staying away from it. Then I seen why, there was that Wolverine, Tas, setting in front of the door. I looked over at Clancy, "Why don't they just shoot Tas?"

"Oh, they've tried that. It has no effect on him, like it would have no effect on me. So now they give him a wide berth." I looked closer at Clancy, he was fading in and out.

He said, "Do you see what I mean?"

"Yeah, that's a neat trick, you'll have to teach it to me sometime."

"I'm afraid that would be impossible. You're stuck with what you were born as."

"Yeah, I know that. But I guess, I'm pretty happy in this here skin that holds these bones together. In fact I've become quite fond of them."

Sometime after midnight, it got quite. There were body's laying dead drunk all over the place. I left my rifles with the horses, the only gun I took was my .357. Of course I had my knives. My moccasins were guiding my feet, if there was a twig they stepped over it. I wasn't even thinking about it, they were doing that on their own.

There were men and women locked in sexual embraces, just as they were when they passed out. It was a little bit comical. But not really, it was more pathetic than anything else.

Clancy was walking ahead of me. He went up to Tas. "Well," Tas said, "It took you long enough." Tas looked at the store door, you could hear the lock click open as he looked. I asked Clancy, in a whisper, "I suppose you can't teach me that either?"

He didn't answer. I guess he deemed it beneath his dignity. We went into the store. I guess you could of called it a General Store. Because it looked like it had about everything that they could pirate or scrounge.

Tas headed for the back room. It had a padlock, that clicked open as he approached. Sleeping in the bed was Mary Jane and Iris. The three of us stood beside the bed and waited, Mary Jane opened her eyes.

She looked at me, "Tas said you would be coming." Mary Jane said as she sat up and the covers slipped away. It was the same old Mary Jane, naked as a jaybird. I was glad to see that Iris wore pajamas. She got up and bent over the bed, shaking Iris, "Come on Honey, it's time to go." She said.

"Is Clay here?" Iris said, as she rubbed the sleep from her eyes. She seen me and held her arms out to me. I picked her up. I glanced at Mary Jane, "do you have any clothes?" I asked her.

"Not really, they're torn and dirty, but I'm sure there is something that will fit me out there." She said as she padded toward the main store. We followed along behind the swing and sway. She went through the clothes, picking out some for her and Iris alike.

She slipped into them, then said, "Just a minute, I have to get my knives. Iris, where are your knives?" She said to Iris in passing.

"There in my Teddy Bear, under my pillow." Iris wanted down, she went with her mother, when they came out they were dressed in Army Fatigues. They both looked sort of cute. We , all five of us, went outside.

"Clancy, why don't you and Tas take the girls back to our camp, I have a little chore to do." They headed that way. I watched them go, there was something not very congruous about a little girl dressed in Army Fatigue's dragging a Teddy

Bear behind her. It wasn't the Teddy Bear that was out of whack, it was the Fatigues.

They were all setting around eating some pemmican, when I got back. I sat down, nobody said anything. Then I got up and went to the spring and washed my knife. I came back again, I looked at Mary Jane, "Say, what happened to that Pete Frank, I thought he was sweet on you?"

"Well, I guess he was for awhile, but one day, he just wasn't there anymore. I asked around, but was told he just didn't fit in. Whatever that meant. I was getting a little bored with him anyway." Mary Jane said, with her head turned.

"Yeah," I said, but to myself I thought, 'like so much'. We still had about four hours to go before the dawn, so we set out. Mary Jane and Iris's horses had followed them up the hill when I left them to do that little chore. So they had their own saddles and everything.

At dawn, we stopped and got a little sleep; two hours or so, then we headed out again. I knew there was nobody around; so I felt safe in traveling in the daylight. We got back to camp an hour before sunset.

Faith was some surprised to see Mary Jane and Iris. They fell into each others arms. Alita and Iris, were the same. Rosie came up and gave me a hug, "Glad you're back safe Dad." She said, with relief in her voice. "Where did you find them?"

"At Fort Smith, Clancy said that was the reason we went there; is to get them. It's sort of a long story, ask Clancy he'll tell you all about it, he likes to talk." Rosie walked over to where Faith and Mary Jane were still jawing. Rosie joined the conversation, Faith glanced over at me, then came my way. I was unsaddling the horses. She came and started to help.

"That was something, finding them. Are you hungry? I have some leftovers?" She said.

"Yeah, I could eat something, I suppose Mary Jane and Iris

are also."

"Rosie is already taking care of that. Is food the only thing you're hungry for?"

I kept unsaddling, then I laid the saddle under the lean-to, taking my wife by the hand, we headed for the warm spring. You know why, I don't have to tell you....

Afterward, while floating around on our backs, Faith asked, "What happens now? Are we still going to the Judith Basin?" I had to think about that question. Had things changed? For some reason I had a feeling that they did somehow.

But it's hard to think on an empty stomach, it was growling at me. We shook off and got dressed. Then went and joined the rest, who were already eating. We filled our plates and went and sat down beside Clancy.

"Well Clancy, Faith wants to know what's next, are we going on to the Judith Basin?" I queried him.

"If we do, you are going to have running battles all of the way. The evil one has a firm grip over the land." He said, while chewing on some beef jerky.

"What about those at the Foundation? Are they Okay?" Faith asked.

"Sure, no one can get at them, not even the Evil One. We can go if you want to, but really there is no need."

"Well, if we don't go there, what are we supposed to do?" Faith said, with an edge to her voice, "Hang out with the *meek* ones?"

"No, you all are not part of the meek ones." Clancy said, completely ignoring her sarcasm.

"Uh...just who or what are we?" I asked.

"A tool, a rather blunt one at times, but still very useful."

"You answered who or what you consider us to be, but you didn't answer about what we are supposed to do." I said.

"It is not I, that said you were a tool. I am but a go-between, Gabe and I both are. Wait a minute, I misspoke, I am the one that said you and Gabe and I, are tools, in that we are used to get things done. But it is the Great Spirit and his Son, that are taking back heaven and earth."

"You've been dancing around and around the question, I'll ask you once more, What are we supposed to do now?" I said, with a slight hint of exasperation.

Faith had been pacing back and forth, she said, "Don't answer that yet, answer me this first: What has happened to or is going to happen to our loved ones in New Mexico?"

While she was asking that question, Gabe had settled down beside Clancy, he cleared his throat, if an Eagle can be said to clear their throats. "Uh, maybe I can answer both of those questions at the same time. It seems that your expertise is needed at the Ranchos de Chama. But you have accumulated quite a retinue. Whom we will have to separate." He paused and looked at Clancy, he took over.

"Yes, Elizabeth will arrive the first thing in the morning, to take everyone, except for you and Faith, and of course, Rosie, Alita, Lacy, Mary Jane and Iris. Oh, yes, Tas will be going also. The rest of the bunch will be going to the Carmel Foundation."

"What about our Horses and Mules? And just how are we supposed to go, cross country or what?" I said…

"Oh yes, of course the livestock will go with us. The Worm Hole, will open up at exactly nine in the morning." Gabe said.

"Worm Hole? What the hell is that?" I asked.

"Oh come on, haven't you ever watched any of those science fiction movies? They weren't all fantasy, you know." Clancy said.

"I thought they were just between Universes or something." Faith said.

"There are different kinds and magnitudes. This is just a simple earthly one. Doesn't take much power at all, it will only remain open for fifteen minutes. Enough time for everyone and the horses and mules to be transported to New Mexico."

Most of the women and children didn't have any druthers either way. All except Seven Tosh and her children, Jessica and Peter. But when we explained that Poppy and Hank would be going with them also, they acquiesced.

Hank had mixed feelings, he wanted to stay with the livestock, but the pull of seeing his Mother and Tiffany won out. When it came to Harry and Patty, they were more than glad to get away from Faith and I.

The next morning everyone was up early. They all helped pack the horses and mules. Breakfast was over when Elizabeth de-cloaked and settled down.

I was a little taken back, when a beautiful naked woman stepped out. Faith whispered in my ear, "I know who she is, it's Elizabeth, she's figured out a way to have a body, something she's always wanted."

I walked up to her, I put out my hand to touch her, expecting her to be a holograph. My hand touched her breast, she smiled at me. I pulled my hand back, "I thought you might be a holograph, where did you get this body?" I asked, my face turning red.

"It's a time of miracles, they thought I deserved one, after all I'm five thousand years old." Elizabeth said.

Faith came up and said, "Uh, just perhaps you ought to put some clothes on, some of these people aren't used to nudity."

"Oh yes, of course." She raised her arms over her head and when she brought them down over her body, clothes appeared.

Faith said, "Hey, that's pretty neat, can you teach me that?"

"Not yet, perhaps someday you will learn, maybe after the thousand years."

"The *thousand years*, what's that?"

"I am sorry, I have said too much, please forget what I have just said. Please everyone hurry, we need to get underway." She said, as she more or less started hustling everyone into the copter. After they were aboard, she stood in the door, naked again, she did a little bump and grind and gave us a wink, then the door closed.

Alita looked at Faith, "Mommy, can you teach me how to do that dance?"

"No Honey, Elizabeth was just teasing us. But when we get time I will teach you how to Ball Room Dance." Faith said, Lacy spoke up, "I can teach better moves than that."

I looked at my wife and said, "You know how to ball room dance?" While ignoring what Lacy said.

"Of course, I learned it in college, didn't you?" Faith answered, she too ignored Lacy's comment.

"No, I, oh, let's just say I had other interests. Come on let's get ready, when that worm hole opens we only have fifteen minutes." I said.

Lacy stood there with her hands on her hips, "So, you're ignoring me, huh? Well let me tell you I was good at what I did. I made more money than any other girl. And I did it straight too."

Rosie spoke up, "Grow up Cousin, we all know you can dance. It's just not the type they want Alita to learn. Come on and help me with the animals, we have to be ready. Alita, Iris, Mary Jane, you all can help also."

Leave it to Rosie to get things organized. Just like the old Oil business, we used to have, she ran it mostly all by herself. They all trooped off to see if the horses and mules were ready. Faith and I stood there looking at each other.

Faith came into my arms and I kissed her, she laid her head on my shoulder, "Where is all of this going to end?" She asked.

366

"I don't know sweetheart. We've been on this roller coaster since we got married. I, for one would just like to slow down and watch the sunrise and set, in all four seasons, in one place."

"Yes, but, are you sure you wouldn't be bored." Faith said, kissing me again.

"No, not bored. My Grandfather said, it was impossible to be bored, if you had a brain. Or I guess it would be better to say, *use your brain.*

Faith rubbed herself against me, "Does this bore you?" She asked. Of course before I could answer, the rest of our family was on their way back....

While we were waiting for our ride, so to say, I asked Clancy, "You said that this so called wormhole doesn't take much power. Just how much and where does it come from?"

"As you probably know, every living sole has their own electro-magnetic field. The worm hole runs on our own energy. If it's just one soul going, the field is only big enough and strong enough for that soul. Now being there is a lot of us going, especially the horses and mules, this worm hole can be big and strong."

"How long has this been around?" Faith asked.

"If you mean this mode of transportation, it has been around for ever, I guess. But it's only been accessed by those that know of it. Which now, I guess that includes all of us here today."

"You mean that from now on we can get around this earth, using the wormholes?"

"Yes, once we share the know how with you. But it doesn't work for everybody. It depends on your heart condition."

"Do you mean our hearts have to be physically fit?" I said.

"No, that's not what I meant. I was referring to your spiritual heart." Clancy said.

"Well, who's the judge of that?" You?" Faith said.

"No, not me, that would be the man upstairs. Don't worry, you wouldn't of gotten this far, if he didn't approve of all of you. Sort of." Clancy said.....

"But, you and Gabe said that we weren't part of the meek one's who are to inherent the earth. So just where do we fit in?" I said.

"Still the blunt tool, aren't you? Isn't it enough that he sees fit to use the lot of you? At least you are alive." Gabe said.

"Leave it alone, Honey." Faith said, then to Gabe and Clancy, "don't worry, we aren't complaining. We can take things day by day."

Clancy cleared his throat, "Yes, in about two minutes the worm hole will appear. The horses and the mules will go in first, Tas will go in with them. You will be happy to know that you humans will go in last, we know you have a penchant for riding drag. There has to be at least two minutes apart between humans and animals."

"Why is that?" I asked.

"Do you remember your old television shows, that science fiction one? Where they beamed around? I see by your expression that you do. Anyway, your molecules and DNA and stuff get scattered around, we can't have animal and humans get mixed up, can we?"

"What? Is that dangerous, how do we know we get our own stuff back?" Faith asked.

"Hummm, that is a conundrum, isn't it? I'm only kidding, of course you get put back together again." Clancy said, then I heard him say under his breath, "mostly, anyway." No one else heard him, I choose not to make a big deal out of it. He knew I heard him, he winked at me.

"I was wondering, can we summon this wormhole anytime we want it?" I asked.

"No, we have to summon it. But if it appears when we are not around, that means they are summoning you, and you had better answer."

"You said before that you would show us how to answer, or use this worm hole?"

"Okay, the code number is simple, it's 777. You really don't have to use it, since they have your DNA, that's what it goes by. We just use the code to cater to your simplicity."

"I don't know for sure, but I think you just insulted me. Did you?" I said....

"No, when you tell someone the truth, it's not an insult, tactless maybe, but no insult. Besides it's a compliment to have a simple eye. The more you keep your way simple, the better off you will be."

"Alright, forget it, you're giving me a headache. Is that the wormhole, forming over there?" I asked as glassy like waves started to shimmer close to where the horses and mules were standing. Then Tas told the animals to go in, they did and they disappeared from our sight.

As we waited our turn I asked Clancy, "Can you disembark from that thing anywhere you want to?"

"No, it's preset as to location. That makes it a little bit unhandy sometimes. You can't take any little side trips. That's where space ships like Elizabeth come in handy. The wormholes are beneficial in other ways, though. They have a sort of biological filter that filters out any impurities or diseases. That's nice isn't it?"

It came our turn, Clancy and Gabe both said for us to go on in, that they would be two minutes behind us. We stepped in as a group, bunched together. No one wanted to be first.

Faith and I, with Faith holding Alita, then Rosie, Lacy, Mary Jane and Iris right behind us. We stepped in....all seven of us.

The first sensation was one of weightlessness. Then a tingling all over. Looking at our extremities, first we could see right through our hands. Then we just started to come apart, literally. There was no pain.

We couldn't understand how we could still be seeing all of this, when we had no eyes? We were just a big bunch of swirling molecules. You notice that I said 'we'? It wasn't I, anymore. We were *one central intelligence*! That must have been why they wanted to keep the species separate.

We each were part of the whole. We knew not only what we were thinking, but all of the past memories or feelings that of which we were. There was no female or male, we were simply *human*. But yet somehow we were still individuals.

I bet you have a question, don't you? What happened to our clothes, weapons, etc.? They were circling around separate from us. Although some of the same elements that made them what they were, were the same kind of elements that made up our bodies.

There was no scientific explanation for what was happening to us, because it was supernatural.

I, as a man, was a trifle uncomfortable, knowing all of the secrets that a woman kept to themselves. Even as to how they felt when they had orgasms. That really blew my mind so to speak. I can't explain it to you, for how can a man explain a woman? I suppose the reverse is true. In fact I now know it is. For I was privy to all of their thoughts, as they were to mine.

As an individual, I was a little uncomfortable with the young ones, Alita and Iris, knowing things that only adults should know. But I suppose exceptional times breed exceptional children. As it turned out, I need not of worried.

Chapter Twenty Two

We felt ourselves becoming more dense. Now that didn't refer to our intelligence, but to our bodies. The swirling colors were slowing down. We were starting to pull ourselves together.

Do you remember that I said, that I needn't of worried about the children? Why? Because they were no longer children. As we materialized, there were two grown, beautiful women, where there used to be two lovely children.

The color's settled down to a light purple mist around us. We, all seven, stood there with no clothes. I looked down, our clothes and weapons were stacked neatly at our feet. I was feeling some unsettled, was I still me? Looking at myself, I seen it was still there, I gave a sigh of relief.

The six women seen me look down, and they giggled at me. I said, "Well, it's no laughing matter, what we just went through and knowing all of your women thoughts, I just had to check."

We hurriedly pulled our clothes on. We had to share some clothes with Alita and Iris. Why weren't their old clothes made big also? We stepped out, waiting for us was the Animals. They looked a little different. And then it hit me, where they went in as horses and mules, they came out as something in-between. Since a mule was a cross between a Donkey and a Horse, now they were more horse than mule, or was it vice-versa?

And standing with them was a man, that we hadn't seen

before, but I knew who it was. It was Tas, his hair had the same design and color scheme as the Wolverine, he used to be. "What's with all of this change-a-roo stuff?" I asked him.

"That's the price we pay whenever we use those wormholes, they're somewhat unpredictable. But as to me, there's more to it, you'll find out more later."

"Yeah, it looks like someone has a sense of humor. They didn't mess with any of our supplies on the pack horses, did they?" I asked.

"No, they're intact. I hope you don't mind, I had to borrow some of your clothes. I also have some extras for Clancy and Gabe, I suppose they will come out different also." Tas said.

The worm hole shimmered and out stepped Gabe. Tas handed him some clothes. I kept looking for Clancy. Gabe said, "He won't be coming, he has a family you know. He has to stay with them."

"Well Crap, he didn't even say goodbye. I got pretty attached to that furry mutt."

"Don't worry, you'll see him again." Gabe said. His nose looked a little like an Eagles beak, sort of handsome. He had the same piercing eyes, that he used to have.

I kept looking at them both, Gabe and Tas. "So," I said, "just what species are you two supposed to be?"

"What we've always been, Human."

"Bullshit," I said. If you're human, you are not human's from earth."

They looked at each other. Gabe said, "You're right, we're not from earth. Earthlings think they're the only humans, but are not. You think the Almighty God would put all of his eggs in one basket?"

"You have a lot of esplaining to do Lucy." I said.

"Huh?" Gabe said.

"Oh, that was just a line from an old TV show. But you do

have some explaining to do. What are you doing down here?"

"We were sent down here to be, what you would call 'trouble shooters'. We have been here for thousands of years. We do the hands on work, that Angels don't do." Tas said.

"What are you, 'shape shifters'?" I asked.

"Maybe, to some extent I guess. Our civilization is a million years old, we've learned how to do some stuff, with Jehovah's help."

"How come he helps you guys so much?" I asked.

"Because we were obedient from the start, we didn't have the Adamic sin. He's been helping earthlings from the start, he made the ransom possible. It's all being worked out now."

"Where do we fit in this scenario of the time of the end." Faith asked.

"Well, I'm afraid, you guys are what could be called, the odd man out. In that you're not of the meek who will inherit this earth. At the same time you're not of the wicked that will be destroyed." Gabe said.

"What about our loved ones here in New Mexico?" Faith said.

"That's also who we're down here for. The Carmel Foundation, an organization of ours, has been gathering a lot of you folks in. But there has been a lot of Maverick's like you and your families, that have resisted being inside of the foundations compound.

We could just let you be destroyed, but there's that gray area that you fall into. We've been given permission to remove you from this earth."

"Remove us huh? Does that mean kill us?" Lacy said.

"No, of course not. Why would we work so hard to keep you alive, like we have done, to simply kill you?" Tas said.

"I don't get it, why? Why are you trying to keep us alive?" Mary Jane said.

"Do you remember that Gabe said, that you were not of the meek, nor of the wicked that will be destroyed? Well let me qualify that. There is no fence in God's new system of things. So you cannot sit on it. You will have to admit you're not part of the meek. So if you stayed here on this earth, you would be classified as part of the wicked. That's where we come in, your talents and ability's are useful, but not on earth anymore."

"Alright, so where are we supposed to go, the Moon?" Rosie said, with a hint of sarcasm.

"One step at a time," Gabe said. "The first thing you have to do is to get those at the Ranchos de Chama. They have been told that you are coming. Not only are Karl, Felicia, Alona and Jake there. But also Miguel and Ester and their children, but Gail Pretty Otter is there also. They have been able to stand off the Devils spawn so far, but their supplies are getting low."

"I recognize where we're at now, we're only about two miles from the ranch." I said. "I see by the sun that it's close to going down, we could go in tonight."

"Yes, but I think it would be better at dawn." Tas said.

"Alright, I guess it wouldn't hurt to get a little something to eat and some rest." I said. I looked around at the rest of our party. Party, that's a ambiguous word at times. We sure weren't having one, but looking at Iris and Alita, who were less than half dressed, could have been having some kind of a party. They looked a trifle uncomfortable with their new bodies. For the first time I got a close look at the rest of us. We looked a little younger than we used to. We all looked like we were in our middle twenties.

I brought this fact to the attention of Tas and Gabe. "You are younger, while the young are older. And Oh yes, by the way, if you don't screw it up, you are on track to live a very long life." Gabe said.

Faith said, "Well what about those at the Ranch?"

"No, not yet. They have to go through the wormhole, like you folks did."

"How are they going to do that?" I asked.

"There are various ways, they haven't decided that." Tas said.

"They, they, they! It's always they, isn't it?" Rosie said. Gabe just pointed at the sky. "We are just tools, the same as you." Gabe said.

"Oh, I know that," Rosie said, "but it just gets so frustrating. It reminds me of all of the governments of the world, always passing the buck."

"This earth is coming under Theocratic Rule. There will be no passing of the buck. It is the same where I come from, we have been under Theocratic Rule since the beginning. It has been a very good thing. So don't worry, *they* won't let you down."

Faith, being the matriarch of our family, said, "Enough talk, lets get some clothes for ourselves off of the pack horses and get something to eat. I see a spring, that flows into the river, I think we can drink that water safely."

And that's what we did. We took the pack saddles off of the horses. Alita and Iris had pulled off what little clothes they had on and were trying on clothes. I felt sorry for them. They didn't know exactly what to think of the voluptuous figures, they had became. I looked away and went and started a small fire and put some side bacon on. Yes, we still had some meat, when that ran out, there would be no more....

All nine of us sat around the fire and made small talk. No one wanted to discuss anything heavy, ignoring the Gorilla in the trees. When the fire burned down, the seven of us cuddled close, while Tas and Gabe disappeared. I think they went to scope out the morning's task.

When all had fallen asleep, except me. I got up and worked

on my weapons. Cleaning my guns and sharpening my knife. I didn't have to worry about the women's stiletto's, they were always razor sharp. I wondered about that scripture, 'beating the weapons into plow shares'. When would we be able to do that?

A couple of hours before dawn, Tas and Gabe came back and found me asleep bent over my rifle with the cleaning rod still in the barrel. Gabe touched my shoulder, I became instantly awake. "Sorry, I guess I should of stayed awake, we didn't have anyone on guard."

"No need, the camp was being monitored from space. You would have been woke up, if the need would have arisen." Tas said. "Go back to sleep with the women, we'll wake you up in an hour."

They were as good as their word…We had just enough time to eat some pemmican before we mounted the horses. Tas and Gabe rode also. I asked them:

"Aren't you guys going to go back to being animals?"

"If the need arises, that served it's purpose. We were only animals to disguise our being on earth." Gabe said.

"Then I take it that Clancy was one of you. He told me he had a family, were they Coyotes in disguise also?"

"Sure, but now all of them are back to normal. He is at the foundation in the Judith Basin, along with his family."

"Do you two have families?" I asked.

"No, we're single. Maybe some day, we've been looking forward to the possibility."

"Let me ask you this; these ones who are laying siege to the Ranch, are you both okay with killing them, if we have to?"

"No, we can't, but you can. The prime directive says that we can't physically interfere. We can advise you though. This prime directive only applies here on earth. If we're in space, we can." Gabe said.

"That's pretty convenient, how many of the Devil's advocates are there in space, none?" Faith said.

Gabe and Tas looked at each other. "Uh, more than you would think. But that's another story. One you will be told about later. First we need to concentrate on this mission."

I had a thought, which I do at times. But anyway, I asked them: "Since you guys are so advanced, you must have some kind of weapon that will just disable and not kill?"

"Sure we do. But it was pretty hard to carry them with us, when we didn't have any pockets. Or opposable thumbs to use them with." Gabe said.

"So, I guess we're stuck with these primitive weapons that we have." I had to shut up, cause we were coming up on their camp. We stopped our horses in the trees.

Their campfires were nothing but coals. They were laying all about, in different stages of sleep, caused by their excesses, with drink or drugs, it didn't matter much. They made it pretty easy for us.

I got off of my horse and picked up a tree limb. I motioned for the women to follow me. I whispered to them: "I will knock them over the head, you guys tie them up, use whatever is handy to do that."

I simply tapped them over the head. A few had started to wake up, before I put them back to sleep. I sort of felt sorry for them, but not too much. There must have been at least fifty of them, I didn't count. We did pick up their weapons and tossed them in the river. It was sad that they had sunk so far down in their depravity, that they no longer functioned as a fighting force. It would of probably been more humane to just kill them all. But my Mother always taught me to be kind to dumb animals. Except one, Dipper Tick, I was going to cut his throat, but I just kicked him in the head. I guess I was going soft.

We reached the ranch house just as the sun was coming over the nearby hill. They weren't sleeping. As soon as we rode into the yard, out they came. The first thing Felicia said was: "Where is Alita?"

Alita got off of Matthew, her horse, who used to be a Mule and said, "Here I am Grandma, don't you recognize me?"

"What? It is you, what in the world, how did you get so big?" Felicia said as she hugged her.

"It's a long story Grandma, we don't have time to tell you right now. You're all supposed to get what you can and come with us." Alita said, looking around at the rest of our loved ones.

Dad, Jake and Alona, pressed in close. Dad said, "What happened to your hair, you look like some kind of Mountain Lion or something?"

"Just battle scars, I guess you could say. We don't have too much time Dad, Alita is right, we need to get away from here."

"We're ready, we were told that you were coming. The horses are already saddled in the barn. It'll just be a few minutes. Gail has to get her medicines out of the cooler. It's in the creek, we haven't had electricity for over a year."

It only took them about fifteen minutes. Twenty of them altogether. We went back the way we came. All of the mob were still knocked out. Jake looked at them and said, "I hate to think this bunch will take over our ranch, what scum they are."

"They won't have it long, the end is coming fast. We have to leave before it does." I said.

"The end? What do you mean?" Jake asked.

"The end of this system of things. We have to leave, or we will be caught up in it." Faith told him.

"How do we leave if the whole world is involved. Where do we go?" Jake said.

"That we don't know for sure, perhaps you should ask Tas or Gabe, they're up ahead, go ask them." Faith told Jake, he kicked his horse up and caught up with them. He talked awhile with them and then fell back beside me. He didn't say anything, I didn't press him.

Alona fell back beside him, they talked. Alona's expression became worried. I knew when we got back to camp, I would have to explain things to the whole bunch of them. But explain what? I didn't know the whole story myself.

Gabe and Tas fell back beside me. I guess they knew I wanted to talk. "So, you guys haven't told me everything, have you?"

"What do you mean?" Tas said.

"About why we have to leave earth. Now it seems to me there are only two sides to this good and evil thing. And that you're either on one side or the other. So using that as a paradigm, if we ain't part of that meek bunch, then we are part of the other."

Gabe moved uncomfortably in his saddle, "Alright, we might as well tell him. That reasoning would hold true, if you, the bunch of you, were all earthlings. But what we haven't told you is: You're not!"

"What the hell, you trying to tell me that we're not human?" I spat back at him.

"Oh no, you're all human alright, just not one hundred percent humans from earth." Gabe said.

"What do you mean, we're not a hundred percent human, or not a hundred percent humans from earth?"

"The latter. You see you were told before that we have been on earth for thousands of years. Well, humans being humans, no matter where they're from, we, uh, sort of had relations with humans from earth. That being the case there were progeny from these unions. I know, I know, we weren't supposed to. So the crux of the matter being, the intermixed ones do not fall on the good side or the bad side. Hence we have to leave earth, us and all of our progeny, no matter how slight the connection." Gabe said.

"And what if we don't want to leave earth?" I said, a bit truculently .

"Well, since you're not part of the *meek*, then you would be on the side that is to be wiped clean from the earth, I guess you know what that means?"

"Yeah, I know." I said, meekly. "What about those that are gathered in the Carmel Foundation compounds?" I asked, as an afterthought.

"Yes, they have to leave also. Sounds rather simple, doesn't it? But it's not, you see, you earthlings and terrain breeds are deemed too violent to be allowed to settle on Terra. You just wouldn't fit in. And the truth be told, we're no longer welcome, either." Gabe said, looking at Tas.

"What are they going to do, just dump us in space somewhere?"

"No, no they can't do that. It would be inhumane." Gabe said.

"Hey, I know. What about Viking Valley?" I said.

"Well, you see, it doesn't really exist, well it does, but then again it doesn't. It exists in conjunction with time and space. It's there sometimes and sometimes it's not." Tas said.

"Maybe we don't exist, maybe we just think we do?" I said.

"You exist alright, we all do. But we just don't know *where* we will exist. We haven't been told." Tas said.

"Who is supposed to tell you?" Faith said.

"The authorities on Terra. We hope to hear in the next couple of days. In the mean time, I guess we just wait." Gabe said.

We had reached camp while we were jawboning. Everyone

pitched in to make supper. The sun was going down earlier and earlier, now it was setting around six. One thing I had learned, was not to stare into the fire at night. It made you night blind. I asked our mentor's, "Should we set the guard tonight?"

"Of course, the Devil would like nothing better than to have his disciples do away with us. He's been mad that Jehovah didn't let him corrupt the Terrain's, like he did to Adam and Eve. And he's really pissed that he has been confined to earth since 1914. He's been after us Terrain's for a very long time. You see, like we told you, we're not supposed to be here. Jehovah God is going to protect the *meek*, we are on our own." Gabe said.

"Alright, I think we can depend on our hy-bred Horses to warn us if anybody comes around. Their almost human anyway. Now that their genes are mixed with the Mules, their smarter than ever. I'll tell them, they can set the guard." I said, as I left the ring of light that the campfire was throwing at the dark.

Brutus was taking the lead with the rest of them. He allowed as it was no problem. They slept on their feet most of the time anyway. They didn't talk, well not yet anyway. But we could communicate. I guess some of those Terrain traits were coming to the surface on us breeds. One thing, I was used to being a breed, half white and Indian. But now I was a earth-terrain breed. I wonder what kind of breed I would become next?

Before I got back to the fire, Gabe and Tas stopped me. "We are going to shape-shift, and check out our surroundings." Tas said.

"Yeah, Okay. Say how long have you guys been able to do that?" I asked.

"Oh, for quite awhile. That trait was one way we escaped the Devils wrath, for so long. I, for one, will be glad to get off

of earth. The tribulation is about to start, I don't want to see it."
Gabe said, as they walked into the dark. I heard the sound of a
big bird taking off and the rustle of the brush as some kind of
animal ran through it.

It took us till late in the night to explain to the rest of our
family what had been going on in our lives. And also vice-
versa. Dad and Felicia couldn't get over how Rosie and Alita
had changed. I was having a hard time getting used to my little
girl, being a big girl, in every way....

She wasn't getting used to it very fast. Faith had to keep
reminding her to keep her clothes on. When she was small it
didn't' matter too much. Of course Rosie was pretty much
grown anyway. So it wasn't too much of a change for her.

We spread our bedrolls under the trees. Faith, myself, Alita,
Lacy, Rosie, Mary Jane and Iris, we were all close together.
Dad, Felicia, Jake, Alona and the rest of their bunch were
gathered under a tree close by...

I woke up an hour after we all fell asleep. I set up and
looked around. The fire was burnt down to glowing coils. The
stars were extra bright this night. Or was it because they were
somehow more important now? The moon hung low and
bright, almost like day. I looked around at everybody,
everything looked right, but was it?

Some of the stars didn't look quite right, one of them was
moving, when it shouldn't of been. It was curious, I should
have been alarmed, but I wasn't. I always slept naked. I stood
up and found my knife and ammo belt. My 30-30 was leaning
against the tree trunk by my head, I picked it up.

There was a clearing about 500 yards from our camp. I
headed over there. Somehow I knew it would land in that
clearing. I stayed in the trees, waiting. I heard a rustle behind
me, I turned with my rifle up.

Faith, Alita, Rosie, Lacy, Mary Jane and Iris stood there.

"Well, at least you remembered your weapons, if not your clothes," I said to them.

"What about you, where are your clothes?" Rosie said. I looked down, then I pulled my ammo belt around a little bit, that put my knife scabbard in front of me.

Faith said, "Oh yeah, like that helps."

"Well, at least I tried, you guys aren't even trying to cover up."

"Why should we, everyone here has seen all of us naked. What's the big deal?" Alita said. I looked at her. She was standing there with one hand on her hip. Yep, I think she was getting used to her new body.

I looked up, the *star* was getting closer. I looked down, Gabe and Tas just appeared. "Were you going to tell us about this?" I said to them.

"Looks like we don't have to. They should be here in about fifteen minutes." Gabe said, he looked around at us. He added, "at least you're dressed right. How did you know?"

"Know what?" Faith said.

"That they would be sans clothes." Tas said.

"What do you mean, they don't wear clothes?" Rosie said.

"That's right, Terrains have never wore clothes. They were created naked just like Adam and Eve. The only thing is, they never sinned. To them wearing clothes is more of a sin than being naked." Gabe said.

"How come you guys wear clothes?" Alita asked.

"We sort of got in the habit here on earth, people would of done us harm if we wouldn't of." Tas said. Then he chuckled, "but it was nice when we changed to animals, it felt pretty good not to have to wear these rags."

"Now that, this changing thing, do they all do that?" I asked.

"No they don't. Only a few of us, so we could protect our

people. You see, like we said before, the Devil really hates us. God gave us this ability to thwart the Devil. I suppose when we leave earth, we won't have this ability anymore." Gabe said.

Tas cleared his throat, "Uh, one more thing, Terrain men don't go to space, as a rule. A few of us did. Most men think it's a woman's job."

"Do you mean to say that the crew members of that approaching ship are all women?" Mary Jane said.

"Mostly, I would bet. There might be one or two men that were brave enough to make the trip."

"Do you mean to say that the men are scared to go into space?" Faith said.

"Heavens no, their scared at what the other men on Terra would think of them. It's not manly, they think."

"What about the three of you, that includes Clancy?"

"We were children, we came here with our mothers." Gabe said.

"Where are your Mothers?" Alita asked.

"They are at the various Carmel Foundations. We'll all be together pretty soon."

"Oh? Have they told you where we are going?" I asked.

"No, not exactly. We do know there is an 'M' class planet where they might send us. It's uninhabited. We don't know for sure." Gabe said....

I was watching the approaching star (space craft), it winked out. "Hey where did they go?" I said, pointing to the sky.

"They just cloaked themselves. No sense drawing attention to themselves or us. We should be sure and stay in the trees and stay off of the meadow. The ship is a big one, wouldn't want anyone to get crushed when they land." Tas said.

"Have you ever seen any of these ships from Terra?" Rosie asked. Leave it up to her to get down to brass tacks.

"Uh, well yes and no. Our mothers told us about them. We

generally use the Wormholes to travel around. But like we already said, the draw back with wormholes is that they go from point A to point B. No stops or detours. The ships are a lot handier." Gabe said.

"Oh yeah, one more thing," added Tas, "the rest of your family and friends from here have to go by Wormhole. They need to be cleansed like you guys were."

"Go? Go where?" I asked sharply.

"We thought we would send them to the Foundation Compound in the Judith Basin in Montana. The ship isn't due for another fifteen minutes, so we have time." Tas said, as he went over to where Dad and them were standing. They had brought a few head of horses and mules with them from the Rancho de Chama. So I guess they would go with them, like our animals came with us.

I walked over, well all of us did, to say goodbye. Gabe said as we approached, "Don't worry, we are going there too, it's just that they have to be run through the biological filter. The children will be grown when they come out, just as Alita and Iris were. Plus your Dad and Felicia will be younger, just as you guys are."

Miguel and Ester's children and grandchildren were a little leery about entering the wormhole, but when the horses and mules entered without any fuss, they followed along.

The last one to enter was Gail Pretty Otter, before she entered she looked back at me. I went over to her. She said, "I'm a little bit leery about this, do you think it's safe?"

"Sure, we went through it, believe me you're going to feel a lot better, physically and mentally." She laid her hand on my arm, looking down, she smiled, "You know that knife is not hiding anything, you wife is one fortunate woman." Then she stepped in....

She was right, why should I hide it? I pulled the scabbard

back to my hip, as I walked back to my family I could feel it flopping back and forth.

As we stood on the edge of the meadow, we felt a great displacement of air. Then the grass became flat all across the meadow. Tas and Gabe were taking off their clothes. They seen me looking, Gabe said, "It would be disrespectful of us to leave our clothes on, in fact a sin to the women on board the ship."

Do you remember that I told you that Gabe had an aquiline nose? You know from his time as an Eagle. But now it was straight, both Tas and Gabe were perfect specimens of the human form. The female members of my family were giving them the once over. I said, "Girls stop your drooling, it's not seemly."

Faith was standing beside me, "I wasn't." she said. "I know you weren't." I said, as I pulled her around in front of me. Rosie, Alita and Iris's cheeks had turned a bright red, but Mary Jane was still gawking at them.

Iris whispered at Mary Jane, "Mom, for heavens sake, haven't you ever seen a naked man before?"

Mary Jane came out of her trance, "Yes, of course. But those two are single, their fair game."

Faith said, "Yeah, but by the looks of it, you're going to have plenty of competition." As we were talking a hatch had opened and standing in it were a bunch of naked beautiful women, as we watched a gangway came out and down to the ground.

The ship itself was still cloaked, it looked weird, a hole in the sky with these women standing in it. They came down the ramp. Gabe and Tas walked forward to meet them. Mary Jane stepped out right behind them. Just as they stopped, Mary Jane pinched Tas on the butt. He jumped. Mary Jane stood there smiling.

We came up behind them, Iris pulled her mother back beside us. "Mother, you're shameless, behave yourself." Iris said.

The woman in front was evidently the boss. As the rest of them were standing a step behind her. The tone and timber of her voice would have made a Grizzly bear behave himself. It was all woman, but with a hint of command that I had never heard before.

Her eyes went over our party, as she hugged Tas and Gabe, her eyes met mine. I winked. She blinked. Faith was still standing in front of me, Faith looked at the woman then up at me. She stepped on my instep, I winced.

I whispered in Faiths ear, "I wasn't flirting with her, I just wanted to see what she would do when I winked at her." She whispered back, "I don't care about the wink, your thing is swelling."

Damn, it was. "Sorry, that damn thing has a mind of its own. Don't move away from me till it goes down." Faith leaned her head back again and whispered, "Don't blame it any, look at that bunch, they almost make me hot."

Rosie poked me in the ribs, "Look at Gabe and Tas." We both looked, shucks, I didn't feel so bad, both of them were saluting, if you know what I mean. Strange thing though, they weren't the least embarrassed. What in the world were we getting into?

The woman from the ship were ignoring their condition. Outside of a slight smile on their lips. I guess they took it as a compliment. Which in a way, I guess it was....

The Captain stepped around them and came over to us. "You must be Clay, and this woman stuck to you is your wife Faith?"

"Yep, I reckon you're dead on." I said. I held my hand out

past my wife's abundant breast. She took it and shook, just the right pressure. Then she took Faiths hand in hers. "I've been looking forward to meeting you and your whole family, we have been following your exploits, quite interesting." She said, then she individually greeted each member of our group.

We already had the horses packed, Faith and I went to check their loads. I reached in my saddle bags and pulled my journal out. We sat down behind a tree and brought it up to date. I thought for a minute, then decided to write these next few lines.....

"I am leaving this journal for whoever may find it. It appears we are going to leave this earth. They say it's for another 'M' class planet. As you probably know, we all desire to leave something of ourselves behind when we finally leave this earth. Yeah, I know it's usually at death we leave earth. But in this case we are alive and kicking. I am going to wrap this journal in oil cloth and plastic and bury it beside this tree. I will mark a blaze on the tree with the date.

Then I handed the journal to Faith, she always checked everything I wrote. Sometimes she even wrote in it; like the time I was in that coma. While she looked at it, I put the blaze on the tree.

She had just handed the journal back to me; when I heard an Eagle flying in mid-heaven say with a loud voice:
"Woe, woe, woe to those dwelling on the Earth because of the rest of the trumpet blasts of the three Angels who are about to blow their trumpets!"

"Did you hear that?" I asked Faith.

"Yes, of course I did. I think we are getting off of this Earth just in time. It's like Gabe and Tas told us; we don't belong here anymore. Here, give me that journal back, I think we should record what the Eagle said, then you can bury it."

She wrote in it, then handed it back to me; she had recorded what the Eagle said, as the Eagle was flying. I was thinking as I buried the journal: Most of our words are recorded in it; but our thoughts and our innermost desires are still floating through the air, just 'As the Eagle Flies'.....

www.ingramcontent.com/pod-product-compliance
Lightning Source LLC
Chambersburg PA
CBHW030353030726
47497CB00002B/320